Praise for She

'This novel is a page-turner and the action is pretty much full on; kidnap, murder, gangster wars, a McGuffin and a decent cop'
– *NB Magazine*

'On show in *Trust Me, I'm Dead* is finesse with character development and plot, in this case thermostatically synced to the reader's imagination'
– *The Westsider*

'Gripping and disturbing, Clark delves into dark places close to home. *Trust Me, I'm Dead* will linger in your mind after you have read it'
– **Leigh Russell**

'This felt like an impeccably planned treasure hunt with tension interwoven into the story to lasso my attention right to the end. I'll be watching for the author's next crime fiction offering!'
– *A Knight's Reads*

'*Trust Me, I'm Dead* is an intense, addictive read with enough action to get your heart beating and characters to die for'
– *Chocolate'n'Waffles*

Also by Sherryl Clark

Trust Me, I'm Dead

Dead
and
Gone

SHERRYL CLARK

VERVE BOOKS

First published in 2020 by Verve Books,
an imprint of The Crime & Mystery Club Ltd,
Harpenden, UK

Vervebooks.co.uk

ISBN
978-0-85730-806-1 (print)
978-0-85730-807-8 (epub)

2 4 6 8 10 9 7 5 3 1

Printed and bound in Great Britain by Severn, Gloucester

For Karen, with love always

1

The sharp crack of gunfire made me jump, even though it was the third time I'd heard it that morning. The orchard owners down the road had bought a new bird-scarer, and the valley and the clear spring air acted like a sound tunnel.

I bent down to pull out the weeds around my snow peas and groaned, cursing the ever-present ache in my hip. The fancy new natural health centre up the road was no better than crusty old Dr Donald, the physiotherapist I'd been going to for several years. That last visit to the kinesiologist had cost me $70. She wouldn't be getting any more of my money.

Mia wandered past me, eating a slice of apple and following the scrawny tortoiseshell cat we'd adopted after it had been dumped on my front lawn. I watched her chase the cat past the gardens and, when it escaped under the fence, she turned back to me. 'Kitty gone.'

'Yep. It must've known you were going to grab its tail again.' That was Mia's favourite trick. I shook my head. She was a different kid from the traumatised two-year-old I'd 'inherited' four months ago. Right now, she was trying to blow seeds off a dandelion head and giggling when it tickled her nose. Not for the first time, I wished my brother Andy could see her now. But since he was dead, it'd have to be his angel looking down that watched over her, if you believed that crap. I still couldn't believe I'd got sucked into going to a kinesiologist, of all things.

'Come on, kid, I've got to get ready for work. And you have to decide what toys you're taking to Aunty Joleen's.'

I didn't want to be working at the local hotel, but I had no choice. My own fault. I couldn't bear to rent or sell Andy's house in Melbourne that had once belonged to our nana, and I was determined not to touch the life insurance Andy had left for Mia. That meant I was continually broke these days, so a job had become a necessity. The pub owner, Pete Macclesfield, known everywhere as Big Macca, had offered me a job managing the place. Macca was great like that, and we'd become good mates. I'd helped him out a few times before, and knew his accounts and paperwork were getting the better of him, so it was win-win for both of us. At least I wasn't stuck behind the bar, pulling beer, although I still did that when it was really busy.

Like today would be. Race day at Bendigo, further north of us, so the accommodation was full up and the Melbourne yuppies who came up for the day in busloads would be sure to include the historic Candlebark Hotel on their pub crawl home. Thank God I had young Billy and Mike Somers who were our security guards on the weekends, and I could call on Connor for urgent stuff, like full-on brawls or visiting bikies. It was handy having the local cop as your good mate!

I bustled Mia into the car with her usual huge bagload of gear and dropped her off at Joleen's on the way to the hotel. Joleen had been a godsend for someone like me who'd never had a kid before, and no idea where to start. She'd also been the one who sussed out that Mia was way too quiet for a kid her age, and got her into play therapy two mornings a week until she started coming out of her shell and talking more.

And all along I'd thought it was me being such a fabulous fill-in parent that was the reason for her good behaviour. Yeah, right. At least she was almost toilet-trained now. That saved me a fair bit of money each week in nappies.

I parked my old Benz around the back of the hotel, out of the way beside the wooden lattice fence that walled off the delivery and kitchen door area. I didn't need any drunks reversing into it. I unlocked and pushed through the side door, making sure to lock it again behind me. Automatic security I'd insisted on when I started work here. Big Macca was too much of a country boy, leaving doors open everywhere. I had my own history of someone creeping in after closing time at my pub in Melbourne and nearly killing me – that wasn't going to happen again.

'Hey, Judi.' Mike Somers came out of the staff toilet, knotting his tie. 'Ready for the war?'

'Now, now, you mustn't think of our valued customers as enemies,' I said, grinning.

Mike laughed. 'Nah, just dickheads and perves, hey?'

'Don't tell me – Suzie is wearing her special black top again.'

'Yep. Billy's been picking up eyeballs left, right and centre.'

I shook my head. Suzie had a great smile and a special low-cut, very tight black jersey top that showed off her bust to great advantage. She claimed that top made her more tips than anything else she owned, and she was probably right. She wasn't the type to chat up the customers and flirt too much though – she had a sharp wit that tended to cut guys down, to size in one sentence. But not until after the tips had been handed over, of course.

I followed Mike out to the bar areas and scanned each one to see what the current situation was. The public bar still had a few locals in it, but they'd leave when the race crowd arrived.

It pissed me off that the locals felt shoved out of their home turf, but the public bar was too big to keep just for them, and it made too much money on race days.

The lounge bar had two small groups in it, punters who'd left the track early, maybe because they'd lost all their money on betting. The bistro was empty, but I could see the chef, Andre, in the kitchen, getting things ready for the onslaught. Racegoers tended to eat late – they drank all day and snacked on rubbish at the track, then got the munchies around eight or nine at night. Andre hated the late rush, and we'd had to promise him triple pay after nine to pacify him. Well, I'd promised him triple. I still hadn't cleared it with Big Macca yet.

I wondered where the hell Big Macca was. He usually liked to be around on race days, hobnobbing with the wannabe rich and famous, but yesterday he'd told me he was going to be out for the day.

'Got a business deal I have to take care of,' he said. 'Sorry to leave you in charge of everything, but you'll be right, won't you?'

'As long as Mike and Billy are here.'

'Yep, the whole staff are on, don't worry. I'll definitely be back by the evening rush.' But Big Macca had looked worried, his eyes shifting from side to side, and I was still wondering what the hell he was up to. I knew the hotel wasn't doing very well. Country race days were a bonus, but there were only half a dozen weekend races a year near us. The rest of the time, it was as quiet as the grave, so to speak.

The front door swung open and a crowd of racegoers fell in, laughing and holding each other up. All young ones, under twenty-five, the girls in Lycra dresses up around their bums and the guys wearing hats that made them look like they'd stepped out of Squizzy Taylor's 1920s gang. They charged to the bar in the lounge area, and one of the guys started yelling. 'Hey, big boobs, how about some service?'

I took a step towards the bar but Suzie already had it in hand. 'I don't serve rude dickheads,' she said. 'Now if you ask nicely, you might get a drink.'

'Ooohhh,' was the reply. 'She's not impressed with me.' The guy took off his hat and bowed, staggering a little as he straightened again. 'Pardon me, madam, may I purchase some drinks in this fine establishment?'

Suzie grinned. 'What'll you have?'

I left her to it and paid Andre a little visit. 'All set for tonight?'

He pouted, and flung his hands out. 'It's wasted on these drunk peasants. Why do I stay here when I'm not appreciated?'

I sighed. He had this routine down pat, and I heard it at least once a week. I wasn't in the mood for it today. 'Because you've got a criminal record, mate, and we're the only place that would take you on. And,' I added, as he looked like he was about to sulk, and I couldn't afford that, 'you are appreciated. We love your food, and if you play your cards right, one of these days one of the peasants will turn out to be a famous food critic, and you'll be made. OK?'

'OK.' He flapped a tea towel and folded it neatly. 'So what do you want for dinner?'

'Whatever you think I'll enjoy,' I said, knowing it would be delicious. For all his tantrums, which were normal for chefs anyway, Andre created bloody good food.

I headed into the office and checked over the paperwork sitting in the in-tray, and cursed. Big Macca was supposed to sort out the bills yesterday, but obviously nothing had been done. I didn't like logging in to the account and paying out money without consulting him first, so I'd have to get on to it as soon as he turned up.

The phone rang, startling me. 'Candlebark Hotel. Judi speaking.'

'Hi, Jude. How's it looking?' It was Connor, checking in.

'Same as usual. The young ones come in first, all drunk. They must get bored, watching horses run around the track.' I took the portable phone with me and peered out into each bar again. 'What time's the last race?'

'Finished around quarter to five.'

'We'll be in full chaos mode in about half an hour then. You calling in later?'

'Yeah, for sure. It's always good to be seen, hey?' Connor liked to wander through the bars a couple of times during the evening as a warning to anyone in the mood for trouble.

'Certainly is. See you later.'

'How's Mia? She at Joleen's?'

'Yes, but if Uncle Connor wanted to call in there, too, she'd be happy to see you.'

'Might just do that.'

Nobody had been more surprised than Connor when I'd returned to Candlebark from Melbourne with a kid in tow, but when he discovered she was my niece, Connor kind of adopted her. He was great with her, better than me, but that wouldn't be hard. I was still referring every five minutes to the baby book Heath had given me.

Heath. Detective Sergeant Ben Heath. We'd met when my brother, Andy, had been murdered, and we'd been at loggerheads from the start. It was just about the worst way to meet someone, and then find out you were attracted to them. Ugh. I'd tried hard enough to pretend it wasn't happening, and so did he, but nothing had come of it anyway. Being over a hundred kilometres apart didn't help, but I had been to Melbourne half a dozen times in the past few months. We just never seemed to get together at the right time, in the right place. Like anywhere near a bedroom. Mia didn't help either. Now I knew why people said having kids killed your sex life.

I shook myself and put the phone back on the cradle, and went to check the guest register to see who was in tonight.

Carl Cammiston and party. Three rooms. He was a horse owner from up the bush, an old mate of Macca's, who had dreams of winning the Melbourne Cup, but he couldn't afford a decent horse so he kept buying long shots and hoping he'd found a gem. Bit like shopping in op shops and hoping you'd discover a Balenciaga. Carl was a good bloke, but his wife was a total pain in the arse. Thought that having a big farm, racehorses and lots of money made her queen of something. After a few drinks, her laugh would strip wallpaper off the walls. I wondered who else Carl had brought with him this time. No doubt I'd find out shortly.

Kevin Benson was a trainer who often stayed with us. The other names were all vaguely familiar, except for Nick Simonetti – he was new.

The front door banged a few times and the noise levels in the bars gradually increased. Time for me to wander around and do the schmooze thing. Big Macca's trick was to ensconce himself at the end of the lounge bar with a glass of scotch and buy drinks for his favourite customers. That didn't work for me and never had, not even when I'd owned the pub in Melbourne with my scumbag ex-husband, Max. I liked to be behind the bar, getting to know people, or chatting to them as I walked around. That way, I covered the lot rather than just the ones

13

who wanted to suck up for a free drink, like they did with Big Macca.

Where the hell was he, anyway? He never missed race days.

I shrugged mentally and thought it would save us a couple of hundred dollars in free drinks, at least. He'd probably turn up later, just in time to upset Andre by demanding steak and chips at midnight.

In the lounge bar, Carl and his wife had arrived and sat at the head of a bunch of tables pulled together; already they had three bottles of prosecco sitting in ice buckets, with a dozen people swigging it down. I filled some bowls with nuts and snacks and took them over. 'Looks like you had a great day, Carl,' I said, smiling at everyone like a good hostess should.

'Two winners, Judi.' Carl's beam could've powered half of Candlebark. 'And a second and a third. All four horses did bloody well!'

'That's great. Melbourne Cup next stop, is it?'

'You never know!' He laughed uproariously, and poured me a glass. 'Here, have one with me.'

'Thanks.' I didn't usually drink with customers, but Carl was worth a bit of money to us so it was a good idea to help him celebrate a little. Mrs Carl was sprawled on the corner seat next to him, and she looked almost ready to pass out. At least she was quiet.

'Where's the big man?' Carl asked.

'Gone out on business, I think,' I said. 'He'll probably turn up any minute. Cheers.' I toasted him with my glass and took a sip. Ugh. Prosecco was my least favourite wine, but I smiled and kept moving.

All the bars had filled quickly, and I moved behind the lounge counter with Suzie who was serving ten people at once, laughing and joking. I stuck to the older punters who wanted a simple beer or a glass of wine and left the champagne cocktails to her.

Mike strolled past me with a nod, and was no sooner out the door towards the public bar than a ruckus started. It was the early arrivals, now scuffling with each other while the girls looked on and screamed and cried. 'Kenny, stop it!' screamed a blonde. 'You're ruining everything!' She was in shocking pink with a fascinator that had taken on a sideways lean so that the feathers poked out behind her left ear.

Mike returned with Billy behind him and within five minutes, the band of travellers were on their way home. Billy came past me and I waved at him. 'Hope they had a sober driver.'

'Yep, someone who was asleep in the hire van. Seemed OK to drive.'

'Good.' We didn't need an accident down the road to be blamed on us. Responsible service of alcohol – it was fine in theory but if people were determined to write themselves off, they'd find a way to do it. Still, I was known as the dragon who took people's keys.

Carl's party wandered off towards the bistro for dinner and I checked my watch – just after 7pm. Andre would be happy. I chatted with Old Jock who lived down near the river and poured him a beer.

'You coming down with something, Jock?' I asked. 'You don't look well.'

Jock started and shook his head. 'Right as rain,' he mumbled.

'Macca should be back soon. He'll cheer you up.'

Jock just nodded and stared into his beer. I turned to find a dark, surly-looking man standing at the bar.

'Can I get you a drink?' I asked.

'No. I want my room key,' he said. His tone made the hairs on the back of my neck stand up, and I took a breath before I answered him.

'Come out to the reception area, sir, and I'll sort you out.' I meant, sign you in, but it didn't quite come out that way. He followed me out of the lounge bar, dogging my heels, and I quickened my steps to get away from him, scooting in behind the desk.

'What was your name?'

'Nick Simonetti. I booked.' He kept looking at me and then scanning the reception area as if expecting someone to be hiding behind the ficus tree or the coat stand.

'Yes, that's right,' I said pleasantly. 'Your credit card?'

He handed over a platinum job that virtually sparkled in my hand. I kept my face blank and ran it through the machine, then gave it back to him. 'You're in Room 7, up the stairs and turn right. Do you need a hand with your bags?'

'Room 7 got its own bathroom?'

'Yes, all our rooms do. It's a suite, which is what you booked.' In fact, Carl had also asked for it and been a bit miffed that someone had beaten him to it.

'Good.' Simonetti took the key and walked off, up the stairs. No bags. Maybe he was coming down later to get them out of his car? I called after him, 'Will you be eating dinner with us tonight?'

'Probably.' He turned halfway up the stairs, glaring down at me. 'What time does the restaurant close?'

'In about an hour,' I said, trying to hold his gaze and not succeeding. The man was a rude pig, but I was used to that. There were lots of them around. This one, however, made me want to take a long step back and then run away. I was

16

trying to think who he reminded me of when it struck me like a falling gum tree – Graeme Nash. Big crime boss in Melbourne I'd come up against through no fault of my own. Same grim face, same flat fuck-you-stay-out-of-my-face tone of voice. I shivered. And hoped I was imagining it.

I debated about whether to warn the girl waitressing in the restaurant tonight, but she was young and I didn't want to frighten her. After all, it might've just been me, and there was nothing wrong with the guy.

I walked through the bars, doing another check, and discovered a drunk woman in the corner of the public bar being groped by an equally drunk guy. I grabbed Mike from outside and he got rid of the guy and called a cab for the woman. She looked familiar, and Mike said she was a local. I shook my head, wondering if the world would ever change. At least I'd learned to stay away from Max. Maybe I was getting too cynical.

I went into the office and checked the answering machine to see if there was a message from Big Macca, but there was nothing. Where the hell was he? I was sure he'd said his meeting was at lunchtime. I hadn't been too surprised when he wasn't back by six, but now it was after eight. Apart from anything else, I was supposed to finish at nine.

I tried his mobile but, as usual, he didn't have it turned on. Kept saying he hated the damn thing, and often deliberately kept it off. I cursed.

As I left the office, I caught a glimpse of Simonetti going into the restaurant and followed him in, pretending to be checking the bookings. Kelly, the waitress, took his drink order and didn't seem to be fazed by him so I left again.

I knew I was wandering around like a bad smell, looking over people's shoulders, watching drunk customers fall over each other. I felt like a wet blanket, and tried to keep a smile on my face, but I was so over this kind of job. Yet it was the only thing I knew. What else could I do in a place the size of Candlebark? Be the postman? A farmer? I couldn't make enough out of my veggie garden to pay the bills, and I didn't want to anyway.

The obvious solution was to rent or sell Andy's house, but I couldn't bring myself to do it – not yet. It certainly wasn't the lure of the weekends in the city with Heath. The weekends that had come to nothing so far. I should just cut my losses and… do what? I supposed I could go back to being a grumpy loner.

I sighed heavily and decided I needed a drink. I poured myself a Cointreau on ice as a treat and sipped it slowly, standing behind the bar and doing some glass stacking and washing, passing the time. I knew that once it got to 9pm and Macca hadn't turned up, I'd have to call Joleen and ask her to keep Mia for a while longer.

Billy walked through the bar, collecting dirty glasses off the tables, and I said quietly, 'Can you do a full car park run now, please?'

'Sure.' He raised his eyebrows but went straight away. We usually left car park checks until nearer to closing time, but I was edgy. I wanted to know why Macca hadn't come back, and to lose this feeling that somehow, in some way, things were slowly moving out of my control.

Billy was gone for nearly fifteen minutes, far longer than it should have taken him to circle the two car parks and check the back doors of the hotel. I kept looking at the side entrance, waiting, and just as I was about to go out there myself and see what was keeping him, he barged back in, half-tripping over the step.

I banged my glass down on the bar and was halfway out to

meet him when he stopped, sucked in a breath and slightly shook his head at me. Then he beckoned me towards him, obviously trying not to alarm any of customers. Already a few heads were turning. I smiled at them and joined Billy outside, firmly closing the door behind me.

'What's up?'

He swallowed hard, his Adam's apple bobbing. 'There's a... body. Round the back.' He pointed to where the kitchen's back door was. 'In the dumpster.'

'Fuck.' My stomach knotted and my hand went to my heart. I could feel it skipping under my fingers. 'Who is it?'

2

Moths flew around the outside light, banging into the bulb with muffled thumps. Out here at the back of the pub the only other sound was the river gurgling.

'D-dunno,' Billy stammered. 'He's face down, in the rubbish. He's not moving.'

'Did you actually check if he's alive?'

'The cops, you know, on TV they say not to touch anything. So I didn't.' He shifted from foot to foot, as if he wanted to run away. 'He... he looks dead.'

'Have you called them? The cops, I mean. Connor.' Now I was babbling myself.

'Yep. Is that OK?' He gazed at me anxiously.

'Of course. Did you tell him you'd found a body?'

'Yep. Don't think he believed me.' His head swivelled back and forth and I realised he was hoping his brother was nearby.

'What made you look in the dumpster? Did you hear something?'

'No, it was because the lid was open. It's never usually open. Seemed weird. I dunno.' His mouth trembled and he turned away quickly.

I made a decision. 'Look, I'll stay here. You go back inside, tell Mike what's happened – and do it quietly. I don't want half the customers out here gawking. Then keep an eye on the place. Last thing we need is a bar fight as well as this.'

'Righto.' Billy made his escape, his face alight with relief.

I stood under the dim halo of light and waited, the moths and bugs flitting around my head and some landing in my hair. I kept swatting them away, and checking my watch. Shit! What was taking Connor so long? Billy might be wrong. Probably it was just a drunk customer who'd thought the dumpster might make a handy free bed.

I knew I should look in the dumpster myself and see if I recognised who it was, see if they needed help, but some gut-deep feeling kept me pinned under the outside light. I knew what a dead person looked like, and I didn't want to be reminded of Andy. Just as I was about to call Connor again myself, his police 4WD pulled into the car park. I waved, and he drove past the parked cars and on to the grass near me, then jumped out and put his hat on. Official business.

'What's up? Billy said he found a body. Was he having me on?' Connor sounded calm but his voice had an edge of excitement. His usual business was petty theft or speeding tickets.

'I haven't checked it out myself. I took him at his word.' I pointed down the side of the hotel. 'It's in the dumpster, apparently.'

'Any idea who it is?'

'Billy said face down – he's got no idea.'

Connor pulled on latex gloves and walked past me; I followed, like he was the Pied Piper and I couldn't resist. No one said I had to look inside the dumpster…

Above the kitchen's back door was another dim yellow lamp, just enough to illuminate the area and no more. The lattice fencing was pocked with dark shadows and the smell of rotting food filled the air. Connor got out his torch and examined the area briefly before going up to the dumpster.

'You're not going to cordon it off?' I asked.

'In a minute. I need to check the person is deceased first. They might be unconscious.'

'Oh. Right. I should have... I thought...' I found myself wringing my hands and tucked them under my arms.

'Bugger.' Connor was reaching down into the rubbish, his legs dangling. 'Can't quite reach.' He dragged one leg up and over, tottered on the edge and, just as I thought he'd fall right in, he caught himself and managed to step down. 'Great. My trousers will stink for weeks.' He bent down and I lost sight of him, could only hear muttering. Then he straightened and grimaced at me. 'I'm sorry. It's Big Macca.'

I jerked back, nearly lost my balance. 'Bullshit. He's away at a business meeting. Been gone all day.' My voice croaked, I coughed, tried to breathe. 'How could it be Macca? Is he dead?'

'Yep.'

'Could it be an accident?'

'Like a heart attack? Doubt it. He's got two bullet holes in him.'

'Oh God.' My knees wobbled and I had to sit down, but there was nowhere, not even a mop bucket. Instead I leaned against the wall, eyes closed, my skin slick with cold sweat.

Connor climbed out of the dumpster, shaking the potato peelings off his shoes. 'Pongs in there.'

'It's a giant rubbish bin. Nothing I can do about it.' Why the hell were we talking about rubbish? My vision blurred and I blinked hard. 'Now what?'

'Now I cordon off the area, call in the big boys. They'll send a Homicide team up from Melbourne. And the crime scene officers.' He glanced at me. 'This is going to be tricky. I know you don't want to close the pub – it'll cause a riot – but someone inside might've done this. A drunk racegoer, maybe, who tangled with Macca just as he arrived back.'

I gaped at him. 'I don't even know where to start with that.'

'I have to do my job,' he said. 'We can't let anyone back here. And I need to get people's names and addresses and stop them from leaving, but I can't be in two places at once. Preserving the scene is more important.'

Good. Something practical I could do. 'There are a lot of regulars on race night. I'll try to write them all down for you, and get as many of the out-of-towners as I can.' I straightened, rubbed my face, turned my back on the dumpster and headed for the side door. 'I'll lock this door, OK? And I'll tell Andre to lock the kitchen door as well. He'll have to know, or he'll come barging out with more rubbish to throw in... over... shit. You know.'

'Good idea.' Connor followed me and gripped my shoulder briefly. 'Are you all right?'

'Yes, fine. Let's get on with it. Whatever *it* is.' I went back into the lounge bar, locking the door behind me. Luckily it wasn't a fire escape door. The kitchen door was, but that was too bad. I pasted a smile on my face and made my way through the lounge bar, stopping long enough to murmur to Suzie that the side door was locked and had to stay that way, and I'd explain later. She nodded and went back to serving at the speed of light, alongside our other barman, Charlie. By now, most people were well away and not likely to notice anything odd. Someone had put a Queen song on Macca's vintage jukebox and people were singing loudly and out of tune.

In the kitchen, Andre was bashing pots and pans, and trying

to plate up four meals. I stood back out of his way, waiting until he'd put the plates under the lamps and rung the bell for Kelly. He wiped the bench down with impatient swipes. 'What? Don't tell me there's a party of ten coming in now, for pity's sake. You'll be cooking for them yourself.'

'No, it's not that.' Tears welled in my eyes and I brushed them away angrily. I had to pull myself together. 'I have to lock the back door. You can't go out there.'

'What do you mean? What am I supposed to do with the rubbish?' He glared at me and then slowly it dawned on him that something was seriously wrong. Probably it was the sick expression on my face. 'Spit it out, lovey. What's up? Must be bad.'

'It's Big Macca. He's dead.' I waved one hand vaguely in the air. 'He... he's out there.' I couldn't stop the tears now. 'He's in the fucking dumpster.'

Andre turned nearly as pale as his chef's jacket and the long, thin scar down the side of his face stood out like a silk thread. 'What was he doing in the dumpster? Did he have a heart attack or something?'

I shook my head. I couldn't get the words out. 'I...ah...' I coughed, cleared my throat, wiped my face. 'Someone killed him.' I held up my hands. 'Don't ask me why, or how. I don't know. Connor's here. He said keep the door locked, don't go out there. All right?'

'Yeah, yeah, of course.' He picked up a knife, put it down again. 'Can we close the restaurant now? No new customers?'

'Yes. No problem.' Suddenly I realised Big Macca was a couple of metres away, on the other side of the wall, and I needed to get out of there. I steadied myself, and went into the bistro. Kelly was taking another drinks order from Carl's table, and I was relieved to see Simonetti was on coffee already, so he'd be out of there shortly. Hopefully, he'd go up to his room. When Kelly came over to me, I said, 'I'm closing the bistro now. Once these people are finished eating, that's it. You can set up for breakfast.'

Kelly half-shrugged. 'Sure. Will Suzie need a hand in the bar later then?'

'Maybe. We can't afford to be rude so we'll see how it goes.'

She gave me a quizzical look but even though I knew I wasn't making much sense, I wasn't in the mood to explain. She'd work it out later, no doubt. I grabbed the notebook we used for bookings and checked we had everyone's names and phone numbers. That was a start. But if they wanted to leave, I could hardly bar the doors.

Going back into the lounge bar and acting normally was the hardest thing I'd had to do in a long time. I didn't want to freak everyone out. Why was I so concerned about the customers and the rep of the pub? Big Macca wasn't in a position to care. That thought made my throat close up and I coughed. I gulped down a mouthful of my Cointreau – luckily by now the ice had melted so it was half water – used the notebook and scribbled down all the names of people I recognised so Connor would know how to contact them later. Then I went into the other bar and did the same. Lots of strangers, but when I tried asking them for their names and addresses, they brushed me off like I was trying to sell them something. There wasn't much I could do about that. No way was I telling anyone there'd been a murder. Connor was right about starting a riot.

Finally I rang Joleen and explained there was a problem at the hotel and was it possible for her to keep Mia overnight? 'No worries,' she said. 'Mia's already asleep and not likely to wake up until breakfast after the amount of running around she did with my two boys.'

'Great, thanks.' I hung up before she could ask me what the problem was. Joleen was a great help, but also very nosey.

I was tempted to go out and see how Connor was going, but I knew he'd call if he needed me. If I hadn't been watching out of the side window I probably wouldn't have noticed a police van arrive, and then two dark sedans driving around to the rear of the pub. Detectives, I guessed. I wanted to know what was happening, what they were doing about poor Macca, but more importantly they needed to deal with the pub crowd as people were starting to leave.

At least the ones staying upstairs weren't going anywhere, but I didn't relish having to tell them what'd happened, especially Carl and his mob. Carl was a good mate of Macca's. I was tempted to slip him a drink that would knock him off his feet, but he'd fall in a heap soon enough. Mrs Carl had staggered off already, and I was glad to see Simonetti hadn't lingered in the bar. If any of them noticed the police out the back and came downstairs to see what was going on, Connor would sort them out.

A few minutes later, I heard raised voices coming from the front car park and hurried out to see what was happening. The police Connor had called in had taken over and were talking to people as they left, recording names and addresses. One young man had arced up and was protesting loudly, but his mates were calming him down, their faces worried. Probably about being accused of drink-driving.

The police tape at the rear corner of the pub looked to me like it was made of neon lights but nobody else seemed to notice. I went back inside, glad to leave things to the police, still reluctant to tell anyone. Judi the Big Chicken.

Suzie eyed me hovering at the end of the bar. 'How come you're still here?' she asked, as she stacked glasses in the dishwasher baskets.

I had to tell her but I didn't want her to create a big fuss. How big a drama queen was she? Not at all, from what I could tell. She chatted a lot from behind the bar, but it was all light stuff about sport and what was on the news and getting the regulars to talk about themselves. She would've made a good therapist. 'Listen, I've got some bad news. But I need you to keep it to yourself right now.'

'Righto.' She frowned at me. 'That bad, huh? Someone rob the joint?'

'No.' A small shock ran through me. I hadn't thought to check the safe, but all the takings for the day were ready to go in. 'At least, I don't think so. It's, um, Big Macca. He's... passed on.' I hated euphemisms, but I lowered my voice all the same. 'He's dead.'

'Crikey.' She hunched her shoulders, her arms folded under her boobs. 'Heart attack?'

'You'd think so, wouldn't you?' I grimaced. 'No, murdered. Two bullets, Connor said. Out the back.'

'What? Did it happen here? In the pub?' Her voice had gone all squeaky and her chin quivered. 'Oh, the poor man! Who'd wanta do that?'

'I don't know where it happened, but his body's out there.'

Immediately her eyes went to the side door. 'That's why you locked it. Connor didn't want anyone going out that way. I wondered how come he didn't do his usual walk-through tonight.'

'He's cordoned off the area and more police have arrived.

Detectives, probably, and crime scene officers.' I shouldn't know this stuff, but I did, and it sent a crawling feeling up the back of my neck.

'Hope it's not that arrogant prick from Bendigo,' Suzie said. 'Detective Constable Barney. He couldn't detect a stick up his arse.'

I couldn't help laughing. 'Don't hold back.'

'Well, he came out when my sister got bashed by her husband. Only reason Bendigo got involved was because they thought he'd robbed a couple of service stations.' She grabbed a cloth and started wiping down the bar with short, sharp movements. 'Wasn't him at all. And Barney decided he couldn't be bothered dealing with a domestic so he sent her file somewhere or lost it, and when she went to court for a restraining order, there was no police report so they told her nothing could be done.'

'What did Connor have to say about it?' I gathered up the canvas bags of takings and made a move towards the office. Time to put the money away, and check nothing was missing.

'He was great. Better than a restraining order. Went and had a word with my sister's husband and he ended up going to Sydney. Haven't seen him since.'

'Uh-huh.' I held up the takings bag. 'I'll be back in a minute.'

Suzie kept on with the tables, and Mike and Billy were picking up the last glasses in the public bar. I knew Andre had gone home as soon as he'd finished, his face still pale with shock, saying he needed some time alone to get to grips with what had happened, and I hadn't argued. I was a hundred per cent sure he hadn't killed Macca, but the police wouldn't be happy. They'd want to question him, seeing as how the dumpster was right outside the kitchen door.

In the office, I locked the door as usual and twirled the dial on the safe to open it, half-expecting to see it empty, but it looked the same as usual. A few bags of change, yesterday's takings, about $400, and the cheque book. Nobody had touched the contents as far as I could see. The motive wasn't about robbing the pub then.

I locked the current day's takings in the safe, wishing there were more race days. We had nearly $3000 in cash, plus what had been charged on credit, and then all the money the in-house customers would owe. Knowing Carl, that'd be another grand or so. Race day every week and Big Macca could stop worrying about the bills.

Like that would matter to him now.

I sat down heavily, my legs shaky. What about me? Did this mean I no longer had a job? Who would the hotel belong to now? I wondered if he'd made a will. He could've left the place to his ex-wife, Wendy – they were still good friends. Trading was fair, not a wild money-making venture, but I couldn't see how he wouldn't make a small profit.

Maybe he had a niece or nephew he'd left it to – I knew he didn't have kids of his own. If he hadn't left a will, it'd take months to sort out. His solicitor might have to step in, if he had one. Experience told me that if I could show the place was making money overall, they wouldn't close it down because they'd want to see the dollars still rolling in while they did all the legal stuff.

Oh well, no point getting my knickers in a twist over it.

I locked the office door and put my head in to the bar to see Suzie sitting with a drink and her feet up on a corner buffet. 'Connor came in and said to wait – they wanted to ask me some questions. Just routine, he said.'

'Has anyone else come inside yet?' I was ready to go home; I considered sneaking out like Andre had, but I'd probably get Connor into trouble.

'Yeah, the cops from Bendigo, including Smarmy Barney.' Her mouth twisted. 'He wasn't happy to see me here.'

'I'll go and see what's happening,' I said. I used the front entrance to get outside, and halfway around to the back I was stopped by a tall, skinny cop in a leather jacket. His hair was slicked back and he had a three-day growth, which always irritated the hell out of me. What is so cool about bristles? These guys usually end up looking like they needed a good scrub down.

'You can't come around here, madam,' he said, officiously. 'Area is cordoned off.'

'I know that. I was here when Macca was found.' I glared up at him. 'I gather you're Constable Barney.'

His face reddened. '*Detective* Constable Barney. How did you know?'

'A calculated guess,' I said. 'What's happening? My staff want to go home.'

'They can't leave until they've been questioned, just like everyone else.'

'Suzie was in the bar all night. She didn't see a thing. The only ones worth talking to will be Billy, who found Macca, and Andre in the kitchen. And Andre's gone.'

'What?' His head made little irritated jerks. 'Who said he could leave?'

'He's been here since eleven this morning. He was tired.'
'You should've known better than to allow him to leave a crime scene.'

'How about you fetch your boss for me, Constable?' It was satisfying to see him colour with fury again. 'I need to sort a few things out with him. Unless you lot want to pay the overtime?'

'Detective Sergeant Withers is busy at the moment. This is a murder investigation.'

'I know. We found him, remember?' I was itching to punch the smartarse, but just in time a guy I guessed was his boss came around the corner.

'You can't come this way, madam,' he called.

Oh, for fuck's sake. 'Why would I want to?' I snapped. 'I'm the manager on duty tonight. I want you to question me and my staff and let us go home. It's been a very long, upsetting day.'

Withers was a heavy-set man with a bulbous nose and greying sideburns, and his expression was sombre. He came up to me and gave me the once-over before answering. 'If you could gather everyone in the lounge bar, we'll come and talk to them in a minute.'

'She's let one of them go home already,' Barney said.

Tattletale. 'I already told you – he'd done a twelve-hour shift, and he has to be back for breakfast tomorrow.'

After some muttering, they decided Andre's questioning could wait. Connor was right – they were really waiting for Homicide to arrive, and any questioning now would be repeated tomorrow.

Barney and another young detective followed me back to the lounge bar, where Billy and Mike were now sitting, chatting to Suzie. 'Is this your whole staff?' Barney asked.

'Kelly's not here,' Suzie said. 'I think she left with Andre. And Charlie went at ten thirty as usual.'

'Shit,' Barney said. 'This is bloody hopeless.' He looked at me as he said it.

'It's Candlebark, Constable,' I said. 'Do you think some of us are going to make a run for it?'

'It's not proper procedure,' he said.

'Come on, Barn,' the other detective said. 'Let's get the questions done. Homicide will be here in half an hour, and we'll look a bit pathetic if we haven't even got that far.'

Barney shot him a venomous look and took Mike and Billy off to the other end of the bar, leaving Suzie and me with Detective No 2. He introduced himself as Detective Constable Hawke, and kept his questions to Suzie short and sharp, once he established she hadn't been outside since she arrived at 3pm. She was allowed to go, with the proviso that she stay available for Homicide to question her further tomorrow.

Then it was my turn. I told him everything that'd happened since I arrived at work.

'You didn't go near the dumpster? Look inside?'

I couldn't hide my shudder. 'No. I took Billy's word for it that Big Macca was dead, although we didn't know who it was then. Connor – Senior Constable Byrne – told me it was Macca and confirmed he was... gone.'

'Were there any strangers in the hotel tonight? Anyone acting suspiciously?'

I laughed shortly. 'It was race day at Bendigo today, so we were flat out with punters and parties heading back to Melbourne. They were nearly all strangers, and acting like the usual drunk racegoers we get here.' I had a flash of Simonetti and it must've showed on my face.

'You don't seem a hundred per cent sure about that, though.'

He was quick, this one. 'It's just one of our house guests – a Mr Simonetti. Never seen him around here before. But he wasn't acting suspiciously, just being rude.'

'We'll be interviewing all the house guests as well,' he said. 'I'll make a note about Mr Simonetti.'

'You're not going to get them out of bed, are you?' That'd do the pub's reputation no good at all, not that murder would help either.

'We've talked to those who were capable of coming downstairs. For the others, the hotel exits are secured, so if anyone tries to leave, they'll be stopped.' He checked his watch. 'They'll be interviewed first thing in the morning, when they're sober.'

I handed him the notebook with the names I'd written down. 'I thought this might help Connor, er, Senior Constable Byrne. But like I said, a lot of the customers were strangers from the city.'

'We took the names and addresses of everyone who was leaving the premises as soon as we arrived,' he said. 'It caused less fuss that way. But thanks. No doubt we missed a few.'

The door opened and Bob, Macca's weekend night manager, walked in. I'd completely forgotten about him – it appeared he'd had no trouble getting past the 'secured exits'. The lines in his face looked deeper than usual, and his face was grey under his bushy white eyebrows. He seemed to already know Macca was dead, but I briefly explained what'd happened, finding his body, and Bob had to sit down for a few minutes to recover. Macca had been a long-time mate of his, and I wished I could've broken it more gently. I got him a brandy while Hawke waited, frowning.

'Now, as you're the person in charge of the hotel, we'll need you to stay around, maybe all night. Do you live on the premises?'

'No.' I had organised Mia for the night, but I didn't fancy sleeping in the tiny box room. 'Bob's the night manager, and he'll be here – do you really need me to stay?'

'Er... possibly not,' Hawke said. 'But can you wait until

Homicide get here?' He seemed a little apologetic, whereas Barney was now hovering in the background, glaring at me, clearly wanting to butt in.

'Yes, OK. I'll go and do the upstairs check on the guests, Bob, and you stay here in case the police want anything.' I hesitated. 'Macca lived in the pub.' I pointed above my head. 'Are you going to prevent access to his rooms?'

'I'm afraid so. I'll go up with you and lock them.'

I nodded. If I had to stay, the maid's box room at the end of the corridor was the one that everyone said had a ghost. Great. Upstairs check was done quickly, and Hawke locked Macca's room and pocketed the key.

I checked the time again – it was nearly midnight, but thankfully the other staff had been allowed to go. It was just me, Bob and the cops.

And whoever was knocking at the front door.

I hoped to God it wasn't Carl wandering out for a pee under the trees, or one of the locals deciding they wanted another drink. Both had happened before. Barney went to open the door; he'd have to deal with whatever was out there. I heard voices, Barney saying, 'It's all secured. We've done everything by the book.'

Must be his favourite sentence. If I was going to be interviewed again, maybe I'd have another Cointreau first. I stood, debating whether that would be seen as cooperating or not, and not really caring. Just as I took a step towards the bar, the lounge door opened and Barney came in, followed by two men in suits – a couple of the Homicide squad, arrived from Melbourne. The first guy was gazing around, noting the surroundings, but the second scanned the room in a second, and focused on me, a slight smile tilting his mouth.

Heath.

I should've guessed, but it still caught me like a punch to the chest. I stopped breathing for a few moments, and it took all my concentration to force my happy smile way back down where it wouldn't escape. For now, I didn't want any of these cops finding out I knew Heath. He could tell them, if he wanted. I waited to see how he would play it.

He gestured at me and said to his colleague, 'I know Ms Westerholme from another case.' He came over, held out his hand, shook mine. 'You're the manager here?'

Right, I got it. 'That's right. I didn't find Macca, though.'

Barney butted in. 'The bouncer found the body. Billy Somers. I took a statement and let him go home. Told him he'd have to come back in the morning, though. My boss is outside with the crime scene officer. He's waiting for you.'

Heath pulled on his right ear. I knew that sign. It meant Barney was talking too much, instead of waiting to be asked. 'Thanks,' Heath said. 'Who questioned Ms Westerholme?'

Hawke raised his hand. 'I did.'

'I'll see what she said in a minute. Unless she saw the killer running off?' He raised his eyebrows at me and Hawke and we both shook our heads. 'Good. We'll go and take a look outside then. I assume Mr Macclesfield's body is still in the dumpster?'

Sadly, yes. I felt sick to think of him left out there, even though I knew it was standard procedure.

After they'd left, I relaxed a little, poured myself another Cointreau, and then I sat with a sigh, putting my feet up on the buffet seat. What a hell of a night.

Now I was alone, I was able to think more clearly, trying to remember what Macca had actually said to me. I'd told Hawke that he'd said he had a business meeting but he didn't tell me with whom. That was correct, but had he said more? I closed my eyes, visualising Macca at the office door the night before, his face furrowed in a deep frown.

'It's just a meeting, won't take too long, I hope. This place is quiet in the middle of the day when the races are on. Sammy can cope.' Sammy was the day barman.

'You sure you don't want me to come in early?' I'd said, hoping he'd say no. Maybe it'd been obvious on my face.

'Nah. I'll be back before the main race crowd turns up, for sure.'

'Not selling the place, are you?' I'd been joking, but Macca turned a bit pale.

'Not if I can help it.'

I'd seen the accounts, and he didn't owe the bank a cracker. Connor had told me once he thought Macca had bought the Candlebark pub for less than $200,000 – it'd been closed for nearly a year but it was still a bargain. Maybe someone had been putting the hard word on him. Had he borrowed from the wrong people?

He'd given me no clue as to who he was meeting. I wished he had. It might've been them who killed him.

It hit me again, and I sagged against the cushioned back. Macca was dead. Somebody killed him. There had to be a reason. Candlebark wasn't overrun with murderers – I couldn't even think of any locals with a grudge against him. And that was exactly what Heath asked me ten minutes later.

'No,' I said. 'Macca got on with everyone around here, amazingly enough. He wasn't having it off with anyone's wife, he hadn't thrown anyone out of the pub who wanted his head for it. His ex-wife has been gone ten years, but they're still friends.'

Heath sat down and loosened his tie, eyeing the dregs of my drink. 'Do you want one?' I asked him.

'Later, maybe. I'd better not while I'm on the job.' He got out his notebook. 'Tell me what he said about this meeting.'

I went through it for him, adding, 'Macca didn't keep a diary. If it was something he thought he might forget, like a dentist's appointment, he wrote it on the wall calendar.'

'Was this meeting noted there?'

'No.'

'And you've no idea who he was going to see?'

'No. I wish I did.'

'His car's not here, apparently. And the evidence suggests he wasn't killed here. Someone brought him back and put him in the dumpster.'

'Bit risky, wasn't it?' I visualised the back of the pub. 'Anyone could've seen them. Andre might've opened the back door at the wrong time.'

'Daylight saving hasn't started yet, so it's likely they put him in there after dark.' He checked his notes. 'The local coroner's been – said it was too hard to give a time of death. He guessed at least six hours ago, probably more.'

I looked at the clock. 'Six pm? If the person he was meeting with killed him, surely it would've been before then? Macca was supposed to be back here by six at the latest.'

'There are no indications he was bashed before they shot him.'

My skin crawled and I folded my hands tightly in my lap. 'You think he was ambushed somewhere, like a carjacking?'

'Out here? I doubt it. But we'll know more by tomorrow afternoon. Or should I say later today.' He stood. 'I'd better go and check what's happening. We'll need to do a door knock first thing, and follow up on the interviews of everyone who was here.'

I decided not to mention all the city strangers who had already left. 'How many of you are there?'

'Me and George Swan. A senior sergeant, Joe Mezzina. A couple of others will come up tomorrow. The Bendigo detectives have gone home. Barney will be back in the morning to help.' He yawned so widely I heard his jaw crack. 'God, I didn't need this. We've got a double murder on the go in Melbourne. Father and daughter shot, the daughter's ex on the run.'

Unreasonably, irritation flickered inside me. Didn't he want to be up here with me? But that was stupid. It wasn't about me, it was the way his job went.

'Look, do I really have to stay here tonight?' I asked.

'Of course not. Who said you did?'

'One of the Bendigo detectives said he thought I should.' I yawned myself, rubbing my eyes.

'No, you can go home.'

'In that case, there's a small bedroom upstairs here that one of you can have.' I waited to see what he'd say. I wasn't going to suggest a thing, but yeah, all right, I was hoping.

'Someone in Melbourne will have booked us all into a motel, probably in Heathcote. That'd be the closest, I guess. We may be here all night anyway.' He scanned the lounge bar and sent me a look. 'These seats don't look too comfortable for a nap. Don't suppose there'd be a spare bed at your place?'

I grinned. 'Plenty of hay in the shed you could make into a bed. No, I do have a spare room, as it happens. Swan can have it, if he wants.'

'Very funny,' Heath said, faint pink creeping up over his collar. 'Like I said, we'll be here a long while and your mate, Connor, will have to stay as well.'

'What? To keep an eye on Macca? He's not going anywhere.' That was a bit harsh, and I felt immediately guilty.

'No, but we have to keep the scene secure. Can't afford to have curious locals wandering around. The techs have started work, and they'll be here for hours. When daylight comes we'll do a more detailed search of the area. And start the door knock.'

Strange to think all this had been going on quietly behind the pub while we'd been inside. 'Do you need to talk to me again?'

He finally smiled. 'I think I will need to come and take a proper statement, just to get it all in writing. I might have more questions by the morning.'

'I'll have to give you directions. My place can be a bit hard to find.'

'Fire away,' he said, opening his notebook again. 'No idea what time I'll be there but it might be early.'

Early was fine. I might still be in bed. Heat swamped my face and I turned quickly to go behind the bar and rinse my glass out. 'That's all right,' I said, and explained how to get to my house. 'I'll be off then.'

'Thanks.' His eyes crinkled at the corners, and I suddenly wondered if he'd been thinking the same thing as me. 'See you for breakfast.'

I'd given him my landline and mobile numbers, which he should already have in his phone, but I didn't want anything to go wrong with him making it to my place. My hands trembled on the steering wheel when I drove out of the car park, and I tried to breathe normally as I headed home.

How stupid was I? Probably really, really stupid. We'd never come anywhere near sleeping together so far. I was sure it was in both of our minds, but times and places had conspired against us.

Now perhaps they were conspiring for us. And I was terrified.

3

Heath had never been to my house in Candlebark. Every time we'd met initially it had been about the investigation into Andy's murder in Melbourne. Violence and death weren't a good start to any kind of relationship. Now there'd been another murder of someone close to me. Was it an omen?

By the time I parked in my driveway, I'd pulled myself together somewhat, after a severe talking to. Inside the house, I started gathering up the toys lying everywhere, and considered washing the few dishes in the sink, then I thought, Stuff it. If he doesn't like it, too bad. I'd never been to his place. Maybe he was a total pig, with crap everywhere. Maybe he didn't care. Or maybe he was a neat freak.

Showed how little I knew about him, really. Which was why this chicken-without-a-head act was so pathetic.

I stepped under the shower for a few minutes, put on some comfy sweat pants and a long-sleeved T-shirt, some face cream, and made myself a toasted sandwich. I was starving. I hadn't eaten since Billy told me about finding the body, and before that I'd scoffed down some crackers and cheese for afternoon tea. I'd put some music on – an old Bruce Springsteen CD – and drank chamomile tea to settle myself down. When I finally crashed into bed, my brain kept trying to conjure up a picture of what Macca would've looked like in the dumpster. It was probably worse than the reality.

I slept badly and was awake again before six. I'd made toast and strong coffee and was sitting at the kitchen table, my brain foggy, my eyes drooping, when Heath opened the back door and frightened the crap out of me.

'Sorry,' he said. 'I knocked at the front door and nobody answered, and I thought something might've happened to you.' He sounded stressed, which strangely enough relaxed me a bit.

'It's fine. I don't use that door much, and this stone house dampens sound.'

He eyed the coffee pot longingly and I poured him a mugful. 'Have you got more questions?'

'Not really.' He grinned. 'Good reason to come and see you, though.'

'Oh.' Heat washed up my neck and into my face, despite my efforts to stop it. 'Good.' Lame.

He glanced around my kitchen and I was glad I'd cleaned up this morning after all. 'This is great. Did you do the renovations?'

'No, the owners before me. They were into preserving history, so all the beams are from an old wharf somewhere, and they replaced a lot of the bluestones and repointed them.'

Inane renovation conversation. I sighed. I was hopeless at this. 'No clues about what happened to Macca?'

He drank some coffee and then leaned over the table and pinched my last bit of toast. 'Not yet. No idea where he was killed, or why he was moved. The Bendigo detectives are coming back this morning – they said they might have some information.'

'About?'

He shrugged. 'Not sure.'

Which meant he did know but he wasn't telling me. A little flicker of irritation slid under my skin. 'Would you like some more toast?'

'That'd be great,' he said. 'Then I have to go. Can't leave it all to Swanny. Do you have to work today?'

'I'm not rostered on, but I'll have to go in, since Macca's... dead. I'm not sure what to do. Should I keep the place running?'

'You've got guests, who we have to interview first thing. When the pub opens, we'll also talk to the regulars who come in, and Macca's mates. It'll actually help if you don't close the place, although no one will be allowed past the cordon.'

'OK.' I suddenly realised that Carl might have no idea about Macca – he'd followed his wife off to bed around ten, after putting away a lot of bubbly. I'd heard him snoring like a freight train when I did the upstairs check. He often only made it at the last minute for breakfast. Would I have to tell him? Maybe I could be a wuss and leave it to the police.

Heath rinsed his plate and mug in the sink, and dried his hands as he talked. 'Best bet would be to ring Macclesfield's solicitor if you need to know what to do about the legal situation. Did he have a will?'

'I'm not sure.' I'd pulled on jeans and a warm top earlier but I couldn't go to the pub like that. 'I'll get dressed and come in shortly. I'll have to go and pick Mia up first. I'll need to take her to the pub with me.'

'Right, I'm off then.' He came over and suddenly put his arms around me, holding me close; a little thrill rippled through me. I breathed in his smell, that male thing of cologne and sweat and something else, and tried not to groan with delight. These moments had been so rare. Then he kissed me, his mouth warm and hard, for long enough to make me wish we could hop straight into bed. Suddenly, he was gone, I felt cold and bereft, and the house was echoingly empty.

As I got changed and ready to go, I wondered if Connor was still at the hotel. Hopefully, by the time I arrived, he'd have been allowed to go off duty and home to sleep. This investigation would be a big event for him, and he'd want to do well, maybe earn some Brownie points. Not that he had plans to become a city cop, but he wouldn't want to look like a country bumpkin either.

Would Heath ever come and visit me here? I wasn't holding my breath. It had taken a murder to get him here this time. Our lives were so different, and his job was so demanding. I hoped he'd find more time to drop in again. Dinner and a sleepover? I snorted.

Better to put those ideas about tomorrow and next week and next month right out of my head. That way I wouldn't be disappointed when it didn't eventuate. I was used to pushing things down into a box and shutting the lid, and I'd make sure that's what I kept doing.

Mia was happy to see me, launching herself at my legs, and then whining to be picked up. 'Just for a moment,' I said, hefting her on to my good hip. 'Any problems?' I asked Joleen.

'Nah, she was as good as gold,' Joleen said. Her eyes widened. 'I heard that Big Macca got murdered. Tell me it isn't true!'

'It is true.' I grimaced. 'Didn't take long for the grapevine to start working.'

'Yeah, phones have been running hot, and someone posted it on the Candlebark Facebook page.' She sniffed. 'Did you see him?'

'Who?' I didn't want to give her a millimetre.

'Macca. You know – his body. Someone said it was buried out under the apple trees in Charlie's orchard.'

I shook my head. 'I don't know where these stories start. Whoever killed Macca put him in the dumpster out back by the kitchen. Don't ask me any more – I don't know.'

'You will later, though, won't you?'

'So will everyone else. It'll probably be on the news.' I took Mia's bag off the table and headed towards the door. 'I have to get to the hotel – we've got a full house of guests.'

'Righto.' She held the door open for me. 'Watch out for those cops from Melbourne. I hear one of them is a real spunk.'

'Is he?' I tried to keep my face blank, and must have succeeded. Joleen waved me off without any more questions or comments, but as I backed out of her driveway, I could feel my face burning.

At the pub I parked my car way off to the side – there were already journalists and a TV crew hovering near the front door. Thank God I had the keys to the side door and sneaked past the crowd without being noticed. They appeared to be waiting for someone to come out of the front entrance and tell them what was happening.

In the lounge bar, I closed the door and set Mia up with toys and a drink in a cup, and put on her harness that let her wander around and play without me worrying that she'd get outside and disappear. I could watch her without having to act like a helicopter.

I started on the receipts from the day before, and finalised accommodation accounts. Pay week finished on Saturday night, but I'd get to that later. When Suzie came in an hour later, she watched Mia while I checked on the rest of the pub.

Andre had finished breakfast and was cleaning up the kitchen. He scrubbed the frying pans with short, angry bursts of the steel pad. 'The cops aren't happy I went home,' he said.

'Too bad,' I said. 'Did you see or hear anything outside?'

'Not a thing. Wish I had. Macca didn't deserve that.'

Bob was at the reception desk and I gave him the accounts. 'Carl and his wife still haven't come down yet,' Bob said. 'His mates had full breakfasts though, after they'd been interviewed. Did we get Carl's credit card?'

'Sure did. And I checked it.' I smiled. 'He said he had some winners yesterday, but Mrs Carl didn't last too well in the bar.'

'That Simonetti has checked out,' Bob said, frowning. 'He's a funny bugger. Bloody rude if you ask me. Didn't appreciate being questioned by the cops.'

I was glad to have avoided him. 'Yes. I won't be sorry if he doesn't come back. We don't need customers like him. They upset everyone.'

Bob grunted. 'Well, a bloody murder upsets everyone. Poor Macca. The cops got any idea who did it?'

'No.' I hesitated. 'Did Macca say anything to you about a business meeting yesterday?'

'Not really. He said he was going to lunch with some guy he called a "slimy little empire-builder". I thought he was talking about that guy at the council who was giving him a hard time about sealing the car park with bitumen.'

'I thought that had been settled. And a council employee isn't likely to kill someone, are they?'

'No, that's the province of wannabe councillors up for election,' Bob said. 'Backstabbing bastards, the lot of them.'

I knew Bob had been running a small firewood business and striking all kinds of problems with our greenie council that had stopped tree felling in a lot of places. I didn't want to start him ranting about that again. 'The cops will ask you about it, so maybe have a think if Macca said anything else to you, OK?'

'Will do.'

A loud voice hailed us from the stairs. 'Top of the morning to you!' It was Carl, strolling down like he owned the place. He showed no sign of a hangover. He also showed no sign of being told about Macca. Uh-oh.

'You're looking bright today,' I said, wondering how the hell I was going to break the news.

'I've had a good hot shower,' he said. 'Left the missus in bed with a headache. And now I'm looking forward to a bloody good breakfast. That cook of yours is a real star.'

'I'll tell him you said that,' I replied, thinking it was the kind of comment that sent Andre into a mouth-froth. He liked words such as 'brilliant' and 'talented' and 'gourmet', and struggled with the locals' obsession with chicken parmigiana 'done the normal way'.

I cleared my throat and held up a hand as Carl made to walk into the bistro. 'Hang on, Carl. I, ah… we need to talk.' I could hear a voice in the bistro and was sure it was Barney. Damn!

Carl raised his bushy eyebrows. 'Sounds ominous. My credit card didn't spit the dummy, did it?'

'No, I…' I gestured to the office along the corridor, and then grabbed Carl's arm and urged him to come with me.

'What's going on?' Carl asked, but he allowed himself to be less than gently pushed into the office. I shut the door and leaned against it.

'Carl… God, I don't know how to say this.' I took a quick breath. 'Macca's dead. I'm sorry.'

'What?' Carl stared at me, his skin paling, his freckles standing out like pock marks. He swallowed hard, his Adam's apple bobbing. 'How?' His voice was a rasp.

'He… he was shot. On purpose. I mean, murdered.' I shook my head, and a tear slid down my face. 'I'm sorry, so sorry. I know you've been mates for years.'

'Shit, I told him…' Carl clamped his mouth shut as if he'd been about to say something he shouldn't.

'Told him what?'

'Nothing.' He folded his arms tightly and stared down at the floor, his jaw working.

'The police are here. They'll want to question you.'

'Me?' His head jerked up. 'Why me?'

It was a slightly odd response but I ignored it. 'Billy found Macca out the back last night, so they need to interview everyone who was here, either working or staying.'

'Oh, right.' He let out a long breath. 'Right.' He was silent for a few seconds. 'I never saw him. I went to bed quite early for me. Had a bit too much bubbly and decided to call it a night. The missus was snoring, totally out of it. We should both stick to beer, eh?'

I forced a small smile. 'Why don't you go and get some breakfast? Try and eat before the police come for you.'

He grimaced at my words. 'Don't know about eating. I need some fresh air.'

I hoped he wasn't planning on taking off. Barney would blame me again. 'As long as you don't go near the crime scene,' I said. 'Go out the side door – avoid all those journalists – and head down towards the river.'

Carl nodded and left the office but I could hear Barney's voice coming from the front desk area and guessed he'd nabbed Carl as soon as he saw him. It didn't sound like Carl was arguing, thank goodness, and if he had nothing to tell them, he'd be sitting with bacon and eggs in front of him in no time.

I filed Simonetti's paperwork in the day's folder, noting that he'd given an address in Melbourne. Why had he come all this way when apparently he hadn't gone to the races? Or had I misunderstood? I'd passed on that I thought he was odd, but maybe I'd mention him again to Heath. Or if it sounded too picky, I'd just forget about it.

I went in to get Mia – it was time for morning tea, and I was hoping Andre had made his usual Sunday morning cake.

When we arrived in the kitchen, Andre was nowhere in sight. Bob was helping himself to the brewed coffee on the hob. 'One of those cops came and wanted Andre for questioning.'

'Heath?'

'Nah, the smartarse from Bendigo.'

'Are all of them back again?'

'Just Barney and Hawke. The Melbourne coppers decided they want a local base – Connor has gone home to get some sleep, and then he's setting up the station for them. Called it an "incident room".' Bob slurped his coffee. 'How long do you want me to stick around for?'

'You can go now if you want.' Unless he didn't want to go early. Maybe he needed the money. But he seemed happy to shove off.

'Good, I want to dig over my veggie garden today and get it ready for early tomatoes.'

'We usually get a frost in October or November – I wouldn't be risking it.'

That started a discussion about home-made hothouses and Bob promised to come and show me how to build one. Just as he was leaving, Andre came back in and slammed a cup on the bench, slopping coffee onto it, wiping the spill with a savage swipe. 'Who the bloody hell do they think they are? Fucking fascists.'

'What's wrong?' I hoped I wasn't going to hear a tirade against Heath. I was still feeling rosy about him.

'That bloody Barney for a start,' Andre said. 'Talk about a big-headed prick. Who the hell made him a detective?'

'Mm, I've heard that line before,' I murmured, waving to Bob as he sneaked out.

'He got all toey because I said I hadn't heard anything. What did he want me to do – make it up?'

'I think they're pretty short on ideas about who might've done it,' I said. 'Did Macca say anything to you about who he was meeting?'

Andre shot me a filthy look. 'Don't you start,' he said. 'No, no and bloody no. Now piss off and let me think about lunch. At this rate, I won't get my usual Monday and Tuesday off this week, and I have something on.'

'We'll close the dining room like we always do. We're hardly turning away a huge crowd.' I sighed. Sometimes I felt like closing the whole pub Monday and Tuesday, except the local regulars in the public bar would lynch me. Macca had stopped trying to organise a fill-in chef for Andre.

'Can I get a cup of coffee?' Heath was right behind me and I jumped.

'Help yourself,' Andre said, in a sarky tone that suggested he hoped the coffee was poisoned.

Heath raised his eyebrows at me and poured the black liquid into a mug, then sipped it. 'Great. I needed that.'

'What have you been doing?' I asked.

'Sitting in on the interview with Carl Cammiston and then watching the techs sort through a whole dumpster full of garbage. Glad it's not a hot day.'

'Have you finished interviewing everyone?'

'Just about. Mr Cammiston has left – said to say goodbye to you.' Heath frowned. 'He was pretty upset about his mate, and bustled out of here as soon as we were finished with him.'

'Did you interview his wife?'

'Yes. She seems to have spent most of the evening so inebriated she doesn't remember it. We're moving across to the police station, now that Byrne's set up an incident room. It's small but it'll do.'

Andre busied himself with pots and ladles, banging them around far more loudly than he needed to. I took the hint.

'I've got to check on Mia and then do the rest of the paper-work.'

'OK, I'll see… where we're up to.'

I guessed he'd been about to say 'see you later' and realised Andre was listening, despite the noise.

I bit my bottom lip and sidled out of the kitchen. Mia was grizzling and I groaned – it was impossible to concentrate when she was carrying on. I was sorely tempted to ring Joleen, but it already cost me a fair amount of money every week for babysitting, and I knew I needed to simply pay Mia more attention. Some days it was easier than others.

Suzie was behind the bar, and it was less than ten minutes until the doors opened. Hopefully it'd be a quiet Sunday trading, the regular half a dozen. Suzie jerked her head towards the door. 'Have you looked outside?'

'No. Why?'

'There's eight cars out there already – they're lining up, waiting to get in.' She folded her arms – today she had on a black high-necked shirt and black jeans. 'There's journalists, too. It's like we've become a TV reality show. They all want to sticky-beak and find out about Macca.'

'Not much to tell.' I shrugged. 'They'll have to ask the police. In fact,' I said, smiling nastily, 'tell them to go and ask Constable Barney for the latest information. That'll make him happy and keep him out of our hair.'

'Yeah, I saw he was back,' Suzie grumbled. 'Good idea.'

As soon as the doors opened, it was like a flood. And most of them were gawking tourists – even the regulars looked avid for gory details, which made me cross. A couple of the journalists tried to badger Suzie for information, but she shrugged and moved to the other end of the bar. I picked Mia up and took her into the office, where I sat for a while, staring at the bills and paysheets, trying to will myself to finish them. I should just take them all home and do them there while Mia had an afternoon sleep. But Heath was outside somewhere, and here I was hanging around like a lovesick teenager.

Definitely time to leave then.

Suzie's crowd had thinned, so I assumed some of them had left again when there was nothing salacious to be heard. I told her I was going home to work and she could ring me if it got busy. I thought about telling Heath I was leaving, decided against it, changed my mind. I was the manager now, me and only me, so he needed to know.

He was out the back again, watching the techs finish up, standing with his hands in his pockets staring into mid-air.

'Come up with anything useful yet?' I asked.

'Not a cracker. Just a lot of very smelly garbage. His car might hold some clues, if we can find it. There were a bunch of phone numbers in his pocket on pieces of paper, but they all looked old – the bits of paper were worn and creased.'

'That was Macca's address and phone book, I think. Nothing

on his mobile phone?'

'We were told he didn't have a mobile,' Heath said.

'Who told you that?' I frowned. 'He hardly ever used it, but he did have one.'

'Barney said you'd told him.' Heath eyed me and pulled on his ear. 'Did you?'

I tried to think back. What had I told Barney? I couldn't remember. Last night was a bit of a blur now. 'I'm sure I wouldn't have told him Macca didn't have a phone, when I knew he did. I had no reason to lie about it.' I shook my head. 'Maybe Suzie told him and he got confused.'

'There was no phone on Mr Macclesfield's body. Any idea of the number or who his service provider was? We should be able to get hold of a call record.'

I went back into the office and found his original mobile phone packet in a cupboard, complete with all the information. Heath wrote the details down, and said, 'Can you talk me through his finances and files?'

'Yeah, sure.'

He pulled up Macca's old office chair across the desk from me. 'Show me the money.'

'Very funny.' I gave Mia a container of cut-up fruit and sat her on the floor with some toys, then pulled out the various files with bank statements, suppliers and invoices, and pushed them across the desk.

Heath scanned the bank statements. 'That's all he's got?'

'These are the operating accounts, the only ones I have access to. I don't think he had a mortgage on the place, or any big loans. I only did the basics.' Mia heard the edge in my voice and came over to me and patted my knees. I picked her up and held her on my lap; she grabbed the calculator and started pressing all the keys.

Heath pulled open the filing cabinet, riffling through the files, muttering to himself. 'Insurance, bills, bills, staff records, WorkCover... all very tidy.'

'That was me. They were all over the place before I sorted them out.'

'Any big bills not paid?'

'No, surprisingly. Usually someone who keeps their paper-work in a big box is in financial strife through being dis-organised, if nothing else. I think Macca paid things and then threw them in the box, figuring if it was in there, he could forget about it.'

'That works for me.' The last two drawers in the cabinet were empty. 'Not much here, is there?'

'No.'

'Think he kept stuff somewhere else?'

I had a flashback to my brother, Andy, who'd hidden clues and vital information all over the place, hoping I'd piece it all together eventually. Was this what Macca had been trying to do? 'Only the normal places, like his accountant and solicitor. Macca never struck me as the tricky, secretive type.'

'Except he was this time, because nobody knew who he went to meet, or why.'

'True.' I let Mia get down again, opened every drawer in my desk and went through them, but there were only odds and ends of stationery. I'd cleaned the office out when I first started working at the pub. I've never been able to work in a mess. Heath examined the pinboard on the wall, and then the calendar.

'Are you sure there's nothing else here?' he said.

'Have you searched his living quarters?' I'd only been in

Macca's rooms once – they were just another suite in the hotel, a bedroom and bathroom, and the balcony out the front overlooking the car park down to the river.

'Yep. Nothing useful.' Heath eyed me. 'Did you know he was a Vietnam vet?'

'No. How did you find out?'

Heath leaned forward in his chair, picking at his thumbnail. 'He's got two medals. And we found a photo of half a dozen soldiers in a jungle somewhere.'

'Shit.'

'You seem surprised.'

'Well…' I zeroed in on the container full of pens and odds and ends on the desk and picked out a white ballpoint. 'He never mentioned it at all, but this is from an RSL club in Bendigo, so possibly he was a member.'

'Possibly.'

'Keith Scott's a regular here. He was in Vietnam, I think. Surely he'd know if Macca was a vet.'

Heath leaned back. 'None of that tells us who might've killed him, though. Now if it was suicide, the vet thing would be useful.'

Footsteps in the passage and then Connor was standing in the doorway, his steady gaze on me. 'Hi, Judi. Are you OK?' He bent and gave Mia a kiss, and she grinned at him, holding up a piece of apple that he politely declined.

I nodded. 'Yeah, I'm fine. It's all a bit unreal, but… thanks.' I avoided looking at Heath. 'Did you get some sleep?'

Connor nodded. 'A bit.' He said to Heath, 'I've set up things at the station for you.'

'Great.' Heath stood, hands laced at the back of his neck as he stretched in the small space. 'Hope you've got some strong coffee over there.'

I knew Connor had a large tin of no-brand coffee and not much else. 'We can always supply you with caffeine if you need it,' I said.

'I'll, ah, sort something out,' Connor said. He was probably planning to go and buy a coffee machine as soon as he could, judging by the way he was already heading for the front door.

'See you later then.' Heath looked as if he was going to kiss me, but the office door was open and so was the lounge bar door. He backed out and disappeared.

It was time I looked up Macca's solicitor's details – he was in Bendigo, so hopefully an initial phone call could sort out how the pub was supposed to run in the interim.

I started to gather up the record books and papers I'd need to work at home, and hesitated, my gaze drawn to the RSL biro. I knew Macca was about to turn 70 so that meant he would've been in Vietnam in his early 20s, probably. Way too young to be dodging bullets and killing people in a strange country, but then kids of 16 had signed up for World War I so… there'd been a lot in the news lately about the lack of support for returning vets, from all of the wars. Maybe the fact Macca had never mentioned his service meant he'd blocked it out, or couldn't talk about it, or no longer cared. I stacked up the roster records, ready to leave then put Mia's things into her carry-bag, but the questions in my head wouldn't settle.

So I left it all there and coaxed Mia to climb the stairs with me, and went into Macca's rooms. I assumed the police had finished in here since the door was unlocked again, Trying not to breathe in, as the place smelled of stale cigarettes, beer and dirty socks, I prised open the window and sucked in fresh air while I watched the river tumble its way over the rocks and down towards the bridge. It was a lovely view and I wondered how often Macca had stood here, taking it in. Like me, he loved living in the country but unlike me, he was a real part of the community. I sighed and then scanned the room. What was I looking for here?

Maybe some sense of what Macca might have been up to, or if he'd been keeping secrets to save my feelings. He'd cared about me, had offered me a job when he didn't really need anyone, but he'd seen my desperation. He cared about others, too, like Andre with his prison record and Suzie with her brazen attitude and hidden insecurities. Those generous parts of Macca made me doubt the picture of possible criminal dealings that the police were building up. I didn't want them to be right.

Macca's bed was unmade and the sheets looked grubby, so I stripped everything off, throwing the dirty linen out into the corridor and folding the blankets and doona up, leaving them on the mattress. Next I picked up all the dirty clothes and threw them out, too. Mia climbed on to the bed and pulled the doona over her, sucking her thumb, which I hated, but I left her alone. She seemed sad today, like she knew about Macca somehow, and after I'd smoothed her hair off her face, she lay there watching me.

Most of Macca's personal toiletries were in the bathroom, and I hardened myself against the half-used deodorants and aftershaves, throwing them all in the bin. In the small cabinet, however, I found several bottles and packets of prescription pills, and one of them was for Prozac. That pulled me up. Macca had always seemed laidback, relaxed about everything, laughing at people he called worrywarts. Yet here he was on antidepressants, a recent refill according to the label. Perhaps he hadn't put his war experience behind him as well as I thought.

I put them back and carried on. In the bedroom, his dressing-table drawers were filled with worn-out underwear and holey T-shirts; his wardrobe had two musty-smelling suits shoved down one end and a half-dozen pairs of trousers and a dozen plain polo shirts down the other. I spotted a large cardboard box in the back corner and pulled it out, sitting on the floor and taking the lid off.

Here was the army stuff Heath had mentioned; the medals were in two faded velvet boxes. No heroic Victoria Cross or anything ornately important. They looked like ordinary service medals, except that I reckoned just surviving Vietnam made you heroic. The small bunch of photos underneath were mostly of Macca and Wendy in brighter times — their wedding day, on a picnic, at the races. A photo of the pub as a depressing, weathered brown building before Macca renovated it and painted it white, putting gardens along the front and white fences around the car park.

And there was the army photo. I peered down at it, wondering who the six soldiers were. Macca was obvious, with his lanky frame and sticking-out ears. His big lazy grin would've completed it but he wasn't smiling. None of them were. They looked grim and a bit stunned, actually. Who were the others? One seemed familiar and on closer inspection, I decided it was Carl. Same curly hair and stocky build. I turned the photo over and saw names scrawled on the back.

Me, Carl, John Matthews, Phillip P, Sarge, Tuan.

I inspected the soldiers again and saw that one was indeed Vietnamese. I hadn't seen it at first because his hat was pulled low over his eyes, but now I noticed his uniform was different, too. Maybe Tuan had been like a scout or a Vietnamese aide or something. Whatever he was doing with the Aussies, he appeared grimmer than all of them. Maybe if your country was a battleground, you'd look like that, too.

I put the photos back and replaced the box, closing the wardrobe door. There wasn't much else in the room. Standard crap prints on the walls, shoes under the bed, spare hotel keys on a chain and a pile of paperback books on the top of the dressing table. I picked up the books — I didn't think Macca had been much of a reader, but these were mostly history, and two biographies of a film star and a footy player. One book was an illustrated history of Vietnam, another was a history of the Vietnam War. I flicked through the war history, wondering why Macca would want to read about it now. Did he still have questions, or bear old grudges about being sent there? Two pieces of newspaper fell out of the book and fluttered down to the floor. They were small cuttings, from the *Herald Sun* by the look of the typeface, with no photos or dates. I read them quickly and thought for a moment, then dived back into the wardrobe for the box of photos. The names on that photo – surely it couldn't be a coincidence? One article was a brief summary of a single-car accident on a country road near Shepparton, with the dead driver given as John Matthews, 69. The other was a short report on a man found dead in his bathroom with a gunshot wound that police were investigating. His name was Phillip Prender. Phillip P. It had to be. Why else would Macca have cut it out and kept it?

I left the photo out and closed the box again, then tucked the photo and cuttings into the war history book and sat heavily on the bed. Mia had fallen asleep and I watched her face, her slightly fluttering eyelids, her little frown.

In the silence, my heart thumped in my ears and I clutched the book. Three of them dead. So what? They'd all be at least sixty-five years old; they might've copped some Agent Orange, or still suffered PTSD of some kind. Probably why Macca was on Prozac, for god's sake. Why was I getting so het up about this?

Maybe after Andy's murder and all the searching for the truth I'd had to deal with, my antennae about this stuff were on too-high alert. I was probably making a fuss about nothing, about something that was perfectly normal. Except Macca had been murdered, and it sounded like Phillip Prender could have been, too. And a single-car accident? I'd heard they were sometimes suicide, but someone could force a car off the road, or tamper with brakes. Three deaths, all not from natural causes. A coincidence?

And what was I going to do about it anyway? I wasn't the police. I wouldn't know where to start, even if I had any reason to investigate. The best thing was to hand it over to Heath and let him ask the questions.

Yes, that was easy and sensible.

I dumped Macca's dirty clothes and linen in the laundry basket, and left his door open — I'd ask Joyce to give his rooms a good cleanout, and then maybe use them for accommodation for myself, if I needed it.

Except I couldn't imagine myself ever sleeping in that bed, even if there was nowhere else but the floor. There was something still in there. Something that was hovering, waiting for answers or closure, something I didn't want to be close to. I grabbed the book, picked up Mia and cuddled her as I carried her downstairs. I didn't want her close to it, either.

4

I wanted to tell Heath what I'd found, and was glad to see him and Swan entering the pub as I came down the stairs. He looked up at me and grinned, and I couldn't stop myself grinning back. Luckily Swan's mobile rang just then and he stepped back outside to answer it.

Heath waited by the reception desk for me. 'How's it going?'

'OK. I really need to take Mia home.' I shifted Mia on my hip, put the box on the counter and held out the photo and clippings. 'Did you see these in Macca's room?'

He took them from me. 'I saw the photo. Where did you find this other stuff?' He read the clippings quickly.

'Tucked inside that book on Vietnam.' I scanned his face, expecting to see at least a glimmer of curiosity, but he half-shrugged and gave it all back to me.

'What – don't you think it's strange that they're all dead?'

'Not really. They're all over sixty. Par for the course, especially if they were heavy drinkers, which a lot of vets are. Above average for domestic violence as well.' He'd dismissed it already, which bugged me.

'But this one died of a gunshot wound.' I shook the cuttings at him. 'Macca was murdered. How do you know this other guy wasn't run off the road or something?'

At once I knew I'd gone too far – he raised his eyebrows in that sardonic way of his and said, 'You're not trying to be a go-it-alone detective again, are you?'

'No, of course not. I just thought it might help with finding out who killed Macca.'

He shook his head at me like I was Mia's age and had been caught eating stolen biscuits. 'You have to learn to leave this stuff to us. You could cause problems – like last time.'

His tone was so condescending that I could have slapped him. I still remembered how eager the cops had been to let Andy's mate take the blame for his murder, and how little they were able to protect me when it mattered most. The anger bubbled up, fiery hot, and one part of me was surprised how raw it still was.

'No worries,' I said stiffly. 'Happy to leave it to you.' I took the cuttings back, put them inside the book and snapped it shut. 'I'm off.'

'Judi…' he started, but I was already halfway back to the office to put Macca's box in my desk drawer and collect my papers, and by the time I headed for my car, he was nowhere in sight. Just as well.

Mia and I went home, and I tidied up, making my bed and trying not to think about Heath and my earlier silly ideas of romance. *Do not get your hopes up*. Heath would be off back to Melbourne in a day or two if there was nothing more to investigate here. They'd probably leave the follow-up to Bendigo, which would mean more interaction with the charming Barney. At least I knew where I was with a simple arsehole like him.

After a small battle of wills to get Mia to sleep, I completed the paysheets and plugged in my laptop for online banking. It had all been gobbledegook to Macca. His last office person had written cheques for the employees' wages, which had been a real hassle. The move to online pays and banking was something he'd refused to have a part of, but it made life easier for me.

I had access to all of the hotel bank accounts, but not Macca's personal account. I checked each of the business balances. They were low, but that wasn't unusual, although I'd have to do the banking first thing Monday morning to cover the wages and the bill for the beer supply. That would leave me stuff-all to cover the rest of the bills – I was relying on Carl's payment for them. Then we'd be back to the bottom line again.

I sighed. I didn't like running a business this way, with no safety net of spare cash. Maybe Macca had kept that in his personal account. I closed down my laptop and shuffled the bills back into their folders, then went to inspect my fridge for dinner food. Nothing except some sad-looking vegetables and cheese. Sunday night was usually leftovers and odds-and-ends for dinner – Mia and I ate what was left and on Monday, one of my days off, I did all the grocery shopping and stocked up again.

Best idea was to take Mia back with me and we'd eat in the hotel bistro. I never did get dinner from Andre last night, so he owed me something special. He did a mean gnocchi with cream sauce that Mia loved as much as I did. And maybe Heath would join us.

A warm flush crept up my neck into my face and I patted my cheeks. *Calm down, woman.* Mia would be there and she'd probably be new-tooth cranky and cling to me the whole time. Besides, I was still mad with Heath for that patronising thing he pulled on me. Maybe I'd make it clear he wasn't in the good books anymore.

Yeah, as if.

On cue, a squawk echoed from Mia's bedroom, the funny noise she often made when waking up, as if to say, 'What did I miss?' A few moments later, she came out, rubbing her eyes. 'Drink.'

'Hot chocolate?'

She nodded. Lukewarm chocolate was her favourite and, when I'd made it for her, she insisted on giving some of it to the cat. The sound of the cat purring and slopping the chocolate milk around the dish made both of us laugh.

I made sure I had the accounts ready to take back to the pub. What was I going to wear tonight? Usually on a quiet evening shift, it was black trousers and a white shirt and coloured beads, but that made me look too much like an old barmaid. Not that I cared... I shook my head. Schoolgirl stuff again. I settled for charcoal pants and a deep red silky shirt.

I should've listened to my instincts and not bothered. Heath wasn't there when I arrived at the hotel; Swan said he'd taken Barney with him to question a couple of people. 'Now that your guests have left,' Swan added, 'we'll start focusing on locals who live near the pub. Someone might have seen a strange vehicle. Pity you don't have CCTV here.'

I bit the inside of my cheek. This wasn't exactly the Melbourne CBD. 'It hasn't been a priority.' I went upstairs to check all the rooms – every room was clean, beds perfectly made, bathrooms sparkling. The laundry basket was empty and I knew there'd be clean sheets and towels in the downstairs airing room.

Yet again, I silently blessed Joyce and Margot who worked at the hotel – it was like clockwork, how they arrived and did their jobs efficiently and rarely needed to be checked on. Most places I'd worked in the city over the years had had their fair share of slackers and thieves and deadshits who were always stuffing things up. Who needed CCTV when we had people like this?

In the kitchen, Andre was doing his usual Sunday night clean-out, rummaging through the fridges for food that was close to its use-by date. We rarely had more than half a dozen for dinner on Sundays, but his buffet lunch was popular, although nobody knew it was always the week's leftovers that went into the curries and desserts he made. We never knew what was going to turn up on the buffet table – going by the bowl in the sink, today had been trifle.

'You missed dinner last night,' Andre said from the depths of the largest fridge.

'You noticed?'

He emerged with a wilted lettuce and two squashed tomatoes and threw them in the bin. 'I saved you some salmon. Not worth eating now, though.' He sniffed. 'There've been cops in and out of here all day. I've made more lattes than I do in a year.'

'Cops not making you nervous, are they?' I said with a grin.

'Not at all!' He shrugged. 'Well, a little. The big hunky one from the city is very sexy, though.'

I laughed, hoping I wasn't going red. 'I'll tell him you said so.'

'Don't you dare!' He flicked me with a tea towel. 'By the way, I've got a proposition for you. Not that kind, either!' He folded the tea towel into a tiny square. 'Carl is buying a new racehorse, a filly called Cutie Curls, and he's offered me a quarter share. I'm looking for someone to go halves with me.'

'Me? Own an eighth of a nag?' I considered it for one second and then shook my head. 'I'm not into racing. Don't know the first thing about it.'

'You don't need to,' Andre said. 'That's the beauty of it. You feed and train the thing and then it goes and wins you lots of money.'

'If only it was that easy. I've seen Carl come in here with a long face many more times than I've seen him celebrating. Last night was the exception, not the rule.'

Andre pouted. 'He said it was the trainer he had. Now he's using this new guy who's a real whiz with the horses. He reckons he can get anything to win with his special training package.'

'That may be so,' I said, 'but it's still a no from me, sorry. Apart from anything else, I've got no money. If I had, I wouldn't be working here.'

'True,' Andre said. 'But I need something exciting in my life, dearie, and in Candlebark, owning a racehorse is going to be it for me.'

'Murder isn't exciting enough for you?' The sharp voice made both of us spin around. It was Barney, back from his questioning and apparently still feeling the need to make everyone around him suffer.

'Was that comment necessary, Constable?' I asked coldly.

'Seems to me that you're not taking the death of your employer very seriously,' Barney said.

'Another comment that doesn't deserve an answer,' I said.

'Then perhaps Mr Macclesfield's daughter could be spared some of your precious time.' Barney jerked his head back towards the front bar. 'She's pretty upset at the news. Had to hear it on the radio, apparently.'

Shock made my face go numb and it was a few seconds before I could answer him. 'Macca doesn't have a daughter.'

Barney's grin was like a shark's. 'Shows how little you knew him, doesn't it?'

Heath loomed in the doorway behind Barney. 'Can you come and talk to her? She's already had a go at us for not informing her of her father's death.'

My brain leapt ahead of the unasked question. 'I had no idea Macca had a daughter. Did you, Andre?'

He shook his head. 'News to me.'

'There was nothing in his rooms upstairs to indicate a family,' Heath said.

I held up my hands. 'Never heard even a hint of it.' Could things get any weirder?

'If you come with me, we can talk to her together,' Heath said.

That meant the so-called daughter was having a hissy fit and needed someone other than a cop to calm her down. Great. I narrowed my eyes at Heath and nodded. 'All right. But I'm not putting up with any crap from her.'

'Such sympathy,' Barney muttered as I walked past him. He was lucky he didn't get a left hook to his ribs.

It was easy to spot the woman in the front bar, even if she hadn't been red-faced and sobbing into a handkerchief. She was in a wheelchair and looked thin and sallow-faced, her hair lank and oily. Our arrival didn't stop the hysterics.

Suzie was sitting next to her, holding a drink she'd obviously poured as a calmative. A couple of metres away sat a young man with sandy hair and a hard face whose sharp eyes roamed around the bar as if sizing it and all of us up.

'I hardly knew him,' the woman was saying. 'Just one short year, that's all we had. Ooohh, it's so unfair!'

Suzie looked up at me pleadingly. 'Here's Judi now,' she said, jumping up and putting the glass on a nearby table. 'She'll help you sort it out.'

'Thanks,' I mouthed at her, making a face before turning to

the woman. 'Hello, I'm Judi Westerholme. I'm the manager here.'

The woman let out more sobs, but they sounded fake and there weren't any tears. The hanky was dry. I'd seen Mia do the same thing.

'Dad talked about you,' she said. 'He said you were very good at your job.'

'That's nice to know,' I said.

'Yes, so of course you'll stay on until I get the will sorted out, won't you?' Past the hanky, her eyes were alert.

'Pardon?' I glanced at Heath.

'We haven't found a will,' he said. 'I guess it's with his solicitor.'

'That's right,' the woman said. 'Dad said he was leaving everything to me. He said I deserved it after all I'd been through.'

Another fake sob. Maybe I'd had too many years of being cynical. I tried harder to be sympathetic. 'Er, I'm sorry, but I don't know your name.'

'Madeline,' she said. 'Madeline Grant. And this is my brother, or half-brother, Jamie. I should have been Madeline Macclesfield, but my mum and dad never married.'

'So your mum wasn't Wendy?' I asked. I'd met Wendy, Macca's ex-wife, a couple of times. She was good fun, a tall boisterous woman with a deep laugh. She and Macca had parted ways when he bought the hotel and she decided she couldn't stomach living in the backblocks.

'No way!' Madeline snapped. 'That bitch did Mum and me out of the life we could've had with Dad.'

I was possibly getting into deep, dark waters with this woman, but holding my tongue has never been one of my best attributes. Besides, I liked Wendy. 'Macca seemed like he'd had a pretty happy time being married to Wendy,' I snapped. 'And he's never mentioned you or your mother to anyone here in Candlebark.'

Madeline's face pinched up like someone had squeezed her head in a fruit juicer. 'Mum had her pride. She wouldn't tell me who my father was until last year. I'd only just found him and then...' Another fake sob that made me want to slap her. 'I can't believe he's dead.' She reached for her drink and slurped a large mouthful – it looked like our good brandy.

I needed a drink more than she did. On my way to the bar, I sidetracked to see how Mia was going and she let out a happy shriek that drowned Madeline out. She only wanted to show me the picture she was drawing and, although it was a mess of scrawls, I admired it for a few seconds and then poured myself a Jack Daniel's and got Mia a lemonade in her special plastic cup. Two mouthfuls, several deep breaths and I could return to Madeline, who was whispering with her brother, but this time I was going to get some sensible answers.

Heath had been watching me and raised his eyebrows at the glass in my hand. I wondered irritably what his problem was, but then he glanced at Madeline and rolled his eyes at me. I had to bite back a smile. Madeline must have noticed something and she gave him a venomous look, the kind that said *I hate cops*. But what was her problem? Surely if her father had been murdered, she'd be glad the police were on the spot, investigating. The brother lounged back in his chair, hands in pockets, watching and listening.

If Heath wasn't going to question her, I would. 'So, you're Macca's daughter,' I said, and ploughed on, cutting off her next sobby display. 'I gather he didn't know you existed.'

'Mum didn't want to tell me, but no, she didn't tell him either.'
'So then you tracked him down.'
'That's right. Oh, he was so happy, and–'

69

'Funny how he never mentioned you to any of his friends here.' I folded my arms, trying to feel sympathetic but she was damn annoying.

Her mouth thinned and she sniffed. 'He seemed like a lonely man to me.' Implying none of us had been Macca's friends.

'He wasn't lonely. He helped a lot of people around here, and was very well liked.'

'So who were his friends? You?' She looked me up and down. 'No one around here would help him when he needed it.'

'What do you mean?'

The tears welled up in her eyes, and I sighed, but this time they looked a bit more genuine. 'I've got breast cancer, and I need a special treatment. Dad was determined to pay for it but he couldn't get anyone here to lend him the money.'

That explained her extreme thinness and sallow skin. If she needed a wheelchair, she must be on her last legs. 'I'm sorry to hear that, but Macca never asked anyone for money as far as I know. And anyway, all he'd have to do is take out a mortgage on the pub. It's his key asset.' Surely Macca would have told somebody about this. I glanced at Heath; his face was impassive but he was watching her closely.

A dark flush crept up her neck and into her face. 'I don't know anything about that,' she said stiffly. 'I only know he promised me he'd find the money.'

Heath rubbed his chin. 'Judi, you told me you have access to the accounts.'

'Yes, I pay all the bills and wages. I took that over a couple of months ago. Macca said he'd had enough of it.' I thought back to the figures I'd checked a day ago. 'There's not much spare, just fairly standard ins and outs, and the extra we made from race day yesterday. That'll cover the wages for a couple of weeks.'

'What happens in between race days?'

'Macca pays – paid – the bills when he had the money. Otherwise people had to wait.' At Heath's raised eyebrows, I added, 'Possibly there were some cash-in-hand payments, but nothing I noticed as a problem. Are you asking if he'd pulled money out of the pub that wasn't recorded? The answer is no.'

'We're going to be checking it all anyway, as soon as the banks open,' Heath said. 'That plus a visit to the solicitor might shed some light.'

'On what?' I asked. 'Who killed him?'

Madeline let out another fake sob. 'Surely it wasn't about money?'

Heath had once said cynically that most murders were about money or drugs, sex or family hatreds. With all the fake sobbing going on, I was starting to wonder if Madeline had put out a hit on Macca, even though the logical part of me said it was highly unlikely.

Heath backpedalled away from that question. 'We don't want to jump to any conclusions until we know a lot more than we do right now.'

I spotted Andre hovering by the door and said, 'Excuse me, I have to see the staff about a few things.' Suzie followed me out and the three of us met in the kitchen with the door firmly closed.

'What the hell is going on?' Andre asked. 'Is she really Macca's daughter?'

'You've been listening in,' I said.

'Of course,' he said. 'So, spill.'

'She says she is. Reckons Macca had a fling with her mother years ago, and Mum kept quiet about who he was. She revealed the truth on her deathbed.'

'Oooh, just like TV,' Andre said. 'What was all that stuff about money?'

'You've both worked here longer than I have,' I said. 'Did Macca ever say anything to you about a loan, or needing money?'

'Nup,' Suzie said. 'The pub would've made more money if he hadn't been so generous but then that was Macca, wasn't it.'

'If the daughter's talking about that cancer treatment that was so expensive,' Andre said, 'a friend told me the government agreed to subsidise it not long ago. So why would she have to pay full price for it?'

'Good question.' My stomach rumbled and I put my hand over it. 'I'm starving. What are we doing about dinner?' I checked the clock. 'It's nearly six. Have we got any bookings for the bistro?'

'Two,' Andre said. 'Are any of those cops likely to come in?'

'Give Barney some cyanide,' Suzie said.

I realised I hadn't seen him for a while, not since he'd told me to go and talk to Madeline. 'Either he's gone home or Heath has sent him off on another job. Yes, let's have dinner. Except... I get the horrible feeling we're going to be stuck with Madeline.'

Suzie pointed at me. 'You mean you're going to be stuck with her.'

'Mmm. She thinks that Macca left this place to her in his will, but I'll believe it when I see it.' I lifted the lid off one of the pots on Andre's stove. 'Is this chicken or pork?'

'It's possum.' Andre slapped my hand and I dropped the lid with a clang. 'Dinner will be ready in about twenty minutes. There are some tables set, but it's up to you whether you push them together or not.'

'Not,' said Suzie. 'I'm not eating with the drama queen.'

'Now, now,' I said, 'where's your sympathy and compassion for the poor woman?'

She snorted. 'With yours, out the back somewhere. I'll keep Mia in the bar with me and feed her in there, if you like.'

Someone knocked on the kitchen door and Andre pulled it open. Heath stood there, a half-smile on his face, and I knew he'd been eavesdropping. 'Is there any chance we can get some dinner here tonight? Just Swanny and me.'

Andre turned on his most charming smile. 'Of course. It's not full à la carte, I'm afraid. Limited choice.'

'Possum will be fine,' Heath said.

I was highly amused to see Andre's face turn bright pink.

Madeline had made a fuss about wanting to stay at 'her' pub, and I'd been forced to put them into two of the upstairs rooms to shut her up. After I'd shown Jamie which ones they were, I made sure I locked the door to Macca's room.

Just as we were sitting down to eat, Connor arrived to confer with Heath and Swan, and his eyes lit up when he smelt the aroma from the kitchen. I let Andre know we had an extra, and gritted my teeth at what was ahead of me.

Dinner was excruciating. Nothing wrong with the food – Andre had cooked a delicious curried lamb from leftover roast. But Madeline was still in full actress mode, dabbing her eyes and pretending to pick at her food and then scoffing it double-time when she thought no one was looking.

Her brother kept up a steady trail between the bistro and the bar, putting away pots of beer like there was no tomorrow. He was one of those men who wore his jeans barely hanging off the platform of his bum, with the band of his undies showing under his faded, trendy band T-shirt. I wanted to hoist his jeans so far up towards his armpits that his balls shrieked.

Someone had joined four tables together, so we were forced to sit shoulder-to-shoulder. I managed to avoid Connor's eyes, and worked hard to ignore Heath. Since the cops present weren't going to discuss the case in front of us, and no one wanted to talk to Madeline or her brother, conversation was pretty much non-existent.

Until the door opened and Carl bowled in.

'Just in time for dinner!' he said, checking our plates. 'Lamb rogan josh, my favourite.' He bounced over to the door into the kitchen and pushed it open with a bang. 'Andre, mate, got any left for me?'

Andre muttered something that didn't actually sound rude, and Carl returned with a full plate, sitting himself down at the head of the table, on my right. Madeline's expression was a curious mix of annoyance and curiosity and I wondered if Macca had mentioned Carl to her.

'Carl,' I said, 'what exactly are you doing here? I thought you'd be home by now, with your feet up.'

'I was, I was,' he said, shaking a liberal amount of salt on to his food. 'As soon as I walked in the door, I knew I should've stayed, so I came straight back.'

'Yeah, but why?'

He raised his eyebrows at me. 'Macca was my mate, from way, way back. You don't just walk out on a mate.'

'But he's dead,' I went on, over Madeline's manufactured sob. 'He won't know you're here.'

Carl poked himself in the chest. 'I know I'm here. And I'm ready to help.'

'With what?' This time I did glance at Connor and caught his raised eyebrows. Carl was usually the one who needed help up to his room.

'Dunno. With whatever needs doing.' Carl scanned the table and dismissed Madeline and her brother without asking who they were. 'Macca's funeral, for a start. Is Wendy coming up? Has anyone even told her?'

Heath cleared his throat. 'Yes, a police officer went around to her house.'

'Good, good.' Carl shovelled a forkload of food into his mouth.

I hadn't given the funeral a moment's thought, and my skin prickled. Maybe I should ring Wendy and see what she wanted to do. I hoped she wouldn't expect me to organise it. Making arrangements for Andy had been bad enough. But the only other person who might want to was Madeline, and the idea of that made my jaw clench.

'We're not sure when the body will be released,' Swan said. 'But if someone picks a funeral home, they'll sort it out.'

'Mmm,' I said noncommittally. I was still waiting for Madeline to jump in and take over. I could tell she was listening hard, but she kept silent. Maybe she didn't want to have to pay for the funeral – didn't that normally come out of the estate? I'd paid for my brother's, but someone in his partner's family had paid for Leigh's body to be cremated and shipped interstate. Family I didn't know she'd had.

Andre came out of the kitchen, waving a wooden spoon. 'You've got a choice,' he announced. 'Apple crumble or bread and butter pudding.'

Yes, we were definitely on leftovers, but Andre's bread and butter pudding was the best I'd ever tasted. Connor and I were the only ones who chose it, because we knew from experience, although the apple crumble smelled divine, too.

As soon as we'd finished eating, Connor, Heath and Swan went off to the police station to sort things out for the next day. Madeline and Jamie moved into the other bar where the walk was shorter for his beer. They were probably in there casting hexes on us all. Andre joined Carl and I at the table and Suzie brought us port and brandy from the bar. 'Anyone in there?' I asked. When she shook her head, I said, 'Close up for the night, then.'

'It's only eight o'clock. And those two are in there.'

'Too bad. No one's coming in now. We all need a quiet night.'

'Who are they?' Carl asked.

I explained briefly, and said, 'Macca ever mention her to you?'

He pushed his lips out, thinking. 'Nup. But I guess anything is possible, the way things from your past roll up again.'

That felt like a slap, even though Carl had no idea about my family, and I didn't respond.

'Hey, I hope you've still got a room for me,' Carl said.

'Of course. But I'm still not sure what you're doing here.'

'I meant what I said.' Carl swallowed some port and grimaced. 'Never did go much for this stuff. No, I want to help – with the funeral, around here, whatever you want me to do. What the hell am I going to do up there on me own? I've got two managers who do it all for me. I'm bored shitless.'

'I've got plenty of dishes for you to do,' Andre said with a grin.

'Doesn't worry me, mate.' Carl clapped him on the back. 'Once that nag of ours starts running, you'll be able to buy your own restaurant.'

'Yeah, sure,' I said. 'How many horse buyers have said that before?'

Jamie rolled the wheelchair back into the bistro and Madeline sniffed loudly. 'I think I'll go to bed now.'

'Goodnight. Sleep well,' I said, trying to sound like the caring hostess.

'I won't be able to sleep a wink,' she said. 'I'm just too upset.'

I rolled my eyes at Andre, but Carl leapt up, having spotted her wheelchair. 'Can I help you upstairs?'

Jamie eyed him as if assuming Carl's grey hair and pot belly meant he was way too old to lift anything heavier than a beer, but I knew Carl was a tough bugger – I'd seen him heave a horse out of the way as well as lift the back end of someone's car that was stuck in the mud. But Madeline simpered and said, 'That would be wonderful.' Off went Carl to do the Good Samaritan thing.

Suzie brought Mia in and she clung to my legs until I picked her up. She laid her head on my shoulder for all of two seconds and then wanted to play with the leftover cutlery and salt and pepper shakers on the table. I dragged the high chair out from the corner and put her in it, along with a plastic bowl of bread and butter pudding and a spoon.

I began to clear the table, stacking dishes while Andre set out the breakfast equipment for the morning. We had a woman who came in early on week mornings and did continental breakfasts for guests if we had any. I counted up – with Carl coming back, plus Macca's unwelcome new family, that would be three we hadn't expected. As I finished, Andre did too and said, 'I'm off. See you Wednesday.'

I stared at him for a moment until I remembered. 'Right. Enjoy your days off,' I said. 'Doing anything special?'

'The big smoke,' he said. 'A friend's fiftieth birthday dinner. I'm cooking. What they used to call a busman's holiday, whatever that means.' He leaned close to my ear. 'You behave with that nice policeman while I'm away.'

77

My face grew hot but I raised my eyebrows at him. 'I have no idea what you mean.'

He laughed. 'I've got eyes, my dear.'

Oops. I'd have to be super-careful as long as Heath was here. I hated being the target of gossip. Mia had eaten most of her pudding and only put about a quarter of it on the tray and the floor. She waved the spoon at me slowly, her eyelids drooping – great, she'd be asleep before we got home, so I'd be cunning and get her ready for bed now.

I wiped her face and hands and changed her into her PJs, found her teddy bear in the lounge bar, and was about to carry her out to the car when Heath walked in from his organising at Connor's station and offered. 'You're going to lock up first?' he said.

'Bob will be here any minute. He'll stay overnight again, thank goodness.'

While I strapped Mia into the car seat, Heath leaned against the side of my car. 'Can't call in and see you tonight, I'm afraid. Swanny expects me to be in the room next to his all night.'

I'd expected it but all the same disappointment hit me like a slap, and I struggled to hide it. 'Sure. Not a problem.'

'It is a problem, but...' He moved in close, his warm hand under my chin, his mouth like a tease. I took the bait and kissed him back. A seismic tremor ran through me and I pulled back but Heath still had his hand on the side of my neck. He could probably feel my pulse hammering against his palm.

Headlights swung into the car park and across us, and I quickly stepped away. 'I need to check in with Bob. That'll be him now.'

In fact, it was Connor, with Bob a hundred metres behind him. I hoped to God Connor hadn't seen Heath and I so close and cosy by the car, but his puzzled face as he got out of his 4WD told me he had. Damn. First Andre, now Connor. Heath would be off back to Melbourne in a day or two, leaving me to explain myself, and that was something I did not want to do. I marched into the hotel, turning off lights and locking the office door, saying a bright 'Goodnight' to Suzie, who also wouldn't be in again until Wednesday. A young guy tended bar Mondays and Tuesdays, and Macca did the rest on his own.

Except now it looked like I'd have to cover the place until I found out what was going to happen. So I'd have to be here every single day. My heart sank. I needed my time off, and Mia needed time with me. A part of me hoped the solicitor would say 'Shut the hotel indefinitely', but I suspected that even if Macca had left it all to Madeline, it wasn't going to be that easy.

Bob looked better tonight, the grey gone from his face. His garden was good therapy, like mine. I gave him the rundown on everything, adding, 'I know you only usually do a night here and there, but I might need you on a more regular basis until we know what's going to happen.'

'Sure,' Bob said. 'I'll sleep in the small room with me mobile on. Once I've locked up, of course.' He added, 'Coppers getting anywhere yet?'

'Not as far as I know.' Bob had no other questions, and I left with a brisk 'See you all tomorrow', trying to get out of there before Connor cornered me. No such luck. He was waiting out the front.

'Mia's fast asleep already,' he said.

'It's been a long day for both of us,' I said. I jingled my car keys in my hand and edged towards the driver's door. 'At least you don't have to stand guard on poor old Macca all night again.'

'No.' Connor huffed a sigh. 'I'll miss him. He was a bright light around here.'

'Yeah, I know.' I opened the car door, relieved that I was getting off without an inquisition.

'Are you and Heath… he was the guy who worked on Andy's murder, right?'

'Yeah. Hotshot.' I shrugged. 'It's not going anywhere.'

'But you'd like it to.'

'Hey, I live here, and he lives down there. Country mouse and city rat. You think it'll work out? I can't see it.' I brushed aside the suspicion I'd had for years that Connor would like more from me than friendship, because that was never going to happen, Heath or no Heath. Trouble was, I'd never made that totally clear to Connor, and now I was shoving it in his face. That made things awkward, and I didn't want them to be awkward. I wanted our comfortable friendship, same as usual, but maybe I was being selfish. 'I need a decent night's sleep. Tomorrow I've got to deal with Macca's solicitor and the bank, and then his bloody awful daughter.'

'Is she really his daughter?' Connor asked. 'What's that all about?'

'She thinks Macca has left her the pub, which may well be true, but I'm past caring right now. I've had enough of her to last me a century already.' A sudden thought stopped me. 'She'll have to be included in the investigation, won't she? Seems a bit odd that she suddenly came out of the woodwork.'

'You think she killed Macca?' Connor said with a grin.

'Nothing would surprise me!' I sighed. 'See you tomorrow, no doubt.'

'OK.' He stood back and watched me drive off; I could still see him in my rear view mirror as I turned the corner and crossed the bridge.

5

I carried Mia into bed without any trouble, and debated staying up for a while in case Heath managed to sneak away, then acknowledged that I was being stupid yet again. Granny nightie it was, and although I thought I'd be awake for hours, I dropped off in a few seconds. Mia woke me the next morning, trying to shove a grubby handful of cornflakes into my mouth.

'Ahhh!' I jerked back and grabbed her hand, giving her a fright so that she burst into tears. 'Sorry, Mia, come here, sweetie.' She clambered into bed with me, sniffing and spreading cornflake crumbs everywhere. That would've gone down a treat with Heath, if he'd been here. And what would Mia have thought? Hopefully not that her dad had come back. She still asked for him every now and then. At first, I'd decided not to mention his name or Leigh's, but that seemed too strange. Now I kept photos of them in her room, and often talked to her about them – admittedly, more about Andy than Leigh. But she knew who they were, called them Daddy and Mummy, and me Judi. What I'd do as she grew older wasn't something I wanted to think about yet.

After a proper breakfast, I packed a large bag full of everything Mia might need for the day – I had no idea how long I'd be at the hotel, or what I'd have to cope with. I'd call Joleen if I had to. I couldn't help feeling a bit resentful, as I'd been planning to spend the day in my garden, making the most of the mild spring weather. Rain was forecast for midweek and I wanted to get seedlings in if I could.

But as I drove into the pub car park, my pulse rate sped up and fluttered at the base of my neck. Heath's car was still there, so I wasn't surprised to meet him coming out of the dining room but I had to take a couple of slow breaths before I could say hello.

'We're heading to the station incident room,' he said. 'But if you're going to ring the solicitor now, I'll wait and see what he says.' He sounded businesslike but his eyes were saying something else and I was glad I'd worn another nice shirt, dark green this time. I was fast running out of decent clothes though. Tomorrow might have to be trackpants.

I checked my watch. 'He should be in by now. I'll try and see.'

I unlocked the office and sat behind my desk, putting Mia on the floor with some toys before dialling the number on the letterhead I'd found. The receptionist knew who I was and put me straight through, so I gathered they'd all seen the news last night.

Phillip Gillespie managed to be both sombre and friendly at the same time. 'Ms Westerholme, I'm glad you called. I was planning to contact you this morning but you've beaten me to it.'

'You've heard about Macca?' The catch in my voice surprised me and I swallowed.

'Yes, it's terrible news. You must be very upset.'

'Yes.' I didn't know what else to add. 'Things here are in a bit of an uproar. I guess I'm ringing you because I don't know what to do about the pub. Do I close it, or what?'

'That's a good question.' He cleared his throat. 'Can you come to my office today?'

'Um…' I looked at Heath, who just raised his eyebrows. 'I think so. Why?'

'I need to speak to you. I have a letter from Mr Macclesfield for you, and also a copy of the will.'

'Me?' I pinched the bridge of my nose and closed my eyes. 'Why?'

'He came to see me a couple of weeks ago.' I heard him rustle some papers. 'I'll explain it all when you get here. Do you know what time I might expect you?'

I glanced at the clock and then at Heath, who was no help. 'Around eleven?'

'Good. I'll see you then. Goodbye.'

He didn't hang up in my ear but it felt like it. My phone fell into the cradle with a clunk.

'What's the matter? What did he say?' Heath asked, regarding me with a small frown.

'He wants to see me, says Macca left me a letter a couple of weeks ago.' I shook my head. 'No idea why. I mean, I've known him for ages, but not that well, and I've only worked here for a few months.'

'A letter? What about?'

'How the hell do I know?' I flung my hands up in the air. 'Do I look telepathic?'

'All right, calm down,' he said.

I wanted to hit him. 'I have to go to Bendigo. I said I'd be there by eleven.' I rummaged in the desk drawer for the notebook with everyone's numbers in it. 'I'll have to ring the fill-in guy and get him to come in early. All this overtime is going to kill me.' Too late I realised what I'd said and I grimaced. 'You know what I mean.'

'I want to come with you. That letter might be vital information. We need every bit of help we can get right now.' He stood
up. 'We can go in my car, if you like.'

'I have to take Mia, and you don't have a child seat. And what
if Swan needs your car?'

'True.' He pulled at his collar like it was strangling him.

'You don't want to drive with me, do you?' I laughed. 'Tough.
It's me in the Benz or you'll have to walk.'

'It's fine,' he protested, but his jaw jutted out in a way that told
me it wasn't.

Once we were on the road, he finally relaxed a bit. 'These old
cars are quite comfortable, aren't they?'

'Better than your Commodore? Surely not.'

Mia had dropped off to sleep within the first five minutes.
The rest of the trip passed in a light vein, both of us avoiding
anything dark like murder or romance.

Gillespie's office was away from the busy centre of the city,
and had its own little parking area so that made it easy. We
got out, I unstrapped Mia and we went inside. The reception
area was furnished in blue and yellow, which was startlingly
bright, and the air con was on high even though the morning
was cool. The pale, young receptionist sniffled with a cold and
I was tempted to tell her to turn the air con off but settled for
giving her my name instead. She angled a glance at Heath but
didn't ask who he was, just showed us into Gillespie's meeting
room where the air con was just as cold. I shivered and she
noticed. 'Sorry. It's stuck on high. We're waiting for the guy to
come and fix it.'

Heath beat me to it. 'You could just turn it off.'

'And have nothing at all?' She looked astonished at the

thought, and then sneezed. 'You want a coffee or tea?'

'Yes, please,' I said. 'Coffee, black.'

'Same for me,' Heath said, 'but with milk.'

She gave him a confused look and nodded, closing the door after her.

'You're probably going to get tea,' I said.

Just as she came back with two coffees that looked more brown than black, Mr Gillespie came in through another door. He was tall and thin, with greasy black hair combed over a balding pate, and he wore a dark blue suit that was too small for him, showing bony wrists and grey socks. I sipped my disgusting coffee and put it aside. Mia wanted to get down so I put her on the floor with a couple of books and a puzzle, hoping that would occupy her for a while.

Gillespie had one folder tucked under his arm. He laid it on the laminate boardroom table, sat down and opened it. There wasn't much inside, just one thick envelope and one thin one. 'Right. Thanks for coming in, Ms Westerholme.' He looked up at me for the first time and spotted Heath. 'Oh. Who's this?'

Heath leaned over and shook Gillespie's hand. 'Detective Sergeant Ben Heath, Homicide.' His tone was brusque.

'Oh.' Gillespie looked at me. 'Are you…'

'No, she's not under suspicion,' Heath said. 'But there may be important information or evidence in that folder of yours.'

'Oh.'

I took pity on the man. He didn't appear nervous, just out of his depth. 'You said Macca had left a letter for me. Can I have it, please?'

Gillespie handed the small envelope over without a word. I opened it and read quickly.

Judi – my new will might seem strange. Please accept what is in it. I'm sorry if it causes you any trouble, but it's meant with the best intentions.

I've truly appreciated everyone's friendship.

Best wishes,

Macca.

I read it again then handed it to Heath. He skimmed it and asked Gillespie, 'Is the will in that other envelope?'

'Yes.'

'We need to see what's in it. Is that a problem?'

'Well, there should be a proper reading, but...' Gillespie flapped his hands.

'Let's see what's in it, shall we?' Heath said firmly.

Gillespie opened the envelope and unfolded the will document, passing it across the table. Heath picked it up. 'Do you mind if I read it first?' he asked me.

'Go for it.' I wasn't sure I wanted to know what was in it. Macca's note bothered me – it sounded like he somehow knew time was short. I shuddered. It reminded me way too much of Andy's last message to me, a cassette tape that blew my life apart.

I watched Heath's face, waiting for him to nod or say it was what Madeline had told us, but his expression was unreadable for a moment and then his mouth turned up in an ironic smile. 'I'm not sure you're going to like this.'

'Doesn't worry me if Madeline gets the lot, although I doubt I'll want to work for her.'

'She doesn't get a bean.'

'Really?' I tried not to think what her reaction was going to be. Volcanic, probably. Macca must have left the pub to his ex-wife, Wendy.

Heath flicked through to the last page and then looked at

Gillespie. 'This is dated two weeks ago. Why did he suddenly make a new will?'

'Well…' Gillespie's bald head was beaded with sweat and I wondered if he was ill, given the air con must've just about been turning the sweat into icicles. 'It was the second will he'd made in three months.'

'Because?' Heath's tone sharpened. 'You must know why.'

'It's confidential. Client privilege.'

'Rubbish. Your client is dead – murdered. That means I get to know what he said.'

'He… he changed his will three months ago when he found out about his daughter. He told me she had cancer but she was beating it, and he wanted to make up for all the years he'd never helped her or her mother.' Gillespie pulled out a wad of tissues from his pocket and mopped his head. 'He said his ex-wife wouldn't want the pub anyway. She'd told him that ages ago.'

I was leaning forward, listening and eyeing the will that was now lying on the table. Heath saw me and pushed it my way, but for some reason I couldn't bring myself to pick it up yet. Mia must've sensed my tension and decided it was time to cling to my legs and grizzle. I picked her up and sat her on my lap; it felt like I was holding a little shield.

'So how come he changed it again?'

'He didn't say.'

Heath's fingers tapped the table irritably. 'Surely you asked?'

'That's not my job, to question what my clients want in their wills. I can't be seen to influence them.' Gillespie's face had reddened.

I butted in. 'What did he say?'

'He thought there might be some disputes over the new will, so he asked me what would happen if Madeline tried to contest it.' He pursed his lips. 'It sounded like she was being... pushy.'

'You haven't met her?' Heath asked.

Gillespie shook his head. 'I don't know Mr Macclesfield all that well. I've only met him three times, just about his will.'

'Surely he said more than that?' Heath sounded totally exasperated. It seemed he'd had high hopes for clues in the will.

Mia started banging her hands on the table and reaching for the envelope; between trying to shush her and follow the conversation, my irritation levels were rapidly rising.

Gillespie paused for a long moment, his lips pushed out as he thought. 'He did say he'd had help. Somebody called Simonetti.' He frowned. 'It was something about shovelling away the shit.' He glanced at me. 'Er, sorry, but those were his words.'

Heath turned to me. 'Aren't you going to read it?' Snappy, like *what was I waiting for?*

I gritted my teeth. 'All right, all right.' I'd been about to say I knew who Simonetti was but my desire to be helpful had quickly faded. I picked the will up, holding it out of Mia's reach,

and skimmed the first legal part, then got down to the bit where he said who would get the hotel. 'This can't be right.'

'He was very clear,' Gillespie said. 'He'd brought in a piece of paper with your full names and addresses.'

'It doesn't make sense.'

'He said it made perfect sense to him. He said you were the only ones who deserved it.'

I read the paragraph again. Macca had left the pub, along with most of his estate, apart from some money for Wendy, to Andre, Suzie and me. My hands shook and the paper rattled. Andre and Suzie, I could understand – they'd both been with Macca for more than five years, but me?

And why had he changed his mind about Madeline?

Gillespie couldn't add much more, apart from giving me a photocopy of the will. Heath told him that Andre and Suzie would be given the will to read, too, which he seemed unhappy about, until he was reminded that it was a murder investigation.

In the car, I said, 'I suppose this gives the three of us a motive to kill Macca.'

'Possibly. Except that you knew nothing about it.'

'Are you saying Andre and Suzie might've known and said nothing to me?' I sped along the road out of Bendigo then made myself slow down. I had Mia in the back, and I didn't need a speeding ticket either.

Heath pulled his tie loose and undid his top button, then opened his window. Cool air swished around the interior of the Benz, helping to calm me down. I found a tissue and wiped my face. Despite the freezing air con in Gillespie's office, I felt damp and slightly greasy. With eyes like a hawk, Mia spotted a McDonalds sign up ahead.

'Chips! Chips!' She waved her arms and tried to get out of her car seat.

'You feed her that stuff?' Heath said.

'Once in a blue moon. But she's seen the ads on TV so she knows exactly what the golden arches mean.' I flicked on my indicator. 'I used to be partial to the milkshakes. Do you want anything?'

'Ugh. No thanks. I had enough of that stuff years ago, on shift work.'

Thanks to the drive-through, Mia had her fries in about thirty seconds and we were on our way again. The smell of the food filled the car and my stomach grumbled. I should've bought a milkshake and too bad about Heath's scorn.

'When we get back, I'll have to interview Andre and Suzie again,' he said. 'Swanny will question you again, too.'

'What for?'

'The will changes things. Before you were asked about what happened the day Macca was murdered. Now it's got to be about what led up to it.'

I sighed heavily. 'All right. If you think it'll help.'

'Anything and everything is useful, especially when we have no idea who he was meeting that day, or why.'

We drove in silence after that. I was trying to process what the will meant, and wondering how the hell Andre, Suzie and I would run a business together. Maybe the same way it'd been running for the past few months, minus Macca. But the money was a problem. I doubted his estate would have enough in it to pay all the bills, let alone pay for much-needed renovations and unforeseen bills. Macca could've left us with an albatross around our necks.

As for Madeline, I shuddered to think what she was going to say when she found out. I sure wasn't going to tell her the bad news. Maybe Heath could do it.

Only the public bar was open at the hotel, with one of our casual bartenders sitting with two locals, having a beer. He jumped up when I came in, looking embarrassed, and I waved him back to his seat.

'Relax, Charlie. Not like it's busy.'

He nodded. 'Really sorry to hear about Macca.' Heath stood in the doorway behind me, and Charlie must've guessed he was a cop. 'You catch the bastard yet?'

'No.'

I said, 'Do you and Swan want some lunch?'

'I'll get something later. Swan's over at the station. I need to fill him in, and then go find Andre and Suzie. Swanny will come and talk to you, OK?'

'Sure. But don't forget Andre is probably still in Melbourne.' I took Mia into the kitchen and sat her on a spare chair by the back door, remembering it was the one Andre used to take outside when he had a break. There was no way I was opening the door – the dumpster would still be out there, reminding me of what had been in it. I made Mia a cheese sandwich and helped myself to the leftovers of bread and butter pudding, leaving a small amount for her. I knew I wasn't allowed to call Andre or Suzie before Heath talked to them. It'd look suss, like I was warning them, but I was busting to tell them about the will, and find out if they were as shocked as I was.

I was cleaning the dishes we'd used when Swan knocked on the door. 'Can you talk to me now?' he said.

'Of course.' We went into the dining room and I put Mia in the play corner we'd built when I'd started working there. It'd turned out to be popular with all the parents who ate in the hotel, too. I sat at a nearby table and waited as Swan sat opposite me and took out his notebook and pen.

'Detective Sergeant Heath showed me the will,' he began. 'Changes things a bit, doesn't it?'

I hadn't really talked to Swan since he'd arrived, but now I examined his face and the hard tone of voice he'd used. He didn't know me, and obviously didn't know my relationship with Heath, so as far as he was concerned, I was one more possible suspect. 'It does for me, I guess,' I said cautiously. 'Now I know about it.'

'You had no idea what Mr Macclesfield had put in his will?'

'No. I would've thought I'd be the last person he'd leave anything to.'

'Why's that?'

'I've only been working here for three months. I knew him before that, when I came to live here. He was more a… new friend. We got on really well.' My throat closed up at a memory of Macca laughing at one of his own jokes.

Scribble, scribble in the notebook. 'No romantic relationship with him?'

'No.' I half-laughed, hoping I wasn't blushing.

'So why would he leave you a third of the pub?'

I held up my hands. 'No idea.'

'Were you surprised about the others getting a third?'

'Not as much as I was about me.'

'Did they say anything?'

'They didn't know either.'

'Sure about that?'

I gave it a second's consideration. 'Yes.'

'Business been good?'

'Race days are healthy. Other than that, it's pretty quiet.'

'How much did Mr Macclesfield owe on the place?'

'I thought he owned it free and clear. I don't think it cost much. Ask Suzie.'

'How would she know?'

'Macca probably told her. He got a bit talkative when he was drunk.'

'How often did he get drunk and talkative?'

I thought about that for a few seconds longer. 'Actually, very rarely. Once that I remember.'

'But you do remember it.'

I'd been trying to sit still and keep my hands relaxed in my lap, but now I was shifting in my seat and my knuckles were white. Was I feeling guilty? No. But that one night when Macca was blind drunk was horrible, and I didn't like remembering it. 'It was a bit unpleasant.'

'How?'

I blinked a few times. 'He was crying, sobbing. At the end, before he passed out.'

'Why? What led up to it?'

Swan was like a relentless terrier with its teeth in my leg. 'Nothing out of the ordinary. It was… actually, it was a race night. Races up towards the Wimmera, but some people make it a regular thing to stay here on the way back.' I racked my brain to pull out more memories from that night. 'Carl was here.'

'Bit out of his way, wasn't it?' Swan regarded me with cold eyes, his face a mask.

'Yes, but he's an old mate of Macca's.'

'When was this unpleasant night?'

'A few weeks ago, I think. It wasn't that bad. It was just that I'd never seen him in a state like that before. He was usually so jovial and full of fun.' Mia was rattling the gate of the play area and I was grateful for the excuse to go over and tip all of her blocks out of the crate for her. By the time I sat down again, I felt a bit more able to deal with Swan's machine-gun questions. 'How is that relevant to this?'

'Everything and anything might be relevant.' He made another note. 'Is this the first time Nick Simonetti has stayed here?'

I was thrown by the sudden change of subject. 'Er… yeah, I think so.'

'Did you speak to him at all?'

'Only to check him in and give him his room key. Bob checked him out the next morning. Why?'

I could see him wanting to say, 'I'll ask the questions.' Instead, he said, 'Do you know Simonetti?'

'No.'

'You didn't know he was a private investigator?'

'No.'

'Employed by Mr Macclesfield?'

My skin prickled. That was the 'help' that Simonetti was providing. 'What for?'

Swan smirked. 'Not to investigate you.'

I bit back a snarly retort and took a breath. 'I had never met the guy before. I thought he was rude. And he certainly never said why he was here. Was he supposed to meet Macca?'

'Yes.' Swan snapped his notebook shut and stood up. 'I'll probably have more questions later. You're not going away, are you?'

'No.' I smiled nastily at him. 'I apparently have a pub to run.'

6

I went and sat in the small office, putting Mia on the floor with some toys, but she was bored within two minutes and started trying to climb up on my lap, whining and pulling at my shirt.

'What?' I yearned for the day when she could talk and tell me what the problem was. Instead I fetched a ball from the play corner and we rolled it up and down the hallway for a while. The afternoon was warm and I paused by the open side door, staring out across the car park at the slow brown river beyond, lined with grass-green weeping willows, and wondering what I should do.

I desperately needed someone to talk to and my first thought was of Andre, but I was banned from communicating with him for now. I jumped at a voice behind me.

'We've finished the rooms, love.' It was Joyce, one of the cleaners. Hands on hips, she surveyed the hallway and bistro. 'You want me to vacuum here, too?'

'Yes, thanks. Er… what other work do you usually do?' My job had been managing the bars, the stock and the accounts. Macca had always taken care of the rest, but 'the rest' was also my job now. Andre did kitchen and bistro stuff. Suzie did… bartending. I wanted to pull my hair out by the roots. How the hell were the three of us going to make this work?

'We do a bit of everything really,' Joyce replied, shrugging. 'Whatever Macca said. He vacuumed the bars as soon as he got up of a morning...' She blinked hard and bit her lip. 'We can do that, too. Might have to come in earlier though.'

I made an executive decision, and I suspected it'd be the first of many. 'Good idea. If you and Margot can come in an hour earlier and do downstairs first, that'd be great. Thanks.'

She nodded and went away; a few minutes later I heard the vacuum humming out in the hallway. Mia was grizzling again so I took her to the kitchen and helped her drink some milk out of her little cup. Maybe I should take her home or to Joleen's. There were things I needed to do, and I couldn't with a grumpy toddler around. I couldn't stop thinking about Macca leaving me a third of the pub. I needed to know what that meant financially – whether Macca had been propping the pub up with cash transfers from his own account. There'd have to be a financial trail, surely. Payment records from one account into another, receipts, even a letter. I had the login and password for Macca's account that he'd given me once just in case, so if he had another linked account for auto payments of any kind, I could check. I felt sneaky about it but I had to know.

The sound of high-pitched crying broke into my thoughts and I automatically reached down to pick Mia up, but it wasn't her. Out in the reception area, Madeline was screeching about something. I listened against my will as I took Mia's hand instead and edged towards the back of the kitchen.

'I can't bear it, I can't bear it!' Madeline let out a howl like a banshee and Mia whimpered.

My guess was Madeline had found out about the will. I so did not want to come face to face with her. And how dare she frighten Mia? I picked Mia up and felt for the bunch of hotel keys in my pocket. We could sneak out through the back door and lock it. No way was I getting trapped in the kitchen.

The lock had been recently oiled and the door opened easily. We crept out, me with a finger to my mouth. 'Ssshhhh,' I said.

Mia giggled. 'Sssshhhhh,' she repeated.

I felt like a thief, tiptoeing around the side and checking who was in the main bar before I opened the side door and slipped in. Charlie gave me a puzzled wave and jerked his head towards the entrance where Madeline was still screeching at someone. I shook my head violently and put my finger to my lips again. Charlie grinned and nodded, leaving me to sidle down the passageway to the office, quietly unlock the door and get inside without being seen.

I kissed Mia and put her down. 'You're a good girl.'

She gave me the same kind of puzzled look, but happily sat in the spare chair with a container of a few Smarties I kept as an emergency stash. I had a search to carry out.

I started with the files, going through every single piece of paper, and paying special attention to the bank statements. Nothing unusual. No regular payments to or from another account, just the usual bills, the ones I knew about. I hadn't missed anything there. I booted up the computer and logged in to the online banking portal. Nothing there either, although I noticed Macca's personal account was no longer accessible. Maybe he'd closed it. I checked the copy of the will I had – Gillespie was the executor, so I called him, practising a stern voice as I waited to be put through.

'Ms Westerholme, is there a problem?'

'I think so,' I said firmly. 'I really can't keep running the pub until probate is done. It's not possible.'

'It is legal,' he said.

'But does the estate – the money in it – cover any bills I need to pay? I mean, they might be huge, and the income from the pub might not cover them.'

'Large bills?' He sounded doubtful.

'Or what if there's a loan or another mortgage we don't know about. I can't find any paperwork here, so you must have it, or at least know about it.'

'No-o-o, I don't.' He sniffed. 'Mr Macclesfield told me he owned it free and clear. I had no reason to doubt him.'

'You're the executor – don't you contact the banks and work that stuff out?'

'I… I have to apply to the Supreme Court for the Grant of Representation first.'

'Oh.' I thought for a moment. 'But you have nothing there from Macca to say he had another mortgage on the pub.'

'No. In fact, if I remember rightly, he was adamant that it belonged to him and no one else.'

I thanked Gillespie and hung up. It wasn't a hundred per cent definite but it did make me feel a little better. I eyed the filing cabinet again. It was too empty. Heath was right. Who was Macca's accountant? I found his name and number and called him, too. Once we got past the professed shock and sympathy about Macca's murder, he confirmed what the solicitor had said.

Macca didn't have a mortgage or a loan with anyone.

'He also doesn't, er, didn't have superannuation either, and the veteran's pension was… variable.'

'Variable?'

'Because of the pub, Mr Macclesfield wasn't eligible for a full pension. He had to keep putting in forms to prove his income and assets.' The accountant cleared his throat. 'About three years ago, he had a run-in with Veterans' Affairs and told them to stick their pension where the sun didn't shine. He hasn't applied for or received anything since.'

As bad as bloody Centrelink. 'He was making very little from the pub.'

'I know,' the accountant said. 'But he'd made his mind up. Said as long as he could pay everyone's wages and the bills, he had a roof over his head and could eat from the fridge – if the chef would let him.' He laughed. 'You must have one of those tyrants in the kitchen, eh?'

'Just a small one.' I thanked him and, after some discussion about meeting to go over financial records, I hung up.

I'd done what Heath asked me to – followed up on the financial side of things. Maybe I should go over to the police station and tell him what I'd found out.

I looked around the shabby office. When I'd first started working for Macca, this room had been full of rubbish – boxes of old magazines, empty coffee cups, all kinds of things stuck to the walls including years-old calendars, and a desk chair that wobbled so much I was sure it would collapse under me. Never mind that its leather was imprinted with years of holding Macca's bum. I'd done a massive clean-up to turn it into a decent working space, but really I'd taken all of Macca's personality out of it.

Here I was, ferreting around in his finances and records, all because I was worried about being liable for the pub. The man was dead, for God's sake! I could still see his face the day I said his chair had to go, the dismay and reluctant approval of a new chair. He was a bloody good bloke and I'd been a bossy know-it-all, not appreciating him for who he was – everyone's mate and everyone's helper. My eyes burned and I blinked furiously.

Mia seemed to sense I was upset and came and crawled up into my lap. I hugged her tightly until she squirmed and reached for a pen to draw with. I gave her some paper from my recycling pile and she happily scrawled some circles.

Circles. Which circles had Macca been in? My brain jumped around, always ready to avoid grief if it could, despite the ache in my heart, and I made my own circles on another sheet of paper. Mates in the pub. Bob, Old Jock, Scottie, Jack… Huge circle. Local business people. Smaller. Specifics like accountant and solicitor. Small circle but more would be in there. Employees. Family. I hated putting Wendy in with Madeline, but…

Underneath I wrote other names that didn't fit neatly anywhere else. Connor – he was a bit of several circles but stood outside them because he was police.

Simonetti. My pen underlined his name several times. He was like a thorn in my foot. I put Mia down and found the booking records for Saturday night's guests. There was Simonetti's mobile number. Before I could think too much about it, I called it.

'Simonetti.' He answered so quickly I was briefly lost for words. 'Who's this?' he snapped.

'It's Judi Westerholme from the Candlebark Hotel.'

He was silent for a long moment. 'I'm sorry about Macca.'

He'd used Macca's nickname. 'Me, too.' I sighed. 'Can you tell me what you were doing for Macca?'

'Have they found out who did it yet?'

'No, and they have no idea.'

'I did explain to them why I was there,' he said. 'They obviously didn't tell you. No reason to, I suppose.'

'I need to know. Macca's daughter has turned up here, causing a huge fuss. And Macca has gone and left the pub to me and

101

Andre and Suzie, so...'

Simonetti sniggered. 'Good. She's not his daughter. I got Macca enough evidence so he could pay for a DNA test privately to prove it.'

'Holy shit.' I knew she was lying!

'Macca's always been a soft touch, but he and his ex-wife had tried to have kids and he'd been told it was his fault, so once the shock of Madeline turning up wore off, and even Macca could see she was overdoing the lost daddy act, he asked me to help.'

'Just as well he did.'

'I'd told him about the result, which is why he changed his will straight away, and I'd brought the official test document with me. We were supposed to discuss what he could do to get rid of her.'

'How the hell do *I* get rid of her then?'

Simonetti let out a long whoosh of breath. 'Macca should have the initial DNA results letter there, if he printed it out. I can email you a copy, if you like. Just tell her to leave, and tell her why. If the cops are still there, get them to help you if she arcs up.'

'OK. I'm not looking forward to the hysterical response though.'

'You don't have any choice,' he said. 'She'll stick to you like a leech otherwise.'

'I'll still feel mean.'

He laughed again. 'Don't. She doesn't have cancer either. She's got jaundice and hepatitis from a trip to Bali.'

I thanked him and hung up. The news about what Madeline really suffered from didn't make me feel any less guilty about asking her to leave. All those years of Andy's drug use, and my final refusal to help him, still weighed on me. On the other hand, it did look like she was out to scam anything she could, and even if Macca had put his foot down…

Mia pushed down her pen so hard that the paper had ripped and she looked up at me in consternation.

'I know how you feel, kid,' I said. 'I have to sort it out now, don't I?'

She frowned. 'Cake.'

'Yes, good idea,' I said. 'Cake will be my incentive. Come on.'

I took her hand and we went out to look for Madeline. She was in the bistro with her brother, and it bugged me that she had helped herself to coffee and clearly rummaged through Andre's kitchen to find cake and biscuits. Like she thought she owned the place!

'I need to talk to you,' I said. No point dithering – I'd lose my momentum.

She had two bright red patches on her face and her eyes narrowed as she looked at me. 'What's going on?' she shrilled. 'What have you been up to?'

My hackles rose straight away, but I did my best to stay calm. 'Some information has been passed on to me.' Oh God, I was dithering after all.

'Anything about the pub should come to me. It's my pub now,' Madeline said. 'And I think I don't want any of you to work for me.'

I pressed my lips together tight but it burst out anyway. 'Listen, you stupid girl! You know the will says you don't get a cracker. Macca left the pub to the three of us.'

'Bullshit!' Madeline spat. 'He promised me. He said he'd make it up to me that he left me and Mum in the lurch. And he promised me money for my treatment.'

'Macca might have been a soft touch but even he realised

eventually what a con artist you are. I know he had someone do a DNA test, and it proves you're not his daughter.'

'That's what you think,' Madeline said. 'He got someone to fake that test. I'll see our solicitor and contest the will. We'll tie you up in court for years, not to mention lawyer's costs. You'll be sorry you ever turned Daddy against me.'

My mouth dropped open. 'How could we turn him against you? We didn't know you existed. And you can't fake a DNA test.'

Madeline smiled again, a nasty smirk this time. 'Of course you can. Anyway, I'll still tie you up in legal knots for at least a year. It'll cost you thousands. You might want to consider making me an offer now, before I bankrupt you.' She jerked her head back. 'Come on, Jamie, let's go. The smell around this place is making me sick.'

Jamie glared at me and patted Madeline on the shoulder, then wheeled her out of the bistro. I almost called after them that they owed me for the room, but I stopped myself. No point making it worse. Surely she'd pack up and leave now? I waited a few moments, debating what to do next, but curiosity got the better of me and I went to check where they'd gone. The wheelchair sat at the bottom of the stairs, and I caught a glimpse of Madeline with Jamie supporting her as they went slowly up, a step at a time.

She really was sick, I'd give her that. Nobody had an emaciated body and yellow skin and eyeballs like that unless they were, but I had to harden myself against her. What she had threatened was all too easy to do. Some lawyers specialised in will disputes and she probably had a really shifty one on speed dial.

Heath came in through the front door and smiled at me.

'Didn't expect to see you still here.'

I smiled back, my face warm. 'Keeping an eye on the pub. Listen, I've found out some very interesting stuff, and I've talked to Macca's solicitor again as well as his accountant. You know, he does own this place.'

He frowned, his eyes darkening, and took me by the arm. 'We need to talk.' I managed to pick Mia up before he hustled me around the corner to the office and once inside, shut the door. 'You can stop worrying. We're investigating new information. It's put a whole different perspective on things.'

'What do you mean?' Mia wriggled in my arms and I put her down; pain jabbed through my hip and I gasped, leaning on the desk for a few moments. I really had to stop carrying her around like that or she'd cripple me. Even the physio had warned me. I sucked it up and straightened, facing him. 'What have you found out? Or is it too secret to tell me?'

He'd watched me with a concerned look but now he rubbed the side of his face. 'You have to stop haring off like Sherlock Holmes. It's dangerous, especially when you have no idea what you're dealing with.'

'It's not my fault I've been landed in the middle of it. This is my life here, you know.'

'I do know!' His mouth was a thin line and I sensed he was talking about more than Macca's murder. 'But you're not a detective and you have to leave it to us.'

My face was burning and I nearly told him to get stuffed, or worse – twice he'd made me feel like an idiot. Just like my overbearing father used to. I was finding out things they had no idea about, because they didn't know Macca and they didn't know this community.

'Look.' He folded his arms tightly, his jaw clenching. 'I'm

going to tell you this just so you'll keep out of it. It seems Macclesfield was dealing in chop chop, probably to try and get money for Madeline and her phoney treatment.' He saw my puzzlement and added, 'Chop chop is illegal tobacco.'

'I thought the cops had stopped all that around here a few years ago.'

Mia had climbed up on my office chair and was standing on the desk, playing with my hair. I had a good grip on her to keep her next to me.

'They did, but the price of cigarettes is so high now that the industry has escalated again. Different players but same game.'

I was about to answer him when Mia pulled my hair too hard. 'Ouch! Listen, kiddo, we'll go home soon, OK?' I glanced at Heath. 'How did you find out about the chop chop?'

'Someone from the task force working on it rang us last night. Swanny went over to Bendigo this morning and talked to them. They had Macca on their radar, and said he'd only sold one lot so far, and was supposed to pick up another one.'

'You mean, someone killed him over tobacco?' I shook my head. That didn't make sense to me. Drugs, yes. Chop chop – what was the point? And it didn't sound like something Macca would get involved in. But what did I know? Nothing, according to Heath.

'There's big money in this, you know. Millions. There are Melbourne ethnic gangs involved, as well as the biker gangs. Semi-trailers carrying containers of illegal cigarettes off the docks. Barney thinks the dealer in this area somehow got the idea that Macca was a police informant.'

My mouth gaped open. 'Barney? He couldn't find his arse with both hands and a compass. How would he know something like that?'

Heath ran his fingers through his hair – I knew him well enough to know he wasn't convinced either. 'Apparently they're running an informant out this way, and it came from him. He's a mate of Barney's, so even though Barney's not on the task force, he's linked into what's going on. Says he keeps his ear to the ground.'

This revelation didn't gel with me, but I needed time to think about it. I also needed time to settle down after Heath treating me like a nosy old bat. I opened the door to take Mia to the kitchen and caught a look on Heath's face. 'Don't worry, I won't say a word to anyone,' I snapped. 'I don't even want to know who the informant is.'

'I wouldn't tell you anyway,' he said in surprise.

Huh, I thought, I bet I could find a way to make you. But I didn't say it. Well, from now on, Heath could stick his investigation where the sun didn't shine. I understood that he probably thought he was protecting me, but my experience had always been that not knowing what was going on, what all the facts were, was a lot more dangerous. And bloody frustrating. Plus I hated being treated like I was stupid. I headed to the fridge with Mia trailing behind me, and pulled the large white door wide open.

'Typical. I'm away for one day and you're eating all of our profits.'

I whirled around, a huge smile bursting on to my face. 'Andre! You were having time off.'

'They called me to come back early,' he grumbled. 'Your hunky detective has had me on the rack, torturing answers out of me.' He paused for a moment, biting his lip. 'I still can't believe it. Why the hell did Macca leave this dump to us?'

'Oh, come on, it's not that bad,' I said. 'Now you can call

yourself a publican as well as a chef. You know, with a bit of renovating and some marketing, we could actually make this place pay. You could become one of those trendy country chefs with a listing in the *Age Good Food Guide*.'

He chortled. 'Yeah, right. Around here? Don't you remember the night I made Bombe Alaska and someone called the CFA fire truck?'

'Forget the locals. We'd never make money out of them anyway, not where food is concerned.' A crash and a loud wail spun me around. Mia stood in front of the still-open fridge surrounded by spilled carrots and broccoli and a broken bottle of cranberry juice. Already its sticky red liquid had spread like blood all over the floor.

'Shit!' My raised voice turned her wail into a full-blown screaming howl, tears running down her face.

Andre leaned across the mess, picked her up and handed her to me. 'You take her out to the play area and I'll clean up. And then you and I and Suzie need to talk.'

I nodded and did as he suggested, but it took me nearly five minutes to calm Mia down. It was times like these I really wondered what on earth I was doing with her. I'd seen other mums pick up their kids and soothe them in a minute or two, but lately Mia had gone from being a too-quiet little mouse to a screaming mess. Joleen had told me it was her big teeth coming through, but I wasn't so sure. I was beginning to think it was me – that despite the books I'd read and the stream of advice from Joleen and Suzie, I was failing miserably at this mothering thing, and probably scarring Mia for life.

This time, though, when I'd calmed her down, she clung to me and gave me several big kisses, and then happily sat at the table and ate the cheese and peanut butter sandwich Andre gave her. Maybe I wasn't doing as badly as I thought.

Andre sat down with me and put a couple of his favourite recipe books on the table just as Suzie came through from the main bar. 'I've got Sam in there, filling in,' she said. 'Andre said we were having a meeting.'

'Have you been questioned again?' I asked her.

'Yes, so now they're saying we can talk to each other.' She grimaced. 'As if we had something to do with Macca's death, for God's sake. A third of this place is not enough of a motive, trust me.'

Andre's mouth tightened and he glanced at me.

I opened my mouth to say something about the chop chop and stopped. I'd be very unpopular with Heath if I let that out. Instead, I said, 'I guess they think it's strange that he changed his will.'

'Has anyone told Madeline yet?' Andre asked. 'I got the distinct impression that she turned up here because she thought he'd left the pub to her.'

I grimaced. 'It caused a major hissy fit. She doesn't really believe it.'

'She'll find out when the solicitor has the proper reading of the will,' Suzie said. She pointed at the recipe books. 'Are you changing the menu already?'

'I was looking at summer soups.' Andre angled a glance at me, his mouth twitching. 'The kind of soup you make for the *Age Good Food Guide*.'

'Christ, surely not!' Suzie said.

Andre and I both stared at her. 'What?' she said. 'The locals will revolt if we try to change this place into something trendy, you know they will.'

'Some of the locals are revolting,' Andre said. 'Old Jock

dribbles on the bar all the time.'

'Suzie, we can't afford not to change things here,' I said. 'Either that or we'll have to sell up.'

'But we'll all lose our jobs,' she began, and stopped. 'Except they're not our jobs now, I guess. We're management. We're on the front line.' She sighed. 'Shit, I hadn't thought about it like that. I thought we'd just go on like before.'

'Macca wasn't making a living here,' I said. 'He did own the pub but it was only breaking even. He didn't pay himself a wage, just ate and drank here and took money out of petty cash for extras.'

'It's one of the reasons the menu was so basic,' Andre said. 'And why we had a leftovers night.'

I looked critically around the bistro and didn't like what I saw. Cobwebs in the corners, tatty curtains, red check vinyl tablecloths from the 60s, a carpet that never came clean and scratches on the doors and woodwork. I'd never looked that closely at it all before.

'The thing is,' I said, 'if we stay and try to make a go of it, we'll need a loan.'

'What for?' Suzie said. 'I've got no credit at the bank, and no one is going to give me a cent.'

'Luckily, I haven't given Carl the money for the horse yet,' Andre said ruefully. 'I guess I can cope with being a pub owner instead of a racehorse owner.'

'No, it's not like that,' I said. 'This place is its own collateral. We do a business plan that includes renos and marketing, how much profit we expect to make in the next two to five years, and the bank lends us enough to give it all a go.'

Suzie paled. 'What if we go under? I don't want to lose my house.'

My experience in losing pubs was bitterly won. 'You won't – they'd only give us a small loan, based on the accounts. They'd take this place from us and sell it if the loan defaulted.'

'But we only just got it!' she said.

'There's another problem... maybe,' I said. I felt I had to warn them. 'Madeline has threatened to tie us up in court, dispute the will, just to put us out of business as revenge.'

Andre let out a huge whoosh of breath. 'She is some piece of work. Can she do that?'

I drummed my fingers on the table, thinking. 'It's possible.'

'She'd probably go to one of those no-win-no-pay places,' Suzie said. Her face was pale. 'Look, if it's going to turn into a court battle, I want no part of it. It's not worth it to me.'

'Not even for a third share in this place?' I said. I avoided looking at the cobwebs and sticky carpet.

'Who wants a third share in something that might bankrupt me, let alone keep me awake night after night?' She looked at Andre and back at me again, and shrugged. 'Sorry, but I didn't ask for Macca to leave it to me, did I?' She turned and went back to the public bar.

'Neither of us can afford to buy Suzie out,' I said to Andre.

'No.' He leaned back in his chair. 'But I understand where she's coming from. You know, Macca might've thought he was doing a good thing, but maybe he's handed us a lame duck.'

'A one-legged duck with clipped wings and no beak is more like it,' I said, and we both laughed. 'I should take Mia home. I know we'll be back here tomorrow.'

It was a relief to get away from the pub and all the complications that were building up. I could see Suzie's point of view, too, but she wasn't making it easy for Andre or me. I pulled into my driveway and went to unlock the house before getting

Mia out of her seat. Just as I opened the back door, the phone rang and I picked it up, thinking it might be Heath.

'Hello, is that Judi Westerholme?' asked a voice that sounded vaguely familiar.

'Yes.'

'It's Peter Thompson, your solicitor in Melbourne. How are you?'

'Good.' I frowned. Had he heard about the will already? No, not possible.

'I've... ah... got some not very good news for you, I'm afraid.' He cleared his throat and I waited, dread crawling through my stomach. 'I've been notified that a Mr and Mrs Donaldson have applied for guardianship of Mia.'

I thought I'd heard him wrong for a few moments. 'Mr and Mrs Who?'

'They're Leigh's parents. Mia's grandparents.'

'But they live in Sydney!' It was a stupid answer but my brain had frozen and the words spilled out of my mouth.

'They did. They've moved to Melbourne and put an application in with the Family Court.' He sounded apologetic, as if it were his fault. Maybe it was.

'You told me that what Andy put in his will – naming me as guardian of Mia – was legally binding.' My voice rose. 'How can they do this?' First Madeline's threats, now this. I was gripping the phone so tightly that my knuckles cracked.

'Their argument is that Andy died before Leigh, so that made her the surviving parent, and legally the only one who could assign guardianship.' He drew in a breath. 'Despite the fact she didn't have a will, they do have grounds for their application.'

I sagged against the wall. 'So what happens now?'

'I'll send you the papers, and you'll have to appear at a

mediation meeting. That's mandatory. If that doesn't settle anything, it might go to court.' Papers rustled in the background. 'The mediation meeting is next Monday.'

'So soon?'

'They filed the application a month ago, but the notification was sent to your house in Ascot Vale. You obviously haven't been there for a while to collect the mail.'

'No,' I said dully. 'Haven't had time.'

'I've got a gap tomorrow afternoon, as soon as I've finished in court. Maybe you should come down and we can go through everything. 3pm?'

'That's fine.' I sighed. 'See you then.'

I hung up and sat at the kitchen table, head in hands, my brain spinning. I'd never met Leigh's parents, never had any desire to. Leigh had been bad enough. Had Andy met them? I had no idea. What could I say to them? How could I convince them to change their mind? Why were they doing this?

All questions I had no answer for. Suddenly, a noise filtered through to me, past the chaos in my head. A child screaming. Mia! I jumped up and ran outside, scanning the garden and driveway, trying to work out where she was, then pulled up short.

She was still in the back of the car, strapped in her car seat. Once the phone rang and I'd answered, I'd completely forgotten about her. She thumped her fist against the window and glared at me, tears streaking her face.

As I raced to unbuckle her and get her out of the car, one thought was like a shout – maybe she'd be better off without me.

7

It didn't take long for word to get around about Macca leaving us the pub. By the time I did my first round of the bars the next day, the locals were all asking me about it. Probably Suzie had told her two sisters and from there, who knows? One of them might've even put it on Facebook, which pissed me off – it was our business, nobody else's – and when yet another local in the public bar asked me what we were going to do next, I'd had enough.

'Maybe burn the place down,' I snapped. 'Save everyone a load of trouble.'

His offended expression said it all.

'Sorry, Bert,' I said. 'The last few days have been a bit of a nightmare.'

'That's all right, dearie,' he said. 'You're all still upset about poor old Macca, I'll bet.'

I nodded, and went off to hide in the office. Upset about Macca? The trouble was I'd almost forgotten that Macca was dead. With the police in and out, seeing Heath regularly, dealing with Mia, trying to ignore Madeline, somehow I kept expecting Macca to walk back in and shout, like he always did, 'Cheer up and put a beer on the bar!' That he'd been murdered still didn't seem real.

Grateful that Mia was with Joleen, I slumped into the office chair, head in hands, and let the tears slide down my face. Macca and I had often sat in here, going through the accounts, talking about jobs that needed doing, sharing the latest local news we'd heard in the bar. I'd learned more about Candlebark in this office in three months than I had in the whole seven years living in the place.

I sat up and wiped my face. Maybe that was why Macca left us the pub. He thought the three of us understood its importance to the community and wanted to keep it that way. He hadn't been a very good judge of character then. Suzie was bailing out already, Andre would rather spend his money on a racehorse and I – well, I still wanted a quiet life.

And to be honest, selling the pub would boost my finances. It'd allow me to keep the house in Melbourne, which I should've sold, but I couldn't bear to part with what felt like my only real family history. I couldn't deny money from the pub would be really handy, but I felt disloyal to Macca even thinking it.

I eyed the filing cabinet, thinking I should do the banking paperwork and see what bills I could pay before the next wages were due, but I couldn't be stuffed. The trip to Melbourne hung over me like a shadow. Joleen hadn't been keen on having Mia again but there was no way I was taking the kid. I wanted to be able to concentrate and think clearly about whatever the solicitor had to tell me.

My mind slid away from that and back to Macca. I could almost see his laughing face, the way he'd rub his balding head from front to back a few times while he thought. In all the gossip we'd swapped, not once had we ever talked about chop chop. I knew I'd remember – it was such a strange term. Even if he'd been planning to buy some and wanted to keep it secret, surely at some time it would have come up in our conversation if locals were buying or selling?

We'd known all about Les Miller's two boys growing marijuana, and Les burning it all when he found out, and we'd also heard about the teenagers who went to clubs in Bendigo and bought ecstasy. Connor had had to search their houses and talk to their parents, which had got very sticky. Macca had made it very clear that if anyone tried to sell drugs in his pub, he'd throw them out quick smart. But no one had ever mentioned chop chop.

It didn't make sense to me. But then if Macca had thought he needed the money for Madeline and her treatment... that might be the new information Heath was following up.

As if I'd conjured Heath up by thinking about him, there was a light knock and he came into the office, his face tired and in need of a shave. He sat in Macca's chair and regarded me in silence.

'How's it going?' I said. Remembering too late that I was supposed to leave it all to the police. Even the questions.

'I think we've driven about five thousand Ks, interviewing people. Half of that was getting lost down back roads and having to turn around and start again. Google Maps is no good when there's a reception black hole.' He yawned so widely that I heard his jaw crack.

'You still think Macca was dealing in tobacco?' I didn't think he'd divulge any secrets, but I was curious about how far his chop chop theory had taken them.

'Plenty of ideas, nobody who will talk. The guy that Barney said was selling around here is nowhere to be found. His house looks like it's been empty for months.'

'Mmm.' I wasn't going to get into how reliable Barney's

information was, or offer any more ideas, not after he'd told me to stay out of it.

'A guy who owns the pub at Myrtleford says Macca was in there last month.'

'He was?' I knew I sounded disbelieving but I couldn't help it.

Heath gave me a sharp look. 'Apparently Macca went to see him about this place – whether he'd be interested in buying it.'

I frowned. 'Was he?'

'No, but he put Macca on to some developer in Melbourne who's bought a couple of country pubs and turned them into four star jobs.' He leaned forward. 'Are you sure he never talked about money issues? Selling up?'

'I'm sure! I've been sitting here thinking about our conversations over the past month or two, and none of that stuff ever came up. Neither did anything about chop chop.'

'Well, he'd keep that quiet, wouldn't he?'

I'd had enough. Now I knew what 'blaming the victim' meant. Heath could argue till the cows came home, but even if Macca had been desperate enough to sell the pub, I couldn't believe he would've gone into selling something illegal like chop chop. It just wasn't him. But then I'd been wrong about people before. I changed the subject. 'I have to go to Melbourne shortly – a personal matter.'

He waved his hand. 'No problem. I need to get back to the station and talk to Swanny.'

I wanted to tell him about the custody thing but the words wouldn't come. I checked my watch and was astonished to see it was nearly midday. Time I found my handbag and phone and got ready to go.

We both stood and, as I brushed past him on my way out, he put his arms around me and held me close. I resisted for a moment then gave in, breathing in his warm, familiar scent. The hug was nice, the kiss was brief, like he didn't want to get into anything more. Neither did I.

I pulled away, gave him a rueful smile and went off to check who was around. Andre was sitting at a table in the bistro, feet up on a chair, having a cup of coffee. He'd levered open the doors out into the garden and cool air drifted in, bringing the smell of jasmine and river water. He grinned when he saw me, and offered coffee, which I gratefully accepted. 'I hope you aren't opening for lunch. It's your day off, even if they did drag you back here.'

'No. Madeline and Jamie came in before expecting food but I got rid of them. They can get sandwiches at the milk bar.' He gestured out to the garden where overgrown bushes cast jagged shadows across the cracked paving and weeds sprouted from every crevice. 'We should tidy that up and put tables out there in the summer.'

'Yes, we should.' I sat down next to him and assessed the scrubby lavender bushes and a large, lethal, red oleander that would have to be ripped out. 'Does that mean you're planning to stick it out and do something with the pub?'

'Hey, where else have I got to go? It's the only chance I'll ever have to own something and make a go of it.' He glanced at me, his face serious. 'Why, do you want to sell up?'

'It crossed my mind. I...' I hesitated, but Andre and I had been good mates right from when I started working at the pub, and who else could I talk to? So I told him about Mia and the grandparents' law suit.

He shook his head and whistled. 'Man, that's pretty rough. How long has it been since your brother died?'

'Nearly five months.'

'Would you give Mia up?'

I swallowed hard, delaying my answer, but I knew Andre wouldn't judge me. That's why we liked each other. 'I've been wondering if it'd be the best thing for her, you know? I feel so useless half the time; I never know what I'm doing. World's worst mother syndrome.'

'Hey.' He leant forward and patted my knee. 'You might not be her mother, but you do a damn good job of being Aunty of the Year. I've seen you with her. You love the kid, even if you think that's being soppy.'

'I do not!' I tried to laugh and it caught in my throat.

'Do, too. And it's OK to worry because you always keep trying.' His mouth twisted. 'You could be like my mum and just give up.'

That created a small moment of silence between us, but it wasn't awkward. We'd talked about this before, shared the shit in our lives – the silence was just a space where we both acknowledged that it had happened and we'd mostly moved on.

'I have to go down and talk to the solicitor today, and I should have already left,' I said. 'The mediation meeting is next week.'

'What does he think?'

'I have a feeling he's going to tell me to find someone else. Family law isn't really his thing.' I sighed. 'I'll find out shortly. I'd better get on the road.'

'I'll keep an eye on things,' he said. 'Good luck.'

The drive to Melbourne in the old Benz was fine until I reached the ring road and got caught in a stop-start mess behind an accident. I arrived at Peter Thompson's office ten minutes late, flustered and red-faced.

'Don't worry, I've got nothing else in my diary now,' he said. 'Let's go and have a coffee downstairs – the cafe there is very nice.'

Thank God for a human solicitor. After a wee stop and a latte, I was able to talk and think clearly again. As I expected, he wanted me to take my case to another lawyer, one who specialised in child custody cases. 'I can appear for you if it goes to court, but if the grandparents get militant, it could be very tricky. If you want to keep Mia, you'll need someone experienced.'

'How much is this going to cost – this new guy, I mean?' Might as well ask the big question.

'It depends on how far the grandparents want to take it.' He grimaced. 'The first step will be mediation. It's standard now in family court cases.'

'What's mediation supposed to achieve?'

'You talk things through, with a moderator present. There's an expectation that they would back off on their custody claim in return for access.' He sounded apologetic again, which for some reason annoyed me.

'What does "access" mean?' I pushed my cup away and the spoon clattered across the table. 'They did such a bloody good job with their daughter, why would I want them anywhere near Mia?'

Peter took a deep breath. 'Have you ever met them?'

'No, have you?' I knew I was being rude but suddenly the old anger was bubbling inside me, the anger that came from families who said they loved but didn't, who treated their kids like pieces of furniture they owned and discarded when they got a bit tatty.

Families like mine, and Andre's.

'I haven't, no, but I have spoken to them on the phone,' he said.

'So now you're going to tell me they sounded very nice and reasonable.'

His face coloured and he blinked several times. 'I... I'm just saying it might be worth talking to them. And the court will make you anyway. So going in there with a hostile attitude won't help you.'

'I'm not bloody hostile,' I snapped. 'I'm angry.'

He didn't reply to that, just sat quietly while I stewed. I watched a stream of men and women emerge from the lifts in the office building, on their way to meetings or sneaking off home early. Nearly all of them were in black, with an occasional flash of red or purple from the women. They looked like a bunch of crows setting off for a funeral. I shivered. Mia had come to me because two people died, and here I was, trying to keep her from her only other living relatives. Was I being unreasonable, or rightly careful? Was I allowing my loathing of Leigh, my disgust at her addiction, to influence me unfairly? I had a sudden flash of the morning she died, of finding her unmoving in bed, of hauling her out to the car and then driving madly towards help that was way too late. All while her daughter sat in the car with me, luckily too little to understand what was going on. And once I remembered that, my resolve hardened again.

'Sorry,' I said to the solicitor, 'but I'm not giving her up. Leigh's parents will have to be anointed saints before I budge an inch.'

'Right,' he said. 'We'll see how the mediation goes, then decide whether to bring a specialist on board.'

I left the cafe, expecting to feel relief but it didn't come. Instead, the churning in my stomach increased and so did my anger. Back in the Benz, weaving my way through city traffic, I couldn't help thinking about my now-senile mother and

121

whether I should go and visit her, and immediately dismissed the idea. A session with her asking me where Andy was and wanting to know why her husband never visited her would really top the day off. Andy and Dad were two more ghosts that always hovered just behind me. I didn't need that batty old vulture bringing them front and centre right now.

I stopped in briefly at the Ascot Vale house to collect the mail off Mrs Jones, the elderly woman next door who kept an eye on the place for me. She insisted on me drinking a cup of tea with her, and I forced down half a cup of evil Earl Grey. Then I took a few minutes to walk through Andy's house and check the windows and doors were still secure. The memories came crowding in, the knife through my hand and the bullet shot through the side window. I got out of there as soon as I could. It suddenly seemed ridiculous to hang on to a house that I couldn't bring myself to stay in.

On the drive back to Candlebark, I turned the radio up until the inane DJ chatter and music filled my brain and pushed out everything else. In the pub car park, I spotted Carl setting off for another walk along the river, this time with a long fishing rod case in his hand. I'd heard there were trout further up, but nobody had ever caught one. It seemed a bit late in the day for fishing, with dusk creeping in, but what did I know?

Avoiding the bars and bistro, I headed straight for the office. In there, with the door closed, maybe I could take a few long breaths and get my head together before the evening busy period began.

On my desk was an envelope with my name scrawled across it. Now what? A threat from Madeline? Suzie's resignation? Nothing would surprise me.

I opened it and took out the sheet of notepad paper.

Judi — I've been called back to Melbourne. Another case of mine has had a major breakthrough. Will call you. Cheers, Heath.

I sank down on to the chair and read it again. Cheers? What the hell did *Cheers* mean? It was the final crap thing in a week of shit. 'Well, fuck you, Detective Sergeant Heath,' I said out loud. 'Don't bother coming back.'

8

My stomach was so churned up with inexpressible anger – over Heath, the custody issue, Macca's pointless murder – that I had no appetite and avoided the kitchen. I was glad that Mia was at Joleen's, and I rang to tell her I'd pick Mia up around 9pm. A quick look in the public bar showed me it was a quiet night and Bob and Charlie could deal with any late-staying drinkers.

I sat in the office alone and Googled family law and custody disputes and read more about it all than I ever wanted to know. I even found stuff on grandparents' rights – in the case of a dispute between the child's parents and grandparents, if the grandparents were found to be behaving in a damaging manner with the child, their right to access could be denied. What did that mean for me?

I knew that Andy's will was valid, and I was Mia's legal guardian as he had wished. I could easily argue that Leigh was, at the time of her death, unable to dispute that provision. But the reality was that if she'd lived, and had got off the drugs again for her daughter, I probably would have lost a court case.

The thought chilled me to the bone. Mia with an addict mother. Yet I couldn't be totally hypocritical – at the time I hadn't wanted Mia, and had convinced myself it was just temporary. Now Mia had been with me for four months. The thought of giving her up ripped a huge hole in me, and caused a raw, wrenching pain that I'd never expected to feel.

I tried to imagine letting Mia go and visit two strangers every second weekend. Impossible. And yet... hadn't I just been deeply worried that I was doing a terrible job with her? Perhaps sharing the load with grandparents would make things easier for me. Maybe they'd felt the same about Leigh's addiction as I'd felt about Andy's – raging and helpless and despairing. They'd moved down from Sydney to try and see Mia.

They might even blame Andy for Leigh's addiction, just like I blamed Leigh. I knew Andy was playing around with coke and ecstasy and who knew what other shit long before he met Leigh. I stared at the website photo of a small boy laughing with an older couple as they shared a picture book. Andy was the one who'd got himself in deep with the gangland guys, but he was also the one who dragged himself out and made a home and a family.

I clicked back to the previous page. There was a bronze Justice, blindfolded, her scales in her hand. I swallowed hard and then shook my head. I couldn't think about it anymore. I couldn't sit here fretting and worrying either. I sat up and looked around. *Find something useful to do.* I grabbed a notebook and pen and went into the bistro, turned all the lights on and examined the large room from top to bottom, listing all the improvements it needed. Last on the list was the outside area, as Andre had suggested.

I wrestled with the French door catches and then pushed, but the doors still wouldn't open further than a couple of centimetres. Upstairs, someone turned on a light and the garden was lit with an eerie glow. Something moved in the dank shadows at the back, something big. Bigger than a fox.

Faster than a wombat.

I flashed back to Andy's house, the lounge room and French doors, the feel of the cold breeze sliding around me, the muffled footsteps as two men entered, searching for me. I yanked the doors back towards me and reached up with a trembling hand to push the bolt home again then knelt for the bottom one. Somebody was breathing harshly in my ears. Me.

'Fuck, fuck.'

No, there were people here. Everywhere. Staff, customers, guests. It could've been Carl going for a night walk, Charlie checking the car park, Bob arriving for his night manager shift. I was freaking out over nothing.

Get a bloody grip!

My mobile phone rang in my pocket, and I yelped, a jolt of fear jerking me to my feet. I fumbled for the phone with clumsy fingers, got it out and had to tap the green circle four times before I could answer the call properly.

'Hello,' I rasped.

'Judi?' The voice at the other end was even raspier than mine. 'Who is this?'

'Bob.' A rumbling cough. 'Sorry, Judi, I'm crook. Come down with some kind of chest cold. I won't be able to come in tonight.'

'Oh.' I opened my mouth to say Macca would cope, and the full force of Macca's death hit me all over again. My throat closed up and I couldn't get a single word out.

'Judi? You there?'

I sucked in a breath. 'Yes, Bob. Yes. You sound awful. You, er... stay in bed. It'll be fine. I'll see if Charlie can work through. Don't you worry. I'll sort it out.'

'Thanks. Sorry to let you down, when... you know.'

I forced out some more reassurances and hung up, then went

to talk to Charlie. His face filled with dismay and he shook his head.

'Sorry, Judi, I can't. My mum's not well and I promised I'd stay over with her tonight after work.' He pointed at the two old blokes propping up the far end up of the bar. 'There's only them left, so I was actually going to ask if I could go early. I've cleaned everything up already.'

'Yes, sure, you go then.' I managed a smile. 'I'll sort the till and close up.'

Charlie didn't need any further encouragement. He was out the door a couple of minutes later, leaving me alone. Well, not really alone. The two at the bar ordered a pot each for the road, and I chatted with them for a couple of minutes, but all they wanted to do was talk about Macca, so I made my excuses and left them to it.

We had guests, if you could call them that. Carl, who was getting to feel like a fixture, and Madeline and her creepy brother. They must have all gone to the takeaway up the street for dinner. Andre had put out the breakfast stuff, but somebody, who would've been Macca or Bob, had to get up early, make the tea and coffee and put out the cold fruit juice and milk. I checked the accommodation book. There were two spare rooms, apart from Macca's which I wouldn't sleep in if I was paid to. I let out a loud sigh and called Joleen.

Her sigh was bigger than mine. 'Yeah, I guess I can keep Mia overnight again. But…'

I guessed what was coming. 'I know, it's getting to be an imposition. I'm sorry. Macca's death has thrown everything into a mess here, and it's me who keeps getting landed with all the extra work.'

'You should be making Suzie and Andre do their share,' she

said waspishly. 'Isn't that what co-owners are supposed to do?'

My mouth fell open. 'I don't think…' But she was right. I cut it short. 'We'll sort it out, don't worry. See you in the morning. And thank you.'

Eventually the two old boys staggered out the door, and I waved them off, glad they were walking home. They both lived up the road, in the small retirement home past the primary school. If I went to the wall bordering the front car parking area, I'd be able to see Connor's police station, but tonight it'd be closed, since the homicide detectives had gone back to Melbourne. For a moment I thought of calling Connor and then shook it off. I was a big girl. All I had to do was lock up and go to bed.

I closed and locked the front door, walked through all of downstairs and checked every door and window to make sure it was secure, turning lights off as I went, and collecting a room key and a large-sized black staff polo shirt out of the laundry area. That'd have to do for my PJs. I left the downstairs hallway and reception lights on as usual and climbed the stairs.

The first-floor corridor was lit by three dimly glowing wall sconces that gave off just enough light for me to get my key in the door of Room 4 without making too much noise. I flicked the switch inside the door and closed it behind me, sagging against the wall as the strains of the day suddenly hit me. The bed with its white duvet and green pillowcases looked incredibly inviting. I washed my face, changed into the polo shirt and crawled under the duvet.

Bliss. This must be one of the beds Macca had recently replaced. It felt so comfortable I groaned in delight. And there'd be no small child waking me at dawn to shove cornflakes in my mouth either. She was safely dreaming in the bottom bunk bed at Joleen's.

I must have sunk into sleep almost instantly, and I woke with a start, not knowing where I was for a few seconds. The pub, upstairs, Room 4. That's right. I checked the time: ten minutes before midnight. Something had woken me.

I reached for the lamp beside the bed and stopped, my finger on the switch. This was an old building, and underneath the carpet were equally old floorboards. In the corridor, one creaked. That's what had woken me. Someone was creeping around.

I shivered, a cold chill running down my back. *Ring Connor.* But it had to be one of the guests, surely. I had locked up. I was absolutely positive I had.

Carl wouldn't be creeping. But Madeline or Jamie might be, especially if they were heading downstairs to see what I'd done with the money from the tills.

I still hadn't had time to bank the weekend takings. Shit! The logical part of my brain said, 'The money is in the safe.' The angry part of my brain said, 'Those bastards aren't getting another bloody cent of Macca's money!'

I slid out of bed and went to the door, leaning my ear against it, but the solid oak made it a pointless exercise. I'd have to go out and catch them at it. I turned the snib lock as slowly as I could and eased the door open, stopping and listening hard for a couple of seconds. The corridor was silent, but dark. As I eased through the gap, I realised why – somebody had turned off the nightlights in the sconces.

Still no telltale noises. I crept along the corridor, sticking to the side where I knew there were no creaking boards, one hand on the wall to guide me. Past Room 2, which was vacant, its door firmly closed. I glanced back. No lights showing under the door for either Carl's or Madeline and Jamie's rooms. If it was Jamie sneaking around, he was doing it in the dark like me. I hoped he wasn't back in his room already. I wanted to catch him in the act of… whatever he was up to.

Ahead were the stairs, and the glow from the reception area lit as far as the landing, making that end of the corridor murky but not completely black. To my right was Macca's room. The door to it was slightly ajar. That could be where Jamie was.

I stepped across the carpet and pushed Macca's door open. It swung back and tapped against the dresser behind it, but the room itself was a black pit. I stood there, listening, shaking inside. I couldn't bring myself to go in.

Besides, there was nothing in there. Even Macca's box of memories had been removed.

Maybe I'd heard the ghost, coming out of the box room.

Now I really was going nuts. Go back to bed. Another creak came from downstairs, the kind of noise that was more likely to be the old pub moving, the way it always did at night in the silence. I edged forward and stood at the top of the stairs, my hand gripping the banister.

I really did not want to go down there. The safe was secure, the money inside where nobody could get to it. It could just be Carl, looking for a midnight snack. If Madeline or Jamie were down there helping themselves to the drinks, too bad. No, I wasn't going down there.

I sensed someone behind me and tried to swing around but I was too late. A hand shoved me hard in the middle of my back and I went forward, flailing, my hand slipping off the banister, my feet with no purchase. For a moment I was in mid-air, then I crashed down the stairs, banging, sliding, trying to protect myself, trying to stop, but it was futile.

I think I screamed. Fear. Pain in my arm, then my head hit something and I lay on the landing, stunned. I couldn't move.

Fuck, not again.

9

I lay there, not daring to move. I knew there was a lot more pain coming. When someone had pushed me down the cellar stairs in the Melbourne pub, the angle had been steeper, with concrete at the bottom. I'd had broken bones then. Here my face was ground into the pile at the bottom of shallow, carpeted stairs, but I wasn't holding out any hope of a reprieve.

I forced my eyes open, blinked a few times, tried to focus. Feet pattered down the stairs behind me and I froze. Whoever had pushed me was going to check if I was dead. I closed my eyes, tried not to breath. The footsteps paused next to my head then continued down. I slitted my eyes and peered at the shape as it reached the bottom, but it was like looking at a wraith. All in black, no features, a dark ghost.

The person-shape went left, through the main bar and I strained to hear more. The faint sound of the side door opening, then a bang as it closed. Whoever it was knew their way around, and they were gone. Thank God.

I couldn't lie there all night. My body was twisted, one arm above my head, the other under me. I tried to move my left leg and it hurt, but nothing like I feared. It wasn't broken then. My right leg was bent awkwardly but a small testing move told me it was OK, too.

The rush of relief made me rash. I tried to move the arm above my head and shrieked. That was not all right. Not at all. My legs were freezing, the rest of me was shaking now, probably shock, and I'd kill for a warm blanket.

Surely I wouldn't be forced to stay here all night. I couldn't bear it. Pain or not, I had to get help. If Carl slept heavily, I was doomed.

'Help!' It came out feebly, but the next one was louder. 'Help!' Still too soft. I took a deep breath and screamed, 'Help! Help me! Carl! Wake up! Carl!'

No movement from above. I tried again, screaming until my throat felt raw. But finally I heard a door open. 'Hello?'

'Help! Carl, I'm down here.'

Soft footsteps. 'Who's down there?' It sounded like Jamie.

'It's me, Judi,' I called. 'Wake Carl up. He's in Room 3. Bang on the door. Hurry!'

Footsteps fading, thumps on wood, a door opening. 'Where's the fire?' Carl sounded wide awake.

'It's Judi. She fell down the stairs.'

'Shit. I'm coming.' A few seconds delay, which hopefully meant Carl was putting clothes on, and then he thumped along the hallway. 'Why's it so bloody dark up here? Judi?'

'Down here.'

'Holy crappola!' Carl said. He came down the stairs and knelt beside me. 'Judi? Can you move? Is anything broken?'

The kindness in his voice started tears that leaked down the side of my face. 'It's my arm, or shoulder. Not sure if anything's broken. I don't dare move.'

'I'll call an ambulance,' he said, getting to his feet.

'Can you get me a blanket first?' I asked. 'I'm freezing.'

'Yeah, of course.' He called up the stairs. 'Hey, mate, bring a blanket down, will you?'

He went to the reception desk and used the phone there, three sharp beeps for 000 then a series of short answers to the operator's questions that reminded me Carl was actually an efficient business owner with staff. He said, 'Yes, possible breaks. No, I don't know about a head injury. If she's fallen down the stairs, it's quite possible, too. OK, please hurry.'

He hung up and came back to me. 'They said twenty minutes.'

Footsteps and then a blanket was spread over me, and I felt instantly warmer, the cold night air blocked from my skin.

'You hear anything, mate?' Carl said.

'Nah. I was asleep,' Jamie said. 'Thought I was dreamin' at first with her shouting.'

Carl sat beside me, and I smelled his deodorant and a faint odour of cigarette smoke. That explained his walks along the river – secret smoking.

'Did you trip, Judi? Or miss your step? Who turned off the hall lights?'

'Don't know,' I croaked. I wanted to tell him that I'd been pushed, that I'd seen someone in black run away, but I still thought it might have been Jamie. Everything had been locked up, I was a hundred per cent sure of it. So whoever pushed me had already been inside, surely.

'You warm now?'

'Yes, better, thanks.' I felt suddenly incredibly tired, and contemplated drifting off, but parts of me were going numb. I tried to edge my trapped arm out but pain seared through my other shoulder, so I stopped moving.

A querulous voice above told me Madeline was awake and demanding to know what was going on. Jamie said loudly, 'It's only Judi on the stairs. Go back to sleep.'

Rude, but the last thing I wanted was her out here, making a fuss. A door closed and both of their voices faded, leaving Carl and me in peace.

'Can I get you anything?'

'A new body.'

He laughed. 'Yeah, I could do with one of those, too.' He rubbed his face with both hands. 'I'd go and make us a coffee but then I'd be up all night.' A lengthy silence. Just as I thought he'd dozed off, he said, 'Have the cops said anything about who killed Macca?'

'They're convinced it's all about the chop chop dealing.'

'You think Macca would be into that?'

I couldn't shrug. 'I said no way, but now I've heard all this bullshit about Madeline and her cancer treatment. I can just see Macca getting sucked in and risking everything to make some quick money for her, can't you?'

'Yeah...' Carl didn't sound convinced.

'Well, who do you think killed him then?'

'Dunno.' His answer was too fast and automatic.

I badly wanted to sit up and watch his face, but I was stuck. I debated whether this was a good time to test my theory. Had to be now – I was unlikely to get a better chance, the way Carl kept wandering off.

'I think it's something to do with–'

Loud thumps cut me off. Someone was at the front door who urgently wanted to get in.

'That'll be the ambulance,' Carl said, leaping up and racing down the stairs.

'Make sure first,' I called after him, but he was already turning the double locks and pulling the door open. I waited, my heartbeat loud in my ears, half-expecting the black wraith to charge in, but two paramedics came in instead.

'You were quick,' Carl said.

'Caught us on the way back from another call-out,' the woman said. 'Saved us the drive back. Where is she?'

Carl brought them to the bottom of the stairs and pointed at me. I couldn't wave so I tried a smile; it didn't work. My 'Hello' came out whispery and dry.

The woman was older, her dark hair pulled back into a ponytail, her brown eyes kind. 'Can I take the blanket off for a little while?'

'Yes,' but I started shivering when the night air hit me again.

'Won't be long. Can you tell me what happened?'

The second paramedic knelt on the other side of me, taking my pulse as they listened to my explanation. 'You tripped?' he asked.

I was sick of pretending. 'No, there was someone behind me. I was pushed.'

A moment's blank silence, then the woman said to Carl, 'Have you called the police?'

'No, I thought…' Carl was still at the bottom of the stairs. 'I'll call Connor now, OK, Judi?'

'Yes.' I hadn't wanted to make a big deal out of this, but I could still see the dumpster under the back light, lid gaping open, Macca lying in its filthy black maw. Maybe the two things weren't connected; either way, I had to tell Connor. I was actually glad Heath had gone. I'd been scoffed at by him once too often.

Carl disappeared to make the call, and the two paramedics examined me then gently lifted me to a sitting position, one holding my arm up until they could assess the damage. We went through the processes for concussion, firm, calm fingers

136

poked and prodded, and then my arm was finally assessed as a dislocated shoulder. I agreed we could lower it. 'We' being them doing it slowly while I held my breath. The pain was like knives being thrust through me, but I'd been so much worse on the concrete at the bottom of those cellar stairs that this was almost bearable.

When they said they thought nothing was broken, I almost cried, blinking hard and murmuring, 'Good, right, yes,' while breathing against the pain as they put my arm into a temporary sling.

'But that's an on-site assessment only,' Glenda added. I'd discovered she was Glenda and the younger paramedic was Tyler. 'When we get you to the hospital, they'll do an X-ray to make sure, and the doctor will probably perform a reduction, all right?'

Before I could ask what that was, Tyler added, 'It's just the doctor putting your arm back into its shoulder joint.'

'Plaster?' I asked.

'Probably not,' Glenda said. 'A sling for sure, for a few weeks.'

Bugger. That was all I needed. I tried to tell myself again I was lucky to be alive, lucky to get off so lightly, but I felt swamped by a dreary bleakness that I hadn't experienced since everything fell apart with Max and the pub in Melbourne. I stared down at my hands resting on my bare legs, the blue-ish veins, freckles, my pale skin. People talked about the body as a temple. Mine felt like an old fixer-upper with sagging verandahs and a rusty roof.

'Judi, are you OK?' Connor came to a stop in front of me, his round face creased with worry, his police shirt clean and ironed as usual. He must've pulled a fresh one out of the wardrobe. Good old Connor.

I made a face. 'I'm surviving. As you can see.'

He gestured at Carl who hovered behind him, arms folded. 'Carl said... you said, well, you were pushed.' His gaze was steady. He believed me. 'How did it happen?'

Glenda interrupted. 'We need to get her to the hospital, before her shoulder swells up any more. You'll have to question her there.'

'I was pushed,' I said quickly. 'From behind. I heard someone sneaking around, came out to see what was going on. Whoever it was came down past me and left through the side door.' I hesitated. 'Before you ask, I had locked up and done a thorough check.'

'The hall lights up there were all out,' Carl volunteered. 'That was a bit strange.'

Tyler had brought the stretcher in, wheeling it to the bottom of the stairs and getting it ready. Connor was forced to step back out of the way. 'I can probably walk,' I said, but was firmly told 'No way', and helped on to the stretcher. It was worth giving in for the layers of warm blankets they tucked around me, one of which was to keep my arm and shoulder stable.

I didn't have to be taken to Bendigo; our nearest local hospital was less than half an hour away and they let me sit up so I wouldn't get travel-sick. The one doctor on duty arrived as we did, looking alert, thank goodness. I was given happy gas through a mask, and he was gentle but firm with my shoulder. It still hurt like hell, but it went back the way it was supposed to. I could tell already that I'd be really sore over the next few days, and my shoulder was going to be a damn nuisance. The new official sling felt like a straitjacket, and once I had my painkillers dispensed, I was wheeled through the reception area to the front door to discover a crescent moon was rising over the distant hills.

Connor was waiting for me. I raised my eyebrows at his 4WD. 'Parked illegally, Senior Constable Byrne?'

He grinned. 'A perk of the job, I reckon. How are you feeling?'

'Like I've been ten rounds with a heavyweight boxer.' I tapped my sling. 'This is already driving me nuts.'

'I didn't come in and ask you about what happened – I figured the questioning could wait. The head nurse looked like she was going to beat me off with an IV pole.' He nodded at the porter who'd wheeled me out. 'I'll take her from here, thanks. I'll bring the chair back in a minute.'

He helped me into the passenger seat of his police 4WD, giving me an undignified lift up, and we were soon on the way home. 'I'll let Joleen know,' he said, 'so Mia can stay with her a bit longer.'

Gratitude at his kindness and care made a lump in my throat, so I just nodded.

We turned on to the main road to Candlebark and he glanced at me before saying, 'You want to talk about it, or wait for formal questions? I need to take a statement.'

'You're not taking me home?'

He hesitated. 'I'm not sure where the safest place is for you right now. Your house is pretty isolated, and you're still in a mobile phone black spot there, aren't you?'

'It's not too bad outside the back door.' I wanted to go home, to my familiar little house where I felt safe. How could it not be safe there? The pub was the problem.

'Hmm.'

'Have you checked the pub? Who was it? Was there any evidence of a break in?'

'I did, on my own, and then I called Sergeant Withers from

Bendigo about it, and he'll send Barney and Hawke back early this morning, along with crime scene techs again.'

'Barney again,' I said, trying to be nice.

'I've been questioning Madeline and her brother,' Connor said. 'Jamie was an obvious suspect, since you insisted you'd locked up properly.'

'I did!'

'OK, I know you did.' He sent me a curious look. 'You said you saw or heard someone go down the stairs past you, and out the side door. Are you sure?'

'Yes.' I hesitated. 'It was someone in black. I know it was dark upstairs, but the light was on in the reception area. They were just this black shape. Like they were wearing black clothes and... I don't know. A black hat?'

'Balaclava?'

'Maybe. They didn't turn around, so no idea about things like eye holes.'

'Height? How did they match up against, say, that painting of the old homestead on the wall?'

I tried to remember, tried to visualise the moment again, the black shape that paused and turned, walked quickly away. 'They were the same height as the roof of the homestead. And they weren't fat. Or skinny. Slim build. No curves. I'd say it was a male.'

'That helps, thanks.'

We were at the 50 sign outside Candlebark, and Connor slowed, putting his indicator on. 'I'm going to take you to the station so we can do a formal statement in peace. I get the feeling you won't want Barney butting in.'

I didn't like the sound of that. 'Don't tell me, Barney will think I made it up. That I tripped and fell on my own.'

Connor flushed. 'Something like that. Just ignore him.'

I sighed. 'If only.'

I'd been in Connor's small country police station plenty of times, but somehow it was different to be there as a victim of a crime. He used official police stationery and made official-looking police notes as I answered his questions again, and then he typed up an official report on his computer.

'When he came past you on the stairs, did his feet sound heavy?'

I thought back, eyes closed. 'No. Not child-light, but light-footed. Someone who knew how to walk quietly. The creaking floorboards upstairs were what alerted me.'

Connor frowned. 'So where could he have been hiding?'

I thought he was doodling but he was sketching out a plan of the upstairs rooms. It jogged my memory. 'He must've been in Macca's room. The door was open but it was really dark in there and I wasn't game to go in.'

'Not surprised. You might have been attacked.'

I squirmed in my chair. 'Thanks for that.'

'Did he want something in Macca's room? Did you interrupt him?'

'You mean, maybe I just got in the way?'

'Mmm.'

Another lightbulb went on in my head. 'Macca's room should've been locked. *Was* locked. I did that to stop Madeline and her brother snooping around.'

'So this guy – or woman – can pick locks. That explains how he got into the building, I'd say.' Connor wrote down what I'd said. 'Going out would have been simple. Same as if you left through that side door. Just a matter of opening the bolts and latch.'

'I can't deadlock it with a key because of the fire exit rules, surely.'

He sighed. 'True. Can you think of anything else?'

I shook my head.

'Do you…' He hesitated. 'This wouldn't be anything to do with Andy's murder, would it?'

My mouth gaped for a moment. 'You think that?'

'Nah, not really. I was just… exploring possibilities.' He shook his head. 'Cancel that thought. But if this was connected with Macca and the chop chop dealing, why would they come into the pub and attack you?'

'Looking for money?'

'That doesn't make sense,' he said. 'If Macca never made the deal, or he was attacked afterwards, whoever did it took everything. Or we think they did. We haven't found his car yet.'

'So there's nothing more they could gain.' I rubbed my face, exhausted. 'I still haven't banked the takings in the safe. Now it's really worrying me.'

'I can take you to the bank. I'll just type this up and lodge it. Bank won't be open yet anyway.' He banged the keyboard for a few minutes while I wandered around, reading posters and newsletters and feeling twitchy. I couldn't see anything pinned up or lying around related to Macca's murder; maybe Connor had put it all out of sight before bringing me here.

I adjusted the sling again and winced. I had no idea how I'd pick Mia up with my shoulder like this. She was going to do a lot more walking now.

'You're sure Mia is OK at Joleen's?' I called from the front counter.

'Yep.'

'I need to check how things are at the pub, too. Madeline will

142

be making a fuss. Andre will be making a fuss. Carl's probably thinking about making a fuss. Sheesh.' To be honest, I just wanted to be doing something, anything but sitting here feeling useless. The painkillers were wearing off, and I wanted a strong coffee and some more pills. I also wanted to rip the sling off and throw it away but I knew that would make my shoulder worse.

'You're not thinking of walking down there?' His face came around the side of the computer screen, furrowed again.

'It's my arm that's sore, not my legs,' I said.

'All the same, I said I'd take you. Nearly done here and then you can sign it. Besides, I want to see what Barney and Hawke are doing.'

Oh joy. I'd forgotten they'd be there now. I checked the clock; it was only 8.10am but it felt more like five in the afternoon to me.

Shortly after, we set off on the hugely long drive to the pub that took all of three minutes, and found both detectives in the bistro, drinking *my* coffee.

'I hope you left some for me,' I snapped.

They both sat up straight, Barney scowling and Hawke looking guilty. 'I can pour you a cup,' Hawke said. 'How do you have it?'

I nearly said no thanks and thought better of it. 'Thanks. Just black.' I sat across the table from Barney and adjusted the sling a bit before searching in my bag for the painkillers. 'So, Constable Barney, how is the investigation going?'

Barney muttered '*Detective* Constable' under his breath and glanced at Connor, who kept his face blank. 'The crime scene tech said there were faint scratches on the door lock of Mr Macclesfield's room, which might indicate it was picked. No new fingerprints, he says. Apparently one of the cleaners wiped down the doors and frames upstairs after the original crime scene techs were finished. There wasn't enough to indicate picking marks on any of the outside door locks – too much wear from other keys over the years.'

'Was there anything damaged or missing from Macca's room?' I asked.

Barney shook his head. 'We've talked to the cleaning staff this morning – they can't see anything missing from anywhere else, either.'

Connor said, 'What did Jamie Grant have to say for himself?'

'He was in his room asleep,' Barney said. 'First he knew of it was Ms Westerholme shouting for help. Madeline Grant said the same.'

'Any other signs of whoever broke in and pushed Judi?'
'No.'

I watched Barney's face but his expression was bland. Perhaps he did believe I'd been pushed. I sipped the coffee that Hawke had handed me, wishing I could have some sort of brainwave that would tell me what the hell was going on, but my mind was a mess. Would Graeme Nash, the Melbourne gangland boss, really send someone up here to get rid of me? I couldn't see why.

Much as I wanted to blame Jamie for what happened, the black wraith's departure out through the side door didn't gel with it being him. That left me with Connor's belief that it was something to do with the chop chop.

A loud horn sound made me jump. It was Barney's phone, and took me a few seconds to recognise the ring tone as the end-of-game footy siren. About what I'd expect from him. He answered, listened, said, 'Where? Send me the GPS?

144

Yeah, when we get there.' He hung up and stood. 'Someone's found Macclesfield's car, down an embankment in the bush. A walking group by the sound of it.'

'Have the crime scene techs left?' Hawke said.

'Yeah, but they've called them back.' Barney glanced at Connor. 'They need you to set up a cordon. There could be anything in that car.'

'Right.' Connor bent down to me. 'Don't go anywhere.'

10

The painkillers the hospital gave me were taking a while to kick in, and with every stab of pain, I became more and more tetchy. I didn't want to snap at Andre, so I went and hid in the office, called Joleen and received a brief update on Mia before Joleen launched into questions.

'Did someone really try to kill you?' she asked, managing a gasp before I could even answer.

'No. Who said that?' They might be right but no way was I admitting it to Joleen.

'Someone posted it on the Candlebark Facebook page.'

'Who?'

There was a small silence. 'I can't remember.' Joleen wasn't good at lying.

'What else did they say?' I tried to tell myself I didn't want to know, but I couldn't help it. Besides, there might be clues in there somewhere. I was supposedly a member myself but I never checked it. I turned on the computer as I listened.

'Some idiot is saying the pub is cursed,' she said. 'How stupid is that?'

'The ghost in the box room might not think so.'

She gasped again. 'Oh, that's just a silly story… isn't it?'

'Of course it is.' Damn it, I couldn't remember my Facebook

password. I started the tedious process of retrieving it. 'I suppose they're all talking about Macca.'

'Not so much. It's sad really.'

'What is?'

'All they can talk about is who killed him. Nobody mentions all the good stuff he did, the charity raffles he ran at the pub, how he sponsored the footy team.'

'Human nature, I'm afraid.' I sighed. Now I couldn't remember how to get into my email account. Oh, that's right, I'd changed my password to MiaAndAndy1. I tapped the keys and peered at the instructions from Facebook. 'So who's the prime suspect, according to the locals?'

She giggled. 'You and Andre.'

'What bloody moron said that?' Maybe I'd give Facebook a miss.

Another silence. The moron must have been one of her friends. 'A few people reckon it was this woman who claims to be Macca's daughter, but she's in a wheelchair. Coulda been her brother, I suppose.'

The gossip network was up to speed as usual. I wondered how much of this had been passed on to Heath and the other detectives. These days they probably monitored social media anyway, as a regular part of the investigation. No need for me to 'butt in' then, as Heath put it.

'No locals you've heard of that were having a dispute with Macca?'

'Nup. Listen, I have to go to Bendigo today. Can I drop Mia off at the pub?'

'Of course. I'm sorry you've had to look after her so much. It's been chaos around here. I hope it all calms down now.' Aha, finally the Candlebark Facebook page came up.

'And, um, would you have any money? You know, to pay me for the last week?'

'Sure.' I had almost none on me, though. Maybe I could borrow some from Andre. 'What time will you be here?'

'Around eleven.'

I said goodbye and spent a few minutes scrolling down the Facebook page, half-marvelling at and half-cursing the stupidity of people who thought they knew more than the police. Not that I was any better! But people had been out and about taking photos – someone had taken a photo of the dumpster with the crime scene tape in the foreground – and posting them with commentaries as if they were real detectives ferreting out clues.

There was indeed a whole stream of stuff about Madeline and Jamie, but most people felt sorry for her, and nearly everyone believed that she was Macca's long-lost daughter. Only one post by someone who called themselves Eternal Flame said, 'Macca didn't have a daughter, not even one he didn't know about, and the sooner the police tell her to shove off, the better.'

I nodded at Eternal Flame. *You and me both.* I couldn't begin to guess who Eternal Flame was – most people used their real names. Perhaps the person was a 1980s Bangles fan. I sighed and closed it all down, then sat with my head in my one good hand. The pain had ebbed away and I was ready for food. Anything would do. It might help me think more clearly.

Before leaving the office, I opened the safe and checked the weekend takings. Nothing had been touched. I hesitated a moment. I needed to pay Joleen, and I could easily borrow from the safe and pay it back when I went to the bank. After all, I was a part-owner now. But all the same, I couldn't. It didn't feel right. I pushed the door closed and turned the dial, checking it was locked again. Connor wouldn't be driving me to the bank any time soon. I'd have to ask Andre or Suzie. I headed to the bistro and pulled up short in the doorway. Madeline and Jamie were in there again, she with cake in front of her and he with yet another beer. I ground my teeth, knowing they'd have no intention of paying for either.

Madeline looked up and saw me, and scowled. She muttered something to Jamie, and he did the same. I couldn't have cared less. When Andre emerged from the kitchen, carrying a large fancy glass filled with chocolate milk and topped with whipped cream and a strawberry – his special iced chocolate – I lost it.

As he placed it in front of Madeline, I marched across the bistro and stood next to him.

'Make the most of that, Madeline, because when you're done, I want you two to pack your bags and get out.'

Andre sucked in a breath but said nothing; he folded his arms and stood taller, backing me up.

Madeline's face turned tomato-soup red. 'You can't do that. I'm entitled to stay here until that fake will is sorted out.'

'Actually, I've had legal advice and as a co-owner of this establishment, I can kick out any guest I want who is causing trouble. I'll even call in the local police to evict you if I have to.'

She looked at Jamie but he kept his head down, staring into his beer. No help there. She almost spat at me. 'Fine, then. But when this place is mine, you're all fired.'

'I look forward to it.' I turned my back on her and stalked into the kitchen, Andre close behind.

'My God, you were amazing,' he said in a loud whisper. 'What brought that on?'

I pointed at my sling. 'I've had just about all I can take at the moment, and getting rid of her can only improve my day.'

His eyes widened. 'Connor said you were pushed. Is that

true?'

I nodded. 'I was pretty sure it was Jamie, but now I've had second thoughts.' Seeing him cower like that a few moments ago had made me realise he probably wasn't capable of trying to kill me, even with Madeline egging him on. 'The cops think someone broke in – picked the lock, probably on the side door, or that one.' I pointed at the back door out of the kitchen.

'Can we put another lock on every door then?'

'We don't need to. But we have to install internal top and bottom bolts. The best lock picker in the world won't get past those.'

He peeped out through the serving hatch. 'Ooh, look, they've gone. Yippee yahoo.'

'Talking of security, I'd better make sure I get their room keys.'

'Yes.' He pursed his lips. 'Bet you don't get any money out of them.'

'It'll be worth it to get rid of them,' I said.

In the main hallway, Madeline's wheelchair stood waiting and the sound of their voices drifted down the stairs. I hesitated, unwilling to go up to the rooms and pass the place where I fell. I wasn't superstitious, but…

While I was sitting at the reception desk, waiting for them to come down, I tidied up. Bob apparently didn't think being a receptionist was part of his night manager job, and I couldn't blame him. Macca asked people to sign in on photocopied forms that asked for their names, addresses and contact details, and then got them to fill out what looked like a large visitors' book. It was a doubling up process, but the visitors' book stayed on the counter and when they left, people wrote in comments like 'Amazing history' and 'Never saw the ghost!'

Carl hadn't filled out a new form when he came back so I

filled it in for him, taking his information off the previous one. Thankfully, that bill had been paid in full. I leafed through the forms for the past fortnight, checking that I'd entered them all into the accounts along with their payments, clipped them together and put the pile aside for filing.

The large, shallow drawer under the desk was full of rubbish, everything from old bar coasters to dried-up pens and odd paper clips. I managed to ease it out and fetched the small rubbish bin, tossing everything in as I went. More drink coasters advertising a beer we didn't serve anymore, a stamp that said PAID and a packet of roll-your-own tobacco. I checked the tobacco but it looked like the stuff anyone could buy from a shop. I left that in case it belonged to Bob.

At the back of the drawer were some old guest sign-in forms, folded and dusty, and I almost threw them straight in the bin. Macca probably shoved them in there instead of giving them to me, although they looked like they'd been there a while.

I unfolded them and glanced at the names. One was dated four months ago, the other was almost a year ago. They'd both been clipped with a bunch of others at some point because the indent marks were clear. It was the names on them that sent a shock through me.

John Matthews and Phillip Prender.

Macca's two army mates who'd died, the ones in the newspaper cuttings. They'd been here! And very likely not long before they'd died.

Had Macca killed them?

I gave myself a mental slap. That's what I got for reading those stupid Candlebark Facebook posts. It was clearly catching.

But this linked Macca with the other two in more than a coincidental 'I knew these guys and read that they'd died' kind of way. It didn't tell me anything about who might have killed them all. I needed that photo of the group of them in Vietnam. Maybe one of the others was guilty. Carl was one of the others. TV shows always talked about motive, and clearly there was one. I just had no idea what it might be.

Carl might know. But if Carl was the killer...

I groaned out loud. Maybe Heath was right – I should stop playing amateur detective. But it was personal now, because someone had tried to kill me, too.

That brought me back to Carl. He'd been in his room, supposedly, and Jamie had woken him up. Or had he? Carl might have been wide awake, having just pushed me down the stairs. But it didn't explain the person in black who went out the side door.

My circling ruminations were interrupted by Madeline and Jamie coming slowly down the stairs, both of them glaring at me. I wanted to say, 'Watch your step' but I didn't need another tirade from Madeline. So I sat quietly while Jamie helped Madeline into the wheelchair, pushed her along the hallway and out through the front door, slamming it after him. He didn't return so he must've loaded their bags into his van already.

Silence. It surrounded me like a mist for a few moments, and then noises started to slowly filter through. Andre running some kind of machine in the kitchen, the hum of beer fridges in the main bar, a car pulling up outside and doors closing.

Then the front door opened and a little blonde-haired girl ran in, stopped and looked around, her face alight. 'Juddy?'

It was like a little happy sunbeam had run in. 'Hey, kiddo.' I went towards her and knelt to give her a big hug with my one good arm. She threw her arms around my neck, her warm face pressing against mine, and I blinked hard. 'Have a good time at Joleen's?'

'Her kitty scratched me!' The bottom lip quivered for a moment until I'd inspected the tiny scratch and kissed it better. 'What's that?' She touched my sling.

'Silly Judi fell over and hurt her arm,' I said. 'The doctor said this will help to fix it.'

'Hmm.' She pulled at it and inspected the folds and pins. 'Sore?'

'Yes, sweetie, it is.'

'No more hugs?'

'Plenty of hugs,' I assured her. 'But gentle ones for a while.'

'OK.' She whirled away from me. 'I can do dancing!'

'Beautiful.'

Joleen came in behind her and helped me up from the floor. 'That sling looks serious. How are you going to manage?'

'The doctor said I can take it off in a few days, but no heavy lifting for at least two to three weeks.'

'Right.' She paused, waiting.

'Money!' I said. 'Hang on.' I raced through to the kitchen, mentally adding up the hours I owed her for. Too many. But what alternative did I have? Andre was pulling bags of frozen chips out of the freezer, surrounded by similar bags of peas, beans and carrots.

'Andre, would you have any money I can borrow, please?'

'Probably. How much do you need?'

'Two hundred. It's for Joleen, for babysitting.'

'Goodness, I might have to take up childcare as a second job.' He made a face as he reached for his wallet. 'On second thoughts, they couldn't pay me enough.' He handed me four crisp fifty-dollar notes.

153

'Thanks a million. I'll pay you back as soon as I get to the bank. And I do need to do our banking, too. It's getting urgent. There are suppliers' bills to pay.'

'No problem, we can go after lunch.' He waved a hand at the bags of frozen vegetables. 'We won't need to order any of this stuff for a while. There are mountains of it.'

I paid Joleen and waved her off just as Charlie arrived for his bar shift, followed by a couple of locals for early beers. When I got back inside, the phone was ringing with a booking for lunch, and then again for a mostly-polite query about why we hadn't paid our gas bill. When I explained about Macca's death, the woman was consoling and extended the due date another ten days. It was a handy breather for one bill, at least. Instead, I called the nearest locksmith and organised the door bolts, relieved he could come straight away.

Pub life went on. No police in sight as they were all dealing with Macca's car. I left the chatting with the regulars to Charlie and helped Andre in the bistro as our waitress, Kelly, only came in Wednesday to Saturday nights. Mia watched me carry plates, one at a time, and demanded to help, so I sat her in the high chair and let her have a go at filling salt shakers from an almost-empty salt container. Ten in for lunch, including four passing tourists, wasn't bad for a Wednesday, but it wasn't going to keep the place running.

When Andre, Mia and I sat down to eat fish and chips after the guests had left, he agreed. 'I wasn't joking about the locals objecting to fancy food, but I really don't know how Macca has kept this place going for so long.'

'He never paid himself,' I said. 'But race days and local events have helped.' I held up a perfectly cooked, crispy chip. 'There will always be customers for great chips, but we have to do more. Those four tourists today only found us by accident.'

'None of us are any good at marketing,' he said. 'Do you think we should hire someone?'

'Maybe.' I ate another chip. 'But not while all this shit is going on. We don't need a guest murdered. When they said no publicity is bad publicity, I don't think they meant murder.'

After we'd eaten, it was time for the bank. Andre had to drive my Benz so Mia could sit in her car seat, and it was as if he was about to embark on the Dakar Rally, minus the sand dunes. We made it to the bank at Heathcote with relatively few dramas and, after I withdrew some money from the ATM and paid Andre back, we went in to deposit the pub takings. The teller frowned as she called up the account.

'You do realise this account will still be overdrawn?'

'Even after the deposit? Are you sure?'

She checked again. 'There was a recent large transaction.'

'Who by?' My voice was too loud and a few people turned and stared. I should've checked the statements again.

'Er, I imagine Mr Macclesfield,' she said. 'It's his account.' She narrowed her eyes at me. 'You're not a signatory, so...'

'The bank should have been notified that Mr Macclesfield is dead,' I snapped, and Andre nudged me. 'Sorry, that's not your fault, I know.'

'When someone dies, proof of death has to be supplied to the bank, and then the account is closed.'

'No, you can't do that,' I said. 'We need that account to keep the pub running.' I took the bag back off the counter.

Andre nudged me again. 'Judi, if the account is in the red, it doesn't matter.'

'Oh, right.' I thought for a moment, watching Mia playing with all the loans brochures and tidying them up while putting them all in the wrong holes. 'How much was withdrawn?'

'I can't really tell you that,' she said. 'You'll need to speak to the manager.'

Honestly, why did banks operate like they were Fort Knox? Probably because they were. I sighed and we followed her to the balding manager's office where I explained everything. He called Macca's solicitor and efficiently confirmed everything, and a few minutes later I had a printout in my hand that told me Macca had withdrawn $5,000. 'Would he have been allowed to take that much out and create a debt?'

The manager pushed his glasses up his nose and shrugged. 'He had arranged a temporary overdraft, a short term one, with the branch in Bendigo. The paperwork was a little delayed in processing. That's all I can tell you.'

'OK, thanks.'

We left the bank and walked slowly back to the car, Mia stopping to pick a pink petunia out of the street flowerbox. 'Now what?' Andre said. 'How can we keep the pub running with no money? We can pay some of the bills with the takings, I suppose.'

'Just as well I didn't deposit them.' I stopped Mia from picking all of the flowers just in time. 'They'll last us a week, if we're lucky. Maybe we will have to close the pub down.'

We stared at each other for a few moments, then he said, 'Bugger it, I'm not giving up that easily. How much spare cash have you got?'

'Not much, in fact almost none.'

'I've got a bit saved. I guess a third of a pub is a better bet than an eighth of a racehorse.'

I laughed. 'Hey, that was a quarter of a horse. I said no, remember?'

'What do you reckon Suzie is going to say?'

'I don't think she's got any money to spare.' I glanced back at the bank. 'If Macca had an overdraft, the bank might not be so keen on lending to us. Maybe I could draw down on the loan for Andy's house.'

'Pity Macca didn't leave us a secret stash of cash somewhere.' He bent down to Mia, who had shredded her petunia and was about to eat some of it. 'Want an ice cream, Shorty?'

I spluttered, 'You can't call her that.'

'Course I can. She'll grow out of it.'

'Now the bad jokes. I think we all need an ice cream.'

We sat outside the ice cream shop in the spring sunshine, analysing the various cafes in Heathcote and what their food specialities were. Andre knew everything. 'Have you been sneaking over here and checking out the competition?' I asked.

'Actually, I have.' He smirked. 'Making sure I'm a better chef, too. Seriously, though, I bet I can come up with a menu that will put us on the food map. All the things I wanted to try that Macca said were too fancy.'

'Seriously?' I'd always enjoyed Andre's meals but I'd never stopped to think about what he wasn't allowed to cook. 'Like what?'

'If you just look at what's produced around us – goat's cheese, venison, organic beef, lamb, duck, local wines – I could do a heap of dishes with those. And, you know, we should be supporting the local producers, not paying all our money to frozen vegetable suppliers.' He was waving his hands around so much that Mia got the giggles and then clapped her hands.

'Oh fine,' he said, pretending to be offended. 'Laugh at me then.'

'I'm not laughing,' I said. 'I think you're totally on the right track. But we'd better get back and sort out stuff for tonight. At least we won't have to worry about the two freeloaders.'

Halfway back to Candlebark, we passed a tow truck with a grey Ford Territory on the back of it, followed by a police car. I craned my head to get a better look. 'Wasn't that Macca's 4WD?'

'Yeah.' He was silent for a moment. 'I wonder what they found in it.'

'Barney would rather choke than tell us.'

'I'm sure we can get Connor to spill the beans.' He grinned at me. 'You never know, now they've found Macca's car, that hunky cop might come back.'

'Huh, as if I care.' Which told him all he wanted to know, and he laughed so much that Mia got the giggles again.

11

We arrived back in Candlebark, hoping to find out more about Macca's 4WD, but the town was empty of police yet again; even Connor was nowhere to be seen. I wondered where the hell they all were, and what they'd found in Macca's car that kept them so totally occupied.

That night, Andre stayed at the pub with Mia and me because I wasn't quite ready to go home, and we made sure all of the sliding bolts were put to use, as well as the extra pins on the sash windows. Carl was the only guest, and he helped us barricade the place.

'I can sleep with my door open, if you want,' he said. 'And if you hear anything, you just need to yell.'

I wasn't sure that was a good idea, and I was even less sure he'd hear me, but in any case, I had Mia with me. Anyone creeping around could creep to their heart's content. They wouldn't tempt me out of my room. I was glad Andre had agreed to stay, though. Carl sat in the main bar with some of the locals all night, even eating in there, and I never got a chance to ask him my questions.

The painkillers I was taking worked well to give me a reasonable night's sleep and I didn't feel the shoulder so much, but the rest of me felt like I'd been ten rounds with a kick boxer the next morning. All the bumps and knocks had blossomed into spectacular bruises, like huge purple flowers. Mia and I had a shower together, because she refused to go under the water alone, and she pointed to the one on my hip with her little brow furrowed.

'Big ouch?'

'Big ouch,' I agreed.

Then the ones on my legs, her lips pursed. 'Big ouch, too?'

'Big ouch, too.'

'Poor Juddy,' she announced.

'Never mind, I'll be better soon,' I told her.

After breakfast, Andre and I sat down in the bistro and started going through all the accounts and bank statements, this time with an eye to working out what the place had cost Macca to run, and where the money went. Through the French windows I noticed Carl walking past with his fishing rod in the carry bag and pointed him out to Andre, who frowned.

'Fishing? Can't see Carl fishing for carp. Are you sure that's a rod?'

'What do you mean?'

'That looks more like the kind of carry bag you'd use for a rifle.'

I gaped at him, and rushed to the window but Carl was already disappearing into the bush down by the river. 'It's not hunting season, is it?'

'No idea. It's probably always hunting season for ferals like cats and foxes. Maybe he's bored and that's what he does on the farm.'

I sat down again. 'Why doesn't he go home? The funeral isn't organised yet, and it's not like he's helping with anything else. I wonder...'

160

'Yeeees?'

'Where was he when Macca was killed?'

'Here. In the bar, with Missus Carl.'

'Are they sure Macca was killed later in the day?'

'Even if he wasn't, Carl was at the races surrounded by thousands of people.' Andre tapped the bank statements. 'Do you see these amounts here?'

'The withdrawals?'

'No, those match up with these accounts paid by cheque. I mean the deposits.'

I focused on the pages where he'd asterisked several deposits of round figures. $1000. $2000. $1000. 'Did he round off the takings and keep what was left for his own expenses?'

'No, the takings are these.' He pointed at other amounts deposited Mondays, Wednesdays and Fridays. 'You can see when there's been a race day because the amount is much bigger. You didn't notice this stuff before?'

'These are older statements. When I started doing the books and accounts for Macca a couple of months ago, he only showed me the very recent stuff. I had no reason to go further back until now.'

'I think either Macca or someone else was topping up this working account with cash.'

'Really?' I sat back and thought about it, and my gaze fixed on Mia in the corner playground, studiously stacking blocks, but I wasn't really seeing her. I was seeing Macca give me the box of paperwork, and joking about how the place needed taking in hand, and 'It's all in there but I'm not good at filing. I know you'll do a great job, mate.'

'He knew, damn it!'

'What?'

'Macca knew the shit was probably going to hit the fan, sooner or later. And yet… how could he know more than two months ago?'

'Slow down. Know what?' Andre got up and headed to the kitchen. 'Coffee time. My brain needs caffeine before I hear this.'

I followed him in and poured some orange juice for Mia and cut up an apple for her while I sorted through the bits of the puzzle in my brain. Half the bits were still missing, but Andre knew Macca better than me. He'd fill some of them in.

Back at the table, I spread the statements out. 'Those deposits are Macca feeding money into the pub to keep it going.'

'That's not a good sign,' Andre said. 'It means the place wasn't anywhere near paying its own way.

I grimaced. 'I know, but we'll work on that later. I'm pretty sure he had no other money. If he had some in his personal account, surely these deposits would show up as a transfer from one account to another. So where did this money come from?'

'He was blackmailing someone?'

'Ha, very funny.' I hesitated, then ploughed on. 'The cops are convinced that Macca was dealing chop chop.'

Andre sighed dramatically. 'Yeah, I heard that one. I never saw any sign of it.'

'If he was, these little amounts are nothing. Look, add them up. Over the few months, they only come to about ten grand in total. Surely chop chop, the way the cops go on about it, would net Macca ten grand or more *at a time*? Probably more.'

'I guess so.'

'But not if he was in it with a group of others, and they were sharing the profits.' I lobbed that bombshell at Andre and let him work it through for himself. He frowned, pushed out his lips, shook his head a little, and then slowly his face lightened and he nodded.

'It does fit, you know.' He went to slap my arm and pulled back, patting my hand instead. 'You're a bloody genius! But who would he be working with?'

'I wouldn't be surprised if it was a bunch of old buggers from around here. I've spent plenty of time listening to them complain in the bar. The aged pension is too small, or they've been landed with some big unexpected bill they can't pay... Bob's a prime example. He got scammed by some so-called investment expert and lost half of what little superannuation he had.'

'What, you mean like that movie we saw with the old guys robbing banks?'

We gazed at each other in astonishment and burst out laughing. 'Oh God,' I groaned, 'I shouldn't laugh so hard, it's killing me.'

Andre sobered. 'It's not really funny, is it?' He snorted again. 'Except it is. Bloody funny.'

'It's only me supposing. I might be completely wrong.'

'Nah, I think you're a hundred per cent right. So, you gonna schlep on over to the cop shop and tell Connor and Barney and the rest of them? Hunky Pants might even be back by now.'

'Oh no, no way,' I said quickly. 'I'm not saying a word.'

'Really?'

I remembered Heath's words, and they still smarted, but more than that, I remembered what Joleen had said, about how Macca's murder seemed to take over the local talk and nobody was remembering all the good stuff Macca had done. If it was discovered that he and his 'gang' had been making money out of chop chop, it wasn't coming from me. Let the police do their job.

I repeated that to Andre. 'Heath said they had a local informant. They probably already know.'

'Yeah, but think about this – if Macca was killed because of the chop chop, who did it? And are they coming for the other old buggers?'

Something ticked over in my brain. 'Maybe the guy in the pub who pushed me down the stairs was actually looking for Bob. Except Bob rang in sick so it was me in the way.'

'Why would they kill off their buyers, though? That's not a good business strategy, knocking off your customers.'

'Something we need to keep in mind for the pub.' I gathered up the statements and put them to one side. 'We should add up bills we owe, and what's coming due, and work out how much money we'll need to keep our heads above water. Without any funding from chop chop.'

'Good plan,' Andre said. 'And call me paranoid, but have you checked the insurance coverage for everything here? I wouldn't put it past Madeline to come back and accidentally-on-purpose fall over so she can sue us.'

I wrote that on my To Do list and we set about adding up figures and working out our financial situation. When Mia got bored with her blocks, I turned on the TV in the corner and she watched some kids' shows.

The accounting work didn't take long. I wrote the last total on my notepad and showed it to Andre. He blew air out slowly and rubbed his face with both hands. 'Man, that is not very healthy, is it?'

'No. The question is, can we turn it around?'

'And then the question is, how much do we need to put into it to make the turnaround possible?'

'Suzie is a third owner,' I began.

'And Suzie says she has no money.'

Charlie came through from the main bar. 'You want me to open up? It's just gone eleven.'

'Yes, thanks,' I said. I started to gather up the documents and statements, keeping our calculations sheet separate.

Andre stood up and stretched. 'I need to start on lunch. Why don't we wait until Suzie comes in and talk to her about all this? If she says a flat out no, then we'll have to decide if part of the plan is how to buy her out. Or if we cut our losses and try to sell.'

'OK.' I was relieved to be able to put it aside for a while. The thought of taking out a loan again was scary, despite what I thought about the pub being its own collateral. I understood how Suzie felt about her home. I didn't want to lose Andy's house. I wanted to keep it for Mia, or keep the money from the sale for her. This would be going against everything I'd planned. As she danced around to the music on the TV, oblivious to my dilemma, I saw my brother in her all over again. The laughing eyes, the fluffy blonde hair, even the little happy jumps and hops.

No, I wasn't risking what little I had for her future to invest in yet another pub with no real future. I didn't know how I'd tell Andre, but I was more like Suzie than I'd realised. Stick with what you have, what's safe. Surely I'd learned my lesson about that.

'Unca Connor!' Mia ran across the bistro and launched herself into Connor's arms.

'Hey, Mia Moo, how are you?' Connor gave her a hug and carried her across to where I sat. 'And Judi, too.' He grinned. 'Like my rhymes?'

'Brilliant,' I said. 'They let you off the cordon at last, did they?'

'I was off that by last night.' He sat and kept Mia on his lap for all of five seconds before she wriggled to get down and go back to the TV.

'Where did they find Macca's car?'

'About ten Ks away, up on Dobles Road. Where you can drive into the state park and camp. Bushwalkers found it down in a gully.'

'That's odd. What would he be doing way out there?'

'It's not that far from here as the crow flies.' Connor pulled out his phone and showed me on the map. 'Have you ever been there?'

I shook my head. 'I didn't even know there was a state park with a camping ground there.'

'Lots of tyre tracks everywhere, which wasn't helpful. It's a popular spot for trail bike riders as well, with tracks running all the way up to the lake.'

'Are you still working up there?'

'No, I've been running stuff at the station for the detectives, answering the phone and managing some of the paperwork.'

'We saw Macca's 4WD on the tow truck. What did they find?'

'Some weird stuff,' he said. 'Hang on, I'll just order some lunch.' He went over to the kitchen and spoke to Andre, then came back and sat down, unfolding a serviette and carefully lining up a knife and fork. 'Did you see Macca's 4WD come back to the pub on Saturday night?'

'No, but then I wasn't outside until Billy came and fetched me.' I watched his face, the little furrow, the way he kept lining up the knife and fork again. 'Macca couldn't have come back here. They said he was already dead.'

'He was. But he didn't die here, did he?'

166

'No. The crime scene people said he'd been put in the dumpster later.' I was trying hard not to remember that open lid.

'The techs found blood on the ground in the forest parking area – it took them a while. It'd all been covered with dirt and leaves. The evidence in the 4WD suggests that it was used to bring his body here after dark, then driven back and dumped down the gully.'

'Oh.' I stared at him blankly. 'Why would the murderer do that? Why not leave him in the 4WD? Surely it was a big risk bringing him back here?'

'Good questions.'

Andre paused on his way back from taking a plate of chips to the main bar. 'What questions?'

Connor sat back, folding his arms, eyeing both of us. 'At the moment, they're re-interviewing everyone who was here that night about the 4WD, whether they saw it in the car park at any point.'

'I never went outside,' Andre said. 'I've already told those homicide guys.'

I tried to remember if I'd seen Macca's car that night but nothing came to me. 'Billy and his brother might have seen something – they do the car park checks.'

'Yep, we've talked to them. Nothing. They said they usually do the checks at certain times, like a routine. Billy went out and found Macca while he was doing an extra check.' Connor cleared his throat. 'Said you told him to.'

'I was getting really worried about Macca. I don't why I thought checking outside would help. Maybe I thought he might be asleep in his car, or outside talking to someone. I don't know.'

'They're going to come and re-interview you today. If you're up to it, with the painkillers you're on.'

I eyed him for a moment. 'Am I under suspicion for something?'

'No, of course not!' But the pink rising from his collar made a liar out of him.

I had a motive, I suppose. The fact I had no idea about being left a third of the pub... they only had Heath's word for my shock and surprise in the solicitor's office. 'Where's Heath? Is he back yet?'

'Yes, he came back late yesterday afternoon.'

Great. Without saying a word to me. 'Does he think I'm a suspect?'

'Your name is on the board, that's all. And I shouldn't have told you any of this.' As Andre placed his steak in front of him with a flourish, Connor turned to him in relief. 'Great, thanks, mate. I could eat a steer, I reckon. I've had nothing but stale sandwiches for two days.'

'Now, would you like it as much if I told you it was organic Angus beef from that farm near Heathcote?'

'Er...' Connor examined the meat on his plate. 'I guess. But would I like the price?'

'Therein lies the quandary,' Andre said, and left.

'Can I eat it now?' Connor asked me.

'Go ahead. We've been looking at the pub finances, that's all. It's making a loss, so Macca has basically landed us with an albatross.' I shifted in my chair, my aching bruises making me groan. 'On the bright side, it means I don't have a motive for killing him, do I?'

I shuffled Macca's bank statements into a pile. 'Can I ask you where the investigation is up to with the chop chop Heath mentioned?'

Connor finished his mouthful. 'Well... no. Sorry.'

I almost told him about our 'old buggers' theory, but I didn't want Connor giving me a lecture on interfering as well. Besides, we'd just been throwing ideas around.

'Surely you can tell me if we're in danger here.' I held up my sling. 'Are the detectives...' I couldn't help putting an edge on the word. 'Who do they think pushed me down the stairs?'

'They're not sure it's connected.'

'What? You're kidding. Don't tell me Barney persuaded them I was hallucinating.'

Connor heaved a sigh. 'Don't get mad at me but...'

I waited, trying not to grind my teeth.

'Barney suggested you were drunk. Said every time he sees you here, you have a glass in your hand.'

'That fucking smarmy lying little shit!' I was so mad I could've grabbed Connor's steak knife right then and run across to the station and attacked Barney. 'I hope you stuck up for me!'

'Of course,' Connor said mildly. 'So did your... detective friend. Although he kind of made it worse. Said you'd been under a lot of stress.'

'That's just bloody wonderful, isn't it.' I sat there, fuming. 'Stuff them then.'

'What does that mean?' Connor was struggling to cut a tough bit of his steak but he knew me well enough to pick up something in my voice. 'Come on, spit it out.'

No. I wasn't saying anything. Not about the old men's group, or anything else I'd sussed out. Not that it was much, but I knew there was more to it all. OK, I understood the whole thing about chop chop and how much money it was worth. I'd even reluctantly go along with Macca dealing in it. But something else was going on, something that felt very close to the pub and the people in it. And I was keeping all of it to myself for now, even though it meant fibbing to Connor.

'Don't worry about it,' I said, forcing myself to sound casual. 'Can you tell me about chop chop dealing then? In a way that doesn't get you into trouble with the others.'

Andre came back to the table with three plates on a tray and sat down to eat with us. He put Mia's chips in front of her on the high-chair tray. 'There you are, Shorty. Half-cold, just the way you like them.'

Mia gave him a big grin and started cramming chips in her mouth. I ate more slowly, listening to Connor; Andre did the same, his expression intense.

'It used to be illegal tobacco growing, mostly around northern Victoria,' Connor said. 'There's some of that started up again, but now it's more that the stuff is coming in from overseas. Not just tobacco but packaged cigarettes. They look just like normal cigarettes but they have brands like Winchester and Spoonbills. You'd know the difference straight away because they don't have the horrible anti-smoking photos on them. And of course they're less than half the price of the legal ones.'

I glanced at Andre but he was focused on his food. 'Well, I've never seen Macca selling ciggies like that,' I said. 'In fact, we only have the one machine here that sits near the side door. I suppose you've checked that.'

'Yep, it's fine.' He contemplated us both for a moment. 'So you've never seen any packets of smokes around here other than legal ones?'

'No. Well, I...' That made me think. Had I seen odd-looking packets? 'I haven't noticed anything. They have to go outside to smoke these days. It's not like ancient times when everyone sat with their smokes on the bar and lit up when they felt like it.'

'So what's the bigger problem you're not telling us about?' Andre asked.

'I might go for that organic Angus beef after all,' Connor joked as he gave up on the last bit of steak. I glared at him and he faltered. 'The problem is who runs the illegal selling. Gangs. Around here it's looking like biker gangs.'

'Bikies don't come in here,' I said.

Andre coughed loudly.

'Yes, they do,' Connor said. 'They may not roar in in a mob, covered in club colours and brandishing guns, but they do come here regularly. Mostly the older ones, nearer Macca's age.'

'How do you know that?' I asked. 'Do you spy on the pub?'

'A bit. It's my job. But Macca told me about a few of them. They're usually old army mates.'

'So you knew he was a Vietnam vet,' I said.

'Yeah, I did. But not many other people knew. He didn't like to talk about it, like a lot of vets.' He pushed his plate aside.

I busied myself picking up Mia's dropped chips and putting them on my plate, out of her reach, while I thought. 'So are the detectives putting two and two together – Macca being a vet and some of his army mates being bikies – and getting what they think is four?'

'They're thinking along those lines.'

Andre leaned forward. 'Have we got anything to worry about here?'

'I don't think so,' Connor said. 'But keep the place well locked up all the same.'

'That's no help if they come during the day.' But my mind had jumped ahead. 'Are you saying that Macca was killed by the bikies who were selling him chop chop?'

Connor's mouth got all pinched up. 'See, this is what happens when you keep asking questions. I can't talk about it.'

Too bloody right, I was asking questions. 'That means they found either the chop chop or the money in Macca's 4WD. Am I correct?'

Connor reddened but didn't answer.

'I bet it was the money.' I flipped a hand at Andre. 'Have you got a coin on you? Let's toss and see what comes up. Either one will do, if Connor doesn't trust us to keep our mouths shut.'

'Judi, that's not fair,' Connor snapped. He sucked in a breath. 'Geez, you'll be the death of me. It was money, all right? Ten grand, hidden in a special pocket he'd made under the driver's seat.'

A part of me had stupidly assumed the police were making up all this crap about Macca, but Connor's seriousness shocked me, and I had to finally acknowledge the truth. 'So he really was dealing.'

Connor didn't say, 'Der,' but he might as well have. Instead, he stood and said goodbye, and went back to the station. No doubt Heath and the others were all there, crammed in and compiling all the evidence to prove it was Macca's own fault for dealing and he should've known better. And as for drunken Judi falling down the stairs, well, what can you expect, and let's go chase some bikies and solve this damn thing.

I was so caught up in my little fantasy about them that I barely heard Andre speaking. 'Sorry?'

'Carl just went past the window.' He pointed to the front door. 'Check out your fishing rod.'

I got up, wincing as my shoulder protested the sudden movement, and went into the hallway. Carl was just coming through the front door, the straps of the long bag slung over his shoulder.

'Hi, Carl, how's the fishing going?'

He jumped as if the hotel ghost had tapped him on the back. 'Oh, Judi, hi. I, er, not much happening.'

I pointed at the bag. 'So you brought a fishing rod from home then?'

He flushed. 'It's, ah, I haven't been fishing exactly. This here is my, er, rifle. Don't worry, I have a licence for it. It's all legal.'

'What on earth have you been doing with it?' I waited but there was no answer, just a fair bit of foot shuffling. 'Andre said you were hunting ferals or foxes or something.'

'Yeah, yeah, that's right.' His look of relief was a giveaway. 'Making myself useful, you know, and foxes are still worth ten bucks each. And it's always good to get rid of feral cats, too. They kill a hell of a lot of wildlife.' A small pause. 'Have you set a date for the funeral yet?'

That threw me. 'No, not yet. I... I need to find out when his body will be released.' For Andy it had taken about a week, but maybe they still needed Macca for forensic work or something. 'I'll ask. Are you sure you want to stay around until the funeral?'

'Oh yeah,' he said quickly. 'No problem.' He glanced around but there was nobody else in sight. 'Listen, you don't need to have someone stay on staff here overnight. It's just me, you know. I can lock up, keep you or the cops on speed dial, I can even get me own breakfast.'

'Really?' It would save a lot of hassle, especially since Bob was still sick as far as I knew. 'If you're sure...'

'I am. I'll be right as rain,' he said firmly. 'Now, I haven't missed lunch, have I?'

'I'm sure Andre can find you something.' We went back into

the bistro together, and Carl propped his bag up against the wall behind him. When Mia showed interest in finding out what was in it, I asked Carl to take it up to his room and he did so, although reluctantly. Maybe he was one of those gun-obsessed guys, although he'd never come across like that before.

As he came back in, I was gathering up all of the statements and accounts and putting them back into folders. 'Looks serious,' Carl said. 'Are you going to sell the old place?'

'We might have to.' Andre was still in the kitchen and I felt wary about revealing too much, given Carl was after racehorse investors. 'Doesn't look like Macca was making a living, from what we can see.'

'No.' He sat down with a thump.

There was a short, uncomfortable silence. 'So have you actually bagged any foxes?' I asked.

'Too quick for me,' he said. 'The bush is pretty thick around here, not like out in the paddocks. And I don't want to accidentally shoot a wombat or a wallaby.'

'No, I suppose not.' Or anyone else?

Andre came back with a plate of steak and chips just as Mia started pulling at her pants and muttering, 'Wee-wee,' so I made my escape to the ladies toilets and left Carl to his meal. Suzie was due to start work at 3pm, so I called her and explained about Carl looking after himself.

'Great,' she said. 'I'll sort it out with him tonight. When are we going to get together with Andre and talk about the pub again?'

I explained what we'd been doing that morning, and she sighed. 'That bad, huh? Maybe I'll start buying Lotto tickets.'

'Look, let's meet tomorrow,' I said. 'I'll show you the money situation, and we can all discuss our options.'

She agreed and I updated Andre before taking Mia home. The glorious spring afternoon stretched out before us, with rain not forecast until the evening, so I couldn't wait to get working on my garden. My shoulder and sling hampered any real digging, but I could kneel and weed, and Mia chased the cat around until it got snarky with her, then she played for a while with a big plastic ball I'd bought her. I'd planted carrots, beans and radishes early in raised beds, and put plastic over them to make a temporary greenhouse, and the carrots were already finger-size so I pulled two for Mia to eat. After all the pub food and chips, we needed some greens so dinner was a big pot of vegetable soup that used up a lot of winter leftovers from the garden.

An afternoon in the garden put me in a relaxed, happy mood, and I poured myself a glass of wine with barely a thought for Barney's 'she has a drinking problem' opinion. I'd just put Mia to bed with three stories and ten kisses, and checked she was asleep, when the phone rang.

I froze. There was no reason to think it was bad news, but everything from the past few days suddenly flooded in on me.

Who's dead now?

12

I forced myself to pick up the phone. 'Hello?' I croaked.

'Is that Judi Westerholme?' The voice wasn't officious, it was soft and tentative.

'Yes.' I cleared my throat. 'Yes, who's this?'

'It's Geoff Donaldson.' Pause. 'Leigh's father.'

'Oh.'

'I'm calling because, well, the mediation meeting is next Monday, and…'

'Yes?' I said stiffly. What did he want?

'I don't know why I'm calling, to be honest.' He stopped talking and I could hear a woman in the background, then he said, 'My wife didn't want me to.'

'So why…'

'I wanted you to know we only want the best for Mia, and we know you're doing a great job of looking after her.'

'I am.' Most of the time.

'But we're her grandparents, and now we've lost Leigh…' The woman in the background sounded angry, like a buzzing bee.

'You want to replace her.'

'No. Not really. Maybe a little.' His breathing was heavy. 'We just don't want to lose her completely, and if you…'

'If I what?' I hated how flat and rude I sounded, but it was

SHERRYL CLARK

like I had no control of the words coming out of my mouth. I tried to loosen my death grip on the phone.

'If you refuse... never mind. I can see this was a bad idea. Thanks for your time. Goodnight.'

He hung up in my ear, and a second later I slammed the phone down so hard the cat jumped. Bad idea was the bloody understatement of the year. How dare he call me out of nowhere like that? How did he even get my phone number?

On the internet, of course.

My whole body was shaking. What was the matter with me? Maybe it was colder in here than I realised. I poured more wine, wrapped a blanket around myself and sat back on the couch, soothing the cat with a few trembling pats, but it sensed my upset and moved to the other end. I drank some wine, but my heart was still pounding and I couldn't sit still. I went into Mia's room and sat in the old story-reading armchair I'd put in there. Her nightlight cast a soft pink and purple glow around the room and I leaned forward, watching as she stirred and threw one arm out from under the duvet.

Her green stuffed frog sat on her pillow, and her old one-eyed teddy bear was tucked up with her. Other stuffed toys leaned against the wall, their beady eyes on me. She had been so unexpected, so instantly precious, and so easily lost by me, the one who was supposed to take care of her. That was in the past now. But she was also proof that my brother had found a way to move on from our childhood and teen years with our dead-hearted parents. Mia had created the cracks in his armour that let out the hate and bitterness and let in love and caring.

I'd been so determined that wouldn't happen to me, that I'd do my very best to take care of her and honour Andy's memory, but I'd keep my guard up all the same. Nobody would find my

177

vulnerable heart, not even a small girl who looked just like her dad. And yet... she had. I reached out and smoothed her hair away from her face; her eyelids flickered but she didn't wake. I wanted to pick her up and hug her tightly, feel her little arms around my neck, and never let her go.

I felt calmer now, and my heart had stopped its thumping. Leigh's parents could say what they liked. Mia was staying with me, and I'd fight them with everything I had.

As I sat back down on the couch with the cat and my wine, there was a quiet, insistent tapping at my door. I wanted to turn the lights off and pretend I wasn't home, but it could be anyone. Perhaps it was Connor. Oh well, he was used to seeing me in my old gardening clothes.

I stopped at the door, my hand on the deadlock key. 'Who is it?' Connor would be very admiring of my new security precautions.

'Heath.'

'Oh, shit.'

'Sorry? I know it's getting late. I...'

'Don't tell me, you have some questions for me about Macca's car.'

'Well, yes, but... are you going to let me in?'

For a moment I almost said no. Then I sighed heavily and unlocked the door, pulling it open just far enough to see his face. 'I didn't think you were coming back.'

'It's a homicide investigation. I had to come back.' His tone was terse. That wasn't a good sign.

'All right, come in.' I opened the door wider, let him pass me and then locked the door again.

'I see you're being cautious. Good move.'

I don't need your approval. 'Go through. The lounge is that way.'

'Right.'

I followed him and sat on the couch again while he was still trying to decide the best place to sit. If he chose the couch, then this wasn't such a formal visit after all. He took the armchair furthest away from me.

All righty then.

'Do you want a glass of wine, or a beer? Coffee?'

'No, thanks. I've had enough coffee lately to send me into orbit.' He gazed around my lounge room, stopping at a painting of the rocky hills around Tooberac. 'That's great. Is it by a local artist?'

'Yes, from the gallery in Heathcote.' I'd had enough of polite conversation already. 'What do you want?'

'Senior Constable Byrne – Connor – mentioned that you felt we weren't taking your fall down the stairs seriously enough.'

'Fall? I was pushed. It was the middle of the night, I hadn't been sitting in my room secretly drinking and I did see the person who pushed me. But not their face.'

'Right. I read all of that in Connor's report. Except the bit about not drinking.'

'Because it wasn't necessary to spell that out, I thought.'

'No.' He stared down at his fingers knotted together, released and flexed them back and forth. 'Madeline and Jamie Grant have left.'

'Yes, I asked them to leave. I did think originally that it might have been Jamie who pushed me, but then I decided it wasn't possible.'

'Because...'

'He couldn't be in two places at once. I'm sure there was someone else in the pub as well.'

179

'Right…'

Was he sounding sceptical, or was I being paranoid? 'Your crime scene tech said locks had been picked.'

'There were small scratches that indicated that as a possibility.'

'Possibility.' My heart was beating in my ears again; I drank some wine and tried to think *peace and calm, peace and calm.*

'I just wanted you to know that we are taking it seriously. It may or may not be connected with Mr Macclesfield's murder.'

'Have you found who was selling him the chop chop yet?'

'No. Have you…'

'Connor already asked Andre and I about whether we'd seen illegal cigarettes in the pub and we said no. He also asked if we'd seen Macca's 4WD that night and we said no. So there you are.'

A puzzled look crossed his face. 'Are you mad at me?'

I opened my mouth and closed it again, huffed out a breath and said, 'Probably.'

'Why?'

I lined up all my reasons, gave each one a quick brush-up and then pushed them aside. 'I feel like this – us – is a waste of time. You're in the city, I live here. The only time we meet is when someone dies. That's a pretty poor reason for rom – a rela – getting together.'

'Yeah, I know.' He scratched his head and sighed. 'It's the job. You know that. It's why I'm not married. Plus I'm pretty bad at relationships anyway. I don't blame you for wanting me to just shove off and leave you in peace.'

'Well…'

'Seems like I can't though.' He grinned. 'Technically you're still a suspect, according to Barney.'

'That little turd!'

'He's all right. He's smart, but not as smart as he thinks he is.'
I bit back a rude reply.

'So I thought I'd pretend I was questioning you, informally.
For some background information. Probably not by the book,
but… it got me through the door, didn't it?'

He stood, and my stomach lurched. He was leaving already.
I'd done a great job of putting him off then.

'Am I permitted to sit next to you?' he asked, and this time it
was uncertainty in his face and voice, and it softened me, just a
little.

'I suppose so.'

He settled down, squeezing in between me and the cat. The
cat opened one eye and then went back to sleep. Heath moved
his arm to the back of the couch and turned so he was facing
me. 'You've got dirt on your face.' He made to brush it off and I
flinched, just a tiny bit, then stilled and let him touch me. His
fingers were so gentle it was like being brushed by swan grass.
I couldn't speak.

'Is your shoulder still sore?'

I nodded. 'The painkillers help,' I whispered. 'Can't take the
sling off yet.'

'No, of course not.'

'Have you got any more questions?'

'Yeah. Why do I seem to spend so much time thinking about
you?'

I tried to breathe normally but I sounded like an asthmatic.
'Er, I'm suspicious?' That didn't come out right and my face
burned.

'Suspiciously beautiful,' he said, and leaned in to kiss me.
His mouth was warm and soft, and kissing him turned out
to be quite addictive. The heat in my face moved south to my

neck and chest, and a voice in my head from way back in my distant past tried to scoff and say, 'You're not pretty at all, miss,' and I squashed it down and kept kissing him. It was the most delicious thing I'd done in a very long time. It was as if all the other times we'd kissed, which weren't nearly enough, were just a practice run, and this was the real thing, warm and then hot and then urgent.

I knew where this was heading and I didn't care. I wanted to make love with him. I wanted him to hold me close, skin to skin, I wanted, needed, to feel totally connected to him, to feel I meant something, to feel loved, to feel taken up and taken away from myself, to be a different, loving me.

He broke away and stood, helping me up, folding me in his arms. This was what I wanted, to feel him against me, holding me. 'Are we...?' he asked.

'Yes.'

In the bedroom, he undressed me carefully, unpinning the sling first. 'Tell me if it hurts.' I could only nod. I'd happily dislocate it again and not say a word. My clothes were laid over the chair, and he helped me into bed. Not like an old lady. Like he didn't want me to be in pain. The glow from the lounge room was enough to light him from the side as he pulled off his clothes and tossed them on top of mine. Enough to show his muscled arms and shoulders, his back, the two shiny scars on his shoulder and thigh. I stayed quiet, watching as he slid under the covers and faced me.

He laughed. 'You look like someone waiting for their walk to the gallows.'

'Oh God, do I?' How embarrassing. I tried for a smile but it was shaky. It had just hit me how terrified I was. How did people do this?

'Are you OK?' He stroked my face gently.

'Yes, I… I'm out of practice. And you… aren't.'

'Sorry? Oh, you think I sleep with lots of women.'

'Do you?'

The grin again. 'No. I'm not interested in notches on my belt.' He let out a breath. 'We could do that thing, you know, where we sleep together but nothing happens. Unless you want it to.'

'That makes me sound like a sixteen-year-old virgin.' Funny thing was, that's how I felt.

'It'll be fine,' he said, his hand brushing over my stomach. As I turned, his fingers moved up, and when they touched my breast, I flinched.

I couldn't help it. I was scared to death.

'Are you sure you want this?' His face was in dark shadow and his voice had changed – was he angry, hurt or rejected? He didn't sound happy.

I was so unused to being vulnerable that I could sense my brain wanting to throw up the walls, back off, get the hell out of there. But another big part of me wanted him and was prepared to push caution out the door. I'd never allowed myself to think of him and me as 'us', or imagine any kind of future. We didn't seem to fit in that way. But it had been an aeon since I'd last made love with anyone, and this might be my one opportunity. Even if it all went to crap after this, I wanted it.

'Yes.' I moved in close to him, touched his face, ran my fingers down to his chest. He kissed me, his mouth warm and soft again, then hard, and I kissed him back with everything I had. I felt like I was drowning in sensations – mouths, tongues, hands, skin – and I wanted to cry. It had been so long since someone had held me like this. I was alive from hair follicles to toenails, with the centre of me aching and burning so much I thought I

183

was going to burst into flames.

I clutched him closer, ignoring the twinge in my shoulder, wanting to feel all of him against me, hungry for skin, and then doubly hungry to feel him inside me. My leg hooked over his hip, my hand guided him in – if he wasn't ready, too bad. But I knew he was, hard and hot and suddenly urgent. He moved over me, inside me, long strokes that went on and on until I was ready to scream, and then something broke like a wall crumbling and I was drowning and gasping, shuddering, crying, tears streaking down the sides of my face.

He came a few seconds later, with a long, exhaled, 'Oh God.'

I could've stayed like that all night, but he was heavy and my shoulder was aching. I shifted a little and he moved off me, still holding me close. We didn't talk for a while, but he wasn't sleeping; his hand continued to soothe and stroke, his fingers following my bones and contours, pausing on my scars.

'From your accident at the pub in Melbourne?'

'Operation scars, yes.'

'You never told me what happened back then.'

'Same old, same old.' I tried to laugh but it came out strangled.

'Seriously, what happened?'

I didn't want to tell him. It'd spoil tonight for me, to bring up old crap like that. 'I'll tell you another time. You've got scars, too.'

'Yeah, comes with the job, unfortunately.'

I shuddered. They'd both looked like knife scars to me. 'How's the investigation going? Honestly?'

'Finding his car was a big help. Also meant we found where he was killed.' His fingers had stopped moving. 'Can we talk about this tomorrow?'

'You'll be here tomorrow?'

'Yeah, but not... here.' He sighed. 'I can't stay, I'm sorry. I know that makes me look like a hit-and-run kinda guy, but...'

'The others will know.'

'Yep.'

There was a patter of little feet and a voice said, 'Daddy?'

I didn't know whether to laugh or be horrified. Instead I struggled to sit up and Heath stayed where he was, thank goodness. 'Mia, sweetie. No, it's not Daddy. It's...'

'Ben. Hi, Mia.'

She looked at him solemnly for a couple of long seconds then focused on me. 'Wee wee.'

'You want me to come with you?'

She nodded and backed away from the bed, then waited for me to get up. I grabbed my fluffy dressing gown from the wardrobe hook and wrapped it around myself, then followed her to the bathroom. *Thank God she didn't come in while we were...* she didn't need help sitting on the potty but I did have to take her nappy off first, and then she wanted an audience.

'Good girl,' I said when she'd finished. 'That's brilliant, isn't it?'

'I got up,' she said.

I put a new nappy on and led her back to her bed, tucked her in and gave her a kiss. 'You're a very clever girl. Night night.'

She watched me leave the room and I hoped she'd drop off again quickly. As I'd feared, Heath was up and dressed, ready to leave.

'I know,' he said, 'bad look.'

'It's fine.' He wrapped his arms around me and held me close. I could only hug him with one arm; the other one was giving me grief now but I said nothing about it. One more long kiss and I wanted him again, but he extracted himself gently and stepped towards the door.

'See you tomorrow?'

'Yes, I'll be at the pub,' I said. I grimaced. 'Owners' meeting with Andre and Suzie.'

'Take care,' he said. 'I mean that. Stay alert and let us know if you see anything suspicious.'

'OK.' I waited until his car drove away, then I managed to take some painkillers and get the sling back on, and the ache in my shoulder started to fade. Finally I checked every door and window again before climbing back into bed. The sheets felt cold and unwelcoming, and Heath's last words echoed in my head. I didn't sleep well.

13

In the morning, I woke with a start to the sound of king parrots prancing around on my roof. Mia came into my room, tentatively, as if checking first whether 'that man' was still there. My brain had already begun to churn, trying to scold me, to tell me what a fool I'd been, so I shut it off by jumping out of bed and getting her dressed, turning the music up loud while I prepared breakfast. It wasn't until Mia and I were eating, and I was cutting up toast for her that it suddenly hit me. No contraception.

I dropped the knife with a clatter. Surely even I couldn't be that unlucky. It wasn't anywhere near the danger time of the month.

No, I refused to do this to myself. Last night had been amazing, and I couldn't bear for the ghosts of my past to crowd in and ruin it for me. If I couldn't quietly remember all the lovely moments without them being tainted, I just wouldn't think about them at all. Still, my body knew. Somehow I stood straighter, I felt like dancing at odd moments, I smiled for no reason. *Just enjoy it.*

I dropped Mia off at Joleen's on the way to the pub; it was a prearranged childcare day and besides, I wanted to be able to concentrate when Andre and Suzie and I talked. Some big decisions were on the horizon.

I half-expected to find the place in a mess, seeing as how we'd left Carl to his own devices overnight, but all the breakfast stuff was tidied away and it even looked like he'd wiped down all the tables. The man himself was sitting with the French doors open, spring sunshine pouring in as he read the daily newspapers. He had both the local and the Melbourne ones, as if he was looking for something.

As soon as he saw me, he tossed his paper aside and rose. 'Good morning, Judi.' He waved a hand around. 'Spick and span. You could give me a job here.'

'Maybe I will. And you got the French doors open, too.'

'Yep. They were a bit stubborn, sticking at the bottom. Damp must've got to them. They just needed a bit of coaxing.'

'Great.' The paving outside was dotted with weeds and the shrubs were all drooping over or leggy and bare, but I could fix all of that. Andre was right – put up a shade sail in the summer and it would make a great eating and drinking outdoor space. 'Don't suppose you made coffee as well?'

'Of course.'

I raised my eyebrows but I wasn't going to complain at how he'd taken over. He could look after himself every night if he wanted to. I had a feeling there were no more accommodation bookings for at least a week. I fetched a coffee for myself and sat down with him, stretching my legs out to the sun. 'No trouble last night?'

'Quiet as the grave.' He ducked his head and cleared his throat. 'Sorry, didn't mean to be flippant.'

'It's fine. And you were right yesterday. It's time we found out when Macca's going to be released and organised a good send-off for him.'

'Too right!' Carl said. 'We'll have a bloody big party, and I'm paying for it.' When I protested, he held up both hands. 'No, no, it's the least I can do for an old mate. We go way back.'

This was my chance. 'I saw the photo of you all as soldiers – taken in Vietnam, I think, wasn't it?'

His smile disappeared. 'Where did you see that?'

'It was in a box of Macca's things. There were medals in there, too, but I guess they'd be service medals. You'd have some, too?'

'Yep, that's right. That was well over forty years ago now. Hard to believe.'

'Are all of you still around then? Will the others come to the funeral?'

For an instant, something hard as flint flashed in Carl's eyes, then he shook his head, his mouth downturned. 'No, more's the pity. We're all getting on a bit. I think a couple of the boys are no longer with us.'

'One of them looked Vietnamese.'

Carl's jaw clenched. 'Yeah, a guy called Tuan. He was like a scout. He stayed behind. We never saw him again.'

I smiled brightly at him. 'You never know – there were so many Vietnamese immigrants back in the 70s and 80s. He might be here and you'd never know.'

'Nah, doubt it,' he snapped.

'Hey, you got the doors open!' Andre said cheerily behind us. We both turned to greet him as he stepped over the sill and inspected the messy garden. 'Looks like a job for a gardening kind of person. Do we know any?'

'Very funny,' I said.

Suzie came in with a cheery wave and headed for the kitchen for coffee, greeting Carl over her shoulder. He didn't hang around, muttering something about walking and foxes and

189

disappeared up the stairs.

'He's super keen on the fox hunting, isn't he?' Andre said.

I collected the paperwork from the office and we settled down to lay it all out for Suzie and talk about our options. When she saw the transfers of money Macca had made, she nodded. 'I had a feeling something like that was happening. There were days here where the few locals who came in were barely covering my wages, let alone anything else. There have been a couple of old pubs in the area that have been done up and become real competition for us. Even Macca noticed the drop in numbers and takings.'

'This is the problem,' Andre said. 'The country gourmet pub is becoming more and more common, and people are doing day trips out of Melbourne and Bendigo. We need to give them a reason to come here. I can do the food part, but what else can we offer?'

We all gazed around the shabby bistro and the overgrown garden. 'Stuff all at the moment,' Suzie said. 'But to do the place up and then have a go at the marketing – we haven't got any money for that, have we?'

'We could borrow,' I said. 'But you weren't keen.'

'No,' Suzie said. 'But neither of you could buy me out either.' We shook our heads.

'At least you got rid of those two leeches,' she added. 'That's one less drain on our running costs. Bet they didn't pay you a cent for their rooms and food, did they? Or the litres of beer he put away.'

'No, but you're right, it's great they've gone.' I tapped the pile of paperwork. 'We're covered for insurances for another five months. But we have suppliers' accounts to pay, and we need to keep paying wages, including our own.'

Suzie leant forward and whispered loudly, 'Is it true that Macca had thousands of dollars hidden in his car? Is that money part of his estate?'

How had that leaked out to the local gossip network? 'No idea.'

'Probate will take ages,' Andre said. 'No point thinking about it. Really, we have two options. One is to keep going, and do a whole bunch of small, cheap things to try and increase our customers. Suzie, your son is the right age to be into social media and how it all works.'

'Yeah, I can't get him off it, and now they're doing things at school on it.'

'We could pay him to do us a basic website and Facebook page, and a social media campaign. If he's not interested, maybe one of his friends is.' He gestured around the bistro. 'It wouldn't take much to tart this place up a bit. I can change the menu – leave the usuals for the public bar, but come up with some specials for the bistro, and promote them on the website.'

'And the other option?' I asked.

'Put it on the market and sell it as soon as probate is through.'

I thought for a few moments about what he was saying. 'Logically the bank will want us to keep trading. A closed, derelict pub is no good to anyone. We could ask for a small loan to do some renos, and if we end up selling, we'll pay it back then.'

A laugh boomed out behind us and we all jumped and turned as one. In the entrance of the bistro, a thickset man in jeans and a leather jacket stood with his arms crossed. Blue and red tattoos curled up his neck, and his long grey hair swept back from his forehead into a braid. Behind him hovered a tall, dark-skinned man whose black hair was shaved at the sides and bushy on top. The hairstyle I called 'toilet brush'. Somehow I knew he wouldn't like me saying so.

'Before you get all excited about renovating,' the thickset man said, 'you need to work out how you're going to pay me back.'

I gaped at him, struggling to grasp what he was saying. 'Are you one of Macca's suppliers? The beer? Meat?' Those were two bills I knew were overdue.

He walked over to our table and loomed over us, folding his arms again and deliberately trying to dominate. His mate stood behind him, copying his stance like they were The Menacing Clones. 'Mr Macclesfield and I had a private arrangement. He owed me a lot of money.'

'What for?' Andre asked.

The man's eyes swivelled up and around, and I realised he was scanning for listening devices or cameras. There were none, but the corners of the room were so dark and dingy it was hard to tell. He decided to play it safe. 'I supplied him with goods. He paid for them. Now we are in a *situation*. A situation I don't like at all. It's very difficult for me.'

'You're saying Macca took your "goods" and didn't pay you,' I said. 'Tell us what they are and we'll give them back to you.' I had a horrible idea this thug was talking about chop chop. Where were Heath or Connor when we needed them?

He smiled and one of his teeth flashed with an embedded diamond. For fuck's sake, talk about pretentious.

'Your dead mate has stashed the goods somewhere. You'll have to find out where.' He unfolded his arms and placed his hands solidly on Suzie's shoulders. She tried to squirm away but he locked his fingers and forced her to stay where she was. Her face was white with fear.

I flashed back to the threats and the violence I'd suffered over

SHERRYL CLARK

Andy's video, and the scar in my hand twinged.

'The goods might be in this hotel.' His gaze arrowed down to the cellars. 'Or they might be hidden away somewhere else.'

'We have no idea what you're talking about,' Andre said. 'You'll have to help us out a bit more than that.'

'Either the goods or the money for them,' the man said.

'How much are we talking about?' I said.

'Initially I would have settled for twenty thousand.' He beckoned his mate over and murmured in his ear. The dark guy nodded and stepped back. 'But due to the circumstances under which Mr Macclesfield reneged on our deal, I will need sixty thousand dollars, in order to be compensated for my... distress.' He smiled again and squeezed Suzie's shoulders so hard that she cried out.

'Hey!' I snapped. 'Let her go. And you can stop talking bullshit. There are no cameras or microphones in here. The cops have got no reason to bug us.'

The man let Suzie go and stepped around the table to me. He bent down and his breath was like rancid cheese. 'Bit mouthy, aren't you?'

I stared back at him. Put this arsehole next to Graeme Nash, underworld boss, and I knew who would come out on top, and it wasn't Smiley here. But that didn't get us out of the shit we were in with this guy right now.

'I'm not mouthy,' I said. 'I'm being straightforward because you're threatening us and we have no idea what you're talking about. You want something? Spell it out. Otherwise we'll just report your visit to the cops across the road, and move on with our *renos*.' Brave words from me. Inside my guts churned like frogs in a blender.

'Spell it out, eh?' The whites of his eyes were yellowish and

193

bloodshot, a sign of something wrong with him. Like being a threatening thug wasn't enough. 'Fine, then. Your mate ran off with both the money he owed me and the goods – the cigarettes he'd ordered. So the twenty is for the goods, and the forty is for inconveniencing me. I don't like having to chase people who owe me. Whether they're alive or dead.'

The words popped out of me. 'We thought you killed him.'

'Piss off,' he hissed. 'Why would I do that, and lose everything I'm owed at the same time? You think I'm fucken stupid or something?'

I wisely kept my opinion to myself.

Andre said, 'But we had no idea what Macca was doing. How is it now our responsibility? We haven't even got enough to keep the pub running.'

Thankfully, Smiley straightened up and took his foul breath with him. 'That's not my problem. I happen to know he left you this place, so you have collateral. I want the money by Sunday night, or else.'

'We don't have it,' I tried one more time.

'I. Don't. Care. Find it.' He pointed at his mate. 'There's more where he came from, and we'll be back. Don't run squealing to the cops, either. Any of you. I have ears to the ground around here, and I'll know. Then you'll be doubly sorry.'

We sat in complete silence as their footsteps receded down the hallway and the front door slammed. A few seconds later, two deep, throaty motor bikes started up and roared away.

Suzie burst into sobs and lowered her head on to her arms, her shoulders shaking. Andre jumped up and went to comfort her, kneeling and hugging her, then patting her gently. I sat and watched, feeling numb, thinking I should do something, anything, but I had no inkling of what that might be. I didn't

194

think I could even say a coherent sentence right then.

Suzie calmed down a little and blew her nose loudly into a tissue. 'That's it, I want to sell. It's like Macca has cursed us.'

I wanted to tell her she was being stupid, but I couldn't find a good argument against what she'd said. Andre came to my rescue.

'Don't say that. Poor old Macca made a mistake, and he made it because that scheming little bitch, Madeline, tried to con him. If anyone should take the blame for this mess, it's her.'

'And she's gone, so we can't offer her up as compensation,' I said.

'God, I wouldn't pay ten dollars for her, let alone sixty thousand!' Andre said.

I almost laughed but we were in deep shit. I was just glad Mia wasn't here. I didn't need bikies getting it into their thick brains that she would be a good bargaining chip. I was never going to let that happen again. Which made me think Suzie was right – we should sell.

'Are we going to tell Connor?' Andre asked me.

'I–' I stared at him blankly. 'I–'

'That guy said he had people around here who were telling him stuff,' Suzie said in a small voice. 'What if he finds out we've been to the cops?'

I looked around the bistro, I thought about Mia, about my house, and how my life had been going OK. Not fabulous but OK, mostly. I refused to think about the mediation meeting. This was here and now. Andre and Suzie were my friends. I'd left things to the police before and in the end it was me who fixed them.

But this was different. Wasn't it?

I'd trust Connor with my life, I'd thought in the past. Now

I wasn't so sure. The thug had said don't tell the cops. The 'or else' threat was about violence. We only had his word that he wasn't responsible for Macca's murder. Next time it might be Andre in the dumpster. Or me.

I shuddered.

But we didn't have sixty thousand dollars. And I'd vowed I'd never let gangsters rule my life again.

I pulled out my mobile phone, rubbed the dust and handbag fluff off it and tapped my contacts list that had all of four people on it. That one. Tap. Tap. It rang.

'Hello.' The sound of his voice made my face heat up instantly, but this wasn't the time for romantic crap.

'Can you pop over to the pub? Now?'

Something in my voice must've got through to him. 'Sure. Be there shortly.'

'Come the back way past the school. I'll open the kitchen door for you.'

'Right.' He sounded puzzled but he didn't waste time asking questions. 'On my way.'

I hung up and found Andre and Suzie sitting like statues, watching me with barely a blink. 'You sure about this?' Andre asked.

'No, but I think it's the less risky of two dangerous options.'

He sighed. 'If it wasn't so early, I'd hit the scotch.'

'I don't care how early it is.' Suzie's face was still white, blotched with red from crying. 'I'm having a bourbon and coke.' She went to the bar and came back with a glass of ice and bourbon. 'Coke seemed unnecessary,' she said, and managed a shaky smile.

'Better open that door.' Andre unbolted the kitchen exit and a couple of minutes later, Heath came in and they shut and bolted the door after him. I'd shut the French doors and the bistro door – it felt like a meeting of a secret society. The bistro was gloomy enough.

'Right,' Heath said, when we were all settled around the table, 'what's up?'

'This is confidential,' I said. 'Just between us for now.'

'But–' he started.

'We're serious, mate,' Andre said. 'Confidential or we don't tell you.'

Heath got that mulish look on his face I'd seen a few times, but finally he nodded. 'OK. For now.'

I let Andre explain what had just happened, the threats, and the bit about 'local ears' that were passing on information. 'We decided we should tell you,' Andre said. 'Even though he said not to. So you'd better not let us down.'

'We need protection,' Suzie said. 'What if they come back for us?' Her mouth trembled and she sipped her bourbon again.

The only protection we were likely to get was already here, investigating Macca's murder. Was Barney's informant really someone who was passing on info to the bikies as well? 'Don't tell Barney or the Bendigo cops any of this,' I said.

'It's going to be difficult not to,' Heath said. 'What this bikie guy has told you is pretty significant for us – if it's true.'

'That somebody stole both the money and the cigarettes?' I asked. 'But you found a lot of money in Macca's car.'

'How did you–' Heath frowned. 'Never mind. Yes, we did, but clearly that wasn't all of it. We've heard a rumour that Macclesfield was the front man, that there was a group of them trading in chop chop.'

The old buggers. I didn't dare look at Andre. 'So you think Macca had twenty grand on him and the guy who killed him took half? Why not all of it?'

Heath shrugged. 'The money we found was well concealed. Macclesfield might have been planning to hold half back until he saw the goods.'

'Do you think it was the bikies who killed him?' I said. 'It couldn't be. Otherwise that thug wouldn't have come in here demanding payment.'

'Well, we're working on…' He stopped. 'You don't need to know.'

Andre leaned forward, his face more serious than I'd ever seen it. 'Listen, this is our lives you're talking about. Suzie here is frightened to death already. Keeping us in the dark doesn't make us feel better about telling you. We could have kept quiet and tried to deal with it ourselves.'

Heath couldn't help it – he glanced at me. I glared back, my chin in the air.

He let out a long, exasperated sigh. 'All right, but it stays in this room. We think maybe one of Macclesfield's group double-crossed him. This person – it could've been a woman – went with him to the pick-up place and took a gun. They held up the delivery men and things got out of hand. Macclesfield might've known about the gun, or he might not. Either way, he got shot.'

'By one of his own mates?' Suzie said. 'A mate wouldn't do that.'

'If the two who just threatened you are telling the truth,' Heath said, 'it had to be whoever was with Macclesfield, because according to them, that person took the chop chop and half the money.'

It kind of made sense to me, but there were still bits that didn't. 'So where did the bikies go who were there?'

'Probably they were forced to leave. It's a wonder it didn't turn into a shoot-out.' Heath sat back, but he looked like a cat about to bolt. 'Hence your visitors now wanting their chop chop back.'

'Or compensation money,' Andre said. 'Which we don't have.'

'It's extortion,' Heath said.

I didn't care what the correct term was. I wanted it all to go away. 'So what do we do when these guys come back on Sunday?'

'I think you should close the pub and go down to Melbourne for a few days,' Heath said.

What would that solve? Surely they'd just come back later. Plus we were already teetering on the edge of bankruptcy, and he wanted us to close down. 'He's coming back on Sunday, he says. Why don't we keep trading until we close Saturday night, then shut down for a few days. We can do without Sunday, Monday and maybe Tuesday.' Andre nodded; Suzie sat with her head down. My guess was we wouldn't see her in here again until the bikie problem was solved.

'What if he returns before then?' Heath said. 'It's a big risk.'

'You're all still here, you and the Bendigo cops. And Connor,' I added. 'Surely you can protect us until Saturday night?'

Andre glared at Heath. 'We've given you important new information, you said. So you'll surely be investigating the bikie link to Macca's murder and the chop chop anyway.'

'Yes, we will,' Heath said carefully. 'There's a task force already working on it. We don't want to get in their way.'

Suzie exploded. 'Well, bloody tell them to come and protect us then!' She gulped more bourbon, and I wished I had a glass of it, too. I knew Heath was doing his best, but this police rules and procedure stuff gave me the shits. Waiting around for people to tick boxes...

'All right, all right.' Heath held up his hands. 'I need to go and report in on all of this.'

'Go back the same way you came,' I said. 'And while you're there, try to find out who the local snitch is who's feeding everything you guys do to the bikies.'

'It's not one of us,' he snapped.

'I never said it was.' Wow, that warm fuzzy feeling from last night hadn't lasted long, for either of us. 'We're staying open tonight and Saturday. We have to, or we'll go under. They're our two busiest nights. We'll close then for a couple of days and disappear, and see what happens. All right?'

Heath made the kind of noise that said, 'You're not being sensible but I can see there's no point arguing,' and left us to it, going out via the kitchen again. When Andre had bolted the door, he came back to our table.

'It's after eleven. I have to get things moving for lunch. And the bars have to open.'

Suzie still looked frightened but there was colour in her face, even if it was bourbon-shaded. Better than nothing.

'Let's show them,' I said. 'Yes, they frightened the crap out of us, but if we freak out now and give up, we lose both ways.'

'Yeah,' Suzie said shakily. 'I mean, what can they do? If they kill us, there's still no money.'

'If they kill us,' Andre said, 'they'll be very welcome to harass Madeline instead.'

On that cheery note, we all went off to deal with Friday's regulars.

While I moved around helping wherever I was needed, pouring beer or restocking the bar fridges or clearing the few occupied tables in the bistro, my brain did a lot of mulling. I've never been good at mulling. Charging in, all guns blazing, is more my thing. But we were in a pickle, and there was nowhere to charge. Nobody to tackle. Unless I wanted to sit here on Sunday night and argue with two bikies. Nup.

Whatever really happened with Macca's chop chop deal that went wrong, it wasn't our fault. I wanted to trust that Heath would find a way to protect us, but for now, the only defence was knowledge. Who did it, why, how and where. Connor had said the attack happened in an isolated area in the bush. It would have been sometime Saturday afternoon, and then the killer presumably, according to the police, brought his body to the back of the pub after dark and dumped it.

Why? When they could've left it in the 4WD or dragged it into the bush. Was it a warning for someone else? But only the bikies had a reason to kill Macca as a warning. I played it out in my mind. Macca turns up with half of the money, they turn up with the chop chop. A shoot-out happens. Macca is dead. Are any of the bikies dead?

No. I thought those thugs would have told us. In fact, that visit would've been payback and one of us might've been dead by the time they left. But that's not what they said. Their guys had been chased off, presumably by someone with a gun. Had Macca had a gun?

I couldn't see it. But then I'd been pretty naïve about Macca and what he was up to right from the beginning.

All the same, it was very likely that someone else had been with Macca, just as Heath had said. Who? Our little joke about the old buggers floated through my head again. It was a ridiculous idea, but...

I didn't buy Heath's scenario that Macca's mate double-crossed him. I debated that with myself for a while, trying to be cynical about it. But Macca himself made that unlikely. He was everyone's mate, but more than that, he helped people, often at his own expense. Look at Madeline. Only Macca would've got sucked in by her.

Maybe whoever was there panicked. Maybe they'd taken a gun – why not, I had one locked in my cupboard – just in case, and the bikies tried to rip them off somehow, and Macca's mate shot him accidentally. The bikies made a run for it, and the killer didn't want to leave Macca there so they brought him back here.

And put him in the dumpster? That wasn't very kind of them. Why didn't they leave his body in the 4WD around the back? Because they needed it to get back to their own car.

There were a few holes in my theory but mostly it hung together. The big question was who that person was. I would've voted Carl to the top of the list, being someone who knew guns and would undoubtedly back Macca up, but he wasn't there. He was at the races surrounded by dozens of witnesses. Probably that's why he was still here at the pub, trying to help. He felt bad about not being here to back Macca up when he needed it. I kind of wished he'd go home to his wife, even though the money from his room was handy.

I sighed, and started setting the bistro tables for dinner. We only had one booking, but the locals often dropped in when they didn't feel like cooking. By the time I'd finished, I'd made up my mind. Someone was getting a visitor this afternoon, and some questions that I suspected they might not want to answer.

Someone whom I had voted into the top three on my list.

14

As I got more movement and less pain in my shoulder, the Benz was becoming easier to drive, although without the automatic gearbox things would have been different. I pulled up in my target's driveway and admired the neat borders and trimmed green lawns. I could see the little hothouse out the back and a section of a large thriving vegetable garden. Bob must pay to have water delivered – he couldn't keep all this up on the two tanks he had, surely.

The front window curtains rippled so I knew someone was home. Hopefully it was Bob. I knocked hard on the front door, avoiding the oval stained glass panel. I didn't want to put cracks through the enamelled kookaburra grinning at me with his big beak. After a few long moments, just as I was about to knock again, I heard footsteps coming down the hall and then the door opened, but only enough for Bob to peer out at me. His white hair looked like he'd been out in a hurricane.

'Judi. This is a surprise.' Bob wasn't smiling, and his voice had no croakiness at all. Must've been the fastest cold recovery in history.

'Bob, just seeing how you are.'

'Well, you know, still not right. I'm sorry to let you down but I just can't manage–'

'Sorry to hear that. Can I come in?'

He didn't seem at all surprised by my rude tone. He sighed and opened the door wider. 'Yes, all right. I suppose you'd like a cuppa.'

As long as you're not going to poison it. 'That'd be nice.'

I followed him down a long dimly-lit hallway, lined with old paintings and sepia photos, past a large vase filled with half-dead gold banksias and red proteas, the kind that cost a fortune in the city but he'd probably grown himself. The house smelt musty and the kitchen reeked of something burnt. The pot was soaking in dirty grey water.

Bob sat heavily at the table and pushed aside the dirty plates and newspapers. 'Sorry about the mess. Things have been getting on top of me since... I got sick.'

'Bob...'

'Yes? Things all right at the pub?'

'Not really. But that's not why I'm here.' I took a breath. 'Was it you who was there when Macca got killed?'

To my horror, Bob's mouth trembled and his eyes filled with tears. But instead of confessing to me, he said, 'My Phyllis would have my guts for garters if she could see the state of this house, you know. It was always her domain, and I did the gardens. We were a great team. Bloody dementia. It's a curse.'

'I'm sorry, Bob. It must be awful for you.'

'Macca always helped. He'd come around in the mornings and sort things out for me, get Joyce to clean now and then. Wouldn't let me pay.' A tear rolled down his cheek and dripped on to his shirt. My own eyes filled, too, and I patted his hand with its pattern of blue veins and dirty fingernails.

'Is Phyllis...'

'In the nursing home up the road,' he said. 'Costs a fortune, but the other one closer to Heathcote is even more expensive. I wanted to keep her at home, but it got beyond me.'

'You managing the fees for the home OK?'

'Mostly. Some weeks I live on sandwiches and what Andre feeds me.' He managed a smile. 'He's a bonza cook, that Andre.'

Bob still hadn't answered the key question, and I needed to know. 'So, you were there when Macca was shot.'

He opened his mouth and I waited for the Yes. Then it was as if somebody whispered something in his ear. His eyebrows went up, he glanced around the kitchen and up to the ceiling, and shook his head slightly. Then he stood abruptly. 'Good to see you, Judi. Thanks for calling in. I've got to water my seedlings. You can see yourself out, can't you?'

He turned and went out through the back door, closing it behind him, and I heard a key turn in the lock. From the window, I watched as he picked up the garden hose and stood by his vegetables, his back to me, but no water was coming out. It was a clear message: Go away.

The burnt smell was singeing my nose; the pot had charcoal fragments of potato floating in it. I left, resisting the urge to slam the front door and stop that kookaburra laughing, and climbed into the Benz. I could go and harass the old man, take the hose off him, even beat him with it if I'd a mind to. But I didn't. Bob had probably answered my question without words.

Now I had to decide what to do with the information.

I wrestled with it all the way back to the pub. I'd be dobbing Bob in with no evidence, other than my gut feeling based on what he'd just refused to confirm. Heath would laugh me out of the police station, or I'd get another lecture on 'interfering', or both. I couldn't bring myself to do it.

I found Andre in the bistro, drinking coffee and leafing

205

through some recipe books.

'I didn't think you used recipes,' I said.

'Simple stuff, no, but if I want to come up with a trendy new menu, I'll have to be more adventurous. I do need to try things out first, though.' He pushed a book across the table to me. 'Everyone's into pork belly and lamb shanks.'

I peered at what looked like ordinary old stew to me. 'This is special because?'

'It's venison with red wine, both of which I can get locally. Same with stuff like mushrooms and asparagus, organic beef, goat's cheese – you and I could go around the farmers' markets and see who the best local suppliers are. Do deals with them.'

'Sounds good,' I said. 'As long as we can pay them.'

He took the recipe book back from me. 'So what have you been up to?'

'Do I look guilty?'

'No, more like you've found another problem to worry about.'

I made a face. 'Yes, I think I have.' I explained to him about Bob, describing the strange reaction and shutting me out.

Andre stacked up his recipe books, lining them up neatly. 'You think Bob shot Macca?'

'Sort of. No, not really.' I pressed my palms into my eyes, trying to picture Bob's expression, and recall his tone. 'I think he knows who did, though. I think our silly idea about an old buggers' gang wasn't as silly as we thought.'

'So now what?'

'That's the dilemma. Do I tell the cops, or keep quiet? I'm not sure, so how can I set them on to Bob if he's done nothing wrong?'

He leant forward. 'If you had a word with Connor, would he be obliged to pass it on?'

'Probably. Maybe.' I threw up my hands. 'I don't know.'

'I love how decisive you are,' Andre said with a laugh. 'Why don't you wait and see? Connor's coming in shortly. He rang up just before you came in and ordered a steak sandwich.'

'All right.' I pointed at a brand new dark blue notebook on the top of his pile. 'What's that?'

'One of my ideas. There've been so many times one of the local ladies has eaten here and we've ended up having a conversation about family recipes and old favourites. I'm thinking I'll ask them for their best, with permission, and credit them on the menu if they work out.'

'Like Mrs Parsons' buttered parsnips?'

He lifted one shoulder. 'Hey, nothing wrong with buttered parsnips. And it might get more of the locals to eat here, which would really help our bottom line. Can't just rely on tourists.'

'True.'

I was struggling to open the French doors again when Connor arrived. 'Let me do that,' he said. 'You don't need to wreck that shoulder again.'

'Yes, boss.' I stood back and let him shove the door open.

'It's sticking because the wood has warped. You need to take a bit off the bottom of both doors, see?' He pointed to the marks on the sill. 'I can do that once this investigation has closed down.'

'Closed down? Are they giving up?'

'No, but there's only so much they can do before leads run out and it all goes quiet.' Andre came out carrying a large paper bag, which Connor took carefully and breathed in the aroma. 'That smells great, thanks.'

'Have they interviewed everyone around here?' I asked.

'Mostly. All the ones who were in the pub Saturday night,

plus they've been talking to a few others about the chop chop.'

'And?' I refused to look at Andre.

'Nobody's saying a word. They all reckon it's a Bendigo thing and nobody here is involved.'

'What do you think?'

'I've never seen anyone buying them at the shop here, but I have occasionally seen people with the packets.' He held up his sandwich. 'Can I go and eat this while it's hot?'

'Sure,' I said. 'So you don't think Macca was part of a gang. What do the Melbourne detectives think?'

'I didn't say that. We're keeping all avenues open. Look, I've got to go. I'll see you later when I do my rounds. Are the Somers brothers working tonight?'

'Yes. Why? Do you think the bikies will come back tonight?'

'No reason why they should.' He looked at Andre. 'But make sure you keep that kitchen door bolted, all the same.'

We waited until we heard the bistro door shut.

'Did he just fob us off?' I asked Andre.

'Yep. He's talking police-like, all official and no-comment.'

'We're keeping all avenues open,' I scoffed. 'I think that's police-speak for "we haven't really got a clue".'

'There's nothing we can do about it,' Andre said. 'You don't want to tell him about Bob, so...'

'Who's the one person I haven't talked to? The one who's here all the time without being here, who wanders around with a gun and talks about foxes.'

Andre's mouth pursed. 'Carl.'

'How many times has he stayed here over the years?'

'I've been here more than five years,' he said. 'And Carl and his wife were staying over on race days way back then.'

'That's the usual routine.' I went and found the two old

accommodation forms and showed them to him. 'Do you remember either of these guys?'

'Macca said they were old mates. They both stayed here a couple of times.'

'Really? What did they do?'

'While they were here?' Andre thought for a moment. 'Ate, drank, sat in the bar with Macca all night.'

'Both of them are dead.'

'You're shitting me! Murdered?'

'Not according to the news cuttings I found. One suicide and one road accident.'

'You think they were running the chop chop with Macca? That would explain why the cops can't find anyone around here who will spill the beans about it. Maybe they're not lying. It's not a local thing.'

I folded up the forms and pushed them into my pocket. 'Same question, though. Why would the bikies kill off their trading partners?'

'This is doing my head in,' Andre said. He did look pretty stressed to me. 'Can we just focus on the pub for now?'

'Sure. But tonight when Carl comes in for dinner, he's going to have me at his table.'

'You go for it, my dear,' Andre said. 'But he's a tough nut and I'm not sure you'll get anything useful out of him.'

'As long as I don't end up buying the back leg of a racehorse,' I said.

In the late afternoon, before it got too busy, I called Joleen to see how Mia was, and the news was not good. 'She's been really grumpy today, and crying a lot. I think she's coming down with something.'

'Oh dear, does she have a temperature?'

'Not really. It might be teeth.' She sounded frazzled. 'I know I said I'd have her tomorrow, but it might also be that she hasn't seen much of you this week.'

'I know. I'm sorry. Without Macca, we're running around in circles here.' I rubbed my forehead where a headache was starting to pierce my skull. 'I'll try to finish up early tonight, and let Andre handle tomorrow so Mia can stay home with me.'

I hung up and sat staring into space. I already knew it was likely that Mia would have to come to the pub with me. Oh well, it wouldn't be the first or last time. It was just if we had another visit from the bikies...

Suzie came in and did a double-take. 'Whoa, you look like you lost the winning lotto ticket.'

'I'm struggling, Suze. Stuck between Mia, who really needs me, and the pub.'

'Welcome to single motherhood,' she said. 'Are Mike and Billy doing security tonight?'

'Yes, they'll be in at seven.'

Her face cleared. 'Good.'

I didn't want to freak her out by saying if the bikies turned up, I doubted very much if Mike and Billy would be of any use at all. They were locals, not authorised to carry guns, and their main job was to make sure drunks didn't drive home, and to break up fist fights. Not protect us from a bikie gang. I thought they'd need a tank and a grenade launcher or two to manage that.

I ate early, and then hovered near the bistro, waiting for Carl to sit down for dinner. Kelly was waitressing and I had to assure her that everything was OK. Finally, after sitting in the main bar for more than an hour, putting away several scotches, Carl ambled into the bistro and took a seat by the window. I waited a bit longer, until he'd ordered his meal, and then went and sat at his table.

'Carl, I want to talk to you,' I said. His face grew suddenly wary. 'About Macca's funeral arrangements.'

He relaxed and leaned back. 'Macca wasn't a churchgoer at all. And the nearest church that's got a minister is down at Heathcote, isn't it?'

'There are things called funeral celebrants now,' I said. 'We could have one of those instead of something religious. But we'd need to write up what we wanted, and do something about a eulogy. You've known him the longest, longer than a lot of people around here. Can you do that part?'

'Me?' He frowned. 'I mean, we were in the service together, but after that... we kinda lost touch for a while, until he bought the pub.'

'I thought all you vets stayed close. I mean, two of your old mates came and visited Macca here a few times. Two that were in the photo I told you about. I thought you might've been here, too, to meet up with them.'

'Nah, I musta been busy.' He swallowed a large mouthful of scotch and the ice jangled in the glass. 'I could write you a little bit, but only what I know. You'll have to ask someone else for the rest. Wendy, maybe. Have you talked to her?'

'Not yet.' I should have. I'd make it a priority as soon as I'd finished with Carl. 'Listen, I need to ask you about a couple of other things.'

'Ye-e-es.' The wariness was back. It wasn't nervousness, more... he was guarded. On alert.

'This is just between you and me. No cops, all right?'

He nodded.

'Did you know Macca was dealing in chop chop? Please, be

honest.'

'Yes, I did. I warned him not to but it was when the pub was doing really badly a few months ago, and then that girl he thought was his daughter... he was desperate, but he wouldn't take money from me. I wish he had.'

I stopped breathing for a few moments. Macca had been a bloody idiot, but I couldn't bring myself to blame him. 'OK, so who was he dealing with?'

'Some guy who came down from Sydney, he said. He never told me his name.'

'Sydney? Not Melbourne or Mildura?'

Carl shook his head. 'Definitely Sydney. That's where the chop chop was coming from, through the wharves there. Hidden in containers of other shit like beauty products, or inside white goods.'

'Was it just Macca?'

'What d'you mean?'

'I've talked to a couple of people and I think there was a small group of them. I don't think Macca was doing it all on his own.'

'You think I was one of them?' Carl's face had gone all blotchy, and his eyes were popping. He was upset, but was that because I'd falsely accused him or sussed him out?

I held my hands up to calm him down. 'I have no idea. And I'm not sure I even care. If you were, I'm not going to dob you in, don't worry. But the cops think Macca wasn't alone when he went to do the deal.'

'That makes sense, I guess.'

'And the Sydney guy you mentioned – he was a front man for the bikies. Which bikies, I don't know. The two that came here weren't wearing gang jackets.'

Now Carl's eyes really were popping. He slurped down the

rest of the scotch and half-stood to go and get a refill. 'Don't get up,' I said. I waved to Kelly and placed an order with her. 'And a Sauv Blanc for me, please.' Talking to Carl was a challenge and I needed some liquid help.

'You didn't hear that we'd had a visit from the bikies?'

'No. What did they want?' A bead of sweat rolled down the side of his face.

'Sixty thousand dollars.'

'What?' he shouted. When heads turned, he ducked his head and muttered to himself. I managed to pick up a few words. 'That's not on me, not on me.'

'What's not on you?' I asked.

'Nothing. Really. I just meant I knew about the chop chop but I had no idea about bikies. Fuck, what was Macca thinking?'

'Maybe he didn't know the bikies were behind it either.' Kelly brought the drinks and I drank some wine, savouring the tang. 'He could've started out dealing with someone local, or someone he knew.'

'Sixty thousand.' He gulped his scotch, his hand shaking. 'I had no idea Macca was buying so much.'

'The buy was only twenty,' I said dryly. 'The other forty is compensation for making them look bad. Apparently they ended up with nothing – no money and their chop chop stolen.'

'Fucken hell. What a balls-up.'

'But it looks like it wasn't them who killed Macca. So… any ideas on who did?' I watched his face carefully; it changed like a weather vane on a windy Melbourne day. Fear, then some kind of thought that made his eyes flicker, then the wariness was back.

'You're saying it could've been one of his mates.'

'Possibly. Could've been an accident.'

'What – they tried to shoot a bikie and got Macca instead?'

'I think that's what the cops are coming around to.'

'Pfft. Maybe.' Carl's dinner arrived, a mixed grill, his plate so loaded with meat that the chips and salad were on a separate plate. A heart attack waiting to happen, especially with his drinking and high colour. He speared a sausage and held it up, wagging it at me. 'Not much of a mate if he shot Macca and then didn't own up to it.'

'People do strange things when they're afraid,' I said. It didn't seem like I was going to get anything else out of Carl so I got up to leave. 'By the way, you're still our only guest. Are you sure you're OK to stay here on your own and lock up when Suzie and the two boys finish?'

'Not a problem,' Carl said, waving his other hand. 'I can watch the footy in the bar, and then call it a night when you close.'

I wondered if he'd still be standing by then, so I had a word with Suzie and she promised to make sure he was sober enough to find his room. 'He'll probably peg out about ten,' she said. 'I can close up with the Somers boys. You go and collect Mia and have an early night.'

It wasn't until I was driving home with Mia asleep in the back of the Benz that I suddenly wondered if I'd get a visit from Heath. I didn't think he'd been avoiding me – after all, it would look strange to the other detectives if he kept hanging around me – but I'd not had a single call or even a text message. Hit-and-run lover – sounded like a song I'd heard before.

All the same, after I'd put Mia to bed and had a short shower and another glass of wine, I waited. And waited. And went to bed alone, calling myself every kind of stupid.

In the morning I woke up thinking about the old buggers' network. If Bob wasn't the one with Macca when he was shot, then who else could've been there?

Macca was supposedly put into the dumpster after dark, so between maybe 7pm and when Mike found him close to 9. Less than two hours – whoever it was cut it fine. But I had sent Mike out earlier than usual, so… and the dumpster had been left open. The killer had to be a 'him' – Macca was a big guy and no woman could've lifted his body up like that. I doubted Bob could either.

The police probably had this all worked out, but Heath wouldn't tell me anything, and it seemed that neither would Connor. I knew who came into the pub and spent the most time with Macca. Bob, for a start. Old Jock, although he would have to be past 80. Scottie, who Andre disliked due to complaints about his steak, but that had been Scottie getting used to his new false teeth. There was nothing wrong with his brain. Either Jock or Scottie, or both, would be in the pub that evening for sure – they hardly missed when there was footy on the big screen.

I'd arranged not to go in to the pub during the day, leaving it to Suzie and Andre. We'd agreed to close from Sunday, for at least two days, just in case. I didn't put my sling on after I had dressed; I was sick to death of it and decided to see how my shoulder went without it for a while. Mia and I did grocery shopping in Heathcote's bigger supermarket, which always took forever since she wanted to help put stuff in the trolley, and then we went for a walk along the rail trail. A flock of pink and grey galahs were eating under the trees, and a kookaburra swooped past us to grab a lizard, which made both of us jump. When another kookie let out its long, raucous laugh, Mia thought it was hysterically funny. Her little round face creased up with laughter, and I wanted to take a photo but my phone was buried in my bag as usual.

Just as we pulled up in our driveway, a familiar grey Commodore stopped behind us and Heath got out. His smile made my stomach flutter but Mia clutched my leg and stared at him uncertainly. Wisely, he didn't try to overwhelm her with a loud, jokey voice. He knelt down and said quietly, 'Hi, Mia. I'm Ben. Remember me?'

She looked up at me to check this was OK. 'You can say hello to Ben.' It still sounded odd to me; I was so used to calling him Heath.

'Hello,' she said, still clutching my leg. Then the cat ran past, desperate to be first into the house in case there was food in her plate, and Mia went after her.

Heath straightened. 'How's your shoulder?'

'OK. But since you're here, you can help carry the groceries in.' I knew I sounded abrupt but something wouldn't let me apologise.

'Sure.'

We carried the bags in in silence, and I put the cold food in the fridge. 'Would you like a coffee?'

'That'd be good.'

'You don't have to rush off?' I turned the kettle on.

'No. I... I would have been leaving today, heading back to Melbourne, but now we'll be here until Monday.'

'Because of the bikies coming Sunday night.'

'Mmm.' He sat at the table, his chair screeching across the stone floor. 'I'm sorry I haven't been around. I was going to call in last night, but I thought...'

'Yes?'

'Another visit where I jump into bed with you and then take off would be a really bad look.' He said it facing me, meeting my gaze, and I sensed he was being honest, although my bullshit detector had been malfunctioning lately.

'No calls? No texts?'

'I did text you. Didn't you get it?'

I shook my head, and dug my phone out of my bag. It was flat again. My face flaming, I plugged it into the charger and when it lit up, there was a burble of pinging and I could see a text waiting to be read. I quickly tapped the screen.

Been totally flat out. Would love to see you tonight.

'Oh shit,' I muttered. I looked up and found he was grinning.

'I forgot you're not in the twenty-first century yet,' he said. 'I thought maybe my hasty exit the other night... that you were mad at me.'

'No. It was just me and my stupid phone. And, you know, the stuff happening at the pub.' And me always assuming the worst when I didn't have good reason to.

He grimaced. 'Yeah. We've been pushed sideways a bit. The excise guys are wanting to buy in. Some of the bikie task force are going to be part of the operation tomorrow night, too. They're hoping those two who threatened you will bring some of their mates, and we'll be able to catch them.'

'And if they don't turn up? Does that mean they got wind of what you were planning?' I swallowed hard. 'Will that mean they know I told you? After they made it clear I shouldn't?'

'It'll be fine,' he said firmly. 'Our guys have got people out there, gathering information and they know how to manage an op like this. We'll catch them and that'll be the end of it.'

I wished I had his confidence. I thought of Bob again. 'What if...' I was going to say, what if there were other locals involved, but that would bring down a barrage of questions, and he'd know I was holding back. I just couldn't put Bob in the frame without evidence. My gut feeling wasn't enough.

As Heath kept saying, let them do their job.

'What's your mate Carl going to do when you close the pub tomorrow?' Heath asked.

'I haven't asked him. Hopefully, he'll go home.' I made coffee and brought the plunger to the table, then the mugs and milk. Mia came into the kitchen and pulled groceries out of the bag, looking for the chocolate biscuits. I took them from her and gave her one, and put the packet on the table. I could've used a plate but I couldn't be bothered pretending manners. She sat up in the chair opposite Heath, her head just barely above the table. 'Milk?' she asked.

'Please.'

'Pleeeeease.'

Heath said, 'Do you think Carl was involved with Macclesfield and the chop chop?'

I stared at him. 'Where did that come from? Carl was at the races all day.'

'True. But the time of death always has a window.' Heath pushed down the plunger and the coffee swirled and steamed. 'He could've met Macclesfield at the park gate and then gone straight on to the pub.'

'What about Mrs Carl? What was he supposed to have done with her?'

Heath didn't answer, and I decided he was just fishing. I poured the coffee and added milk to his, then picked up a chocolate biscuit and bit into it. Creamy and crunchy. I preferred chocolate on its own. Creamy. No extra unwanted elements. Maybe that's how Heath felt about me – I came with extra, unwanted elements, like Mia. Too damn bad.

'Sorry?' I'd missed his question.

'We've interviewed everyone who was at the pub that night, plus all the other locals who knew Macclesfield well. Is there anyone else you can think of that Macclesfield knew or was in contact with?'

I opened my mouth to tell him about the two Vietnam vets and the accommodation forms, but Heath had already told me they were irrelevant, and I guessed they were. I couldn't see how they could be connected to the chop chop, especially if Macca only started dealing it a little while ago. 'You questioned *all* of the locals?' I said instead. 'That must've been interesting. Anyone acting guilty?'

'No. Some of the old guys were pretty broken up, though. They must've been really good mates.' He drank his coffee, his eyes drifting from me to Mia, who'd licked all of the chocolate off her biscuit and was now loudly crunching the rest of it. She wasn't the world's most delicate eater.

'Who was the most upset?' I asked casually.

'Why do you want to know?'

'Looks like I'll have to organise the funeral. I should ask some of them to speak, maybe.'

'Oh, right. I can't tell you names, sorry – there were a lot of them. But I do remember Bob Granger. He works at the pub, doesn't he? He was pretty distraught.'

'Bob, yes. He is.' That didn't surprise me. Silence fell and I kept my gaze on my coffee mug.

'So... you... and me.'

I looked up, as far as the buttons on his shirt. 'Yes?'

'Are we... OK?' His expression seemed hopeful, but I flashed back to the first time I met him, outside the mortuary, snarling into his phone. At the time I'd thought he was annoyed at having to waste time on me. But that had been nothing compared to the moment when I told him what I'd done with Andy's video. I shivered. Were we OK? Maybe that wasn't possible. Maybe I would never be OK with him, not on his terms anyway.

'I guess so. But the distance thing, and our lives.' I smoothed Mia's hair back off her face, but she was so entranced by her biscuit that she barely noticed me.

'It is a bit of a worry when the only time we get together is when someone dies.' The glint was back in his eyes, along with the twitch at the corner of his mouth. That did give me hope.

'As long as it's not me killing anyone, you'll be fine.' I hoped my attempt at humour worked. I knew I was giving him mixed messages all the time, and I really didn't want to. Words just burst out of me, and half the time even I couldn't work out why.

'Good to know.' Heath finished his coffee and stood up. 'I've got to go, sorry. There's a big meeting today with the task force guys in Bendigo. Not enough room here and we don't want to tip off anyone who might be watching the pub.'

My skin crawled and I glanced out of the window. Nothing but paddocks as usual, but there was thick bush on the other side of the house. 'Watching the pub? Are you serious?'

'Yes, so there'll be officers in there tonight, not in uniform of course.'

'Of course.'

He smiled. 'You'll hardly know they're there. And unless there's a good reason why not raised this afternoon, Swan and I will be there for dinner and we'll hang around a bit, too. The locals are used to seeing us, so it won't set off any alarm bells.'

'That's something to look forward to,' I said brightly. A pub filled with cops. I couldn't complain. It'd make me feel safer, but my plan to quiz Scottie and Jock might fall apart if the cops spooked them. I'd cross that bridge later.

Heath gave me a funny look. 'Yes, it will be,' was all he said. 'Bye, Mia.'

'Bye bye,' she said, reaching for another biscuit. I pulled the packet away from her fingers.

'How about a banana instead?' I said, and gave her one from the basket.

I followed Heath out to his car, where he stopped and put his arms around me, breathing into my hair. 'You smell good. I wish I could stay. This place is so quiet and peaceful.'

'You're welcome anytime, you know.' I hoped he knew I really meant it.

'Thanks.' He kissed me goodbye, something that started small and then took my breath away. For a few moments there was nothing but him and his mouth, my hand on his shoulder, his fingers in my hair, and then the world came back to me. Two rosellas swooped out of the gum trees, chirruping loudly as they dived past us, and we broke apart and laughed.

I watched him reverse out on to the road and waved as he drove away, and immediately a little pool of emptiness opened up inside me. I hadn't been honest with him, about anything really. About the old buggers, because I couldn't bring myself to dob them in without evidence. About the gut feeling I had about Macca's Vietnam connection, because even I couldn't see how it fitted or was of any real importance. About my feelings, because God help me if I said those three words and got rejected.

No matter how close I wanted to be to Heath, how much I wanted him physically, how much I wanted him to be in love with me – none of it was going to happen as long as I believed I couldn't be totally honest with him. And I couldn't work out if it was him, or if I was going to be that way with any man.

I went and persuaded Mia to come outside again, bribing her with the promise of planting seeds. I fetched my spade, sharpened the edge and set about digging in my garden, the best way I knew to get rid of my doubts and regrets and anger.

By the time I'd finished and put away the tools, most of my emotions had settled, all except one that still sat in the pit of my stomach – fear. In Melbourne, I'd dealt with that by facing it head-on. It seemed as though here, among friends, I'd have to be a lot more sneaky.

15

There was no way I was taking Mia into the pub, not with everything that was going on. I was worried the bikies might come back a day early, and if Heath and the others were in the pub, anything could happen. I dropped Mia off at Joleen's, feeling guilty yet again at leaving her, but she ran off to watch TV with the other kids without a backward glance at me. Clearly I was no competition against Peppa Pig.

I was surprised at how busy the pub was, until I realised we were into the AFL football semi-finals and everyone was in the public bar to watch the game on the big screen. Macca had invested in a massive unit last year, and there was nothing like watching the game with mates, even if they barracked for a different team. How many of them would stay on for food was debatable. I checked in with Andre, who had been cooking plates of chips and sausage rolls and pies all afternoon.

'Six tables booked for dinner,' he said. 'Including Mr Hunky Detective.' He grinned as my face burned. 'Want to be the waitress tonight?'

'No, thanks. I'll leave that to Kelly.' I peered around the doorway into the public bar and spotted my two targets – Old Jock and Scottie. They both sat at the end of the bar, half-full pots of beer in front of them and weren't talking, just staring at the TV. The game was in the last ten minutes and there was a lot of raucous cheering and shouting as the ball went back and forth, and the scores crept up. The interstate team playing had very few supporters – everyone was barracking for the Victorian players. Everyone except Jock and Scottie, who watched as though it was a boring but necessary documentary on sheep dipping.

I opened the tills, one and then the other, and took money out to put away in the safe. By the time I'd finished counting, recording and closing the safe and returned to the bar, the game was over and those who hadn't left were now loudly dissecting what had happened. The Victorian team had lost, and the discussions were strident and angry. I was glad to see the Somers boys arrive and move through the bar, their white shirts and ties serving as a reminder that it was better to calm down before being kicked out.

I moved down to Jock and Scottie and pasted a smile on my face. 'How are you two doing?' Their glasses were almost empty. 'Can I get you another one?'

They glanced at each other and nodded together. I poured and placed two brimming pots back in front of them, and took their money. As I handed back the change, I said, 'Hard to believe Macca's not sitting in his usual spot, isn't it? He'd have a fair bit to say about that game.'

Jock's hand trembled as he lifted his glass and slurped in some beer, then wiped his top lip. Scottie muttered, 'Yep, he would.'

'Did you… did you see Macca at all last Saturday?' I ventured.

They both looked at me like I'd just contracted a horrible, contagious disease.

'I'm sorry. I know the police have probably already asked you a heap of questions.' I pretended to wipe away a tear, feeling

224

like a scheming con woman, but I wasn't going to stop until I had some answers. 'I just feel so bad about it.'

'Why do you feel bad?' Jock asked. 'You didn't kill him... did you?' He glanced at Scottie who let out a guffaw.

'Course she didn't, you silly bastard. She wasn't anywhere near...'

I almost snapped, 'Near what?' but held back. Instead I said, 'It's the thought of Macca being out the back in that horrible dumpster. Who would do something like that? It couldn't have been anyone around here – everyone was his mate!' Maybe I was overloading the emotion now but it got a reaction.

The blood left Scottie's face and he pressed his fingers to his eyes. Jock took another gulp of his beer and nearly choked on it, coughing hard. I poured him a glass of water and put it in front of him.

'Shit, no, water might kill me,' he gasped. Scottie thumped him on the back and then they both sat stolidly again.

I lowered my voice more, as a few others nearby were watching us curiously. 'Did you hear that the police found his 4WD and the place where he was killed? I mean, what was he doing there?'

Scottie shrugged; Jock said nothing. I had to play my final card. I leaned in close.

'I think Macca was into the chop chop with a few others from around here. And I don't blame them for a minute. But you'd think if they knew anything about who killed him... well, that's what mates would do, I reckon. Let the police know.'

Scottie let out a scornful grunt.

'Or tell someone like me, and I can pass it on confidentially. No comeback then. I only want Macca's killer caught. Couldn't care less about the chop chop.' I straightened up. 'Hope you two got some of those chips and sausage rolls this afternoon. They smelled pretty good.' I gave them both a bright smile and moved away. Let them stew on that for a while and we'd see what came out of it. Probably nothing, but it was worth a try.

I went to see how things were going in the bistro and the next time I passed through the bar, Scottie and Jock were gone. I'd frightened them off. Or maybe they'd gone home to think about it. Or maybe they knew nothing and I was totally on the wrong track.

But Heath and Swan were there instead, sitting at a corner table with pots of beer that were no doubt light. Everyone knew they were cops; there was a space around them and a few glances now and then, but nothing hostile. I guessed everyone here knew they were Homicide and everyone wanted them to catch whoever killed Macca. But a week had passed, and as far as I could tell, there were no suspects apart from the bikies.

I went over to say hello, trying to look both casual and hostessy at the same time. Major fail. I felt awkward and clunky instead. 'Good evening.' Echoes of Hitchcock.

'Hi,' Heath said with a smile.

'Hello, Ms Westerholme.' Swan wasn't smiling. It made me certain Heath had not told him anything about 'us'. Interesting. But understandable.

'Is it just you two?'

'It's better if we don't tell you that,' Swan said stiffly.

For fuck's sake. As if I was going to run around pointing them out to everyone. 'Enjoy your evening,' I said, and walked away.

Within five minutes I'd sussed out who the other two were anyway. Their sharp eyes and way of sitting, as if they were ready to leap up and take action in an instant, gave them away. I felt a bit the same. I kept watching the doors, and walking back and forth through the bars and bistro, until my feet began to ache. I must have done my 10,000 steps in the first hour.

Heath and Swan went into the bistro to eat and whether they liked it or not, they had Carl at the next table. I thought he might have sat himself at their table, but if he had anything to hide, of course he wouldn't. Suzie had the bars under control; Andre had finished cooking and was cleaning up; the Somers boys were patrolling. Heath and Swan finished eating and returned to the public bar. Everything was calm.

It didn't feel right, but I knew that was just me. It was as if the pub was haunted tonight – I sensed Macca hovering, but also Andy and my nana. All good ghosts, if you believed in that stuff, which I didn't really. But I couldn't stop thinking about them all, about how unfair it was they were gone. Nobody murdered Nana, but my parents in effect took her away from us, another thing I was bitter about.

I'd helped to solve Andy's death. It didn't make his death easier to bear, but it gave me a sense of restitution. Not justice or closure. Just restitution. It shouldn't matter as much to me about Macca, yet it did. His life meant so much. His death did, too. Somebody around here had to know what happened, and why.

I kept thinking I'd see Macca stroll in and take his seat at the end of the bar. It wasn't calming at all. It was nerve-wracking. I wanted to go and get Mia and go home and lock the doors. But I'd said I would stay and help Suzie, to keep her calm. I was also the only one who knew the safe combination. Finally I couldn't stand it any longer. My skin kept crawling, and I started to get flashes of falling down stairs, and the scar in my hand tingled. I emptied the tills again, locked the money away and told the others I was going home.

'Carl will be here overnight again,' I told Suzie. We both glanced over to where he was drinking scotch and staring at the harness racing on the TV, but it didn't look like he was actually seeing it. His face was slack-jawed and vague.

'He should go upstairs now,' Suzie said.

I agreed and went to tell Carl he could call it a night. He nodded without looking at me. 'No worries, go up soon,' he slurred.

Heath came over to me. 'Are you leaving now?'

'Yes. Are you staying until closing time?'

'And after. We'll watch the car park for another half an hour, and then Byrne will patrol later on, just in case.'

'It might all happen tomorrow night then,' I said.

'And you won't be here,' he replied firmly. 'Nor will anyone else.'

I frowned at him. 'Will you want the pub open though? Like, lights on at least? Otherwise the bikies will think we're hiding and they'll go away.'

He frowned at me. 'Leave all that to us, OK?'

'It's my pub, or a third of it is. And it was Andre and I who were threatened. Don't you think we have a right to know what you're planning?'

'The main thing is that you are not here, and kept out of danger,' he said. 'Don't worry, we'll let you know what happened.'

As if. We'd be kept in the dark still. There was no point arguing. I would be happy to get out of the place tonight and not feel haunted anymore.

Except when I got home with Mia and had put her to bed, it still felt like things were hovering over me. I sat in the dark on my couch, with a glass of wine and the cat snuggled up, remembering. Andy and Nana and Macca, memories jumbling, pushing the bad ones away and trying to hold on to the good ones.

I couldn't bring myself to go to bed. In the end, I pulled the spare duvet out of the cupboard and curled up on the couch with the cat, lying there, staring into the dark. I'd checked my phone was charged, but I knew I wasn't waiting for Heath to come visiting.

When the phone rang just after 2am, I sat up carefully, pushing the cat aside, and looked at the screen. Connor.

'Hello.'

'Judi, you sound wide awake.'

'I am. What's wrong?'

'Someone has tried to set fire to the pub.'

'Shit! Who? The bikies?'

'No.' He let out a frustrated breath. 'Or we don't think so. We don't know.'

'Is it... has the pub burned down?' There'd been a few country pub fires in the past ten years, most often started by electrical faults in ancient ceilings and walls. But I knew this wouldn't be the case with Candlebark.

'No, it's fine. Well, one side of it is pretty scorched, and I think you'll have to replace the side door, but mostly it's OK. Bit of smoke damage in the hallway.'

'Thank God for that. How come the whole place didn't go up?'

'Well, it was me. Not being a hero or anything.' He laughed. 'I was on patrol. Orders of the guys from that task force. I was to swing past every half an hour or so, until three, and then one of them was going to take over. I spotted the fire, and I had an extinguisher in the vehicle.'

'You are a bloody wonder, Connor.' I closed my eyes and breathed in and out for a few moments to calm myself.

'The CFA guys are here, making sure it's all OK,' he went on. 'No need for you to come, really. Andre is here. It's all under control. And I know you can't just leave Mia home on her own.'

'What about Carl?'

'That's the weird thing.' He paused. 'He wasn't there. He came back just before the CFA truck arrived. Said he couldn't sleep and he'd gone out for a walk.'

'Did you believe him?'

'I don't know. The place was totally locked up, like it was supposed to be. I'm pretty sure he didn't start the fire. The main accelerant was petrol, and he didn't smell of petrol at all, so...'

'But you think it's odd.' I stood and walked around the room, easing the stiffness out of my limbs.

'We'll know more in the morning.' He cleared his throat, which alerted me. I knew Connor's little signs.

'What else have you found? Or what do you think you'll find tomorrow?' I stopped by the window and eased the curtain aside, peeping out. Nothing was moving as far as I could tell, but it was so dark out there, how would I know? 'Please tell me. The homicide cops have been so tight-lipped, and the lack of information just makes it worse.'

'There are three bottles here, also with petrol in them. One had broken on the ground. And I think...'

'Come on, spit it out.'

'I think tomorrow morning we'll find a bullet hole or two in the wall of the pub.'

'Why?' My brain was trying to put those things together.

'Someone came along while the arsonist was in the middle

230

of setting the fire, and shot at him. Those bottles are basically Molotov cocktails, but only one got used. If they all had…'

'The pub would be a pile of ash, probably.'

'Yes. My one extinguisher wouldn't have done much good at all. Especially if they'd been thrown through the windows.'

'Fuck. I don't know how to thank you, Connor.'

He laughed again. 'Just doing my job, madam.'

'Don't you madam me!' I managed a smile, which he couldn't see. I hesitated, but he needed to know. 'Look, Carl has a rifle.'

'Probably his farm one. But good to know, all the same.'

'Thanks for calling me. I'll be there first thing. I owe you big time.'

We hung up and I sagged against the wall. This had to be the bikies getting in first with a bigger threat. Either someone leaked to them that the cops were there last night, watching out, because I'd talked to them, or they'd worked out there was no way we could come up with sixty grand so this was payback in advance.

Whatever the reason, they wouldn't be turning up on Sunday night.

I wanted to get in my car and go down to the pub straight away, but I couldn't. The cat opened one eye and then yawned. 'Yeah, I'm keeping all of us awake,' I told it. 'You sleep and I'll do the worrying. Don't you stress out now.'

Connor said the pub was OK and Andre was there. I debated calling him, and finally couldn't help myself.

'How did I know you'd call?' he said.

'Sorry. Connor rang me first. I just… I can't sleep. What's it look like?'

'Better than you'd expect. They're sending forensics out first thing. Again. It's all cordoned off. Suspicious, so it has to be a crime scene. Again.' He sighed heavily. 'Do you feel like someone doesn't want us to have this place?'

I found myself nodding, and then shook my head. 'No, damn it. This is all down to Macca, you know. I've been trying not to blame him. After all, he's dead.'

'And you shouldn't speak ill, yada yada.'

'Yeah, but... it was all very well for him to leave the pub to us, but... he only did that a few weeks ago. When he knew how much shit he was in.' I was pacing again. 'I'm starting to feel like he's passed the parcel to us, knowing it was full of turds.'

Andre laughed. 'You're not wrong.'

There was shouting in the background, and he said, 'I'm going to go and make sure the place is locked up again, all right? And I think Carl is determined to stay in his room. The smoke has barely got inside, let alone made it that far.'

'Oh, let him. But tomorrow? Carl is going to answer some questions, whether he likes it or not.'

'Agreed. By the way, Hunky Cop is here now.'

'And I should care about that because?'

Andre laughed so hard that I thought he was going to crack a rib, so I disconnected.

I checked on Mia, watching her sleep under the glow of her merry-go-round night light. She didn't have a care in the world by the peaceful look on her face. Yet the kid had lost both parents and was stuck with me. She still asked for her daddy, but less and less as time went on, which I thought was incredibly sad. It didn't bother me that Leigh, her mother, had seemed to fade from her memory, but I wanted to keep reminding her who her dad was with photos and stories.

My thoughts jumped to Monday. I'd almost forgotten about the mediation meeting, with all the drama that had been going on. I'd been told not to take Mia, which was a relief. Joleen had already agreed to have her that day. I wasn't looking forward to the drive down to Melbourne, and the meeting even less so. I was dreading it, actually, and the pub dramas had been a good reason to push it aside. I'd never seen photos of Leigh's parents, hadn't known they existed apart from the obvious – she'd been born to them. I was tempted to Google them but that was pointless and whatever I found would only increase my dread.

Better to swallow a painkiller or two and head for bed. A few hours of sleep were better than none. Mercifully, Mia slept in until after 7am, and I did doze despite the tumbling ideas and theories rolling around my brain. After breakfast I dressed her in old trackies and a top she'd nearly grown out of – if there was ash and dirt around, it didn't matter if she got grubby, although I didn't want her anywhere near the petrol.

The sight of the pub was like a slap. Somehow I'd convinced myself that everything was untouched, thanks to Connor, but the whole side door and the wall above it were black, smoke streaks stretching up. The step and bitumen path were black and blistered, and the bottom of the door was charred.

'Holy shit,' I said.

'Holy shit?' Mia echoed from the back seat.

Now look what I'd done. 'It's fine, Mia, don't worry. Don't say what Judi does. Good girl.'

I parked and got her out of her car seat, and held her hand as we walked across to the side door. Two crime scene techs were there, inside the cordon, so we stood behind the tape and watched them work.

Andre came around the side of the pub to join us. 'Lucky escape, hey?' he said.

'Holy shit,' Mia said.

My face burned. 'Mia, don't say that. It's not nice.'

She gazed up at me as if to say, '*You* said it so what's the problem?'

'Classic,' Andre said, grinning. 'Come on, I've made coffee.'

I was looking forward to a cup until I got to the bistro and found Heath and Swan there, deep in conversation with two others who looked like either bureaucrats or cops: a woman with nerdy glasses and a guy with a hipster beard and haircut. I followed Andre into the kitchen and poured Mia some orange juice while I whispered to Andre.

'How long have they been here?'

'Half the night. Like me.'

Yes, the bags under his eyes were darker than usual. 'You should go home,' I said. 'Get some sleep.'

'We're not open for at least two days,' he reminded me. 'I'll sleep later. We need to talk to those guys about how to protect the pub. We might have to pay the Somers boys to watch the place.'

'The cops won't like that,' I said. 'They're staking it out for the bikies tonight, aren't they? Or have they gone off that idea?'

'We'll have to ask, I guess.'

We ventured out into the bistro together, Mia holding my hand. 'That's Ben,' she announced loudly.

Just what I needed. Next thing she'd be asking if he was sleeping in my bed again tonight. I put her into the play corner and piled toys around her, hoping that would keep her quiet, then went back to where Andre stood, talking to the cops.

'Do you think the bikies set the fire?' he was asking.

'Possibly,' Heath answered. 'Where were you last night between midnight and three?'

234

'Home,' Andre said. 'When Connor rang me, I came straight here.'

Heath and the others all looked at me. 'Home. With Mia. You can ask her if you like.'

Heath's mouth twitched and the others regarded me in stony silence. Stony silence made me grumpy. 'Connor said the person setting the fire was frightened off by someone shooting at them. Is that why you want to know where we were?'

'Just eliminating you from the list,' Swan said.

'Why would the bikies come early?' I asked. 'Did someone tell them I'd been in contact with you?'

'That information stayed with us,' said Nerdy Glasses in the kind of tone that was supposed to make me crawl back where I came from. As if.

'You all attended a meeting in Bendigo yesterday,' I said. 'Was that *information* discussed in the meeting?'

They looked at each other. Swan said, 'Of course. But the meeting was only for those of us involved in this investigation.'

I kept my focus on Swan. If I glanced at Heath, I'd lose my train of thought. 'How many of you attended?'

'That is none of your business,' Hipster Beard said.

'If it turns out that the bikies are responsible for this attack, it will be because that information leaked from your meeting.' This time I did glance briefly at Heath. 'I've experienced the repercussions of leaks before. I'm beginning to wish I'd never told you.'

'This is not a typical bikie attack,' Nerdy Glasses said.

'That means stuff-all to me,' I said. 'Our pub came close to burning down. The only people between ashes and saving it were an anonymous shooter and our local police officer. Where were you guys last night?'

'Hang on, we were here,' Heath said.

Andre added his five cents worth. 'But then you went home. Is that what you'll do tonight?'

'No, we'll be here all night,' Heath said.

Hipster Beard said, 'If the bikies were here last night, they're very unlikely to come back. We may not need–'

'Oh great,' I snapped. 'Well, you won't mind then if I call in our two security guys to keep an eye on the place. I can't expect Senior Constable Byrne to do it all himself.'

'You don't need to do that,' Heath said.

'I think I do.' I stomped out of the bistro and went into the office, Andre following.

He shut the door. 'Wow, you really let them have it.'

'Did you hear that?' I was trying to keep my voice down but I was boiling mad. 'They're not even going to watch the pub tonight. Why are we even bothering to close?'

Andre hugged me. 'Hey, we need the rest, and we need the place to be closed just in case. You don't want those bikies turning up and shooting customers.'

'I guess not.' I sucked in a breath. 'Do you think the shooter was Carl?'

'Pretty likely, don't you think?'

'How did he know? Did he see the bikies arrive? Did he have a plan to sneak out the back and chase them off?'

'If it was him, we need to thank him,' Andre said. 'He saved the bloody pub!'

The phone rang and frightened the crap out of me. I snatched up the receiver. 'Hello, Candlebark Hotel.'

'Is that Judi?' It was a woman's voice.

'Yes,' I said cautiously. It didn't sound like Madeline.

'It's Wendy, love, Macca's ex.'

'Oh, right! Hello. How are you bearing up?' That was a bit lame.

'Oh, fine. I'm really sorry about Macca, he was such a good bloke. I've missed him ever since we divorced, but... you know...'

I mouthed 'Wendy' at Andre, and he nodded, gesturing that he was going back to the kitchen.

'Country life is not for everyone.' Another stupid platitude.

'True. And he understood. We still got together every now and then.'

'That's nice.' Did they? It wasn't surprising though.

'Look, I'm calling about the funeral. Has anything been arranged yet?'

'I haven't been told if the body has been released,' I said.

'It has. They called me. I suppose because I'm the nearest listed family, so to speak.' She laughed shortly. 'I'm glad Macca got the mess with that scam artist sorted out.'

'You knew about Madeline?'

'Yes, it was me put him on to Simonetti, just in time.'

'Right.' I hesitated. 'Did you know Macca left the pub to Andre, Suzie and me?'

She laughed again, and this time it was much friendlier. 'That was my idea, too. I sure as hell didn't want it.'

'Oh.' I sat down. It was all a bit much to take in. 'So if we can have Macca back, what do you want to do?'

'He wanted a send-off in the pub.'

Now I was really glad I was sitting down. 'He *told* you that? Did he know he was...'

'Going to be murdered?' A big sigh. 'No, of course not. That's just too awful to even think about. Have they found out who did it yet?'

'The police are not getting far.' I didn't feel like asking her about the chop chop and all of that. Too much had happened and I wasn't in the mood to explain it all.

'We were talking not long ago. He'd been to the doctor and had to have a prostate exam. Frightened him a bit, because the doc found something he didn't like. It turned out fine, but Macca panicked a bit. That's when he told me what he wanted.' She went on to tell me the other things Macca had decided constituted a decent 'send-off'.

'I guess we can do most of that,' I said. 'When?' After we'd got rid of the bikies, hopefully.

'How about Thursday? Is that enough time to prepare it all?' Four days away. 'I think so.'

We spent another ten minutes working out details and who would do what, and when I hung up, I checked the desk drawer to make sure Macca's medals were safe for the send-off, and then went to tell Andre our plans. The cops had gone, so I could fill him in without worrying about them listening. 'Thursday. Hmm. I'll have to sort out the catering quick smart.'

'Let me know if you need help,' I said. 'We can get Kelly in, and a few others. Suzie will help, too.'

Andre said, 'Now, I was eavesdropping on the cops, so I can tell you some inside info.'

'Good. We need all the help we can get.' I checked Mia but Andre had already given her a snack and a drink.

'The fire that burned the side door – the crime scene techs said it looks like a Molotov cocktail. Probably intended to go through a window.'

'Shit, the pub would've been past saving before the CFA even knew it was burning.'

'Yep.' Andre raised his eyes to the ceiling. 'So if Carl was the shooter, he must've been outside waiting. Not that he heard something and ran out with his gun. He shot the arsonist before he could throw anything.'

'How did he know?' It was a question I wanted the cops to ask him. If they didn't, I would. 'Are the police still saying it was bikies?'

'They are, but there's only evidence of one person. One set of boot prints. The guy stepped in the petrol and then ran for it, so they could track him into the bush.'

'Not to a bike waiting nearby?'

'Motor bike tracks, yes. But a trail bike. And once you get further towards the state park, there are dozens of tracks, so they lost it.'

'Why would bikies turn around and use a trail bike?' I said.

'There's no way you'd get a Harley along a bush track,' he pointed out. 'And Harleys in Candlebark near the pub would be a total giveaway. They're not stupid, those guys. They've been running chop chop around the area, and further north, for several years, and hardly any of them have been caught.'

'Was I right? The cops are thinking they don't have to stake out the pub tonight?'

Andre's mouth twisted. 'They're still talking about it. How much it would cost, is it worth it, risk versus outcome. All that bullshit.'

'In that case they can all fuck off and we'll defend the place ourselves.'

He stared at me. 'You and whose army?'

'I think it's about time the old buggers got their act together and helped us. After all, they're the ones who started all this with Macca.' Mia came over to me and I picked her up, trying to do it with my good arm, cuddling her close. 'But this kid has to be safe at Joleen's.'

'It's not going to help Mia if *you* get hurt or killed,' Andre snapped. 'You're being silly.'

That was the first time Andre had ever had a go at me. I gaped at him. 'I thought you'd be totally on board with it.'

'It's just a building, Judi. It's insured.' He ruffled Mia's hair and she reached out to him, so he took her off me and let her run her fingers over his bristly face. 'Do you really want to put lives at risk? Let the bikies come in and do their worst.' He grinned. 'And then blame the cops for not defending it.'

'Yeah, OK. I suppose you're right. I really would've liked to see Old Jock and Bob and Scottie with their .22s out the front though. I can see them in armour made of tinfoil, looking like Dad's Army.' I gazed around the bistro. 'I just don't want it burned down.'

'Me neither.'

We both sighed.

'How would you feel about watching the pub tonight from somewhere down the street?'

'What?' He looked at me as if I was mad. 'Haven't we been through this?'

'Secretly. Let the cops stake it out or not. Let's just watch.'

'That will get us into a heap of shit, you know. What if Connor sees us?'

'He won't tell... will he? Anyway, it's a free country. They can't stop us.'

Andre gave Mia a kiss. 'Your aunty is a certified lunatic.'

'So you'll do it with me?' I asked.

He hesitated then rolled his eyes. 'Yeah, why not?'

'Can you look after Mia for a little while, please?'

'As long as you're not going out to buy a bazooka,' Andre said.

That wasn't a bad idea. 'No, I'm going up to talk to Carl. Again. Let's see if he's got a better story this time.'

Somehow, for whatever reason, I believed Carl knew a lot more than he was telling, and I was determined to get it out of him.

16

I climbed the stairs to Carl's room and, as I walked along the hallway, I tested to make sure all of the doors were locked. Even Macca's was secured, which made me feel better, despite the fact there was nothing left in there. His medals were probably worth very little – all the same, I was glad the wraith hadn't got his hands on them.

I knocked lightly on Carl's door, got no answer, and rapped loudly instead. There was shuffling and groaning inside, and the door opened just enough for me to see his face. His eyes were bloodshot, his unshaved whiskers were grey and dirty, and his woolly hair was flat on one side. I'd woken him up. Too bad. I needed some answers.

'Can I come in?'

He avoided my eyes. 'It's pretty messy... smelly. I haven't cleaned up...'

I pushed the door open a bit more. 'I don't care about that. We need to talk. I'll open a window.'

He groaned. 'All right.' He stood back and let me in, and I held my breath until I could get to the sash window and try to wrench it upwards. It was hopeless with one arm – it was probably painted shut, but Carl came and helped, and it gradually screeched open enough to let in cool, crisp air. By then I'd had to suck in a few lungfuls of fetid Carl smell, a combination of sweat, old booze and dank earth. Had he had a shower at all in the past few days? It looked like he hadn't let the cleaners in.

I picked up the pile of dirty clothes on the armchair and threw them on the bed before sitting down. 'I wanted to thank you,' I said.

'Me? What for?' He didn't look like he was faking the surprise.

'For helping to save the pub last night. We were close to burning down.'

His face coloured a dirty shade of red. 'I didn't do anything,' he mumbled. 'I was out walking.'

I huffed out a breath. 'Carl, it's me. Stop the bullshit. For whatever reason, you were outside the pub last night and you shot at the guy with the Molotov cocktails who was about to throw them in the windows.'

'Me? Shoot at someone?' His eyes slid around but he managed not to look at his rifle standing in the corner by the dresser. 'That could be taken as attempted murder.'

'I couldn't care less,' I said. 'All that matters is you stopped him.'

'Right.' He wasn't admitting anything.

'But where did you go after that? You didn't come back inside.' I leaned forward. 'Did you chase him into the bush? The cops reckon that's where he went.'

Carl scratched his woolly head. Maybe he was trying to pretend to be a gormless sheep. 'It was a bikie, wasn't it? Didn't he go off on his motorbike with his mates?'

'You know damn well he didn't. He had a trail bike stashed in the bush and he bolted on that. But you were on foot so you couldn't have caught him once he was on the bike.'

Silence. Carl's shoulders hunched and he examined his bare feet with their hairy tops and yellowed toenails that needed trimming.

'Did you see who it was?'

Silence. It was infuriating. Why didn't he just speak up?

'I'm not planning on telling the cops any of this.'

He raised his eyes to meet mine. 'Why not?'

'They've got their theories, and I've been told not to interfere.' I smiled. 'I've got my own ideas, things I'm not ready or willing to share. Yet.'

'What might those be?' he said cautiously.

'I think you knew about Macca and the chop chop.'

'I said I did.'

'But you also knew who else was in on it. Please don't deny it.'

He shrugged.

'It was Bob, Old Jock and Scottie. At least. Could be more. All the old buggers. Am I right?'

He shrugged again, and I wanted to smack him.

'Why can't you just tell me if I'm right or not?'

'Well... aren't you in bed with one of those cops?' He smirked. 'Literally?'

'Who told you that?' It better not have been Andre.

'Just heard it in the bar or somewhere.'

I ground my teeth. This place was like *Coronation Street*. The downside to living in the country. Suddenly I longed for the anonymity of the city. It might be worth the traffic and pollution and feeling crushed on all sides. On second thoughts...

'Look,' I said, 'don't you think it's time you went home? What does your wife think of you being down here all this time?'

'She probably hasn't noticed. As long as she's got her drinking buddies to play with, she couldn't give a stuff. Stupid bitch.' He rubbed at his mouth. 'I can't go home yet. I can't leave things…'

'What things?' Something was bothering him. 'Are you hoping to avenge Macca's death somehow? He really wouldn't want that.'

'How would you fucken know?' He stared at me, his bloodshot eyes rolling a little. 'You all think you're such big mates with him, and you barely knew him. Not like I did.'

'I get the Vietnam connection, wanting to look after each other–'

'You know nothing about it,' he snarled. 'When's the funeral? Have you at least managed to organise that properly?'

I'd had enough. Whatever was getting up his nose was beyond me. 'Thursday. I've been working it out with Wendy, his ex-wife.'

'I know who Wendy is!'

I had to give it one last try. 'Do you know who killed Macca?'

'Fuck off.'

'Right. Thanks for that.' I stood up. 'I'll put your account under the door. The cops are in charge tonight. They'll probably want you out of the place.'

'What?' He gaped at me. 'I thought they were all going to piss off now.'

My turn to shrug and I took great delight in it. 'Why wouldn't the bikies come back? They don't give up easily. You should know that.'

'They're nothing to do with me.'

Strangely enough, I actually believed him. Which was even more confusing. 'Well, if the cops come knocking, you'll know why.'

'What?'

I couldn't tell if it was fear or anger in his face. 'To ask you to leave. For your own safety.'

'Yeah, righto.' He scratched his whiskers. 'They can't actually make me leave, can they? Only you and Andre can do that. Legally.'

'I have no idea,' I said. 'You can ask them yourself.'

I went back downstairs and sat with Mia in the play area for a while, stacking blocks and knocking them over, making her laugh. All the while, I was trying to work out what was going on with Carl. The empty pub was so quiet – usually the bistro would have people eating and drinking by now, and the public bar would be filled with a low buzz. Once we got our act together with the marketing, we could have the whole place filled with tourists and day trippers on a Sunday.

I needed to speak to Heath and Swan, and find out what they were planning. Either they were going to be in the pub tonight, waiting, or the place would stay empty and locked up, and who knew what might happen. That's why I wanted to sit somewhere nearby and watch. Nobody was going to wreck or burn the joint while I was around. I called Joleen and sorted out childcare for Mia overnight, hanging up just as Andre came back.

'I've turned everything off in the kitchen, except the fridges,' he said. 'Same in the bars. Even Macca's jukebox is unplugged. I figured if we have to be closed, there's no point running up the electricity and gas bills.'

'Helloooo,' came a voice from the hallway, and then Suzie stood in the doorway. She looked worn and frazzled, her hair lank, and she wore trackies and a bulky sweatshirt rather than her usual tight jeans and figure-hugging tops. 'I wasn't sure you'd still be here. The outside lights are off.'

'Saving electricity,' Andre said. 'There's coffee still reasonably hot if you want some.'

She shook her head. 'I'm not sleeping as it is.' She came across the bistro and sank down on to a chair, pushing her hair off her face.

'Has something happened?' I asked.

'Does anything else need to?' she said, with a short laugh. 'Someone rang me at dawn to tell me the pub was burning down. I came down here to check, and then I went home again. I noticed neither of you rang me.'

Andre and I glanced at each other guiltily. 'Sorry,' I said. 'It's all been a bit chaotic, and then the cops were here…'

'Didn't do much, did they?' she snapped. 'I heard it was Connor who saved the place.'

'Yes, that's right.' The local gossip had caught up with the facts then.

'You don't need to worry,' Andre said. 'It's safe now, and they don't think the bikies will be back.'

That was glossing over things a bit but I let it go. 'We're about to shut the place up for a few days until this blows over.'

Suzie flapped a hand as if to say *so what*. 'Look, I'm just going to say this straight out. All this stuff has freaked me out. That and the financial side of it. I've decided I want you both to buy me out.'

My mouth dropped open. 'What? But we already said we can't afford it.'

Her face hardened. 'Then we have to sell and split it three ways.'

I couldn't think straight. This was the last thing I needed right now. Mia chose that moment to trip over a toy truck lying on the floor and fall with a scramble of arms and legs. Her screams rang around the bistro, and I rushed over to help her up and soothe her, but she kept going. It seemed to take forever to calm her, while Suzie sat and watched with a stony expression. Andre fetched a couple of crackers with peanut butter from the kitchen and that helped to stop the crying.

By the time I turned back to Suzie, she was standing. 'I've gotta go,' she said. 'I just wanted to tell you now. I won't be able to work here anymore either. I've got kids of my own at home. I can't afford to take risks.'

'But this place could be your financial future,' I said. 'We have plans.'

'Your plans,' she said. 'Not mine.' She pointed at Mia. 'Maybe you need to think about Mia a bit more. What would happen if you ended up like Macca?'

Before I could answer, she turned and left, slamming the front door behind her.

'Oh God,' I said. I ran my fingers through my hair, wanting to rip it out by the roots. When was all this shit going to stop?

Andre had slumped into the other chair. 'You won't like this, but I had actually heard a rumour she'd been talking to the guy who has the pub in Heathcote. Sounds like she's already lined up another job.'

'That's bloody loyalty, isn't it?' I shook my head slowly. 'I don't even know what to do with all of that.'

'Don't do anything,' Andre said. 'Probate is a long way off. So is selling, or loans or any of that stuff. How about we just get through the next few days, and plan a great send-off for Macca? Leave the rest of the crap for later.'

'Good idea. I guess I understand how she feels, but...' I rubbed my face. 'Look, right now, you should go home and get some sleep. Are you still going to keep watch with me tonight?'

'As long as it's in the Benz and not my little car with the awful seats. I'll come to your house, shall I?'

'Yep, about seven. I can't see the bikies turning up early while there might be people around.'

Andre puffed out his lips. 'Unless somebody's tipped them off.'

'That's what I thought the fire-bombing was about.'

'Carl changed your mind?'

'There's something weird going on with him, something to do with Macca. Or maybe he's gone a bit crazy, or blaming himself. But it's not about the bikies. I couldn't get him to admit it was him who scared the fire-starter off.' I got up clumsily, bumping my shoulder against the wall. 'This bloody arm is driving me nuts.'

'But it is getting better?'

'Too slowly,' I grumbled. 'I can still sit in a car for a few hours though.'

'Right, I'll see you tonight then.' He left, and I collected up my belongings, ready to head home. I didn't want to stay in the pub alone. Carl could sort himself out. I strapped Mia into her seat and loaded everything in the car, then sat for a few seconds, cursing myself. I had every right to go and ask Heath what their plans were for tonight. It was me that had been threatened, and me that co-owned the pub. With Andre and Suzie, of course. But still, I had rights, and it was only because of the stupid sex that this was all mushrooming into a situation where I couldn't do what I wanted. Bugger it.

I put the Benz in gear and headed for Connor's police station. Even if Heath wasn't there, Connor would talk to me. Or else he'd be sorry. Heath's Commodore was in the driveway and I parked in the street, my heart already hammering in my chest. But my nervousness just made me angrier with myself. I helped Mia to get out of her seat and held her by the hand.

'Going shopping?' she asked, gazing up at me. 'Lollies?'

'Not right now, kiddo. Uncle Connor maybe.'

Her face glowed. 'Unca Connor!' She half-dragged me towards the police station entrance, and I was happy to open the door and let her go first. She rushed in, shouting, 'Unca Connor, Unca Connor!' I hid a smile and let the door whoosh and close behind me.

Connor appeared behind the counter with a grin on his face. He pretended not to see Mia in front of the high counter. 'Hey, I can hear Mia. Where is she? I can't see her.'

'Down here, down here!' she shrieked.

He leaned right over and beamed at her. 'There you are.'

She'd been here lots of times and knew we had to go around through the side door to get in. I doubted Connor would let her in today. I spotted Heath and Swan at the back of the adjoining room, their faces turned towards us, but I kept my focus on Connor, as if I couldn't see them.

'Hi, Connor,' I said. 'Just checking in about tonight.' I couldn't keep the edge out of my voice. 'Thought it would be good to know what was planned now we've had to close the pub.'

'It's for your own safety,' he began.

'Yet it seems there'll be nobody there tonight?'

'Well...' He glanced over his shoulder. 'They're discussing that now.'

'Mm-hm.' Mia was trying to climb on to the counter, her little fingers clutching at the edge. 'You can't get up there, Mia.' She let go and ran to the side door, banging on it, and I tried to ignore the noise. 'Thanks again for putting out the fire. We could've lost everything.'

'No problem. Are you heading home now?'

'Yes. But I do really need to know what's going to happen tonight.' I jerked my head in Heath's direction. 'They're supposed to keep me informed, aren't they?'

'Yes, I know, I just...' his face took on the pained look I knew so well. Connor hated being put on the spot. 'I'll get one of them to call you. I promise.'

'Please make sure they do.' A thought struck me and I paused. 'Have you seen Bob recently?'

'No, why? I heard he'd been sick.'

'I might pop in and see him. I'm a bit worried.' God, I hoped he hadn't contacted the bikies on his own, or even with the other two. Or was it them who had the chop chop stashed somewhere? 'Do you know yet who was with Macca when he was killed?'

'Pardon?' Connor stared at me, and then lowered his voice. 'How do you know anyone was with him? Who told you that?'

Oh shit. I couldn't remember what I'd said and who I'd said it to. Clearly, not Connor, and it was also clearly something the cops didn't know about. Surely by now they'd worked out Macca wasn't doing the dealing on his own.

I faked a big 'no idea' shrug, and I knew Connor wasn't fooled, but I kept going. 'Nobody. I just thought maybe someone else had been there. Don't worry about it. Probably local gossip that came across the bar.'

'What is?'

Heath was right behind Connor.

'Gossip. Not worth worrying about,' I said. But now that he was right in front of me... 'What's happening tonight? Are you going to look after our pub? Or should I get the CFA on standby?'

Heath's eyes narrowed. 'It's all in hand.'

'The pub is locked up tight. Except Carl is still in there.'

'What? Why?'

'He's staying there. He's a paying guest.' I wasn't going to say I'd told him he'd have to leave.

'He can't be there tonight,' Heath snapped. 'If the bikies turn up, he'll be in danger.'

You think? Carl will probably shoot them all.

I smiled. 'I'll leave that one with you, then. I'd appreciate a call when you've decided what you're doing.'

I took Mia's hand, bent down and whispered to her, 'Lollies.' I knew with that she wouldn't kick up a fuss about leaving. We exited and were soon cruising away towards home to where the lolly jar was hidden on a top shelf, ready for occasions like this. I might even have a jelly baby or two myself. And bite their heads off.

As I passed the turn to Bob's street, I took my foot off the accelerator, braked and then wrestled the wheel to turn. I was on the wrong side of the road for a few seconds but as usual, Candlebark streets were empty. I pulled up in front of Bob's house and scanned the front of it. No sign of life, but it had been like that the last time I was here. I got out, and decided to leave Mia strapped in for the two minutes it would take. I doubted anyone would answer my knock, but I made it loud and long.

To my great surprise, Bob answered the door. Same as before, I only saw a few centimetres of his face around the edge of it, but he looked better – his hair was combed and he was freshly shaved. He muttered, 'Judi, hello.'

'Hello, Bob. Just wondering how you were. If you were feeling better yet.'

'A bit.'

'Right. That's good.' I paused, trying to peer past him but the hallway was dark. 'You heard about the pub?'

'Yep.'

'Sounds like the bikies won't be back,' I said brightly.

His face shuttered, as if I'd accused him of something. 'That's good news. Cops gone then?'

'Not yet. They might still be staking the pub out tonight, just in case, you know.'

'Yep.'

'So we've closed for a few days.'

'I heard. Not permanently, though.'

'No, of course not. We'll still have need of your services.' I tried a laugh but it was weak.

'Good-o.' He made to shut the door and I pushed against it, feeling like a vacuum cleaner salesman. I tried one more thing.

'I wanted to let you know about Macca's funeral.'

'Oh yes.'

God, this was like squeezing blood out of a rock. 'Thursday. At the pub. Not the church. Macca didn't want a church service, apparently. Would you say something?'

He frowned heavily, his face creasing into deep furrows. 'What about?'

'Macca. You know, a bit about how long you've known him, that kind of thing.'

'I suppose. I'll have to think about it.' The frown was still there. 'I've got to go. I'm off to visit my wife.'

'Right, good, OK. See you Thursday then.' I gave a silly little wave and let him close the door. For someone who was supposed to be a good mate, Bob was being weird, too.

I drove home and thankfully Mia went down for a nap, giving me time to think in peace. Not that it led to any great breakthroughs. It cemented my determination to watch the pub though. The insurance was only a backup. I wasn't going to abandon the pub to destruction. I had Connor on speed dial, if the worst happened and Heath was a no-show.

I went out to my vegetable beds and stood there, contemplating where I was up to with crop rotations. It never paid to plant tomatoes in the same place twice, and even though they wouldn't be going in until late October, I needed to work out planting now. Once upon a time, it was considered a huge risk to plant before Melbourne Cup Day in early November, in case of late frosts. Now that was mostly ignored, thanks to climate change.

I dug over one bed with a fork and added my three manures like I always did, and turned the soil again a few times. My shoulder ached but I needed two arms for garden work, and I was careful. It was so good to be doing something with the earth again. I trimmed the parsley back, and breathed in the aroma of the leaves as I gazed out across the neighbour's paddocks.

'I thought I'd find you out here.'

Heath's voice made me jump and I spun around, spraying parsley cuttings across the ground. 'I didn't expect to see you.'

He spread out his hands, a rueful expression on his face. 'Here I am. I thought you should be updated on what's happening, what will happen.'

'Meaning Swan and the other two didn't agree with you.'

'No, but Connor did.'

'I'm surprised you didn't send him instead.' I took a breath. 'Sorry. I'm on edge about the pub and... you know.'

'I do know. You feel powerless and you think we're not doing enough. I promise you, we are working this – from all the angles.' He gestured at my garden seat under the tree. 'Can we talk?'

'Sure.' I brushed off the leaves on the seat and we settled on it, not so close we were touching. 'Away you go, then. What do you want to tell me?' *And what are you going to leave out?*

'First, we will be in the pub tonight. Leslie is going to pretend to be you, and sit in the bar and wait. We'll see who turns up, but we all think it'll be a no-show.'

Nerdy Glasses was going to be me? That was like Lady Gaga pretending to be Queen Elizabeth. Or vice versa. 'She doesn't look like me.'

'She'll wear a wig and contacts. It'll pass at a distance, through the windows.'

'What if they try to burn it down again? Or bomb it? Or drive into it with a bulldozer?'

His eyebrows shot up. 'A bulldozer? Are you serious?'

'Didn't you hear about that guy who didn't want his ex-wife to get the house so he bulldozed it?' I wasn't serious about it happening to the pub, but I did want to stir him up a bit.

'I'll keep that in mind. We've asked Carl to leave, for his own safety.'

'Did he go willingly?'

'No. He said we had no right, and he'd be back tomorrow.'

'Great.' Not. I wished Carl would go home. I was beginning to think he was staying here because his wife had chucked him out. Maybe I should call her to see what was going on.

'If nothing happens tonight, we'll be going back to Melbourne tomorrow.' Heath sounded tentative, as if he wasn't sure what I'd say. I hesitated before answering, and decided to be honest. I wasn't good at pretending at the best of times.

'I'll miss you.' I kept my gaze on the garden beds, feeling my walls start to crumble. 'We almost got something working…'

'I know.' He laced his fingers together and his knuckles went white. 'The night I spent here with you… that was the best… it's the best I've felt about my life in a very long time.'

'But?' I didn't want there to be a but. For once, I wanted this to go right.

'No buts. You and me… we've talked about this before. We both have pretty solid armour, good defences, good at shutting people out.' He unlaced his fingers and sat back. 'The problem is, when we open up to each other, it's only a crack. It's enough for us to see the possibilities, that's all.'

'And then we pull back and close the crack and pretend it wasn't real.' I didn't dare touch him. This conversation needed to play out to the bitter end. 'So are you saying we should stop trying?' I could feel the tears behind my eyes, threatening to leak out, and blinked hard.

'No. I think we should try harder. But I don't quite know how.' He turned to me. 'I just know I want to try. But you have to want to try, too.'

'Right.' This wasn't what I expected and it scared the shit out of me. But he cupped my face with his hand, and his hand was so warm. His eyes were warm, too, the opposite of their usual flinty glare. I couldn't breathe. I could only look at him.

'So, do you?'

'I… yes. But I'm hopeless at this stuff. Surely you've noticed.' He grinned. 'A bit.'

I didn't know what else to say, so I leaned forward and kissed him hard, putting all the words I didn't know how to say into that feeling of my mouth and his, warm and inviting and exciting and sexy. I wanted to take him into my bedroom right then and there. To hell with everything else.

The kiss was glorious. It went on for ages, and was over too soon. We both pulled back slowly, and he let out a long breath. 'I'm glad I came. I was afraid you'd tell me to piss off.'

'I might've. But I didn't.'

'You know I have to go back now. Duty calls, as they say.' He rubbed at his temple. 'I hope tonight goes like we think – that nothing happens.'

'Me, too. I don't want the pub damaged any further.'

'If it stays quiet, I'll be finished with my watch by midnight, so…' His mouth twitched in that way I'd come to recognise so well.

'You'll call in to, er, update me?'

'Of course, madam, I'll be at your service.'

'Oh, you have no idea of how much service I'll require,' I said, and laughed. He laughed, too, but he still had to go. And after the sound of his car had faded, I wondered if I should've told him I'd be staking out the pub tonight, too. Hmm, probably not.

A squawk from the house told me Mia was awake. Good timing. We'd eat early and I'd take her to Joleen's, and then get ready. Despite everything Heath had said, I had a feeling deep in my guts that something would happen tonight – I just didn't know what.

17

Andre arrived on time, and we set off in the Benz, with coffee in thermoses and blankets in the back. 'Have you worked out where to park?' he asked.

'It's tricky,' I said. 'And it doesn't help that this car is so noticeable. But there's a spot under some trees near the public toilets. I think if I angle the car a bit, so we're mostly hidden behind the toilet block, we'll be right. There's a hedge along the side, so if we need to get out and sneak towards the pub, we can crouch down behind that.'

'Get out of the car? Sneak behind the hedge?' Andre pursed his lips. 'You said we were just watching.'

'We are!' I hoped we'd sit there all night, bored to death. I knew I should be at home but I wouldn't be able to stand it. Not for a minute. Even though I knew what I was risking with Heath. I didn't want another lecture about interfering, not after the rosy encounter of this afternoon. A lecture would make me mad at him again, and I didn't want to ruin things when it was looking kind of hopeful. I drove into Candlebark and circled around to the spot I'd chosen, to avoid passing the pub or the police station. A bit of manoeuvring and we were in a good position to watch the pub and half of the car park, including the side door.

The outside lights were on, and so were the lights in the public bar. I hoped the cops weren't all in there having a party while they waited.

After we'd settled down and I'd poured us both a coffee, Andre said, 'I've been thinking about Suzie, about buying her out.'

'I don't see how we can manage it,' I said. 'If we were going to go for a loan, it'd be for renovations and marketing and stuff. Buying her out would mean we'd have nothing left to fix the place up.'

'We could get someone else to buy her out,' he said.

'Like who?'

'Someone like Carl.'

'What? And have him hanging around all the time, wanting to be the manager? I don't think that would work.' Plus I was beginning to think Carl had mental health problems he wasn't dealing with. I felt sorry for him, but letting him buy into the pub wouldn't work for me.

'Not actually Carl. Someone else. A sleeper investor.'

I laughed. 'Someone with money to waste.'

'No, someone with a genuine interest,' he said in a hurt tone.

'Do you know anyone like that?'

'Maybe. I'll let you know if I find someone.' That's all he would say.

We sat in silence for a while, and chatted a bit, and time dragged on and on. I kept looking at my watch but the minutes were moving like snails.

'This private detective stuff is bloody boring,' Andre said. 'Whose idea was this?'

'Mine. We're looking after our big asset, remember?'

'Right.' He checked his phone. 'It's after eleven. How long are you going to wait?'

259

'I thought about twelve. If they haven't come by then…' I'd have to get home in case Heath came to visit.

'I can't hear any Harleys roaring through the town.'

'No, but… what's that?' I pointed up the side street away from the toilets.

Andre peered through the windscreen. 'Big black 4WD. Going in the wrong direction. Oops, wait, there're two of them.'

We looked at each other. 'Two of them? That's very odd, especially for eleven on a Sunday night.'

'They weren't going anywhere near the pub. Where does that road lead?'

In a flash, I knew. 'To Bob's house.'

'Bob Granger? Why would they… I get it, he's one of the old buggers you were going on about.'

'Correct.' I'd started the Benz and swung out on to the road, heading in the same direction as the two 4WDs.

'So, should we call your hunky cop?'

I debated for a few seconds as I drove. 'Let's wait. I could be wrong. I don't want to call them away from the pub for nothing. Besides, if those are the bikies, they might circle around.' But I knew they wouldn't. Bob's street was pretty much a dead end.

'If they are going to Bob's, does that mean he's got the chop chop they're after?' Andre's voice had gone a bit squeaky. 'Are they going to kill him? Or burn his house down?'

'Can't see why they would.' I took the next corner a bit fast and had to brake. *Take it easy*. 'They'll just want it back. That and whatever money Bob has stashed away.' I slowed right down at the next corner. This was Bob's street, and I had to be careful. I stopped the car, turned off my lights and peered towards his house. Candlebark had never gone overboard on street lighting, but I was pretty sure I could see one of the 4WDs in Bob's driveway. Where was the other one? There, turning at the dead end and coming back.

Had Bob arranged this? Or had the bikies worked out who had the chop chop? I didn't like this at all. What if Bob didn't have it, and they threatened him? If they beat him up, Bob wouldn't last long. If it was Bob who'd been there when Macca was killed, he'd be a witness. God, what if this was about getting rid of Bob?

'They're there. And we're here.' Andre had his arms wrapped around himself. 'I don't like this, Judi. You need to call someone.'

The doors of the parked 4WD opened, two dark shapes got out, and went up the driveway.

'I know. I will.' I thought about Bob's house, who lived next door, the fences, the dogs. And Bob in his little house on his own, against two carloads of bikies. 'You call.' I showed him the number on my phone and he copied it in. 'If Heath doesn't answer, call Connor.' I switched off the roof light and opened my door.

'Where the hell are you going?'

'To have a look,' I whispered. 'Don't worry, I'll be careful. I want to make sure Bob is OK. I don't want him to end up like Macca.'

'Judi, don't be stupid. Let the cops deal with it. Please.'

I hesitated. Maybe I was being stupid. It could be dangerous. If something happened, Heath might be so angry with me that he'd end it with me. That thought nearly stopped me. But Bob might be getting beaten up, or even killed, like Macca. I was already imagining that tall, dark guy thumping the crap out of Bob. I couldn't sit there and wait and do nothing. I just couldn't. If that made me an idiot, so be it. I had no intention of barging in. I had no weapons. I just needed to check what was going on.

I walked quickly down the street, keeping to Bob's side, moving across the other houses' front lawns, under the trees, and watching the black vehicles. Somebody's dog started barking as I passed, then subsided. Nothing moved outside Bob's house. I reached the house next to his and slipped along the side fence towards the back yard. There were lights on in the back half of Bob's house, but I couldn't hear anything. I hoped that was a good sign.

I had no idea whose yard I was in, but I was counting on them being fast asleep. As I reached the part of the fence that was level with Bob's back door, his dog started barking. Bob growled from inside the house, 'Siddown, Bluey,' and the dog quietened, but it tried to come towards me, dragging its chain.

Shit. I hoped the bikies in Bob's house would distract it somehow. I strained to listen, and picked up deep murmurs from inside. They must be in the kitchen area. Nothing sounded menacing. Then one raised voice that sounded like the guy who threatened us in the pub.

'You're kidding, old man.'

Murmur murmur. Must be Bob.

'I've had enough trouble with you lot. My boys nearly got killed last time.'

Now I could hear Bob. 'That wasn't our fault. The shots came outa nowhere. I thought it was you lot–'

'I don't care. I want the stuff back, and then we're done.'

'But I've got half the money. We can still–'

'Keep it. Where's the chop chop? Come on, I haven't got all night.'

'You can't… you have to let us keep selling. We need the money. *I* need it!'

A thump. 'Get off me, you stupid old prick. I said no. And you'd better keep quiet about all this, or you'll be dead.' A pause, some muttering. 'Get him up. Come on, hand it over now or else.'

Where the hell were Heath and the others? Surely Andre had called them by now. They only had to drive a few hundred metres, for God's sake. The back door opened, triggering two security lamps to light up the whole area, and I crouched down behind the fence, listening hard to try and work out where they were going. The dog dragged its chain and yelped as someone kicked it out of the way. They were heading for one of Bob's sheds.

I heard at least two cars stopping further up the street, and then glimpsed dark shapes moving past on the footpath. Cops, at last. I suddenly realised that some of them might do the same as me – head down the neighbour's side fence to gain access to the back yard. I ran across to the rear of the neighbour's house, thankful that Bob's lamps were strong enough so that I didn't crash into the barbecue table and seats that were under the grape arbour. I chose the chair in the darkest corner of the arbour and huddled down, feeling like the lone spectator at a vital footy match.

Nothing was happening, so I chanced standing on the wooden chair, fairly safe in my shadowed corner. Four men in leather jackets and jeans were carrying boxes across Bob's back lawn and down the side driveway, out of sight. Bob stood by the shed door, shoulders slumped. He'd sounded pretty desperate when he'd begged the guy to let him keep selling. That nursing home must cost a bundle.

Still nothing happened. Just when I thought I'd imagined hearing cars pulling up, two men ran up the fenceline, past me, and climbed the fence towards the back, flinging their legs up and over. They disappeared into the gloom behind Bob's sheds, and the dog ran across the concrete, dragging its chain and barking, but nobody took any notice of it.

Suddenly there was a shout, 'Police!', and running feet, more shouting. Two cops ran past Bob, who stood open-mouthed, his face draining of colour. One bikie threw his box of cigarettes to the ground and tried to run, and was tackled like a rugby player, thumping on to the concrete. More cops came up Bob's driveway, chasing the bikie with the long grey hair who tried to leap over Bob's vegetables and smashed his way through a lattice of broad bean stakes. He fell head-first on to a stack of timber planks and appeared too dazed to fight the handcuffs slapped around his wrists.

Inside the house where I was, people moved and things creaked, footsteps shuffled. The ruckus had woken the neighbours. Time to go. I sneaked out of the arbour and around the side, creeping along the wall, dodging the few plants that hooked at my clothes, and trying to see what was going on. Connor's blue and white police 4WD in the street had its headlights on now, lighting up the front yard. I didn't want him to see me. He'd go berserk. The neighbour had a nice bushy lemon tree in his front yard and I sidled behind that. In Bob's front yard, a fight was going on. The headlights made the scene look bizarre; bodies wrestled and grappled, their shadows thrown up on the walls of the house.

Heath was on top of a man, struggling to get handcuffs on him. Two other cops brought the boss bikie down Bob's driveway in cuffs but he was fighting them again. They dumped him face down on the lawn to try and calm him down. Bob was led out, not yet in cuffs but looking crushed and shaky, too scared to protest. I hoped the cops wouldn't thump him on to the ground and handcuff him. It might give him a heart attack, for God's sake. I edged out from behind the lemon tree, planning to sneak back up the street.

Suddenly, another bikie burst out from the other side of Bob's house, making a run for it. Then came Connor, chasing him hard, two pairs of heavy boots thumping along the road.

The bikie headed straight up Bob's street, towards my Benz. Oh shit. I felt my pockets but no keys. I'd left them in the car! I'd left Andre in the car. If the bikie got to my car and got into it, he'd drive it away, maybe with Andre in it.

Catch him, Connor!

I hesitated then moved towards the footpath. No way did I want Heath to see me, but I had to go and help Andre. He probably hadn't seen the keys in the ignition. My fault. The house owners had emerged from inside, coming down their front steps and peering over at Bob's house.

'What's going on?' the elderly woman asked, her quilted nightgown gaping open to show a pink rayon nightie and knobbly knees underneath.

'Police operation,' I said, and took off.

As I passed the second house I veered out on to the street and sped up. I wasn't a runner – hell, I wasn't even a casual jogger. Ahead of me, Connor was still chasing the bikie and not gaining on him. The bikie was almost at the Benz, and he slowed down, changing direction to his right. Heading for my car!

18

I tried to go faster, but my legs wouldn't cooperate. Neither would my lungs. They were already burning and I was puffing hard. The bikie reached my car and grabbed the door handle. The windscreen was fogged up and I couldn't see Andre in the passenger seat. The bikie pulled at the door handle several times, then thumped the roof of the Benz in fury and started running again.

Too late. Connor reached him and sent him crashing to the ground with a flying tackle. I stopped and bent over, heaving and gasping. Maybe I should start going to the gym. Nah.

By the time I reached my car, Connor had the guy in cuffs and was still kneeling on him to keep him from trying to get up again. 'Stay down!' he shouted.

My arrival gave him a start, and he jerked around, probably thinking I was another bikie. 'Oh God, Judi, you scared the crap out of me. What are you *doing* here?' He didn't sound happy.

'Um, out for a drive, you know. I couldn't sleep, and…'

'Bullshit. You were making sure we were watching the pub.' He stood up and moved behind the bikie, ready to grab him if he caused trouble.

'Yeah, a bit of that.'

'So where were you just now?'

I didn't like how angry he sounded, or the grumpy look on his face. 'I was…' Might as well tell the truth. 'I was checking on Bob. We were worried about him.'

Where was Andre? I checked in the car – not a sign of him. I shouted, 'Andre!'

'I'm here.' He was behind me. 'I followed you to Bob's. I know, I know, but I didn't trust you to stay out of it. I wanted to make sure you were safe.'

'First bloody sensible thing I've heard either of you say,' snapped Connor.

Andre handed me the car keys. 'I locked it, don't worry.'

'Thank you.' I gave him a hug then we both looked at Connor a bit sheepishly. 'Sorry, Connor,' I said. 'But I really was worried about Bob.'

He folded his arms. 'How did you know that's where the bikies were heading?'

'We didn't. We were watching the pub, and we saw the two black 4WDs going past. They looked suspicious, and I knew Bob lived down this way.'

'So do a lot of other people. Why Bob?'

Uh-oh. 'I just… I had a feeling Bob might be involved, that's all.'

'That's all? Have you been withholding information?'

'No!' Yes. Oh God, I hated this. Connor had never been angry with me before. But on the other hand, I'd been shut out of what was happening right from the start. That wasn't Connor's fault, maybe it wasn't Heath's either. But if any of them had listened to me, answered my questions, given me some credence for my ideas, then we all might have got a lot further along with the investigation and solving Macca's murder.

I straightened, ignoring his angry gaze. 'I was told very clearly to stay out of it. So I did.'

'We both did,' Andre said. 'Nobody would tell us anything.'

Immediately Connor backed down, dropping his eyes. 'Yeah, well, that didn't come from me. I said you and Andre and Suzie might know more than you realised, and we should be listening to you more.'

Too bad, so sad. Now they had to sort out the bikies and work the rest out for themselves. I assumed arrests and interrogation and all that stuff would soon help them discover what had really happened to Macca.

'So you must've realised Bob was there when Macca was killed,' I said.

His head shot up again. 'What? How do you know that?'

Why couldn't I keep my mouth shut? 'I, um, I was over the fence from Bob's place and I heard them talking about it.'

'I don't even know where to start with that,' he said dismally.

Luckily, he didn't get a chance. The big black police van pulled up next to us and two uniformed officers got out, picked up the cuffed bikie and loaded him in. They murmured to Connor for a minute and then drove off. I peered past Connor and saw people moving down Bob's end of the street. There was no way I was hanging around for Heath to tell me off again.

'We're off,' I said. 'Aren't we, Andre?'

'Yes, right, we are.' He ran around the other side and hopped in.

'See you tomorrow,' I said to Connor. I jumped into the driver's seat, started the engine and pulled away as fast as I could without spinning wheels in the gravel. In short order time, we were a block away, and turning down a side street to avoid being seen. I pulled up where we started from, next to the toilet block.

'Great,' Andre said. 'After all that excitement, I need a pee.'

While I waited for him to return, I reviewed the events of the night. Connor was angry with me but hopefully he'd think about it and realise that, without Andre and I, they would never have caught the bikies. They would've all still been sitting at the pub. I hadn't taken any stupid risks, I'd stayed out of sight and not been hurt. I'd learned my lesson in Melbourne about that. The fact my hands were still shaking was the after-effect, that was all.

Andre hopped back into his seat. 'Home now?'

'What happened when you called the cops?'

He held his phone up. 'Hunky Cop wasted a few seconds shouting at me, and then he got his act together and came running.'

So Heath would be mad at me tomorrow. I'd worry about that later.

'They'll be grateful to us when they think about it.' I sighed. 'I feel bad about Bob though.'

'Did he get hurt?'

'No, I don't think so.' I thought back to what I'd overheard. 'He was trying to get the bikies to let him keep some of the chop chop, so he could sell it, but they weren't having it. Demanded he hand it all over, and stuff his money. His wife's nursing home must cost him a fair bit.'

'Yes. Never get old, hey?' Andre said.

'Not me. I'm staying this age forever now.'

'Me, too, but hopefully with more muscles.'

'You can come to the gym with me.'

We looked at each other. 'No way.'

I let out a breath, started the car and drove towards the pub, cruising slowly and looking around.

'I thought we were heading home,' Andre said tetchily.

'I just want to check the pub. Won't take long.'

'Oh, for crying out loud, Judi. We've done our bit for the night.'

'I know. I'm paranoid. But I can't help it. They're all at Bob's place, and the pub could be on fire. They'd never know.'

Andre hmphed a couple of times. 'How could the bikies burn the pub when they're all being arrested?'

'I don't know.' I swung into the car park and pulled up by the front door, letting the Benz idle. 'Stay here while I have a look.'

'No way! Turn the car off and we'll look together.'

I was secretly relieved he'd said that. We stood at the front door, listening. Not a sound, but the lights were still on. I unlocked the door, only having to use one key instead of two, which sent a prickle up my neck. 'Be as quiet as you can,' I whispered.

He didn't answer, just followed me in, almost clipping my heels. I stopped by the reception counter again, listening. A cold draught whisked around my ankles. Where the hell was that coming from?

'I can hear someone,' Andre whispered. He pointed to the public bar. 'In there.'

I froze and cocked my head. It sounded a little like someone groaning, or it could be a door creaking. The door that was apparently open somewhere. My heart was hammering so hard it almost drowned out the next noise, a creaking floorboard overhead.

Andre looked up. 'Who's up there? Surely Carl hasn't come back?'

Another sound came from the bar. Definitely a moan. 'Someone in there is hurt.' Whoever was upstairs could wait. I

270

wasn't going to confront them, not after being pushed last time. I crept into the public bar, staying back by the long wooden counter, glad some lights had been left on in here. No way I'd be venturing in in the dark.

'There, under that table,' Andre said.

It looked like a woman; even though she was dressed in black trousers and a dark blue jumper, the shape of her hips was feminine. I started to rush, and made myself slow, holding my arm out to stop Andre. 'Careful. Check around to see if anyone else is here.'

When I got close, I realised who it was. Nerdy Glasses. Leslie. She groaned again and tried to put her hand up to her head, where blood was seeping out of a cut in her scalp. Red trickled down her neck and in wavy lines across her face.

I knelt next to her and put my hand on her arm. 'Don't touch it. Stay lying down. Andre, call an ambulance. Somebody has hit her on the head.' I couldn't see any other wounds but that didn't mean she didn't have a stab or bullet wound under her clothes. Not everything bled copious amounts.

Leslie tried to speak. 'Someone... behind me. Didn't see, sorry.'

'Don't worry about that now. The main thing is to get you some help.'

'Get me up. I need to...'

'No, you have to stay where you are. You've got a head injury.' I remembered when I'd been hit by Baldie, the pain and horrible nausea, the blurred vision. 'I'll get you something to put under your head.'

Andre was busy giving the ambulance operator all the details, while I found a pile of clean bar towels and chose the softest ones, folding them and taking them to put under Leslie's head.

271

She sighed. 'Thanks. I was... sticking to the carpet.'

Andre came over to us. 'They said twenty minutes.'

'Shit, you wouldn't want to have cut an artery, would you?' I said.

'The downside of country life,' he said. 'How bad is she?'

I checked her head, and then nudged her. She replied she was OK. 'She can cope for now, I think. Should I call Heath or Connor?'

Andre made a face. 'They're both mad at us.'

'This is different. This is one of their people.' The cold air was wrapping itself around all of me now. 'Can you check what door or window is open, please? Or Leslie will die of pneumonia.'

Andre made his way through the bar and around the back to the office and storerooms. 'Side door is wide open,' he called. The huge bang as he slammed it shut frightened the crap out of me. Even Leslie jumped.

'Sorry,' Andre said as he came back, wiping his hands on his jeans. 'It's still got fingerprint stuff all over it. I wonder who left that open?'

'Not us,' Leslie muttered. 'Was closed all night.'

'Oh.' I raised my eyes to the ceiling. 'So that other noise we heard...'

Andre looked like he was about to totally freak out. 'Are you saying what I think you're saying? This is not good.'

'We're not going up there,' I said. I pulled my phone out. Heath or Connor? Heath. Leslie was his team member. I hit his button in Contacts and waited.

'Judi, I hope you're home.' He didn't sound friendly, or even like he was hoping to visit me.

'Um, not yet. I'm actually at the pub.'

'What for? Leslie is there looking after it.'

'No, she's not. She's been attacked. We're here with her, waiting for the ambulance.'

'Shit.' A long, sucked in breath. 'Is she OK? How bad is she?'

'Probably concussion at the very least.' I checked her head. 'The wound has almost stopped bleeding. I don't think there's anything else, like…'

'She hasn't been shot?'

'I don't know. I don't think so. Hang on.' I bent low to Leslie. 'Have you got anything else, you know… Heath wants to know if you've been shot.'

'No, just my head.' She shivered. 'I'm so cold.'

'I'll get you a blanket.' I told Heath what she'd said, and added, 'Look, it sounds like someone is upstairs. But it might be Carl.'

'What? He's… I can't get away from here. I'll send Byrne.'

'Tell him to hurry.' I hung up. I was so over this crap. Delays, waiting while other things went wrong, paperwork, commands and instructions. How did anyone survive being a cop? The army would probably be worse.

There'd been no more creaks from upstairs, but that didn't mean anything.

'Are you game to go up and check if Carl is in his room?' I asked Andre.

'No bloody way! If he is, let him come down on his own. If it's not him, then whoever it is can rot up there.'

I didn't think they would. I thought that sooner rather than later, they'd come down. And if it wasn't Carl, it was very likely the person who'd thumped Leslie. What the hell could be up there that was so important? Had Macca hidden something?

That was a lightbulb moment. We'd looked everywhere obvious. I bet even the cops hadn't really searched the pub. Macca hadn't been murdered here, so why would they? They were only looking for evidence that might tell them what was going on. What the hell could he have left up there that would make somebody break in – twice – to look for it?

If that's what was going on.

Now I was itching to get up there and do my own search. But I wasn't going until I was sure the place was empty. No more being pushed down the stairs for me.

Headlights swung across the windows and a police 4WD pulled up. Door slam, footsteps, rattling at the front door: the sounds were so clear. Funny how silent the pub was without the usual stuff going on, only the fridges humming softly in the background. Andre went to let Connor in, and they came back to the bar, Connor checking around as he walked. His hand hovered near his gun, which was something I'd never seen him do before.

He came over to me. 'How's she going?'

I checked Leslie and her eyes had closed. I didn't like that – with concussion it was better to stay awake. 'She's OK for now, but she needs that ambulance.'

'It's coming. What happened, do you know?'

I explained what Leslie had said. 'And we heard someone upstairs when we came in.'

'No sign of them?'

'No. Could be Carl.'

His mouth turned down. 'Hope not. He said he was going to a motel in Heathcote. I should go and check who it is.'

'What if it's the guy who hit her?' Andre said.

'I should be able to deal with it,' Connor said.

'Another rugby tackle coming up,' I said, and was glad to see him grin.

'Hopefully not. You two stay here.'

'Wouldn't dream of moving,' Andre said.

I watched Connor leave the bar and climb the stairs, his boots moving carefully up one step at a time, out of sight. I couldn't sit and wait. My guts were churning again, and I got to my feet, hanging on to a chair until the pins and needles in my foot subsided. I went to the doorway and listened. Another creak from a floorboard, but was that Connor or the other person?

Then footsteps, running, a thump, a crash. Fuck, what was happening? Somebody had fallen. Another thump and a cry. Oh God, that sounded like Connor! I rushed to the bottom of the stairs.

'Judi!' Andre shouted behind me. 'Stop! You can't–'

More running footsteps, coming down. Somebody in black. The wraith. A wave of pure fear rushed through me, like liquid ice, and I couldn't move. The person in black had a black face, too, no, it was a hood thing, two glittering eyes in the holes. He leapt down, two stairs at a time, full tilt, arms swinging. One caught me on the side of the head and I fell back against the wall.

'Judi!' Andre came running out of the bar and the wraith faltered, punched him, and Andre dropped to the floor. The wraith ran for the front door, which had been left ajar for the ambulance, wrenched it open and was gone.

I staggered over to Andre and helped him up, my own head still spinning a little. 'I'm fine,' he said, rubbing the side of his face. 'Just as well they breed them tough where I come from.'

Andre? Tough? He was the nicest guy I knew, even more than Connor. 'Listen, I think Connor is hurt. I have to go up there.' Even though just the thought of climbing those stairs made my guts clench and twist.

'Be bloody careful,' he said, swaying slightly. 'I don't want to have to come and save both of you.'

'Me neither.' I doubted he'd be able to.

By the time I had made it to halfway up, sweat was dribbling down my back and I had to grip the bannister hard to stay steady. 'Connor? Connor!'

No answer. Then a muttered curse. It sounded like him. I went faster and, at the top, switched on the corridor lights. Connor lay on the floor just past Macca's door. My heart seized up for a moment, but he wasn't dead, thank God. He was trying to sit up without success. I ran to him and knelt, pushing him flat again. 'Don't move. He's gone. Is it your head?'

Two concussions. Just as well the ambulance was coming.

'No, yes, it's... my head and...' He groaned and put his hand to the side of his neck. 'Bastard came out of nowhere and whacked me. Like bloody Bruce Lee. Got me several good ones, and I went down in a heap. Bloody useless.'

'Did you see who it was?' I asked. I was trying to see if he was bleeding anywhere, but there was no sign.

'No, all in black.' He coughed and sucked in a rattly breath. 'Winded me a bit, too.'

Down below, a door banged and voices drifted up the stairs. 'The ambulance is here. I'm going to go and fetch someone.'

'Nah, I'm fine. Let them sort out Leslie. She needs it far more than me.'

'Leslie? On first name terms, are we?' I grinned and patted his arm. 'There's not a little bit of romance blooming, is there?'

I'd been joking to make him laugh and take his mind off his pain, but his face turned a deep shade of pink. I'd been closer to the truth than I realised. I was about to tell him he had no taste, and then shut up. I had no idea what Leslie was like. She was probably really nice under her police clothing.

'Help me up,' he said. 'I want to go and check on her.'

Even more interesting. I did as he asked, and he leaned on me all the way down the stairs until, at the bottom, he straightened with another groan and rubbed his chest. 'Don't tell her what happened. We'll get to that later.'

In the bar, the paramedics were still checking Leslie for concussion and checking her vitals. Connor sat on a chair near her and watched, asking questions that she tried to answer in between talking to the paramedics. He wrote notes and checked his watch, then when she refused to go to the hospital, he overruled her.

'You have to have an X-ray,' he said. 'You know it's standard OH and S. If Heath and Swan knew you'd refused, you'd be in big trouble.'

After more grumbling she finally agreed to go, although she insisted on walking to the ambulance, which made the paramedics cross. Connor made sure everything was locked up and went to report in to whoever HQ was, promising to come back later and check on things. In a few minutes, the bar was empty and Andre and I were left to stare at each other.

'This is getting way too weird, even for me,' Andre said. 'Maybe Suzie was right.'

'No way. She...' I stopped and shook my head. 'Yeah, OK, I know.'

We sat in silence for a while; Connor lying there like that still made me shudder. Another horrible night. I stood and stretched, bones cracking, and checked for my keys. 'It's nearly 2am and I have to drive to Melbourne tomorrow. Today. I need to go home and get some sleep, and so do you.'

'Yep. Home.' We turned out the main lights and shared out the door and window double checks, avoided going upstairs and met at the front door. There was no sign of Connor returning, so we locked the front door and I texted him, as he had spare keys. At my house, Andre was swaying with exhaustion, so I convinced him to stay in the spare room, and we both staggered off to bed.

My last thought was that I'd forgotten to text Heath, but I wasn't sure what to say. After seeing Connor beaten up, I was finally beginning to understand that maybe Heath got mad at me because he was scared I might get hurt.

19

Connor turned up at breakfast the next morning, walking stiffly and grunting as he sat down to grab a cup of coffee while he filled us in.

'Just some big bruises,' he said when I asked him about his injuries. 'Now, I need to take an initial statement from both of you about last night.'

'About what happened in the pub?'

'Not just that, but... it'll do for the moment. Swan is going to question you later about the incident at Bob's house.'

I made a face. That'd be something to look forward to. Between Andre and I, we explained how I'd wanted to check the pub was OK, and how we found Leslie on the floor. I wasn't any better at describing the wraith than I had been before. I was just glad that this time I'd stayed at the bottom of the stairs.

'Have you got any idea who this guy is?' I asked.

'We're thinking he's connected to the bikies somehow,' Connor said. 'There was a possibility it was Jamie, Madeline's brother – that maybe he came back and tried to set fire to the place as well.'

My mouth gaped. 'Really? I never thought of them – I was just glad they were gone.'

'Yeah, well, revenge drives people to do strange and violent things,' Connor said. 'It's a powerful reason for lots of crimes, including murder.'

'But?'

'They both had alibis. They're up on the Gold Coast, actually. At one of those health farms.'

'Probably spending the last of the money they managed to get out of Macca.' I kneaded the back of my neck.

'What did Bob tell you last night?' Andre asked. 'Did he confess?'

'He was caught with the chop chop in his shed,' Connor said. 'And the money. And four bikies on his property carrying the stuff out to their vehicles.'

'So he said nothing,' I said.

It was Connor's turn to make a face. 'Actually, when they were taking him to the police station in Bendigo, he had a heart attack.'

'Shit, is he OK?' Another old bugger down.

'He's in intensive care in hospital,' Connor said.

'What about…' I stopped. I was stuck again. I had no evidence.

'Come on, spit it out, Judi,' Connor said. 'I'm not Heath. I'm not going to tell you to stay out of it.' He grinned. 'As if you could.'

'I don't really know anything,' I said, 'but I hear stuff in the bar, and I see stuff. I wondered if Bob's mates were involved in any way.'

'You mean Old Jock and Scottie?' Connor frowned. 'Jock's got to be over eighty.'

'Yeah, but Bob's nearly seventy. Macca was seventy-one.' I had no idea about Scottie's age, but it'd be similar. 'How did Bob end up with the chop chop? Was he there when Macca got shot?'

Connor shrugged. 'He refused to say anything at all, apparently, and then he had his heart attack. It's likely he was, otherwise how would he have possession of it? But…'

'What?'

'If he was there, and he knew who killed his best mate, why wouldn't he tell us? And why bring Macca back to the pub?'

Andre chipped in. 'Maybe if it was a bikie who killed Macca, which is what everyone thinks, then he threatened Bob. Maybe the bikies forced Bob to hide the stuff in his shed.   He might have been helping Macca but not been selling.'

'That's not what I overheard,' I said. 'Bob was pleading with them to let him keep some to sell.'

'Yeah, that reminds me,' Connor said. 'What exactly were you doing there?'

'Nothing.' I tried to make my tone as injured as possible. 'You thought I was taking silly risks, but I was well hidden.'

'And if it wasn't for us,' Andre reminded him, 'you guys would never have known what was going on. Those bikies would have loaded up the chop chop and left town and you'd be none the wiser.'

That silenced Connor for a while. He pursed his mouth and huffed a bit and drank coffee then he said, 'All right, I'm going. Good luck today, Judi.'

'How did you know?' I asked.

He tapped his nose. 'I knows everything.   Well, almost everything.'

After Connor and Andre left, I checked the clock. I needed to get dressed and ready to go, but my heart was like a stone weigh
t
in my chest. What I really wanted to do was go and fetch Mia from Joleen's, and head to the lake for a picnic lunch. Instead, I couldn't even call in to see her on my way to Melbourne,

because it would get her all excited, thinking she was coming with me. I chose black trousers and a dark purple shirt, put on some makeup to cover the shadows under my eyes, and set off in the Benz. This was a trip I'd been dreading, and the closer I got to the city, the bigger the dread grew, like a dark fungus.

It reminded me of the time a few months ago when I'd made the same drive to identify my brother's body, and that was a horrible memory I'd sooner relegate to the brain bin.

I'd Googled a car park near where I needed to go and booked it, for once thanking the internet. It still cost me big bucks. I arrived at the family mediation office in plenty of time to have a double shot latte first to shore up my determination. I wasn't going to give a millimetre to these people. Every now and then I had a nightmare where I found Leigh again, dead in her bed from an overdose. It was something I would never share with Mia, and to me that meant not sharing Mia with the people who were responsible for Leigh's existence. A psychologist would probably have a field day with me and my hang-ups, but I didn't care. I wanted to protect Mia from ever having to come in contact with drugs again. No excuses accepted.

Just like you wouldn't accept excuses from Andy?

The thought jumped into my head and sent a stab of shame through me. I sat in the cafe, seeing none of the bustling work world around me, taking a few deep breaths. I had fucked up by being so hard and unforgiving. But that was different. Maybe by being so tough on Andy, I'd played some part in how he turned his life around later.

You're making excuses for yourself now.

'Fuck this,' I said out loud, ignoring the startled glances from people at nearby tables. I rose abruptly and pushed past the line of office workers waiting for takeaway coffee, and headed for the mediation place. The sooner I got this over with, the better.

I thought I'd be first there, but Leigh's parents had beaten me and were already sitting at the big oval table, a pile of documents in front of them. I'd brought nothing but a copy of Andy's will that I placed in front of me after I sat down. There'd be no backing down. I stared across the table at the two people who dared to try and take Mia away from me.

Neither of them looked like Leigh. For a start, they were both plump, and well-dressed; she was in a dark red pants suit with a white shirt underneath, her hair styled into a thick bob with a fringe that wasn't very flattering. She looked back at me calmly, as if to say she was as determined as I was to win here today. He had a ruddy face and was balding on top, and he wore a dark blue suit with a tie that had horses dancing across it. He seemed uncomfortable. He met my eyes initially and then starting glancing around the room and shuffling his paperwork.

The mediation woman sat and told us her name was Flora, and smiled encouragingly. Then she introduced us to each other, so I knew Leigh's mother was Lucy and confirmed her father was Geoff. We went through all the guff about meeting today to discuss the Donaldsons' formal request for access to their granddaughter, Mia Westerholme, and how we all had to be polite and follow the rules she laid out for reasonable discussions and so on. I nodded but I wasn't really listening. I was waiting for the first broadside, and it came from Geoff.

He leaned down and picked something up from beside his chair and slid it across the table. A large white stuffed rabbit. 'We brought this along. We were hoping you'd agree to take it with you and give it to Mia. From us.'

I stared at it. They were kidding. Rabbits were pest animals and everyone where I lived was doing their best to kill them off.

'That's a lovely idea,' Flora gushed. 'Judi, don't you think?'

No. I didn't want anything of theirs anywhere near Mia. I swallowed hard. 'Lovely. Thanks,' I gritted out.

'Now, Lucy and Geoff, I think it would be helpful to Judi if you explained why you have taken these legal steps to see Mia, how important it is to you.'

I wouldn't find that helpful at all. They were asking to be allowed to contaminate Mia's life. Anyone who raised a daughter who became the kind of person Leigh was... it wasn't just her drug addiction, it was the way she'd palmed Mia off on to her friend and run away from what happened to Andy. Just when Mia needed her most, she'd abandoned her.

Like your mother did.

I shut down that shitty little voice in my head and tried to focus on what Lucy was saying.

'Leigh was our only child, and it nearly killed us when she died. To discover what had happened to her and that she had a daughter...' Lucy blinked hard. 'It's like a magical second chance.'

'Second chance?' I squawked.

Flora frowned at me and I sat back, starting to fume. 'So you didn't know you had a granddaughter?' Flora asked them.

'No,' Lucy said. 'Leigh hadn't been in contact much, and when we did see her...' her mouth tightened into a little disgruntled button. 'The young man she was with, well, we could see what a bad influence he was. We fought with Leigh about that, and she cut off contact altogether.'

'Bad influence?' I said. 'Are you referring to my brother?'

'We did meet him,' Geoff said. 'He seemed nice, at first. But the drugs... he was using a lot. You must have known. And he got our little girl addicted, damn it!'

No, they were wrong. It was Leigh's fault. She was the real addict.

'Andy was never on heroin,' I said flatly. 'That was Leigh. And she caused all the trouble for him, got him killed. You need to look at the police reports.'

'We have,' Geoff said. 'We're not denying Leigh was at fault, too. If she'd just come home... but she refused. She stayed with him, and she died because she did.'

'Now, just hang on a minute!' I leaned forward, thrusting out my hands, counting on my fingers. 'One, it was Andy who turned it all around, bought a house, made a home for them. Two, it was Leigh who tattled to her cousin and got Andy killed. A cousin who was also a member of your family. Three, it was Leigh who–'

'Judi, this isn't helping,' Flora tried to interrupt.

I wasn't stopping now. I'd been thinking about this for days. 'Three, it was Leigh who left Mia with some woman who didn't want the responsibility, and then ran away and hid. I was the mug who had to go and find her, to save Mia's life, who had to try and get Leigh to the ambulance when she injected herself with even more drugs. Hauling her dead body out to...'

I stopped, because everyone was staring at me, and Lucy's face was awash with tears. She fumbled in her purse for a packet of tissues, sniffing loudly and blowing her nose.

I put my head in my hands. I didn't want to see her distress. I couldn't even stand my own.

Flora said, 'Perhaps if we think about Mia in all of this, about her being in contact with her grandparents and how good that would be for her.'

'Why should I trust them any more than I trusted Leigh?' I burst out.

I was getting too emotional. I had to control myself. This was going to make it worse, and I'd look like a lunatic. I was supposed to be calm and rational here, and make sure they stayed out of Mia's life. I took some deep breaths and tried to order my thoughts into clear, logical arguments again.

'Judi, what do you want us to say?' Lucy said with a catch in her voice. 'That Leigh was bad? That we brought her up wrong? That we should accept responsibility for her actions? We'll do that if it helps you.'

I shook my head. It wouldn't help. I had no idea what would anymore.

Lucy went on. 'You lost your brother. We lost our only child. We've regretted every single day since Leigh left home that we didn't do a better job. We thought we had.' She blew her nose again, and her husband patted her arm. 'We thought we'd done the very best we could, and it didn't seem to matter. I'm betting your family was the same, your parents loved you and did the very best they could.'

Oh God, you have no idea.

'But Leigh… we loved her so much, and it made no difference. Off she went, and we spent half our time wondering if she was alive, if she was OK. When she died… we had no idea about Mia. I'm sorry for what you've lost, but you have Mia. We have nothing, nothing left of our little girl except her daughter. Please. Please don't shut us out. Please don't take Mia away from us. She's a part of us, through Leigh. If we can't be part of her life, I just… I don't think I can bear it.' Lucy sobbed again, jamming her tissues against her mouth.

To my horror, I felt tears rolling down my face. Followed

by an ache in my chest that spread and intensified. An ache I'd thought had finally drained away and left me some peace. I stared down at the table, at Andy's will, its corners all crumpled and bent from the early days when I'd kept shoving it out of sight, unwilling to believe my brother had saddled me with his child. I hadn't wanted Mia back then, had tried to wriggle out of taking her on. That I loved her fiercely now – it hadn't been like that in the beginning.

Think of Mia, Flora said. So I did. I thought of Mia with grandparents, like Andy and I had had Nana when we were younger. Loving, doting Nana, when our lives with Mum and Dad had been so cold and unloving. We thought we'd done the very best we could, Lucy had said. Whereas our parents hadn't bothered trying.

I put my hand on Andy's will. What would he have said, if he were sitting here now? I looked up at Lucy and Geoff, at the pain in their faces, the tears still brimming in Lucy's eyes, at Geoff's clenched jaw as he waited for the worst, for me to say no.

'OK.' I sucked in a breath, and felt the ache loosen and start to fade a little. 'OK, you can see her. Spend time with her. It's OK.' And it was.

The joy in their faces now was almost too hard to bear, but Mia needed more than me. I'd wanted to be everything, but that wasn't what was best for her.

'Oh thank you, thank you so much!' Lucy said. Geoff gave me a nod and then his face broke into a huge smile. He grabbed Lucy's hand and held on tight.

The rest of the meeting was about the first visit, where and how and why. We agreed that they should come to Candlebark, so Mia was in her own home and less likely to be scared or

287

worried, but I thought she'd probably be fine after a little while. As for the rabbit, its pristine white fur wouldn't last long out in the garden or with the cat, but I was pretty sure she'd love it.

20

The drive back to Candlebark seemed to whiz by, the Benz gliding rather than bumping along. Every now and then, a sharp pang hit me. Had I done the right thing? What if they came and Mia hated them?

But I didn't think that would happen. They were decent people, they were grieving, and they didn't deserve another kick in the guts from me. The rabbit sat on the passenger seat, its shiny brown eyes looking out at the sky and the hills in the distance. It had long, floppy ears. Maybe I'd done it a disservice, too. Maybe it was a hare.

On the outskirts of Candlebark, I pulled over. I should go and pick up Mia, but I wasn't quite ready. There was someone I wanted to talk to first. Scottie. I dredged his real first name out of my memory – Keith or maybe Kevin. The online White Pages told me Scott, K was living on the main road out of town, and I'd passed his house without realising. I did a U-turn and went back to the driveway for 139, the numbers hand-painted roughly on a rusty round oil tin with the top half of the lid cut out to receive mail and papers.

The driveway was potholed and overgrown, the house hidden behind an unkempt hedge. I drove slowly along, wincing as the leggy shrubs scratched along the side of the Benz. The house came into view, an old weatherboard bungalow badly in need of painting. The iron roof held large rust patches, and the concrete front steps had a huge crack running across the middle. A shiny new green Holden ute was parked to one side. That told me where Scottie's chop chop money was going.

As I got out of the car, a huge kookaburra swooped down, pounced on a skink in the long grass and took off again. The quick and the dead. High up in the gum trees behind the house, a treecreeper trilled, but apart from that it was silent. Too silent. It gave me the creeps.

I rapped loudly on the frosted glass in the front door, half-expecting Scottie to refuse to answer, but the door opened within a few seconds. A bulky man in his forties stood there, frowning, his mouth already in a half-sneer. 'Yeah? Don't want no religion here.'

'I'm not from a church,' I said. 'I'm a friend of Macca's. I wanted a quick chat with Scottie.'

'Yeah? What about?'

'Macca's funeral is on Thursday, at the pub.'

'Yeah? I guess you'd better come in then.'

He stood back and let me enter; I tried to get past him without actually touching him, sucking in any protruding parts I could. He smelled powerfully of some heavy, sweetish deodorant and I tried not to gag.

'Dad's in the kitchen. Straight ahead.'

I was hoping Sonny wouldn't follow me, and he didn't, veering off to a lounge room where a huge TV was showing a replay of an AFL game. I had no idea whether the grand final had been played yet or not. I didn't care. I'd expected the inside of the house to be filthy and dusty, but it was surprisingly clean, with no clutter and just the basic furniture. In the kitchen, Scottie was smoking a rollie and drinking black tea from a huge mug that'd started life as a soup bowl. I guessed the rollie was made from loose chop chop, but I didn't say anything.

He looked up. 'Judi, what the hell are you doing here?' He didn't sound upset or suspicious, which was good.

'Came to tell you about Macca's funeral.'

He made a face and sucked at his rollie. 'Bad business, that.'

'It was a bad business, wasn't it?' I said, deciding to sit down and face him squarely. 'And now Bob's been arrested, too.'

'Yep, I heard. Bastard cops put him in hospital.'

'Quite a gang you've all had going.'

His face went blank and he took a long time to pick a bit of loose tobacco off his lip and drop it into the ashtray. 'Where's the funeral then?'

'At the pub.'

'Yep, Macca wasn't a churchgoer. I'll be there.'

I bet you will, and it doesn't look like you'll feel the slightest bit guilty about it.

I tried to look relaxed and said offhandedly, 'The bikies told Bob they weren't going to supply you anymore.'

'That right?' He gazed at me for a long moment. 'You going to tell your cop boyfriend all this crap, are you? Did he send you here on a scouting trip?'

'He's not my boyfriend.'

Scottie snorted. 'Couldn't believe me ears when I heard you'd scored a share of the pub in Macca's will. He always was a soft touch. Easily sucked in by any woman with a sob story.'

I leaned forward, my finger jabbing the air. 'I knew nothing about the will!' Too late I realised he'd diverted me from my questions about their chop chop gang. I tried one more time. 'What would you do if the police came and searched your property?'

'Nuthin'. They're welcome to, any time they want.'

So Bob had been the fall guy then, the one who'd stored the chop chop and taken the biggest risks, while Scottie sat back and reaped the rewards. I wouldn't have been surprised if he was the boss of the whole local dealing gang. They might be old buggers, but this one was as cunning as a wild dog. I was wasting my time.

I stood and left without saying goodbye to either of them. I couldn't be bothered being polite. There was no point talking to Heath, either. A search would be a waste of police resources, right now anyway. But I reckoned in a while, I'd have a word with Connor about Scottie and see what he thought. In the meantime, the detectives might solve everything without me. That'd be nice.

I drove straight to Joleen's and collected Mia along with all her toys and clothes. Joleen had the bag ready, a small frown on her face. 'Just so you know she's gone backwards a bit on the potty training.'

Immediately, guilt spiked through me. 'Is that because I haven't been around enough? I'm really sorry. Things will settle down soon.'

She flapped a hand. 'It's not you. It happens. They can be doing really well, and then something sidetracks them for a bit. It might even be Tammy's stupid book.'

'A book?'

'One of those ones with a pink princess doing potty training – supposed to be inspiring. Mia has decided she hates pink.' She shrugged.

'Oh, that's all right then.' Thank goodness the rabbit wasn't pink.

I waited until we got home before I brought the rabbit out. Mia's eyes lit up. 'Bunny!'

'Yes, and it's a present from your…' what did they want to be called? No idea. 'Your nana and grandpa.'

That got me a puzzled face. 'Nanny?'

'Nana. Remember your mummy?' I pointed to the photo of Leigh. Mia nodded solemnly. 'Your mummy has, had her own mummy. And she's your nana.'

The puzzled face didn't improve. It was too hard. I gave her the rabbit and asked her what she'd like to call it.

'Bum!'

God no, that'd make me instantly unpopular with Lucy and Geoff. They'd probably think I did it deliberately. 'Bunny,' I said firmly, and that seemed to stick.

I'd spent a lot of the trip back from Melbourne thinking of things other than grandparents. The pub, for instance. I couldn't see how Andre and I could make it work if we had to buy Suzie out, even if we managed to obtain a small bank loan. It'd have to be small – I wasn't prepared to go into major debt over it, or risk losing Andy's house, despite what I'd told Suzie. If we found a buyer for the pub, some of my money problems would go away. If I rented out the house in Melbourne, that would sort more of them out.

I sat and played with Mia for a while, putting odd-shaped blocks into odd-shaped holes and building stacks, while pondering what to do. Finally I rang Andre.

'How did it go?' he asked.

'A lot better than I expected,' I said. 'They're coming for a visit.'

He whistled. 'That's great. A big weight off you, I bet.'

'Yes. And talking about weights…'

'The pub.' He sighed. 'I know. Now that the bikies have been rounded up, we have to go back to Suzie and make some decisions.'

I agreed and we arranged to meet at the pub after dinner. I'd get Mia ready for bed and take her with me, making sure the meeting didn't drag on, and then we'd come home and call it a night. I was ready for sleep right then.

I pulled up outside the pub just after seven, and Andre was already there. The lights were on in the bistro, and he'd put some ice cream on a plate for Mia. As I was organising the high chair for her, Suzie arrived. She went into the public bar first and then joined us, her nose wrinkling.

'There's still blood on the carpet in there.'

'I'll ask Joyce to clean it tomorrow,' I said. 'By the end of the week there'll be beer stains to cover it anyway.'

She sniffed and sat down, declining Andre's offer of coffee. He poured some for himself and joined us, and for a couple of minutes we all watched Mia sucking ice cream off her spoon.

'So,' Andre said. 'We need to make some decisions about the pub. Suzie, have you changed your mind about selling your share?'

'No. I don't want the drag on my finances.' She stuck her chin out. 'Sorry, but I have to think of my kids and my house. I told you that before.'

I nodded. I was in the same position so I couldn't blame her. Still, it was such an opportunity, for Andre at least. I felt bad about abandoning him.

'Judi?' Andre asked. 'What're you thinking?'

'I'm stuck. I don't really want to sell, but I can't see a way out. Every option means a loan and a liability I mightn't be able to handle. I don't want to lose my house either.'

'But if someone bought out Suzie's share…'

'Really? You have a buyer?'

His face flushed. 'Maybe. I have a few old mates who might be interested – those sleeping partners I talked about.'

'Wow, that's great,' I said. 'But I'm not sure where that leaves me.'

'You'd have to make a decision for yourself,' he said. 'But we could sit down and work out finances first. We'd have to– '

'Sshh!' I waved a hand to shut him up, the hair prickling on the back of my neck. I'd heard something, and it wasn't something I liked the sound of – at all. I was bloody sure I'd heard a door close upstairs. I pointed at the ceiling.

Suzie's face drained of colour. 'I'm not going through this shit again.' She leapt up and headed for the door. A shot cracked outside, a glass pane in the French door shattered and Suzie fell to the floor. 'I've been shot!' she screamed.

I froze for a second, and then I launched myself at Mia, lifting her out of the high chair and diving to the floor, trying to put her down and get us both at ground level at the same time. My shoulder crunched and I gasped in pain.

Fuck, that was all I needed. No matter. Mia was screaming louder than Suzie, frightened by me and by Suzie crying out, 'Help me, help me. I'm bleeding!'

Another shot, another broken pane in the door. I twisted around to see where Andre was. Nowhere in sight. He must be shot, too. No, there he was, on the floor on the other side of the table, crawling towards us.

'Stay down,' he yelled. 'Go that way!' He pointed at the bistro doorway.

'I can't move and take Mia, too,' I said, my voice shaking. 'My shoulder.'

'I'll get her. You go.' He scuttled past Mia, checked over his shoulder, and pulled her with him. That made her scream even more, but we couldn't help that right now.

'What about me?' Suzie was freaking out. Blood stained her T-shirt around the right upper side of her chest, the red growing like a blossom unfolding. A deadly blossom. I crawled across the floor to the doorway where Andre was trying to calm Mia with no success.

'I'll do that,' I said. 'Get Suzie out of there.'

He crawled back and managed to help Suzie to push herself backwards with her feet, groaning with every effort, until she was close enough to the door that he could drag her through.

In the hallway, I cuddled Mia on my lap, soothing her as best I could while my heart thumped like a heavy drum. Another shot, another pane of glass. Why was the shooter aiming at the bistro doors?

Andre answered before I could ask. 'It's because the lights are on in there.' He reached up to the switch and flicked it; the bistro went black.

There was no way that was going to save us.

'If he comes in through the French doors, we're fucked,' I whispered.

'He'll never get them open,' Andre whispered back. 'Bolts top and bottom, and the doors still stick so badly, I don't think they'd budge.'

'What about...' I gestured wildly at the front door.

'I've got it.' He leapt up and ran to the door, turning both locks but there was no floor bolt. 'Side door.' He went down the hallway past the office and was back in a few seconds that felt like an hour. 'All good.'

'Kitchen door?'

'Locked and bolted still from last night,' he said.

'We have to call the police,' I said. 'Connor. Heath. Anyone.' My phone was in my bag, which was in the bistro.

'My phone's in there.' He pointed in the same direction.

Mia chose that moment to struggle out of my arms and run to Andre. God knows why. 'Ice cream,' she said. That explained it. But then she tried to go back into the bistro to retrieve her plate.

'Grab her!' I said, and he managed to stop her despite her squawks of protest.

The only phone was on the reception desk. I crawled along the floor, bypassing Suzie who had stopped moaning, which wasn't a good sign. In the darkness, I couldn't see if she was conscious but I guessed not. Once I got behind the desk I stood up, and bumped my leg against something hard. I felt around me and connected with something long and coldly metallic, leaning against the wall.

A rifle.

What the hell was going on?

I picked up the phone and went to dial Connor, realising halfway through pounding the keys that there was no dial tone. Nothing. The only other option was to crawl back into the bistro and get my bag. I leaned forward on the counter, my arms shaking, my teeth clenched. Mia was crying and trying to get away from Andre.

'It's like trying to hold on to a fish,' he said.

Decision. Make a bloody decision!

Another shot, and the sound of breaking glass came from somewhere above us, followed by creaking floorboards. The shooter was aiming at upstairs windows now. That meant someone was up there. Another shot, from inside the pub this time. Above us.

Carl. It had to be.

Fucking Carl was having a shootout with someone, and we were collateral damage. Mia was collateral damage. Again. Rage surged through me, and I straightened.

'Andre, take Mia into the office and lock the door, and then shove the desk against it. The filing cabinet, too, if you can move it.'

'What do you mean?' He grunted; Mia must have kicked him somewhere painful. 'Why the office?'

'We can't get outside and run away. We don't know where this bastard is. And fucking Carl is upstairs, I'm sure of it.' I picked up the rifle, and put it down again. There'd be time for that in a moment. 'Please – take Mia and keep her safe. Unless you can use a rifle.'

'Not me. OK. But I feel awful leaving you out here.'

'I'll be fine. I think this guy is after Carl, but I don't know why.'

'What about Suzie? We can't leave her here in the hallway.'

I hesitated. 'I'm pretty sure she's unconscious. It's important to get her an ambulance, but Mia needs to be safe first. Sorry, but that's my priority.'

'OK.' Andre got up and lifted Mia into his arms. They were just dark shapes in the gloom. I put my hand on Mia's arm and kissed her.

'Mia, go with Andre. Be a good girl and you can have lollies with your ice cream.'

'Lollies now?' she asked. 'I'm being good. Too dark.'

'Not yet. In a little while.' I let her go. 'Hurry, Andre. Don't rely on the lock. This guy can pick his way into anything, I think.'

'Right-o.' They disappeared down the hallway, Mia still calling out for lollies, and I went to the bistro doorway. My night sight had kicked in and I could make out table and chair shapes. We'd been sitting slightly to the right of the French doors. I figured if I went around the wall and made sure I wasn't silhouetted in the doors, I'd be reasonably invisible. I'd move slowly and see what happened. I couldn't crawl with my shoulder causing me grief.

Stepping into the bistro took every gram of guts I had, which wasn't that much. I held my breath, skittled around the corner and flattened myself against the wall. Nothing happened. Halfway along the wall, another shot cracked, but the bullet didn't come my way. The guy must be still shooting at upstairs. I hoped nobody living near the pub came to see what was going on. They might get hurt or killed, too. *Please, someone, call the cops.* But I couldn't count on that. I kept moving and only crouched down when I reached the table, going on my knees and one arm to where my bag sat under a chair.

I hooked it out and backtracked to the wall, then along the wall to the doorway. Back in the hallway, I sank down on to the visitor's low seat and scrabbled through my bag for my phone. Thankfully it was charged and lit up instantly. My hand was trembling so much that it took me three tries to tap Connor's contact and then call him.

It rang and rang, and my heart started to race again. If he didn't answer...

'Judi, hi.'

I kept my voice low. 'Connor, trouble at the pub. Big trouble. A shooter. We need an ambulance for Suzie, urgently.'

'Shit. Is it the bikies?'

'No idea, can't see. Someone with a pretty high-powered rifle.

299

We're trapped in here.'

'Who's we?'

'Me, Andre, Mia. And I think Carl is upstairs, shooting back.'

He smothered a curse. 'On to it. I'll come now, but I'm still at least twenty minutes away.'

'That long?'

'Sorry. On a call-out.'

'Where's Heath and his crew?'

'Bendigo.'

'Shit.' Too far away to be of help. 'Be careful. I think this guy killed Macca.'

'OK. Hang on. Stay safe. Hide.'

'I'll try.' I hung up.

I didn't want to hide. Well, part of me did. Another part wanted to rip this guy's throat out. I might kill Carl instead.

I went behind the reception counter and grabbed the rifle. If Carl was upstairs, defending the pub or himself, he could do with some help. I could shoot a fox. I could do lots of things, but I wasn't sure I wanted to climb those stairs; all the same, I wasn't waiting here for this lunatic to give up on shooting and try to burn the pub down again. He seemed to be capable of anything.

I held the rifle the way Connor had taught me, barrel down, under my arm, and climbed the stairs slowly to the landing. There I stopped. 'Carl,' I yelled. 'Where are you?'

'Judi?'

Who the fuck did he think was downstairs? Surely he'd seen us enter the pub? 'Yes. Where are you?'

'Macca's room.'

'I'm coming up.'

'No, don't. He's shooting at the windows.'

Obviously. And I don't plan to walk in front of a window, you dickhead. 'I'm coming up. Don't bloody shoot me.'

Silence. I went up to the top of the stairs and did my sticking-to-the-wall trick again along the corridor to the open door to Macca's room. I stopped and slid down to the floor.

'I'm at the door,' I called. 'What's going on?'

'I think the bastard is up a tree, one of the ones at the end of the car park. He must have a night sight on his gun.'

Now he tells me. All my sneaking around the dark bistro... I didn't get shot so it was worth the trouble. 'Who is this guy?'

'Long story,' Carl said.

I wanted answers now. 'Start talking.'

There was a long silence.

'Carl? Who is he? You obviously know.'

'He's... I think he's my son.'

'What? Are you sure? Since when have you had a son?'

He huffed out a heavy breath. 'More than forty years, apparently.'

'You didn't know?' This was like Macca and Madeline, only ten times worse.

'No.'

'And? Come on, spit it out.' The rifle was getting heavy and I wanted to put it down, but I didn't dare.

'It was when we were in Nam. There was a group of us.'

'The ones in the photo?'

'Yeah. We worked together for a while, when it was getting pretty hairy. The Vietnamese guy, Tuan...'

'You said he was a scout.'

'Yeah, seconded to us. Maybe not officially, but he knew the villages and the area. Saved our lives a few times. He had a sister. We went to their house, met the whole family. She was

301

beautiful.'

He said the last three words in a way that made my skin crawl, even though I didn't quite know why. 'Are you saying you had a relationship with her?'

'I tried. She only had eyes for Macca, but he wasn't interested.'

Two more shots from outside, and windows in the room next door shattered. This guy was getting impatient. I had a horrible feeling his next move might be to come into the pub, hunting us. But I desperately wanted to know what was going on, and why.

'What happened?' I asked, keeping my voice sharp, trying to force him to tell me faster.

'One night... we'd all been drinking. We'd been out on patrol and then some of the Yanks got ambushed and we were told to go in and... anyway. We started drinking when we got back and me and Sarge went to Tuan's house. His sister was there and we... I...'

I knew what was coming. 'You raped her.' Sour bile rose in my throat and I swallowed hard.

'I didn't mean to! I was drunk. Sarge was so drunk he couldn't get it up.'

'Then what?'

'The others came, Macca and Phil and Johnno. There was a fight. Macca was drunker than any of us and he went berserk. He smashed up the house. Broke my nose. Later, he said he didn't remember any of it.' He made a choking noise. 'God, I wish...'

I closed my eyes. Young and stupid and drunk. How many times had that combination led to death and destruction? Didn't need a war.

'Are you watching out the window, Carl? Has he moved out

of the tree?'

'Don't think so.'

'Are you shooting back?'

'Can't get to the window now.'

'What do you mean?'

'Bastard got me.'

My throat closed over and I could barely breathe. 'Are you OK?'

'I'll live. It's in my shoulder. He's a bloody good shot.'

That was all I needed. 'Hold on. Connor's coming.'

Carl wheezed out a laugh. 'He won't have a hope. This guy will take him out as soon as he gets out of the car. Connor was lucky last time.'

'Last time?'

'I'd managed to get off a shot before this guy could throw the petrol bomb through the window. I missed, but it sent him running. Then Connor arrived and sorted out the fire. If he'd come a few minutes earlier, the guy would've shot him.'

'How come you missed?'

'I couldn't see what he was up to. When he lit the match, I... I rushed it. I panicked, I suppose.' He coughed, hissed at the pain. 'He'd been inside the pub before, looking for me.'

There was silence from outside. Connor would be ten minutes away now. I tried to call him, to warn him, but the call wouldn't go through. He must be in a black spot. I texted him instead, but he wouldn't get it until he hit reception again. I had ten minutes to somehow stop this guy from shooting Connor. If he was still in the tree.

'Carl, take a shot at him.'

'I'm not near the window.'

Shit. I ducked down and went into Macca's room, staying

below windowsill height. Carl lay on the floor by the bed.

'What are you doing? Stay down.'

'What do you think I'm doing?' I crawled across to the open window and sat with my back to the wall. My shoulder was sore but it was bearable. 'You left this rifle downstairs?'

'Yeah, in case I had to come down and didn't have time to reload.'

'Is it loaded?'

'Yep. Course.'

'Which tree do you think he's in?'

'Why? Do you reckon you can pot him from here? That's only a .22.'

I didn't like Carl's sneering tone. 'Well, it's not like you've done a great fucking job, is it?'

That shut him up. I thought about how to get the rifle over the sill and aim it. I could use the sill to stabilise it.

'Come on, where is he from here? What direction?'

'More or less straight out, and slightly to the right.'

Yes, that'd give him a sightline into the bistro. Made sense. I turned and eased the rifle over the sill, keeping my head close to the window frame. I had no intention of showing myself. I wanted him to do that. I gripped the rifle and fired into the trees, then waited for him to fire back.

Nothing. I was right. He was too clever to sit in the tree now. He'd have to know someone would be coming to help us, sooner rather than later.

He was moving in to kill both of us.

21

In my mind, I could see the wraith creeping around the walls, lock picks ready, rifle over his shoulder. He must really want to finish Carl off, and too bad who else got in the way. Andre and Mia were safe in the office for now, but if this guy tried to set the place on fire again...

My brain felt scrambled with all the possibilities. 'Carl, can you get up?'

'No hope. Sorry.' He groaned. 'Jesus, this hurts. I almost wish the bastard would come and finish me off.'

'Thanks a lot. You're no help.' And he wasn't going to be either. Two down, and Suzie was worse than Carl by a long way, from what I'd seen. This guy might even shoot the paramedics when they arrived. I fumbled with the bolt and reloaded with shaky hands. Panic rose up in me like a black wave and I fought it down. *Stay calm, stay calm! Losing your shit won't help anyone, least of all Andre and Mia.*

OK, he was going to break in. He was an expert. What door would he most likely come through? I had to work it out. I only had a couple of minutes, if that. Front door. Had to be. The others all had bolts on them now, and he'd hardly alert us by breaking a window. Both front door locks were pickable. Fire regulations said we couldn't deadbolt them and stop people getting out.

Would he come up the stairs? Yes. He knew where Carl was. Did he know Carl was shot? Probably not. I could hide behind the reception counter. But if he checked there, he'd find me. I'd have to fire at him as soon as he came through the door.

Shit, what if Connor came in first?

I didn't like the idea of being trapped behind the counter. I'd stay up here. A plan was forming in my head. A stupid, desperate plan that was the only one I could think of.

I whispered urgently to Carl, pulled his shoes off for him, and then went out of Macca's room and along the corridor to the top of the stairs. Thank God for the landing, and the stained glass window above. It'd provide just enough light to create a silhouette.

I sat down, my back against the hallway wall, the rifle lying across my lap, and waited.

The silence felt thick and suffocating, but that was me, trying hard to breathe normally and feeling like an elephant was on top of me. Gradually it was like the air thinned, and I could pull in air again. When the sound came, it was as clear as if it was next to me. A scratching, a snick, another snick, a slight creak as the front door opened. A chilly draught swept up the stairs and I shivered but I wasn't cold. I was frightened sick. I had to put a hand over my heart; it was thumping so hard I thought anyone could hear it.

'Carl,' I hissed. 'Ten seconds.'

I counted them out in my head, and Carl threw a shoe against the wall, as we'd agreed.

Then there was no other sound. I strained to hear footsteps, or a hand brushing the wall. Where the fuck was he?

Maybe checking the bistro or bar first. There was a soft moan

– Suzie! He must've walked into her on the floor, or kicked her perhaps. More silence. He wasn't going to finish her off and alert Carl. Very soon he'd be heading up. I hoped.

I lifted the rifle slowly and aimed it down at the landing. I hoped this guy was in a hurry now. I couldn't hold this gun up all night. My shoulder was already burning. My eyes ached as I tried to see through the gloom. This was the wraith. He might slip past me.

There. A movement. A body shape. Crossing the landing, turning, heading up. The body shape was distorted. His own gun, held at the ready. Ready to shoot. Ready to shoot me.

I gripped my rifle, steadied it. The dark shape grew larger, larger.

I fired. The rifle kicked back hard against me this time and pain arced through my shoulder and down my arm. I nearly dropped it, falling sideways.

The shot echoed around me. He fell with a cry, crashing on to the steps.

I gasped with the pain, edged myself upright, grabbed the rifle properly again.

'Judi, are you OK?' Carl yelled.

'Shut up!'

I couldn't rely on one shot. I might have only winged him. I pushed myself up the wall, standing, biting my mouth against the pain, and steadied the rifle again. Then I took one step forward and aimed down the stairs.

At first I thought there was nothing there, that he really was a ghost who'd drifted away. But then I made out his body, and his arm moving, trying to pull his gun up and aim it again.

'Don't you bloody move!' I shouted.

He kept moving.

I started to pull on the trigger and heard Connor's voice in my head. *Pull the bolt back firmly. Don't wuss on it.* Fuck. I hadn't chambered the next round. My fingers felt like claws, trying to get a grip on the bolt. I pulled it back hard, heard the casing eject, pushed the bolt forward, heard the bullet slide, click.

He kept moving, and his gun was lifting now.

'Stop. Stop!' I screamed.

His gun kept coming up.

I fired again. The gun felt like a cannon slamming back on me, sounded like one. 'Oh God, fuck you, stop moving.'

This time he did.

Vile, burning vomit rushed up my throat and I slapped my hand over my mouth, swallowing, swallowing.

The front door downstairs slammed open, banging against the wall. 'Police! Get down! Stay down! Armed police!' The shouted commands were loud and slightly hysterical.

'Connor!' I shouted back. 'Don't fire. It's me. He's on the stairs.'

'Is he armed? Are you OK?'

'Yes. But I shot him. Twice.'

'Don't aim the gun at me. Put it down. I'm coming up.'

I couldn't put the rifle down, I just couldn't. Not until I saw this fucker in handcuffs and his gun taken away from him. I lowered it, barrel pointing to the floor. My skin felt like it was covered in a layer of ice, and I shivered again, my teeth chattering.

Another shape loomed on the stairs and my heart jumped. 'Stop!'

'It's me,' Connor said loudly. 'Just me. You're not aiming at me, are you?'

'Of course not, I'm not stupid,' I snapped.

'That's my Judi.' I could hear the smile in his voice and relaxed. Connor could deal with this now.

'He's probably only injured,' I said, 'so be careful. Take his gun away from him.'

'I don't… it's OK, I see it.' Connor bent and picked it up, using a latex glove, and stepped around the wraith. He came quickly up the stairs with the gun. It was heavy, a solid killing weapon, the night sight jutting off the top of it. A high-powered hunting rifle. 'Where are the light switches?'

'Just past the corner.'

He found them and turned everything on, and holstered his police revolver. The power-saving bulbs took a tiny while to brighten, and were subdued anyway, but I still blinked hard in the light. Connor went into the nearest room with the rifle and I heard the wardrobe door open and close. He came out and pulled the door shut after him. 'That's the best option right now.' As he went back down the stairs to check the guy lying there unmoving, Carl called out again.

'Everything OK out there? Is the ambulance coming?'

Connor glanced up at me. 'Is he injured, too?'

'Yes, but Suzie is worse. She's in the hallway downstairs.'

'I saw.' Connor bent, felt for a pulse, and the guy moved.

'Look out!' I yelled.

But Connor was ready. He pulled the guy's arm back and twisted it up, kneeling on his lower back. 'Don't try anything.'

The guy moaned something and banged his head on the step.

'What did you say?'

'The worst one got away,' the guy muttered, and then fell silent.

'There's blood all over the carpet here,' Connor said. 'I'm guessing that's your shooting, Judi.'

'Afraid so. Does that mean a whole shitload of paperwork for you?'

'I'm sure I'll cope. This guy… do you know who he is?'

'Carl seems to think he's his son.'

Connor's head jerked up and he frowned at me. 'Seriously?'

I nodded and tapped the .22. 'Can I put this down?'

'Just a tick.' He pulled out a set of handcuffs and cuffed the guy to the iron stair railing. 'That'll hold him.' He patted the guy down and half-turned him, checking for other weapons. It hadn't even occurred to me that the wraith might have a hand gun on him, and I shuddered. 'He's clear.'

Connor came up to take the .22 from me then paused. 'I actually don't want to leave you unarmed, and I need to see how Suzie is. I'll be back. Can you watch him?' He pointed down the stairs. 'I wouldn't ask, but it's only me right now.'

I swallowed hard. 'I think I can do that.' What I really wanted was a large glass of Jack Daniel's. 'But you have to go and check on Andre and Mia. They're hiding in the office. Please do that first?'

'Sure will.' He ran back down, skirting the guy, and disappeared from sight.

'Judi!' Carl yelled.

'It's OK,' I yelled back. 'Connor's cuffed him.'

'He's not dead?' He sounded disappointed. It occurred to me that the wraith being dead would mean Carl had fewer questions to answer. A lot of those questions were mine. Like did he know this guy was coming to kill them all, and if so, did he warn Macca?

I moved a bit closer to the top of the stairs. I could only see part of the guy's face; it was pale and his eyes were closed. His arm outstretched, cuffs linking him to the railing, would be causing him pain, but he was quiet. Maybe he was unconscious. He did look Asian. If he really was Carl's son, he'd be half-Vietnamese. He was dressed all in black, but Connor was right about blood on the carpet. A large patch of blood on his upper back showed up as dark umber, and a rip at the top of his shirt indicated where my second bullet had hit him.

A vehicle pulled up outside and I heard Connor's voice. 'She's on the floor there, pretty bad. There are two others. Is another ambulance coming?'

A murmur of voices that came closer and clearer. 'Up the stairs? Gunshot as well?'

'Yes, .22. Suzie here was a .303, I think. She's lost a lot of blood.'

'How long's she been unconscious?'

'I don't know.' Connor called up to me. 'Judi?'

I couldn't see my watch and it wouldn't help. 'A while. At least ten minutes, probably more.'

'Right.'

A head came into view below me. The paramedic came up swiftly, stopped by the guy and knelt. 'Why is he handcuffed?' she said.

'He's the killer,' I said, 'so be careful.'

She glanced up at me, as I held Carl's rifle. 'He's not still armed?'

'Connor searched him.'

'OK.' She checked all the vital signs. 'He's alive but I need to turn him over. Someone will have to take the cuffs off.'

Connor shouted from below, 'I'll be there as soon as I can.'

She grimaced. 'I'll cut his shirt off then.' She got to work with the scissors and snipped fast, revealing the first bullet had gone through the top of his shoulder, leaving a large hole at the back.

No doubt the bullet was in the wall below somewhere.

'When're the ambos coming up here?' Carl yelled.

If he was shouting like that, he couldn't be too bad, but then again, he'd been shot by a .303. I'd better not be too mean, even though I felt like it. 'There're a couple of people worse off than you, Carl.' Another vehicle pulled up outside, lights flashing. 'There you go, they're here now.'

'Thank Christ for that,' he muttered.

I wanted to go and slap him. Instead, all of a sudden, tears filled my eyes and spilled over. I knew it was probably a reaction to the shock, but I felt stupid and inadequate. I brushed them away and focused on taking some deep breaths.

More voices below, including one I recognised that made me choke up again. Heath.

'Quick report, please, Connor.' He sounded brusque and businesslike.

Connor filled him in on the events – what he knew at least – the rest would have to come from Carl, Andre and I. Then Heath came running up the stairs, barely glancing at the guy and the paramedic working on him. He stopped in front of me, scanning my face and then my body, including the .22. 'Please tell me you're OK.'

'I'm not shot, if that's what you mean.' I managed a wobbly smile. 'Is Suzie going to be all right?'

His mouth twisted. 'I don't know. The paramedic is setting up a transfusion and getting her into the ambulance right now. They'll do the best they can.'

I gestured at the guy on the stairs. 'Is he going in the same ambulance?'

The paramedic answered. 'No, she's urgent. This patient will go next.'

'What about me?' Carl yelled.

The paramedic and Heath both looked at me. I shrugged. 'He's shot as well, but I don't think it's life threatening.'

'The next crew will help him as soon as they can,' the paramedic said.

'God, what a clusterfuck,' Heath muttered.

'Hey, one of you has to uncuff this man so I can treat him,' the paramedic said. 'If he's dangerous, you'll have to ensure he doesn't attack me.'

Heath took a moment to cup the side of my face gently. 'Sure you're OK?'

I wasn't. I wanted to lie down on the floor and throw a massive hissy fit, or run away to my house and hide. I blinked hard a few times. 'Yes, I'll be fine.' Not.

'Right. Let me get this guy sorted and I'll be back,' he said, and went back down the stairs to help the paramedic. I thought it was strange Heath hadn't taken the .22 off me, and I didn't quite know what to do with it. In the end, I managed to get to my feet and put it in the cleaner's store cupboard, among the brooms and mops. The police could collect it from there later. I got back to the stairs just as the paramedic was turning the guy over, with Heath's help. She'd already put a dressing on the shoulder wound and now I could see where I'd hit him first – high up on his thigh. 'Hasn't hit the artery, lucky for him,' the paramedic said. All the same, his leg was soaked in blood.

I'd been putting it off but I guessed I should go and check on Carl. I called to let him know it was me, and that I was turning the light on. He was still lying in the same place, next to the bed, but he'd pulled himself up a bit and put a pillow under his head. He wasn't comfortable though; his face was etched with deep lines and looked grey. The wound on his shoulder was oozing blood, and a thick, congealing puddle stained the carpet under him.

'The paramedics will be up shortly,' I said. 'They've sent two ambulances, but they might need a third if you get worse. Did the bullet go through you?'

'Yep, I was lucky.' He wheezed and coughed, then added, 'A couple of centimetres lower and I'd be a goner. Those .303s are like elephant guns.'

I found a guest towel in the bathroom that one of the cleaners must have put there, and tried to wrap it around Carl's shoulder.

'Ow, shit, that hurts. Leave it. It's not bleeding much.'

Ungrateful bastard. I perched on the bed. 'How do you know this guy is your son? He could be anyone.'

'One of the others in our team heard on the grapevine that someone was asking after us – going to the RSLs, and apparently he went to that Vietnam vets' museum as well.' Carl smacked his lips. 'Has that bottle got anything left in it?' He pointed to the window, and an almost empty bottle of scotch lying on its side.

'It's got about two mouthfuls in it,' I said.

'Give it here, will ya?'

'You shouldn't be drinking if you're going to need an operation.'

'Don't be a nag, woman. Hand it over.'

Oh well, it wasn't my problem if they refused to fix him up until the alcohol wore off. I handed him the bottle and he guzzled the last of the scotch. A few drops dribbled out of the side of his mouth and he tried to lick them up with a yellow-furred tongue. Ugh.

I knew Andre would be taking good care of Mia, but I still wanted to get down there and make sure she was OK, now

I was calm enough not to frighten her. I had about three minutes to get more information out of Carl, before Heath or the paramedics came in, and I didn't want to waste the chance.

'So this guy has been killing you all, one by one.'

'Not Sarge. He died about thirty years ago. Killed himself.'

'But the others? Macca had newspaper cuttings about them.'

'Yeah, Macca knew something was going on, and so did the others. They guessed it was about something that happened in Nam.'

I stared down at him, trying to control the urge to get up and kick the bastard where it would hurt the most. 'So you knew, or guessed, it was your son after revenge. And you never told them.'

'I warned them to stay alert. They didn't need to know why.'

'Of course they fucking did!' I exploded. 'You basically caused Macca's death. If it was you who raped that poor girl, why did he kill the others?'

'He didn't know which one of us it was. He was going by the photo his uncle Tuan left him. The prick sent a copy to all of us. It took me a while to work out what it meant. Then Phil phoned me, said he'd seen an Asian guy hanging around.'

'That's still a big leap to get to your son killing all of you, one by one.'

'Yeah, well…' he shifted on the floor, and groaned. 'Fuck, this hurts.'

'Come on, what else happened?'

Carl's mouth turned down in a sulk. 'He took a shot at me, up on the farm. Missed by a hair. Frightened the crap out of me. I thought it was a roo hunter not paying attention. Then he left me a note in the letterbox on the road. Cocky prick.'

'So all this time, when you said you were going out for foxes…'

'Trying to track him through the bush and get him first. After he killed Macca, well, I was the only one left. It was me or him.'

'Why didn't you tell anyone? You could've stopped all of this – the pub nearly burning down, Suzie getting shot.' Not to mention me being pushed down the stairs.

His chin jutted out. 'It was my fuck-up. I was gonna fix it. Get rid of the scum once and for all.'

'Jesus, Carl, you...' I was so angry I couldn't speak. I couldn't stay in the room with him either. If I did, I'd end up attacking him myself. I stood up and walked out, along the hallway and down the stairs, narrowly avoiding the group around the killer. Two more paramedics now and they were trying to get him on to a stretcher. His eyes were open, and he watched me go past. I barely looked at him. Carl's revelations were tumbling around in my mind, and I didn't know what to do with them.

Still so many questions unanswered. If the guy was Carl's son, why hadn't Carl known? Had the mother or Tuan never tried to contact him? Or maybe they had and Carl had brushed them off. Or denied it was him. That sounded more like Carl.

What had happened in the intervening years to drive this guy to kill three ex-soldiers and have a darned good try for the fourth? Had the guy ever known which of them was actually his biological father? Maybe he hadn't cared. Maybe what had been done to his mother stained them all in his mind.

Heath was downstairs, talking to Swan and Connor. I pushed past them and went straight to the office. It was empty, and my stomach fell like a bird dropping out of the sky.

'Mia!' I called. 'Mia!' No answer. I knew she had to be safe but where was she? Panic rolled through me like a huge, crashing wave. She was dead and nobody told me. She'd got frightened and run away and was out in the bush somewhere. She was...

'Hey, there's Judi,' Andre said brightly. And there she was, in Andre's arms, reaching her little chubby arms out to me. I took her from Andre and hugged her tight, the rush of relief making my whole body tremble. After a few moments she started to squirm; I loosened my grip and gave her a big kiss.

'So you're OK,' Andre said. His tone was strange and I glanced at him. He looked like he was holding something back that he really needed to say.

'Go ahead, tell me I was stupid to go up there,' I said.

'You can be as stupid as you like – when it's just you,' he snapped. 'But what about Mia?'

'That guy had a .303 and a night sight on his gun,' I said. 'If we'd tried to get out of the pub and make a run for it, I think he would've killed all of us.' I nodded at Mia. 'Even her. He was obsessed with killing Carl – and the other soldiers in their team – and he wasn't going to let any of us get in his way. I wasn't trying to be a hero, Andre. I was trying to stop him from hurting Mia and you. And me.'

Andre's eyes had widened at my words. 'What did Carl do to cause this?'

'I'll tell you later. Not in front of Mia. But it was nasty. Nasty and revolting.'

'Maybe that's why Carl had been talking about buying Suzie's share of the pub. He was feeling guilty.'

'I wouldn't have Carl as a partner if you paid me a million bucks.'

The front door opened and what looked like a squadron of police and crime scene techs came in, including my least favourite cop, Barney. His expression was sour as usual, and turned even more sour when he saw me.

'Miss Westerholme, you can't seem to stay out of trouble,' he said.

'Constable Barney, nice to see you, too.'

He opened his mouth to correct me but Heath intercepted him and gave him orders about what needed to be done first. 'The paramedics are bringing the suspect down now. He'll need to be guarded closely – I want two officers on it, and I want him cuffed to the trolley as well.'

'He's been shot?' Barney asked. 'Who by? You?'

Heath glanced at me, and his mouth twitched. 'I believe a member of the public managed to, ah, accomplish the task. Self-defence, and kept everyone here safe. Unfortunately, there were other members of the public injured by the suspect, but she is to be commended for her bravery.'

'She?' Barney's face was a picture of incredulity. He looked at me, and I just raised my eyebrows and smiled nicely. It didn't do anything to reduce his level of gobsmackedness.

The paramedics were coming down, awkwardly angling the stretcher around the last corner newel and into the hallway. The shooter was covered with a blanket and tightly strapped in, with dressings on his shoulder; his eyes were closed but he looked like he could leap up at any moment and fight his way out. I shivered; I didn't know whether I was relieved he wasn't dead or not.

'Detective,' Heath said to Barney, 'follow them out and make sure those officers are on the ball.'

Barney ambled after the paramedics and Heath frowned then turned to us.

'Suzie is on her way to hospital. She's critical, but stable so far. Transfusions are first priority. The paramedics are with Carl now.' He shook his head, his expression strained. 'Judi, you... you could've been killed.'

Not this again. Andre was bad enough. 'We would have all been killed, if I hadn't done something. Look at poor Suzie. Nothing would've stopped that guy. And Carl was in no condition to defend us.' I let out an exasperated breath. 'Jesus, you think I wanted to have to shoot him?'

In my arms, Mia picked up my irritation and patted my face. 'Juddy shouting.'

'Yes, I am. Sorry, sweetie. I'm going to stop now. We're going home.'

As soon as I said that, the events of the day crashed in on me. The mediation meeting, the long drives there and back, but mostly the terror of being shot at, and the endless, horrible moments of waiting for the killer to come up the stairs. Shooting him still seemed unreal, like it wasn't really me who'd done it. I swayed a little then straightened my spine. Mia needed me to hold it together, so I had to, even though I wanted to curl up in a ball and hide.

'Andre, do you need a lift home?'

Heath held up a hand. 'I need both of you to stay so I can take down what happened, and get initial statements from you.'

I'd had all I could take of police procedure. 'Tough,' I said. 'The .22 is in the cleaner's cupboard. You can ask me the rest tomorrow. I have to take Mia home and put her to bed, right now.'

Heath opened his mouth to argue, and Andre jumped in. 'I'll talk to you now, and you can work with Judi later. Come on, mate, you can see she's dead on her feet. I mean...' he stopped, aghasth

I nearly burst into hysterical laughter, but I clamped it down, and simply collected my bag, patted my pocket to make sure I had my phone, and walked out without a word.

22

The Benz took us home, purring all the way, and Mia was asleep in her car seat by the time we got there. I put her into bed as she was, only putting a night-time nappy on her, and with the house finally quiet around me, I sank down on to the couch. Only to struggle up again and light the fire, thankful I'd set it ready a few days ago. As flames licked up the kindling and took hold, I poured myself the long-promised Jack Daniel's and sat on the couch again, arranging cushions and pulling a rug over me.

Strangely, now I was safely home, the urge to cry had faded. I felt almost numb, and the JD was helping me grow even more numb. I poured myself another, stacked more wood on the fire, curled up on the couch and just let myself go into zombie mode. And then sleep.

When I jerked awake, the nasty dream I'd been having clung to me like a bad smell. I'd half-expected to dream of the shooter coming at me again, but instead I was being chased through the bush by a huge man wielding a whip and a thick tree branch, slashing at the bracken and shouting something incomprehensible. At the last minute, his hot breath on my neck, I'd turned and seen my father's face.

That was enough to wake anyone up in a hurry.

Dawn was just stealing across the paddocks, tinting everything a rosy pink. *Red sky at dawning, shepherd's warning.* I hoped that didn't mean another crap day ahead. I'd had enough of crap days. Then I remembered I'd have to be questioned and make a statement today, probably to either Heath or Swan. The thought of it made me cranky before I'd even staggered to the shower to try and wake up a bit more.

As I stood, eyes closed, my face up to the hot water, I felt a cold breeze as the shower door opened.

'What the–' It was Mia, her cold little hand smacking my leg.

'Somebody knocking,' she announced importantly. 'Come on.'

'OK, thank you. Wait there for me, sweetie.' I dried myself and pulled on trackie pants and a sweatshirt as the thumping on the front door started again. 'Yeah, yeah, coming!' I yelled.

I padded to the door, guessing who it would be, hardly caring that I looked like a drowned rat. Yep, it was Heath.

'I was in the shower,' I said.

'Sorry, I wasn't sure, and your car is here, so…'

'Come in. I have to sort Mia out first.'

I took my time washing her face and brushing her hair, then dressing her. I brushed my own hair, put on comfy shoes and we went into the kitchen.

'Coffee?' I called.

'Yes, please.' He came in and stood awkwardly by the fridge. Mia gazed up at him, her bottom lip out as she tried to figure something out. Finally, she got it.

'Ben.'

'That's right.' He crouched down. 'You were a very good girl last night, I heard.'

She nodded. 'I good girl.'

'Hmm, pity your aunty...' he broke off as I glared at him. 'She's a good girl, too.'

'I am,' I said. 'I'm excellent.'

That shut him up. He straightened. 'Can I help with anything?'

'No, thanks. Do you want some toast?'

All the niceties of breakfast went on, along with pointless chatter about meaningless things, until Mia had finished eating and was allowed to watch some TV. Later, we'd go for a nice, long walk in the forecasted sunshine.

'So,' Heath started, pulling out his notebook and pen. 'I need you to run me through everything that happened last night.'

Last night seemed like the bad dream I'd had – distant and somehow absurd. 'Didn't Andre tell you all that?'

'He did, but I need to hear it from you.' He paused. 'After all, it was you who shot Nguyen.'

'That was his name?' Suddenly he became more real again, and I shifted in my chair.

'Yes, Chinh Nguyen.'

'So you know he's Carl's son?'

Heath grimaced. 'Carl is now saying he told you that when he was hallucinating with the pain.'

'What a bullshitter he is.' I laced my fingers together tightly, and tried to take some slow breaths. 'I'll tell you exactly what he told me, and you can work it out for yourself. Try starting with the newspaper cuttings I showed you.'

'Yes, I guess you were right about those.' He at least looked a little bit shamefaced.

'You guess?' My fingers were aching. I forced them apart and launched into a retelling of everything Carl had said, and then my own knowledge and conclusions. 'Why else would Nguyen kill Macca, and then go after Carl? He had to be seriously crazy for revenge.'

'Don't worry, we're checking it all. Nguyen is refusing to talk, but we may be able to track his uncle down.'

'Tuan? Is he here or in Vietnam?'

'He was here. He had to escape after the war ended, to save his own life because he'd worked with the enemy, but his sister stayed behind with their parents. And later Tuan went back, but we don't know where he is right now. Or if he knew what his nephew planned.'

'What a mess.'

'Yes. So take me through last night.'

I started with the meeting, with Suzie telling us she wanted no part of the pub, just the money, and went on from there. When I got to the bit about Suzie being shot, tears filled my eyes. 'Is she OK? Have you heard?'

'Been downgraded to serious and stable. The bullet went through – he was using a deer hunting rifle. Pretty lethal. She was lucky.'

'I doubt she'll agree. She'll blame us.'

'So after Suzie was shot?' he prompted.

I went on and only faltered again when I got to the bit where the wraith – I still thought of him like that, in his black gear with the silent footsteps – came up the stairs towards me. 'I fired once, but he started to get up again. I only had Carl's .22. It was like a horror movie, you know, where the thing just keeps coming. So I fired again. I had no idea whether I'd hit him either time, or whether he was faking it.' I stared into my coffee cup where the dark dregs stained the porcelain. I wanted to find something that would wipe my brain clean and I could forget all of this ever happened.

'Hey, you're doing great.' His hand on my arm was warm, and I covered it with mine, but my fingers were icy.

'Then Connor came, thank God, and the guy did try to get up but Connor cuffed him to the railing. And that's it really.'

Heath scribbled more strings of words, asked me a few more questions, and then told me we were done for now.

'For now?'

'There'll have to be more formal questioning and a full statement taken.' He opened his hands like Jesus welcoming the flocks. 'Sorry, but you did shoot someone.'

'Yes.' That, at least, was sinking in. 'So now you have your murderer, what next?'

'He'll be taken back to Melbourne once he can travel. Charged in Bendigo, initial questioning, but then... we can't keep travelling up here.' His phone made a sound like an angry bee and he checked the text. 'Forensics won't be finished at the pub until later today. I know it's costing you money to keep it closed, sorry.'

'Don't worry, once we reopen, we can run murder tours like they do in America and charge entry fees.' I wasn't really serious but he looked so aghast that I started laughing, and then I couldn't stop. My mother would have told me I was being hysterical, but I couldn't care less. I needed a good laugh. Pity Heath didn't see it the same way.

He got up and put his notebook away, and said stiffly, 'I'd better get back.'

That stopped me laughing. 'So I won't see you again then?'

'It probably won't be me who takes your formal statement.'

'You know that's not what I meant.' I hesitated. In for a penny... 'You could come for dinner tonight.'

He blinked a few times, and nodded. 'I could.' He held up his phone. 'I'll text you, if that's OK. Hopefully I won't get stuck anywhere.'

'Hopefully.' I smiled. 'I'll make sure my phone is charged.'

'You do that.' He gave me a little wave and his mouth twitched, and he was gone.

I spent the day with Mia, trying to make up for everything from the past few days – the neglect, the drama, the danger. I still felt guilty. I made sure we took Bunny with us on our walk, and to the supermarket, and I saved Bunny from being run over by the grocery trolley. I reminded her a few times that Bunny came from Nana and Grandpa and got the same puzzled look. The visit was coming up in a few days, but I tried not to think about that.

Later that afternoon, I'd just poured myself a glass of wine and was thinking about when to start cooking when a car pulled into the driveway. It was Heath, come to tell me he'd been called back to Melbourne.

'Looks like some kind of gang drive-by killing,' he said. 'Likely to be payback, so it's all hands on deck.'

'This is going to be "situation normal" with us, isn't it?' I said.

'Now you know why I haven't been with anyone for a few years.' He made a move towards me and hesitated; I knew it was time I let my walls down. I stepped close and he pulled me into his arms, holding me so tight I could feel his heart beating. 'I know I'm a bloody big pain in the arse, but I want to keep trying.'

I debated the wisdom of pursuing something so clearly doomed for about a second. 'I do, too. Maybe Mia and I can come to Melbourne. Before she starts school.'

He pulled back, his face puzzled. 'But that won't be for... ha ha, very funny.'

'Yes, I'm hilarious,' I said. 'But seriously, I will come down. And with Mia's grandparents having visiting rights now, that changes things, too.'

'Visiting grandparents? When did that happen?'

'I'll tell you about it later. On the phone.'

So off he went yet again but at least this time I felt we'd parted with some hope for that R word – relationship.

Thursday came sooner than I wanted. The funeral was set for midday, and Andre had the food sorted. I'd put away all the expensive spirits and bought local wine cheaply. We'd debated about who to ask to run the whole thing, and Joleen had suggested a funeral celebrant from Bendigo, who'd turned out to be perfect, since he was Macca's age.

I'd done my formal statement after being questioned for several hours by Swan, with Barney in attendance. I'd refused to travel to Bendigo for it, citing Mia and personal mental health as my reasons, and they'd given in. It had all taken place at Connor's police station with Connor nowhere in sight. Swan had been more pleasant than I'd expected, although Barney spent the whole time scowling. I was tempted to warn him about what would happen if the wind changed, but I guessed it wouldn't make any difference.

It didn't matter how many times I went through everything that had happened, when I got to the bit about Suzie being shot, and having to drag her into the hallway, thinking she was dying, my eyes filled with tears and I couldn't speak for a while. She was serious but stable, officially – unofficially the word was she was very slowly improving.

Swan asked me questions about things I hadn't even contemplated. 'Did you know the gun you had was only a .22? How?' Because I had one at home, and yes, it was licensed and locked away properly. 'Were you aiming to kill?' How could I answer that? I was trying to save my own life and other people's. I just wanted to stop the guy. 'Did you know the murder of Mr Macclesfield was connected to his service in Vietnam?' No. Not until Carl told me what was going on, and why.

That last reply received a long silence. I waited for Swan to ask me more, and he didn't, so I added, 'Carl can deny now all he likes that he knew what it was about, and who the guy was who shot Macca, but he confessed to me that night. He just doesn't want you to know how much of it was his fault.'

'I'm not sure fault is the correct word,' Swan said.

'Carl knew months ago what that photo meant. If he'd told Macca, it would have saved his life.'

'Mr Macclesfield was dealing in chop chop,' Barney said. 'That's what got him into trouble.'

'Are you really as stupid as you sound?' I snapped.

'There's no need for that, Ms Westerholme,' Swan said nicely, but he gave Barney a glare that sat him back in his seat.

'Have you questioned the guy – Chinh?'

'Mr Nguyen is still refusing to answer questions,' Swan said.

I knew from Connor that they'd matched Nguyen's gun to the bullets that killed Macca, but not much more than that. 'Have you worked out yet how Macca's body got into the dumpster? Considering he was killed at the meeting point in the bush… why wasn't he left there?'

'Investigations are still under way,' Swan said. And I couldn't get any more out of him, which left me up in the air about how much I said about Bob and Scottie and Old Jock. I wanted to believe that they'd all had such a shock from Macca's murder and the bikies coming to town that they'd given up their life of crime, but somehow I doubted it. In any case, Bob was being released from hospital and the word locally was he might have to move into the home with his wife.

I went to visit Connor the night before the funeral, taking Mia with me; he'd been happy to have the homicide detectives off his doorstep at last. 'You're not planning on shooting anyone else, are you?' he asked me.

'Not right now.' We talked a bit, catching up on our news, and Mia showed her bunny to him, and then I said, 'Look, there's something I need to tell you.'

'Crikey, this sounds serious. *Are* you going to shoot someone?' But he said it with a grin.

'Be serious!' I took a breath, and told him everything I knew about the old buggers and the chop chop, and that I thought it was Bob who'd driven Macca's 4WD back and probably Scottie had helped to put his body in the dumpster.

Connor scratched his head. 'Why would they do that if it was Chinh who killed Macca?'

'They didn't know that at the time. They probably thought the bikies were responsible. Some kind of double-cross. I think they panicked and all they could think about was not getting caught buying chop chop. Putting Macca in the dumpster would throw you off the scent.'

'It did for a while.' He gazed into space, thinking it through. 'How did Chinh know where Macca and Bob would be?'

'You said yourself the parking area isn't that far from here as the crow flies, and Chinh had been camping in the bush. Carl guessed he was out there. Maybe Chinh had seen Macca meet the bikies at that spot before?'

'And you think Scottie is the ringleader.'

'Yes. I think Scottie might have gone back with Bob to the bush spot and they put the 4WD down the gully. Scottie's cunning. He was deliberately confusing things. Except the bikies weren't confused at all. They wanted their money *and* the chop chop back.'

'Jeez, that puts a different slant on everything.' His face looked pained. 'I may have to get the Bendigo detectives here again. Just when I'd got Barney's aftershave out of my nostrils.'

'You don't have to say it was me who told you, do you?' I still remembered Scottie's threats and they made my stomach churn. I told Connor about that, too. 'My bet is they're going to start up again, as soon as things die down. You could wait a bit, keep an eye on them and gather evidence, and be the hero.'

His face went a bit pink, which was curious. 'Well, I'm actually still in touch with Leslie. Just as friends, you know.' The pink deepened.

'Are you now?' I bit my lip to try and hold back a big smile and failed miserably. 'That's... handy.'

'I can talk to her about it. Keep her informed, and then they can run the operation.'

'I feel a bit sorry for Bob and Old Jock,' I said. 'But Scottie is a whole different kettle of fish.' I punched Connor lightly on the arm. 'Yes, you keep Leslie informed and we'll all be happy.'

Now that the funeral service was starting in an hour, I remembered asking Scottie to say a few words – if the guy had any conscience at all he'd keep his mouth shut. Bob had been let out of hospital and was on bail, probably mainly because of his age, and I'd heard a rumour he was going to plead innocence, that the bikies had threatened him and he'd had no choice. Sounded like Bob had no conscience either, but no doubt he was unwilling to be charged as an accessory or moving a body or whatever the police would come up with if they found out what he'd done. I was leaving that up to Connor.

With ten minutes to go until starting time, the bar and the bistro were both packed with people, and they were spilling out into the car park. Andre came bustling through from the kitchen, fretting about his sausage rolls and sandwiches and whether he'd have enough.

I pointed at a bunch of women coming in the front door. 'Andre, never fear, the CWA have arrived.' By the time they'd pushed the tables together and arranged the plates of food they'd brought, there was hardly a centimetre of table cloth to be seen.

In the end, we had the service in the car park, because we couldn't fit everyone inside and the sun was shining. Wendy had arrived, brimming with tears and elegant in a bright pink dress. 'Macca hated black,' she told me. Macca's coffin sat on a wheelie thing, and the men from the funeral place stood back and let the celebrant run everything.

Someone had been in the celebrant's ear and he had a dozen great stories to tell about Macca, ones that made us laugh and cry, and I saw a lot of surprised faces when he talked about Macca's years as a soldier, and a lot more, including mine, when he talked about Macca's years working up in the mines in Mt Isa. It was where he'd met Wendy, and earned and saved enough to buy the pub.

But mostly he talked about Macca continuing to play footy until he was 54, the oldest player in the local club's history, his fundraising for the school and the kinda and the scouts. Then he finished up with: 'Macca was one of those men who was happy to admit when he'd made a mistake. He had no problem with saying sorry, with making amends, with backing down when he was wrong.'

I glanced around at heads nodding, immensely glad that Madeline and her brother had stayed away, had accepted their scam hadn't worked after all.

'Right up to his death,' the celebrant went on, 'he was still trying to help people. If we were mean, we'd say "more fool you". But Macca wasn't mean. He was kind and generous and he kept promises, and I don't know a better sort of person to be. God speed, Macca, this little town will miss you far more than you will ever know.'

By the end, there was a lot of sniffing and hankies pulled out and blowing of noses and dabbing at eyes. Then Mike and Pete stepped forward, Mike with a smartphone held up. 'Macca would have hated us singing hymns, but since this was one he sang all the time around the pub – really badly – we thought this was the right send-off song.'

As music belted out across the car park, I realised what the grey boxes on top of several cars were – Bluetooth speakers. The familiar tune of 'House of the Rising Sun' made everyone smile – if we hadn't heard Macca singing it, we'd heard The Animals on the pub playlist often enough. I could still see his excited face when Mike had shown him a grey-haired Eric Burdon singing the song on YouTube, 55 years after its first recording.

I looked up at the pub and then around at the faces of all of the people of Candlebark, and then finally at Andre, who appeared to be thinking the same as me.

Yeah, Macca, we could make a go of this.

Acknowledgements

People say second books are much harder than first, and I'm thankful this wasn't the case, but it could have been when I discovered the first 25,000 words of *Dead and Gone* had disappeared in a computer meltdown! Luckily I found most of it on an old USB (there are advantages to being a bit of a hoarder).

As any writer knows, a book is a mosaic of many things – words and ideas, yes, but also a huge amount of research, and support from friends, colleagues and keen readers. My fellow writers, Lucia Nardo, Demet Divaroren and Tracey Rolfe, are always willing to read a chapter or three (or sometimes the whole darned thing and help with feedback and questions).

If you're in the country in Victoria and inclined to go looking for Candlebark or the Candlebark Hotel, you won't find it as I created both especially for Judi. But there are a number of historic pubs you can visit to indulge in both their history and their beer. I 'borrowed' a little bit from each one I've been to: the Coach & Horses Inn at Clarkefield, which does have a ghost; the Tooberac Hotel at Tooberac where you can sit in a public bar a little like the one at Candlebark; and the Victoria Hotel in Rutherglen which I'm pretty sure is the one with the stained glass window above the stairs!

My thanks to members of Victoria Police who have helped me in different ways. Firstly, Detective Senior Constable Howard

Beer (Ret) who endured all of my questions in the early days (and still does with vast patience), and then Senior Constable Mark Boysen and Klute at the Victoria Police Dog Squad in Attwood, Victoria; Senior Constable Shane Flynn (ret); Senior Constable Roger Barr; Constable Simon Robertson and Ben, New Zealand Police. Special thanks also to Dr Sandra Neate who answers all of my questions, no matter how gruesome. Thanks to Deputy Chief Coroner in New Zealand, Brandt Shortland, who also answered lots of my questions. Any mistakes are about the plot, not their advice and assistance.

Thank you to the people at Verve Books – especially Clare Quinlivan, whose support and feedback improved this book one hundred per cent. And my agent, Brian Cook, who is always a willing and professional ear. Thanks as always to my husband, Brian, and my sister, Lesley, and brother, John. To my brother-in-law, Johnny, I wrote as fast as I could, and here it is!

I am so appreciative that so many people I've met over the years, as friends, students and fellow writers have read the first book, *Trust Me, I'm Dead*, and let me know how much they enjoyed it. It really does make a difference. Thank you.

About the Author

Sherryl Clark has had 70 children's and YA books published in Australia, and several in the US and UK, plus collections of poetry and four verse novels. She has taught writing at Holmesglen TAFE and Victoria University Polytech. She completed a Master of Fine Arts program at Hamline University, Minnesota, and a PhD in creative writing at Victoria University. Her debut novel, *Trust Me, I'm Dead* was shortlisted for the CWA Debut Dagger Award.

@sherrylwriter
vervebooks.co.uk/SherrylClark

To be the first to hear about new books and exclusive deals
from Verve Books, sign up to our newsletters:
vervebooks.co.uk/signup